MW00778415

Other Books by MaryLu Tyndall

THE RELIANCE

THE RESTITUTION

THE RECKONING

THE FALCON AND THE SPARROW

THE RED SIREN

THE BLUE ENCHANTRESS

THE RAVEN SAINT

CHARLES TOWNE BELLES TRILOGY

SURRENDER THE HEART

SURRENDER THE NIGHT

SURRENDER THE DAWN

SURRENDER TO DESTINY TRILOGY

VEIL OF PEARLS

FORSAKEN DREAMS

ELUSIVE HOPE

ABANDONED MEMORIES

PEARLS FROM THE SEA DEVOTIONAL

CENTRAL PARK RENDEZVOUS

TEARS OF THE SEA

The Ransom

Legacy of the King's Pirates

MaryLu Tyndall

The Ransom
Legacy of the King's Pirates
by MaryLu Tyndall

© 2014 by MaryLu Tyndall

Library of Congress Cataloging-in-Publication Data is on file at the Library of Congress, Washington, DC.

ISBN: 0991092120
ISBN-13:   978-0-9910921-2-3
E-Version ISBN: 978-0-9910921-3-0

Cover Design by Dineen Miller
Interior Layout and Design by Ellie Searl, Publishista®

Ransom Press
San Jose, CA

Acknowledgements

My heartfelt thanks go to so many who helped in the writing of
this book. To my fabulous editor, Lora, (EditsbyLora.com) I
couldn't have done this without you! Special mention to Anica for
help with a sticky plot problem! Many thanks to Susanne Lakin
and Michelle Griep, fabulous authors and friends, who read
through the book and fixed all those little things I missed. Special
mention goes to Dineen Miller, who designed this gorgeous cover,
along with postcards and bookmarks and several other things I
needed. You are one talented lady!

Of course, I would be remiss if I didn't thank my Motley Crew,
several of whom also helped proofread the manuscript, and all of
whom help spread the word about my books. I run a tight ship,
but my crew is the best group of sailors who ever graced the
Caribbean. I love you all and appreciate you so much!
Most of all, I thank God for giving me stories and a platform on
which to share them with the world. I love you, Abba.

Chapter 1

The Cat and the Fiddle Tavern, Port Royal, Jamaica
March 1692

MURK, MIRE, AND MAYHEM. 'Twas the only fitting description for the punch house in which Juliana Dutton found herself. No, not found herself. She had come here on purpose, passed through the display of debauchery once on her way to the brothel beyond, and now, yet again, on her way back to the street. Only this time, the room overflowed with patrons—if patrons was a fitting term for the slovenly-attired men and women guzzling their drinks amidst shouts and curses and a discordant fiddle. What had she been thinking?

But she had to make sure one last time that her friend Abilene was not among the dissolute cullions flooding the room—that the woman had not been hiding when Juliana had passed through before. Or worse, swallowed up in the arms of some foul ruffian. Yet, as Juliana peered from beneath the hood of her cloak, cringing at the visions that met her eyes, her friend was nowhere in sight.

What *was* apparently in sight was her. Dozens of glazed eyes fastened upon her as she wove through tables laden with mugs of Kill-Devil rum, card games, flickering lanterns, and plates brimming with roasted boar and fish pudding. The scent of food joined the odors of sweat, smoke, and bitter spirits, creating a stench that would keep the Devil himself away. Though, from the befouled language and equally befouled sights, it appeared he was already present.

The ensuing whistles and lewd invitations proved her assumption correct. Air fled her lungs. Gripping her throat, she hurried toward the door. A chair slid in her path. A man rose before her, brashly eyeing her from the hood of her cloak to the tips of her red mules. A brace of pistols crossed a chest the size of England adorned with a red doublet trimmed in metallic lace. Two formidable swords hung from each hip. A scar on his neck disappeared behind a stained cravat that bubbled over his shirt like the ale foaming on his mustache.

Pirate.

With a jeweled finger that belied the crusted dirt beneath his nail, he yanked off her hood, releasing her golden waves. One would think none of the men had ever seen flaxen hair on a woman before as groans of pleasure swept through the crowd.

Followed by vulgar suggestions that shocked her and caused her to tremble violently.

"That be a proper fine lady, says I," one man shouted. "Take 'er, Mad Dog."

"She be askin' fer it by comin' here," another man yelled, triggering an outburst of laughter.

Yet the man kept staring at her. Mad dog, indeed. A rabid one from the looks of him.

Juliana was not a timid sort, not a woman prone to hysterics or swooning, but when the rake clutched her arm and leered at her with teeth the color of dirt, her heart nigh burst through her chest.

"Leave her be!"

From behind the brute, a voice boomed like the crash of a massive wave. The pirate glanced over his shoulder, stiffened, then released her with a grunt. Wiping his mouth on his sleeve, he picked up the chair, shoved it beside a nearby table, and toppled onto it like a felled tree.

Moans of disappointment filtered through the mob before the music resumed and the men returned to their drink and games. Tugging her hood back atop her head, Juliana searched for her rescuer, unsure what price his chivalry bore. But no one came forward to claim his prize. Before the man revealed himself, or worse, before Mad Dog reconsidered, she dashed for the door, surprised when no one paid her any mind. No leers, bawdy comments, groping hands, lecherous grins. It was as if she'd disappeared. Mayhap God had made her invisible. She was, after all, on a mission of mercy.

Nearly at the entrance, her gaze latched upon a pair of startling blue eyes—so piercingly blue, they almost stopped her. They definitely slowed her. Mayhap it was the man's coal black hair, dark stubble on his jaw, and sun-bronzed face that made the color of his eyes so luminescent. But no, there was something else within them. An intelligence, an intensity … and now a bit of humor as his gaze remained upon her. He leaned against a thick post, calm, quiet, sturdy—a bastion of control amidst the clamor surrounding him. Rounded, sinewy arms folded over his leather jerkin, Hessian boots crossed at his ankle. His lips lifted in a mocking grin.

Turning her face away, she shoved past a group of inebriated patrons and fled down the stairs onto Thames Street. Pulse hammering, she searched the shadows. Oh, fie! Where was Mr. Pell with her carriage? She'd instructed him to wait for her right here. A blast of wind tore off her hood and flooded her with the scents of salt and brine, roasting fish, and other unsavory odors that glutted the town of Port Royal, Jamaica. Her home for the past four years.

Another distinguishing feature of the town was that a lady should never venture out unescorted after dark, especially near the wharves. Which, of course, was precisely where she was, searching for her wayward footman. Though the sun had barely set, pirates, privateers, and other nefarious sorts roamed the streets, filling their guts with rum, their beds with women, and their hearts with darkness. Slipping into the shadows, she ducked her face within the folds of her hood and hurried down the sandy street, praying for God to watch over her.

She had barely gone a few steps when two men grabbed her and dragged her down an alley. She opened her mouth to scream. A leathery palm slammed onto her lips. She tasted blood. She tasted other things as well. Dirt and rum and remnants of the man's dinner. Her stomach vaulted. She kicked and clawed as the man yanked her farther into the shadows. His friend snickered in anticipation.

So, this was to be her fate? This was the reward for her charity? For her care of Abilene, her work at the orphanage, her undying devotion to a father who had never loved her and a brother who did naught but despoil their family name?

Dear God in heaven, where are you?

The man shoved her against a brick wall. Sharp stone poked her back through her stays. She vainly tried to reach the knife in the pocket of her cloak, but the man held her arms firm.

"I ne'er seen the likes o' such a lady prime fer the takin'," the man's friend exclaimed, his hot, putrid breath saturating her face. She coughed.

The first man clawed at her bodice. "Aye, a rare treat, says I." His voice was coarse with spit. "An' one I richly deserve."

Juliana found her voice. "You deserve nothing but *hell*!" She thrust her body against his, thrashing her legs and arms, but they bounced off rock-hard muscle.

"Aye, a truer word has ne'er been spoken." He chuckled as his friend came to assist him.

"She be a wild cat, this 'ne."

"Do you know who I am?" Juliana shouted, hating the tremble in her voice. Outmatched in strength and unable to reach her knife, all that remained in her arsenal of defense were her wits. And surely she could outwit these fish-brained slugs. "I am Juliana Dutton, daughter of Henry Dutton, one of the wealthiest merchants in Port Royal! He has powerful friends—Lieutenant Governor Beeston among them. And I assure you, gentlemen, he will have you drawn and quartered if you proceed with this fiendish deed!"

Her declaration only further amused the ruffians as they exchanged a hearty laugh. Abandoning her bodice lacings with a grunt, the man reached down to lift her skirts.

Breath huddled in her throat. Her knees quivered. And Juliana did the only thing she could. She screamed with all her might.

Gravel crunched. The dark outline of a man appeared at the head of the alleyway. Her assailant gave the intruder a cursory glance before he continued fumbling with her skirts. The second man drew a sword. A metallic chime echoed off the walls as the newcomer rapidly advanced. After one more glance over his shoulder, the beast who held Juliana suddenly stiffened. Releasing her, he slowly backed away while gesturing for his friend to lower his blade.

Juliana plucked the knife from her cloak and held it before her. It was ludicrous to assume she could defend herself against *now* three assailants, but she would not be ravished without a fight.

"Begone with you!" Authoritative words exploded from the intruder's lips, tumbled down the length of his drawn sword, and shot from the tip with the same impact as if the blade had pierced the men's hearts. With wide-eyes and raised hands, they retreated. "We didn't know she be yers, milord."

"Now you do." The same voice from the tavern chased them down the alley as they scampered away.

So, her rescuer had come for his reward, after all. Juliana gathered her breath. And her wits. She wiped her sweaty palm on her skirts then tightened her grip on the knife.

Ramming it in front of her, she attempted to slip by the man while he sheathed his sword. But he spun on her, saw the blade in her hand, and began to chuckle.

Which only made her thrust it farther toward him. "I warn you, sir. I'm not afraid to use this."

"I have no doubt, milady." He contained his laughter with difficulty. "Though I fear it will be to no avail." Before she could retort, he gripped her wrist with one hand and snatched her knife with the other.

"How dare you? You have no right!" She forced indignation into her tone as she inched away from him. He was naught but a shadow in the darkness—a rather tall shadow. A rather intimidating shadow.

One thing—mayhap the only thing—her father had taught her was never to appear weak in front of your enemies. No matter the fear that gripped her. "Very well, you may keep the knife." She kept her tone curt. "If it pleases you to steal from a helpless woman." Turning, she clutched her skirts and started for the street.

"Helpless?" He matched her pace and they soon stepped into the light of a street lantern. "Nay, I would never call you such."

She faced him: the same man from The Cat and the Fiddle who had kept the wolves at bay. The same coal-dark hair tied behind him in a queue, the same dark stubble. The same piercing blue eyes. Yet standing so close, he seemed much taller, much larger. More ominous. Wind raked a strand of hair across his cheek as he gazed at her with impunity.

Her heart thundered in her chest, and she retreated a step. She took in his white billowing shirt, his leather jerkin, black breeches, knee-high boots, and the cutlass at his side that winked at her in the light.

"You are a pirate."

He gave a mock bow with all the flourish of a courtier. "At your service, milady."

Her breath came fast and hard as she scanned the street for Mr. Pell. This man was no ordinary pirate. He commanded the respect of other pirates—a man who could send the most cutthroat brigands scurrying away with a single word. He must be the Pirate Earl whose reputation had flooded the city. A leader of pirates. A man of great strength and wit with a penchant for cruelty, women, and rum.

Gathering her cloak about her neck, she brushed past him. "I bid you good eve, Mr. Pirate."

"Milord Pirate, if you please." He slid beside her.

She glanced his way, noting the amusement flickering in his eyes. It infuriated her. "The two words side by side reek of profanity, sir. Now, if you don't mind, I'll be on my way." Easing her hood back over her head, she dashed onward, silently praying for the pirate to leave her be—for *everyone* on the streets to leave her be. She no longer recognized her city. Darkness had forced the good citizens into their homes, while luring out the riff-raff to roam the streets with abandon. A man sauntered by, doxies on each arm. Juliana shifted her gaze from the women's revealing necklines. Ahead, a band of men, mugs in hand, sang a ribald ditty that scalded her ears. A pistol shot cracked the night sky. Juliana jumped. Shouts and curses blared atop the clanging of an organ bellowing from a brothel across the way. Footsteps scuffed behind her. She dared not turn around.

Oh, fie, where was Mr. Pell?

Three men approached. A white periwig sat askew on the first man's head, while the other two wore colorful bandanas beneath plumed tricornes. All three were armed with pistols and knives. Juliana stiffened. She lowered her head. Her heart leapt in her chest like a galloping horse.

Not two yards away, the men suddenly halted, nodded at her—or over her—then hurried past without saying a word.

She didn't have to look to know that the Pirate Earl had not abandoned her.

"I told you to leave me be," she said loud enough for him to hear.

"Nay, I believe you merely implied you would be on your way." That deep, husky voice again, authoritative with a hint of humor. It jumbled her insides. He appeared beside her, one hand resting idly on the pummel of his sword.

Halting, she faced him. "What is it you want, *Mr. Pirate?*"

He seemed to bristle at the title. "Merely to inform you that you shouldn't venture near the wharves at night. Nor enter such an ignoble place as The Cat and the Fiddle." He rubbed the stubble surrounding his mouth with forefinger and thumb. "Regardless of the name, a kitten does not fare well in such a place."

"Forsooth! I am no kitten, sir. And oddly, I find myself unscathed."

One dark brow rose. "Yet not of your own doing."

"Regardless." She spotted her carriage. "Ah, there's my footman." Taking the opportunity, she darted between a horse and wagon, several inebriated men, and a wild pig, hoping the annoying pirate would give up his pursuit now that Mr. Pell was found.

But Mr. Pell lay unconscious on the driver's perch. Even her hard shaking did not arouse him. The smell of alcohol hovered over the man like a dismal cloud—a cloud that threatened to storm over Juliana's safety. She should have known better than to trust him. The unreliable footman was always into his cups.

What was she to do? Oh foolish girl! Why did she never think of the consequences before running off on some errand of mercy? She'd put her entire family at risk: her shipping business, her father's health, her brother's future.

The Pirate Earl appeared beside her.

And her own virtue.

"Ah, at last we know what has kept your footman." He chuckled.

"*We* don't know anything, sir," she snapped, staring at the besotted servant. She would have to move him in order to drive the carriage. And since her strength forbade the act—and she refused to ask a pirate for help—she gathered her cloak about her and started down the street.

He clutched her arm. "Where are you going?"

"Home." She tugged from his grip, her ire rising. "I have no money if that's what you want."

He grinned. "I have more than enough wealth, milady."

She stopped and glared at him. "If you intend to ravish or murder me, please be about it. Otherwise I grow weary of our exchange."

Was that a spark of surprise, mayhap even admiration in his eyes?

Without saying a word, he retraced his steps to the carriage, hoisted poor Mr. Pell over his shoulder, and laid him across the passenger seat in the back. Then leaping onto the driver's box, he grabbed the reins with one hand and lowered his other to her.

"Are you now to steal my carriage?" she asked.

"I intend to take you home."

"So you can rob me?"

"Again with the money, milady?" He grinned. "You cut me to the quick."

"By your own admission, sir, you *are* a pirate. Why should I trust you?"

"You shouldn't." He shrugged. "But either way, I intend to escort you home. On foot or in this carriage, 'tis your choice."

She stared at the imposing man, wondering at his purpose. But what choice did she have? She could scream, but no honorable man would come to her rescue in this part of town. She could run, but he'd quickly overtake her. She was completely at his mercy. And she hated that fact more than anything.

As if he could read her mind, one dark brow lifted. "I mean you no harm."

Sincerity shone in his eyes. Regardless, she had no intention of leading this ruffian to her home. She could, however, appeal to a passerby for help should they enter a better part of town, mayhap even her neighborhood, where she knew many who would come to her aid.

With no other recourse, she slid her hand into his and allowed him to lift her onto the seat beside him. Even through her gloves, she felt the strength and warmth of his callused fingers. Their legs touched and she shifted away. He smelled of salt and tobacco and a hint of cinnamon. Nothing like a pirate should smell. He flicked the reins, and the carriage lurched forward.

A dozen reasons filled her mind for his interest in her. None of them good. All of them sent blood dashing through her veins until her head felt light. "Mr. Pell has an affinity for drink, I'm afraid," she said nervously, filling the silence.

He turned the carriage onto Queen Street. "Ah, yes. That explains why you ventured into the most perilous section of town during the night and brought your cupshotten footman for protection."

"You forget I also brought my knife, Mr. Pirate."

He laughed and glanced her way. "Humor amidst fear, a trait that will serve you well."

"Fear?" She raised her shoulders and glanced at the passing shops and houses, a blur of brick mortar and in the darkness. "I am not afraid," she said emphatically.

He snorted.

The carriage clanked and bounced down the street as the sounds of revelry faded behind them, replaced by the call of a night heron and the lap of waves against pilings. Sounds that normally soothed her, but this night, sitting next to this man, going to a place of his choosing, her stomach twisted in knots. Oh, fie, why was there no one out tonight? The street was as empty as a church on Monday.

"Why do you not release him?" the pirate asked.

"Who?"

He jerked his head behind him. "Your footman."

"That is none of your concern." She wouldn't tell him that the price of Mr. Pell's employment was his silence.

Flicking the reins, he turned onto High Street. "What could be of such importance that you risked your life by venturing to The Cat and the Fiddle?"

Juliana clasped her trembling hands together and searched the street for anyone taking a stroll. "I was helping a friend."

"A trollop for a friend?"

Juliana despised that term. Particularly when associated with Abilene. The lady hadn't always been in *the business*. But the loss of her family, subsequent poverty, and an evil man's deception had driven her to the streets to survive. Pride had kept her from receiving help from anyone. Including Juliana. Regardless, Juliana visited her as often as she could, bringing her extra food, clothing, and medicines, all the while trying to convince her to come home with her. But Juliana had not found her today. And that worried her most of all.

Her home was fast approaching on the right. Mayhap her butler, Mr. Abbot, was up and about. Surely he would have waited for her return as he normally did. Or her brother might be coming home from one of his posh parties. "Does it shock you that I associate with soiled women, Mr. Pirate?"

"Milord Pirate. And I am rarely shocked, milady."

"I beg you, do not refer to me as such. I am not titled."

He stopped the carriage before her house, set the brake, and leapt down to assist her. "Regardless, you have the manner and mien of nobility."

Taking his hand, she stepped down beside him in the light of a street lamp and glanced at her dark house. Where was Abbot? Thinking to make a dash for the door, she tugged her hand from the pirate's grip. But he refused to release her.

Her eyes were level with his chest—a rather wide chest encased in leather and crossed with a thick brace, buckled in silver. Her pulse took up a pace again, but she hid her fear behind a playful tone. "Nobility, you say? Idle flattery does you no credit, Mr. Pirate."

He leaned toward her. A strand of dark hair tumbled over his jaw as his breath wafted warm across her cheek. "Pray tell, what would do me credit in your eyes, milady?" He released her hand.

Emotions awhirl, she stepped back, unsure of his next move. "That you leave me be."

"As I always intended." He smiled, those piercing blue eyes of his searching her own, studying, absorbing her as if he knew her most intimate thoughts.

Unsettled, she lowered her gaze.

"What of your Mr. Pell?" he asked.

"Leave him." She inched toward the front steps. "He'll awake soon enough."

Reaching within his jerkin, he withdrew her knife, spun it in the air, caught it expertly, then flipped it—handle extended—to her. "I believe this is yours, milady?"

Swallowing, Juliana took it. The feel of the weapon in her hand gave her some measure of comfort. Mayhap this man truly intended her no harm.

Grinning, he dipped his head. "Sweet dreams, milady." Then turning, he strolled down the street.

Juliana hurried up the steps to her front door before the man changed his mind. Once inside, she locked the bolt tight and peered out the window at his retreating form. She caught her breath and leaned her forehead against the glass, when an alarming thought prickled her skin.

How did the Pirate Earl know where she lived?

Chapter 2

A DISTANT MOAN ECHOED THROUGH Juliana's head. A raspy cough etched the air. Coughing... coughing ... always so much coughing. Her head bounced against the mattress. She opened her eyes. Nothing but red embroidery filled her vision. Another cough. Jerking, she sat up on the seat beside the bed, ashamed she had fallen over asleep. A moan brought her gaze to her father lying prone on the mattress, his face white, his cheeks sunken, feverish sweat gleaming on his brow. The smell of sickness and soiled sheets added to the gloom in her heart. He coughed again and tossed his head in his usual disturbed state of slumber.

Ellie Sims entered the room, tray in hand. "Did you fall asleep agin tendin' your father, miss?"

Juliana sighed. "I suppose." Pain shot through her arms and shoulders as she unfolded herself from the chair and stretched. The last thing she remembered was sitting beside her father's bed to pray for God to heal him. But it had been a long day of paperwork and decisions, a visit to the orphanage, and then her harrowing adventure down by the wharves. She must have drifted asleep before she uttered a single petition.

Ellie set down the tray and tore open the velvet curtains, admitting a flood of light that transformed dust into glitter. Juliana wished her problems would transform so easily into sparkling powder—powder that would blow away in the next blast of trade winds. But she discovered in her twenty years that life was never that easy.

The lady's maid shoved her hands onto her hips. "Just look at your gown, miss. A knot of wrinkles. After I tend your father, I'll 'elp you out of it so I can press it properly."

Glancing down at her disheveled attire, Juliana fingered strands of hair that had fallen from her pins. "I believe I have far worse problems than wrinkles, Ellie, but thank you." She smiled at the woman who had been more like an older sister to her than a servant—a nagging older sister, but at least one who cared. "I am in your debt for all you do, truly. Much more than any lady's maid is required. Especially tending to my father."

"Ah, go on now. You know I love this family as my own, and I'm 'appy to serve. I understand why you don't want the rest of the staff to know your business."

Juliana sighed. Secrets, so many secrets. Her father coughed again, followed by a moan as he pried open his eyes. "Cannot a man have some privacy in his own bedchamber?!" He attempted to growl with his usual force, but the impact fell impotent on his breathless voice.

Lowering to sit on the bed beside him, Juliana took his hand in hers. The strength and resolve that had once permeated his fingers had fled, leaving them clammy, weak, and bony. "Not when you are ill, Papa. You must be cared for."

His eyelids fluttered above a scowl. "Must I be cossetted like a child? Be gone with you all!" He coughed again and a drop of blood slid from the corner of his lips.

Grabbing a cloth, Juliana dabbed it, avoiding his fumbling attempt to swat her away. "Now, now, Papa, we are only trying to help."

"Trying to kill me is the way of it."

Reaching behind him, Ellie assisted him up while she propped his pillows.

"Come now, Papa, you are far too disagreeable for God to welcome in heaven just yet." Juliana set the cloth on the table and stood. "I do believe He may have more work to do on your behalf."

"God, bah!" Her father's exclamation resulted in another bout of coughing that prevented him from continuing his tirade. Juliana would grin at the justice if her heart wasn't so heavy. In truth, there was naught to smile about. What remained of her father's health deteriorated day by day.

After all the years she'd spent cowering beneath his enraged outbursts, cringing beneath his insults, anxiously anticipating his pendulous moods, and fawning over his every need so as not to prick his ire, it felt good to finally speak her mind—to say the things she'd forced behind a wall of suppressed defiance.

She only regretted the circumstances by which she'd gained her courage. And her independence.

Mr. Abbot appeared in the doorway, his normal livery forsaken for a fine suit of black taffeta bordered in silver lace. A brown periwig sat atop his head, while a creamy neckerchief bounded from his neck. How fortuitous that her father and Mr. Abbot were the same size. In fact, if not for his humble demeanor, no one would suspect that Mr. Abbot was anything but an urbane gentleman. Certainly not a butler. And an indentured servant at that.

His eyes skipped over Ellie and Juliana's father and landed on Juliana in an unspoken request.

"And the two of you!" her father barked. "Stealing my business. Robbing me blind while I lay in my bed. I will not suffer it. I tell you, I will not suffer it!" He attempted to rise, but a fit of coughing forced him back to his pillows. When they were spent, he managed to grunt out, "Stealing my clothes too, are you now, Abbot? I'll send you back to the auction block!"

Feeling her anger churn, Juliana repressed it with a sigh. "You're being silly, Papa. Mr. Abbot and I are *saving* your business, not stealing it, so that when you are well again, it will not have suffered from your absence. Now, if you don't calm yourself like the doctor says, you'll only get worse."

He mumbled some obscenity Juliana was glad she couldn't hear, while Ellie drew a cup of steaming tea from the tray and held it to the man's lips.

He jerked his mouth away.

"Papa, you will eat what Miss Ellie has brought you. And you will cooperate with Dr. Verns when he comes to call later today."

"That charlatan! All he knows to do is bleed me." He raised a shaky hand and dismissed Juliana with a wave. "Faith, I'll not have an ounce of the fluid left in me if he has his way."

"I can 'andle 'im, miss. You go on now." Ellie gave a nod, and Juliana knew she *could* and would deal with her father. For some reason the old man favored the woman who had been his wife's lady's maid before she'd become Juliana's. While he flung contempt and mockery upon everyone in the house, he tolerated Miss Ellie, spoke to her in pleasant tones, even confided in her. Juliana could never discern the reason, save that Ellie cared for him with ne'er a complaint, ne'er a bitter word, and accepted his harsh ways.

"I'll check on you later, Papa." Juliana left the chamber before he could respond, falling into step with Abbot down the long hallway. "Have you seen Rowan?"

"Aye, miss. I found him sprawled across the settee in the drawing room when I arose this morning. Me and Mr. Pell carried him to his chamber."

Juliana breathed a sigh of relief. "Thank you, Abbot. I cannot imagine what I would do without you."

"Beggin' your pardon, miss, but if your brother were half the person you are, you would have no need of my services."

She stopped him and pressed a hand on his arm as they reached the stairs. "I will always have need of you, Abbot."

Clearing his throat, he turned away, uncomfortable with her praise. Which was one of the many things she admired about him. "'Twould that Master Rowan would cease his drunken roisterings, miss, for I see they grieve you great," he said as he followed her down the stairs.

"Great*ly*, Abbot," she corrected him as they eased across the marble floor of the foyer and entered her father's study. "Your speech has much improved over the past months. Why, you almost sound like a cultured gentleman, not a butler, and certainly not the shoemaker you were back in England." An odd thought occurred to her regarding the fine quality of the pirate's speech last night, but she shoved it aside.

"All due to your tutelage, miss." He scanned the books lining the shelves on one side of the room. "Learning to read, even just a little, has brought me more joy than I can say."

"I should have taught you long ago, not waited for its necessity. Forgive me, Abbot." She skirted the large mahogany desk and plopped down in her father's high-back chair. One glance at the mounds of documents littering the top caused her remaining strength to ebb.

Adjusting his periwig, Mr. Abbot approached, awaiting his orders for the day. At five-and-forty, he still maintained his youthful appearance and vigor, with but a few lines on his face and select gray hairs to indicate otherwise. He was tall and lithe, and his hands were thick and rough. Not the hands of a butler, but the hands of a workman. The hands of an indentured servant whom her father had purchased soon after their arrival in Jamaica.

Yet Mr. Abbot had never seemed like a servant to Juliana.

"I wish I could relieve you of some of your burden, miss." He scanned the papers.

She sighed as a warm breeze, ripe with the sea, blew in through the open French doors. "I wish you could as well, Abbot, but alas, the task falls to me to keep this business running while father recovers." *Oh, Lord, please let him recover soon.*

"The task fell to you, miss, because the good Lord knew He would equip you with all you need to best handle it."

"Some days I wonder. I truly wonder." Rubbing the back of her neck, she retrieved the document she'd set out for her immediate perusal. "I wonder how long I—no, we—can keep up this charade."

"No one seems the wiser, miss." He hesitated. "Though several merchants and a few of your father's workmen have asked why he doesn't come to the docks anymore."

"And what have you told them?"

"Just what you said, Miss Juliana, that your father made me his manager of business affairs while he enjoys a more leisurely life at home."

Juliana nodded. "Good."

"My only fear is that I will make a mistake in my dealings, misread something, or miscalculate monies due, and the ship owners will demand to see your father."

Juliana skimmed the bill of lading as familiar fear began shredding her nerves. Should that happen, should anyone discover a woman was running Dutton Shipping, all her customers would flee like bats before the sun. She'd eventually lose everything: their three ships, their income, the house, her father's medical care, and probably even his life.

And the rest of them would be cast onto the streets.

She could not allow that to happen. She *would not* allow that to happen.

"We expect the *Esther's Dowry* to sail into port this afternoon," she said, shifting beneath a sudden pang to her heart at the name of the ship—her mother's Christian name—and the second word that exposed to all the world the only reason Juliana's father had proposed to her. What an insult to her mother while she lived, and now to her memory, to have her only perceived value painted in red on the hull of a brig.

"This is an important shipment, Abbot. We stand to make twenty pounds if all goes well, which you know we desperately need at the moment." Rising, Juliana circled the desk and laid the document before the butler. "Here"—she slid a finger down a list on the left—"are the items we purchased in England and France. See my marks on the side? That will help you determine what they are should you have trouble reading them." She assessed the butler's worried expression as his eyes peered at the writing and then over to the code they'd worked out for him to use until he learned to read well enough.

She pointed to one symbol. "What is this?"

"Oak chest of drawers."

"And this?"

"French tapestry."

"Indeed! Well done, Abbot, and over here are the prices the merchants who ordered them agreed to pay, their deposits, and the amount they still owe us upon delivery."

He nodded and swallowed nervously. "I've never dealt with so huge a shipment. What if I forget? What if I can't read these numbers? What if they try to cheat me?"

Juliana forced her breathing to settle. "Captain Greyson, along with father's warehouse managers, will assist you as always."

"Of course. I pray I learn all this soon enough, miss. I fear someone will sense my distress."

"I predict you will find yourself an expert in no time, Mr. Abbot. I am sure of it." Her voice rang confidently, though she felt none of that surety within her at the moment. Every man in her life had let her down. She believed Mr. Abbot wouldn't do so intentionally, yet she feared he would as well. Nevertheless, what choice did she have? She folded the paper and handed it to him. "The task fell to you, Mr. Abbot, because the good Lord knew He would equip you with all you need to best handle it," she said, repeating his prior statement with a wink.

He chuckled. "How do you say … ?" He scratched his periwig, setting it askew. "It's a French word … Tu—"

"Touché?"

"Yes. Touché, miss. Touché." He drew a deep breath and adjusted his neckerchief.

Standing on her tiptoes, Juliana set his wig straight and gave him an approving nod, then watched as he strolled from the room, shoulders slumped, nervous twitch in his fingers.

Her own pulse began to twitch, and she tossed a hand to her throat. Though Abbot had successfully handled several minor shipments, the one sailing into port today was by far the largest and most important. These merchants were friends of Papa's, had dealt with him for years. If Abbot didn't satisfy them with the same exemplary service, if he didn't answer their questions with the utmost alacrity, then Dutton Shipping would be certain to fail, and all their lives would be forfeit to the cruel fate of Port Royal's outcasts.

Chapter 3

JULIANA ROSE FROM HER FATHER'S desk, rubbed her eyes, and gazed at the half-eaten meal of turtle stew and biscuits Cook had brought her at noon. Four hours ago. Exhausted, she moved to the open French doors, allowing the afternoon sun to slide warm fingers over her skin and knead out the kinks in her shoulders. How had father kept up with all the paperwork required to run his shipping business? No wonder he'd spent hours locked away in his study and then even more hours down by the docks. Thank the good Lord that Juliana had inherited his mind for numbers, for it hadn't taken her long to determine his system of managing things. If she hadn't ... she shuddered at the thought and closed her eyes, absorbing the sun's warm rays instead.

Her mother's familiar scent drifted past her nose, and for a brief second—one brief, glorious second—Juliana's heart leapt with the hope that when she opened her eyes, her mother would be standing before her. But her mother was long gone. Dead and buried in the cemetery just outside the Palisadoes gate. Three years ago, yet it seemed like fifty. Juliana felt as if she were nearing fifty years of age instead of twenty.

Wandering into the garden her mother loved so much, Juliana inhaled deeply as she wove among the flowering bushes—gardenias, poinsettias, and hibiscus—finally stopping at her mother's favorite, heliotrope. She lowered her nose to the tiny purple flowers that smelled so much like her mother. Sweet scents of vanilla and cherry swirled around her like a healing balm, and she closed her eyes as happier times danced on the edge of her memory—moments that, if she didn't bring them oft to mind, she feared they would slip into oblivion. Already, she had trouble picturing her mother's face. The details of her lovely complexion, green eyes, and fair hair blurred like the heliotrope Juliana now stared at through teary eyes.

She slid onto the stone bench and hugged herself. "Why did you have to leave me, Mother? Just when I needed you the most." She knew her mother was in heaven now, for if anyone was in heaven, it would be her mother. Kind, loving, generous, with ne'er a disparaging word for anyone, even when father treated her as if he'd purchased her like he had Mr. Abbot. Yet instead of wallowing in the misery of a bad marriage, her mother had become a patron to the neediest in the city. She'd given generously to the poor and hungry and donated hours of her time assisting the children at the Buchan orphanage when the preacher who had been sent to care for them had left them to starve. Juliana had much to live up to if she was going to see her mother again and be welcomed in that celestial city.

Air heavy with fragrant moisture swirled about Juliana, and she shifted on the seat as the heat of the day dampened her skin. "I have kept my promise, Mother. I have continued your work at the orphanage." Though time had not permitted a visit today, Juliana went as often as she could. How could she not? 'Twas her mother's dying wish, her last lucid thought from a feverish brain before the ague took her home. A disease she had caught from the very orphans she begged Juliana to now care for. But she didn't fault the needy children. Caring for them came easy. What didn't come easily was the time she must sacrifice away from her father's books.

"Mother, I am running a shipping business!" Her exuberance rang across the garden, and she quickly glanced up to ensure no one had heard her. No one was about at the moment, but she needed to be careful. After her father had become ill, she'd released most of the staff and had told only those upon whom she sorely depended for help. And those she trusted to keep quiet about her father's condition. The less people who knew that Juliana was in charge of Dutton Shipping, the less chance the truth would be unleashed.

Still, Juliana woke up every day and fell asleep every night with the bitter taste of fear in her mouth.

"Mother, you would be proud," she whispered. "You taught me to be independent and strong. For that I thank you."

The sun slipped behind the stone wall that bordered the garden, dragging her thoughts to the prior night and her encounter with the Pirate Earl. A most unusual man. Dangerous, intimidating, a scoundrel by all intents, yet he spoke with a gentleman's tongue. And, like a gentleman, he had left her with both her virtue and her money. Alas, what sort of pirate did that? Especially one of his reputation.

No matter. She waved her hand through the humid air, shoving aside the thought. No doubt 'twas God who stayed the vile man's hand. Besides, she would be more careful the next time she paid Abilene a visit. Providing the poor lady was still ... oh my—Juliana's fears of Abilene's fate resurged. Lifting up a silent prayer, Juliana determined to inquire after her soon.

Perspiration slid down her back, and she realized she'd not had her morning toilet nor changed her attire since yesterday. Her mother would be so ashamed. Her father would berate her. Miss Ellie would simply shake her head. Yet the lady's maid had not come to retrieve Juliana all day. No doubt she'd been busy with Juliana's father. *Oh, fie!* Juliana had forgotten all about the doctor visit, and she had so wanted to be present when he examined her father. She hoped Dr. Verns had some good tidings for a change. She hoped Abbot's business at the dock was a success. Her head spun with all her concerns, and she reached up to rub her temples. She hoped to spend a quiet evening at home and retire early.

But that was not to be. No sooner had Juliana sat at the table in the dining hall with a cup of hot tea and a plate of corncakes—which she'd all but begged Cook to relinquish before supper—than Miss Ellie entered the room all aflutter. Before she could say a word, Juliana inquired whether Mr. Abbot had returned, but Ellie shook her head. "Miss, I forgot, you 'ave the soiree at Lady Stevenson's tonight." She moved toward her, hands wringing and eyes sparking. "We must get you bathed and ready to go."

A ball? Juliana sagged in her seat. She had no energy left for a ball tonight. Besides, Miss Ellie looked as though she'd not taken a moment's rest all day. "Come sit." Juliana pulled out a chair and patted the seat. Hesitating at first, the maid finally slogged forward and sank onto the cushion, shoulders slumping.

Juliana sipped her tea, then set the cup on the saucer with a clank. "I will not go and leave you to tend my father alone. You need your rest."

"He is sleeping," Miss Ellie replied. Though only fifteen years Juliana's senior, the strain of the last few months had leeched the youthful glow from the maid. Tiny lines formed at the corners of her mouth, and the luster had faded from her brown eyes. Even her normally tight cotton gown seemed loose around the waist. Juliana hated that her family's problems had caused so much turmoil for the woman.

She laid a hand on her arm. "You aren't eating enough, are you? We have plenty. There is no need to fear."

"I know, miss. I 'aven't the stomach for eating these days. Besides,"—she glanced at her plump middle and chuckled—"I 'ave plenty to spare."

"Still, I insist you take care of yourself. Which is why you are to take the night off and get your rest."

"I will, miss, but you still must go to the party." She fingered a wayward strand of dark hair that had escaped from her mob cap. "The doctor gave your father laudanum, so 'e'll sleep through the night and be no trouble to me."

The doctor, of course! "Pray tell, what was Dr. Verns's report?" *Please Lord, allow me some measure of hope.* But the frown on Ellie's lips crushed any chance of that.

"He bled 'im as usual, miss, though Mr. Dutton was none too pleased. Then 'e instructed me to boil some milk with barley and rum."

"Did my father drink it?"

"Some. I'll give 'im some more when 'e wakes."

"The doctor gave no indication that my father improves?"

Miss Ellie shook her head.

"So there is no excuse not to attend the soirée tonight," Ellie said. "Miss Akron's maid inquired about you. Said there is talk among society that somethin' is amiss 'ere at Dutton house."

Fie! Wasn't it hard enough running a business and a home, caring for orphans, tending a sick father, and dealing with a wastrel brother? Did Juliana also have to keep up pretenses just to stave off meddlers?

As if on cue, Rowan sauntered into the dining hall, looking no worse for his night of wanton dissipation. In fact, dressed in a doublet of violet taffetas, silk breeches and hose, with a plumed castor on his head, he cut a fine figure, charming as ever as he winked at her, plucked an Ackee fruit from a bowl, and bit into its juicy flesh. "What is this, Sister? Why are you not dressed?"

"The question should be, *Brother*"—Juliana couldn't help but grimace at the mischievous innocence claiming his features—"why are you inclined for yet another evening of revelry so soon after dragging yourself home in the wee hours of the morning?"

"I never drag, sister dear. I merely move rather slowly, and upon finding something resembling a couch or bed, I gracefully fall upon it."

Juliana flattened her lips. "'Tis a wonder you can find a resemblance to anything in your condition."

"Condition?" Rowan strode to Miss Ellie, leaned over and planted a kiss on her cheek. Shrieking, the maid stood and batted him away. "For shame, Mr. Dutton." Red infused her face as she bobbed a quick curtsey and darted from the room, shouting over her shoulder. "I'll await you in your chamber, miss."

Grinning after the flustered maid, Rowan faced Juliana, his eyes sparkling. "What condition is that, Sister?" He took another bite of the fruit. "Alack, the one wherein I find my pockets empty yet again. Is that the horrid condition of which you speak?"

Frustration mounting, Juliana rose from her seat. "I just gave you a shilling two nights past."

Shrugging, he stole one glance over his shoulder at the sideboard then faced forward and tossed the rest of the Ackee over his head. It landed with a plunk in an empty pewter pitcher.

Juliana shook her head. "How do you *always* do that?"

"Skill." He grinned.

"'Twould that you had equal skill in keeping your money."

"I *am* keeping it. I am merely investing it."

"In what? Cards, women?"

"In truth, I find I have a talent for Faro." He gripped the back of the chair Ellie had vacated and for a moment the humor fled his blue eyes. "And soon my investment will pay off. You will see that even *I* can help out with expenses." His mirth returned as he waved a lace-swathed hand across the room. "Besides, you have plenty of money. Father's shipping business is thriving, is it not?"

"No thanks to you."

"When are you going to realize that I am the beauty and you are the brains, dear sister?" He brushed dust from his coat.

"We are both beauty and brains, my twin. Trouble is, you use your beauty for harm, while I use my brains for good. Which one of us do you believe will ultimately provide a suitable living?"

He pointed a finger at her and smiled. "Ah, it delights me that you brought up the topic, for tonight, you and I will have a chance to prove that beauty is far more lucrative than brains."

"Whatever do you mean?" She narrowed her eyes at him.

"At the soiree, of course. You are of marrying age. Faith now, how many wealthy men vie for your hand?" He waved his hand around exaggeratedly. "All you must do is choose one. Then you'll no longer have need to work so hard every day."

Juliana bristled. "Father will get well."

"What if he doesn't?"

"Then I am perfectly capable of taking care of us. As I have proven. Besides, I don't wish to marry." Not if women were to be ignored, bullied, treated as property, and forbidden to use their talents in lucrative endeavors.

"Pshaw, Sister! Why be such a bore? Come now, go up and refresh yourself and put on your best gown. I have a surprise for you this evening."

While the word *surprise*—spoken from her brother's charming lips—may have delighted a thousand other women, bringing to mind jewels or trinkets from the Orient or romantic interludes, it did naught but douse Juliana with foreboding. "Rowan, I will not suffer another matchmaking scheme. Especially not with that fawning looby, Captain

Nichols. I will attend the soirée with you but only for a short while. That is all I can promise." She need only make an appearance to assuage the wagging tongues.

"That is all I ask." He gave her a sheepish grin then turned to leave. "I'll retrieve my allowance from Father's strongbox."

"Please try to not spend it as fast as I can make it, dear brother."

Halting, he pressed a hand on his heart. "Nigh impossible, for you are very good at making it, dear sister."

As he strode from the room, a whistle on his lips, Juliana swallowed a lump of apprehension. He had resigned his case far too easily. There'd been no arguments about her staying through the night, dancing with this wealthy baron or that rich merchant, fluttering her fan at a handsome inheritor or an affluent naval officer.

One particular boorish officer came to mind, Captain William Nichols. Her brother had been foisting the man on her for months now, spouting his praises at every occasion, alluding to his noble pedigree, his estates back in Hertfordshire, the vast fortune Nichols had inherited from his Viscount father, and all the while proclaiming that the man had taken a fancy to Juliana. Of the latter she could attest. The captain had been relentless in his pursuit of a courtship between them. A bitter taste rose in her mouth. She supposed he was handsome enough, particularly when attired in his dark blue naval suit, but he seemed ill-tempered and mawkish, and she found herself avoiding his company. Not only that, his prying persistence invaded her life in such a way that she feared he'd discover her father's illness, uncover her deception …

And bring them all to ruin.

Yes, she must definitely stay as far away from the intrusive Captain Nichols as possible.

Nevertheless, her brother's real reason for matchmaking was not lost on her. No respectable woman with a dowry would marry him, so that left her to procure a steady stream of wealth to fund his gambling and wenching. Especially should father continue ill and Juliana fail at business. Which is what her brother no doubt expected from a woman! But she would prove him wrong.

She would prove them all wrong.

Still, nagging doubts assailed Juliana as she soaked in a bath until the water grew cold. They continued as Miss Ellie helped her on with her corset and multiple petticoats, small hoops, and underdress. Misgivings persisted as Ellie flung a mantua over Juliana's head—a gorgeous emerald satin that draped over her shapely figure and was held snug by a stomacher all aglitter with jewels and pearls. She stared at her reflection in the tall looking glass, unsure whether to be happy at her appearance or peeved that women were forced to go to such lengths to please men.

"You look stunning, miss." Ellie put her hands on her hips and admired her handiwork.

Juliana sighed. "Thank you. I'm not entirely sure I wish to look stunning tonight." Why attract a man if she had no need for one? Yet she must keep up the facade of the bored daughter of a wealthy businessman. 'Twas the price of her independence.

"Miss, 'old still an' I'll apply your powder," Ellie said as Juliana took a seat at her vanity.

"None for me tonight, Ellie. I cannot tolerate the stuff." Candlelight flickered across her reflection in the glass, accentuating the shadows beneath her eyes. Good. She looked as tired as she felt. That should keep some of the wolves at bay.

"But your skin is too golden from the sun. What 'ave I told you about carrying your parasol?"

"I am usually carrying too many other things to worry about my skin. Such as food and clothing for orphans." Juliana raised a brow, regretting her curt tone.

Ellie frowned. "Still, miss, if you are to keep up appearances ..." She grabbed a string of pearls then layered them over Juliana's coiffeur. "Mayhap a patch?"

Juliana's jaw tightened. How she hated the silly things! Yet, she couldn't very well steal all her maid's joy for the night. "Very well. But a small one. Mayhap a star on my forehead."

"But that means you're—"

"I know. 'Tis what I want it to mean." She gave Ellie a stern look, and the lady completed her ministrations without further protest.

Rowan nodded his approval at her appearance as she descended the stairs a few minutes later. He proffered his elbow to escort her to the door, a rather pleased grin on his face.

"What are you about, Brother?" She halted and eyed him with suspicion. "I will brook no further intrusion into my personal life, do you take me? I will court whom I will court when I will court." *If I court anyone.*

Her only answer was a look of abject innocence above a sly grin.

"Besides, I intend to merely make an appearance tonight. I'm tired, Rowan. Surely you can understand." She allowed him to proceed.

"Indeed, I do. Hence, your carriage awaits." He waved her forward.

"Have you summoned Mr. Pell?"

"No need."

She faced him at the door, wondering if Mr. Pell was already in his cups. "Who is driving us?"

"Do give him a chance, Juliana."

"Give who a—"

Before she could finish, Rowan opened the door to the smiling face of Captain Nichols.

Chapter 4

A S SOON AS CAPTAIN NICHOLS turned to address Mr. and Mrs. Billingsworth, Juliana slipped away from the exasperating man. She'd not had a moment to escape ever since he appeared at her door—thanks to her conniving brother. She had a mind to withhold Rowan's weekly allowance for such a dastardly deception. That would teach him! Yet as she wove among the chattering guests, she knew that was not possible. Being heir to their father's dwindling fortune, Rowan had access to every asset.

Seeking a corner wherein she could find a moment's peace, Juliana sank against the wall and surveyed the ballroom. Carved mahogany decorated the doorways, window moldings, and ornamental arches between rooms. Silk wall covering painted with pink rosettes lined the walls all the way to high ceilings whereupon hung glittering chandeliers. An orchestra tuned their instruments on a loft above the room, while guests—decked in the finery of their class—vied for attention from the most influential members of Port Royal society.

One of them, her escort Captain Nichols, settled into his station with unabashed pride as several people approached him, no doubt asking his opinion on this matter or that. Opinions he was evidently delighted to shower on all those around him. In fact, during the entire carriage ride to the Stevenson's home, he had regaled her with tales of his many courageous exploits at sea. She'd merely smiled and nodded at the appropriate times while secretly kicking Rowan from beneath her voluminous skirts as he sat across from her. Once they'd arrived at the party, her cowardly brother had abandoned her, dashing off to find a game of cards, no doubt.

Captain Nichols turned, saw she wasn't beside him, and began surveying the crowd. She must find somewhere to hide. A cluster of young gentlemen glanced at her with interest. A few she knew. A few she did not. All of them she longed to avoid. The warmth of a tropical breeze swirled around her from glassless windows as she dodged an incoming gentleman. Nodding her greeting at Lady Bain, she held up a hand to a servant holding a tray of French macaroons and finally spotted a group of her friends.

"Lady Anne," Juliana said as she approached. "Do allow me residence beside you for a moment." She squeezed in between the woman and Miss Margaret while casting a glance over her shoulder. Good. She'd lost Captain Nichols again.

Lady Anne swung an arm draped in ribbons and lace around Juliana, and tucked her close, dousing her in a cloud of French perfume. Juliana withheld a sneeze as the woman leaned in to whisper. "Hiding from that handsome naval captain? You really should give the man a chance, Juliana. He's obviously lovesick for you."

The other ladies agreed with sly grins. Miss Margaret, Miss Aston, and Lady Anne were Juliana's only friends on the island, though she wondered if they were truly her friends. She doubted they would come to her aid should trouble strike. They certainly hadn't been willing to help Abilene when she needed them the most. "The captain is sick, I'll give you that," she replied. "But I doubt love has much to do with it. Besides, how do you know 'tis him I'm hiding from?"

"We saw you enter on his arm." Miss Ashton pursed her rouged lips. "Did he escort you to the ball?"

"Yes ... No ... I mean I was tricked into accepting his company."

"I should be so tricked." Miss Ashton sighed dreamily and waved her silk fan about her face, sending brown curls dancing. "You must be mad, Juliana. Captain Nichols is wealthy and handsome and every bit a gentleman."

"Then you may have him," Juliana said a bit too tersely. But she meant it. 'Twould that Nichols would grow tired of the useless chase and find another victim to hound.

The orchestra began a lively tune, melding with the cacophony of chatter.

"None of us stand a chance with the captain when you are in the room." Margaret adjusted the lace lining her belled sleeves. "Ever since his intended, Miss Caroline, was suddenly shipped back home to—"

"In disgrace," Lady Anne interjected with a critical brow.

The other ladies gave disapproving nods. "Regardless," Margaret continued, "ever since then, the captain's interest has had but one focus."

A gentleman approached Lady Anne, but she waved him off. "I'm waiting for Lord Canton to ask me to dance," she responded to her friend's curious stares after he'd left.

This seemed to satisfy the ladies, though Juliana had no idea who Lord Canton was. Some wealthy buck newly arrived in Jamaica, no doubt. Indeed, she must attend more functions or she'd be conspicuously devoid of enough gossip to keep up her charade.

"Ah, there is your pursuer." Miss Aston dipped her head to the left, causing her pearled fontange to waver slightly, and for a moment Juliana feared the stiff tiers of lace would slip from her tower of hair to the floor. But she had bigger problems. Nichols was combing the crowd at the edge of the dance floor just a short distance away.

Miss Margaret looped her arm through Juliana's, giggling with glee at the subterfuge. "Let us seek out some refreshments, shall we?"

Much to the dismay of a bevy of young gentlemen—who had been desperately trying to gain the ladies' attention for the past several minutes—Juliana and her friends wove through the throng and emerged onto a triple-arched Georgian portico. White-clothed tables, laden with all manner of drink, fruit cut in fanciful shapes, and coconut sweet cakes stretched across the tiled porch. Beyond, palms and cedar trees waved in the breeze beneath a moonlit sky while the scent of the sea joined the smells of wine, lemon, and coconut in an exotic dance beneath Juliana's nose. Her stomach stirred but then tightened again. She hadn't eaten in hours, yet none of the delicacies appealed to her. Pressing a hand over her jeweled stomacher, she declined a piece of cake Margaret offered.

"Where have you been of late?" the red-haired lady asked as she loaded her plate with food. "You missed our ride into the country last week, and yesterday, croquet."

"Busy." Juliana grabbed a glass of lemonade, hoping it would settle her stomach.

"Busy?" Lady Anne sipped her punch wine. "What else is there to keep us busy save these banal entertainments?" Her bored gaze took in the mob circling the table, no doubt seeking her Lord Canton.

"I am helping the children at Buchan orphanage." Juliana's palms began to sweat at the half-truth and she nearly dropped her glass.

"Oh, lud. Whatever for?" Miss Ashton quickly smiled and fluttered her lashes at a passing gentleman. Then she frowned. "Those dirty little children have diseases don't they? Didn't your mo—"

Margaret nudged Miss Ashton to silence.

But the reminder had already pricked open the wound on Juliana's heart. She forced civility into her angry tone.

"Those *dirty little children* are in great need, while we lack for nothing."

Lady Anne shrugged. "My father gives to charities, what more can we do?"

"It would behoove you to accompany me on a visit to the orphanage some time. These children not only need food and clothing but love and instruction."

"How sad." Margaret tossed sculpted balls of melon into her mouth.

"If you don't stop eating, Margaret," Lady Anne said, "you'll be as fat as a whale, and then no man will have you."

Margaret frowned as Anne turned to Juliana. "'Tis the orphan's lot in life, Juliana." She tightened her lips, causing a tiny crack to form in her powdered makeup. "We cannot save them all. Besides, it appears you have neglected your own wellbeing in the process. You look tired dear, too thin, and your face is far too dark. Why are you not properly made up?"

"If you're not careful, someone may hand you a tray and ask you to serve." Miss Ashton quipped and they all chuckled.

Margaret stuffed a sweet cake in her mouth.

"And your patch is in the wrong place if you wish to attract a gentleman. It suggests you are haughty and aloof."

Juliana fingered the star on her forehead. "Exactly what I wish to portray."

"You are incorrigible, Juliana," Lady Anne declared with a skeptical chuckle. "God gave you such exquisite beauty for one purpose and one purpose alone—to snare title and wealth."

"Alas, what did He give me a brain for, then, I beg you?" Juliana snapped.

They all gaped at her as if she'd asked why they had legs. Did she even know her friends at all? Did they *know* her? "I care not for my skin—" she began, but male laughter drew all gazes to an arched entryway where Lord Munthrope floated in on a cloud of opulence surrounded by a gaggle of toadies who laughed at his every witticism.

"Now, *there* is a man we should set our cap for." Lady Anne pressed a finger on the tiny heart at the corner of her mouth—the position of the patch proclaiming her interest in finding a lover. "He's wealthy beyond belief and the eldest son of an earl."

Juliana curled her lips in disgust as she took in the man. Earl or not, he carried himself like a pimpish fop. Even now, he waved his arms about in a flourish as he spoke, nearly swatting bystanders in the face with his wide lacy cuffs. Tight curls from a white periwig framed a powdered face dotted with various patches, while a foam of mechlin bubbled from beneath his chin. Loops upon loops of colorful ribbons lined his gold-embroidered doublet and continued marching down his breeches, trimmed with Flemish lace. A lady clung to one arm while his jeweled walking stick hung on the other. His voice was too high for his size, and the shrill tone grated over Juliana.

Revulsion hissed in her whisper, "I wouldn't marry him if he were the king of England."

Lady Anne gasped and Margaret almost choked on her cake. From across the room, Lord Munthrope's eyes unexpectedly met Juliana's, and an unusual sensation prickled over her. Turning her gaze away, she brought up a question she'd been meaning to ask.

"Have you heard word of Abilene?"

Lady Anne's nose pinched. A red hue stole up Miss Margaret's face, while Miss Ashton looked away.

"Why would *we* have heard from her?" Lady Anne finally said, her tone ripe with disdain.

"Because she was our friend," Juliana snapped, her anger simmering, "and she is now in a bad way."

Miss Ashton snorted. "Is that what you call it?"

Ignoring her, Juliana continued, "I went to The Cat and the Fiddle last night looking for her, but she was nowhere to be found."

"Forsooth! You went to that haven of pirates?" Lady Anne shrieked, though her tone brimmed more with excitement then fear. "By yourself?"

"My footman was with me but he … he … got lost."

"Lost? My dear, how utterly terrifying!" Lady Anne took the last gulp of wine and set down her glass. "Were you accosted?"

Eyes full of anticipation sped toward Juliana as if they all wished it were so, if only to relieve their boredom.

"Nearly, but someone … a man came to my rescue."

"A man?" Margaret asked.

"A pirate, if you must know. I believe he might have been the Pirate Earl."

"Do say!"

"This is most exciting!"

Miss Ashton leaned toward her, a twinkle in her eye. "I hear he's quite handsome."

Juliana stared at the silly woman, aghast. "He's a *pirate*. What does it matter if he's handsome?"

They all frowned at her declaration. She wouldn't tell them that he was, indeed, very handsome—dangerously handsome.

"Oh, dear, you do have such grand adventures." Lady Anne sighed.

Too many adventures to Juliana's way of thinking.

"Miss Dutton, I couldn't help but overhear." Captain Nichols stepped beside her, drawing quite a few gazes—feminine gazes. Juliana had to admit, the man was dashing in his blue cambric coat with gold braid, white breeches stuffed in tall black boots, and his cocked hat atop a curled brown periwig. Yet his face was anything but handsome at the moment, as his brown eyes were aflame with incredulity. "You encountered that scurrilous Pirate Earl all alone? He is a reprobate of the fiercest kind!" He seethed, barely acknowledging the other ladies. "'Tis unheard of! A lady wandering the streets at night. Does your father know of this?"

Juliana opened her mouth to tell him 'twas none of his affair, when he shook his head in exasperation. "We shall address this later. Lady Stevenson is asking where you are. She wishes to dance a minuet with us." Without awaiting her response, he took her hand, forced it on his arm, and escorted her back into the ballroom. As they passed the entryway, an odd awareness brought her gaze up to see Lord Munthrope in the midst of regaling his sycophants with some embellished narrative.

His stark blue eyes followed her every move.

Chapter 5

LORD MUNTHROPE FINISHED HIS PARODY with mock precision, sending the crowd into a tumult of laughter.

"Munny, you are too much, too much, I say," one of the bystanders announced, hardly able to contain himself. *The fatwit.* Pasting on a smile, Munthrope bowed elegantly and excused himself, much to everyone's dismay.

In the ballroom, his eyes grazed over the pearl-laden coiffures and plumed castors, seeking the object of his interest, Miss Juliana Dutton. He'd noticed her the minute she'd entered the room on the arm of that buffoon, Captain Nichols. He'd watched her as she'd ducked away from the man and hid in the corner, saw her join her goose-brained friends, and then he'd followed her onto the portico. Why? He couldn't say. Mayhap because her skin glowed like amber amongst the pasty white faces of her powdered friends. Mayhap because her golden waves warmed him like sunshine. Though it could be because when he'd gazed into those blue-green eyes of hers that reminded him so much of the sea, he'd found courage and kindness.

Yet 'twas more likely because he hadn't been able to force her from his thoughts after he rescued her last night. And now, from the look on her face, she was in dire need of rescuing again.

He stopped before Miss Wilson, whose flirtations could finally be put to use. After asking her to dance, he swept her onto the floor beside Miss Dutton and that pompous whiffet, Nichols. When she saw him, the corners of her fair eyebrows knit together in the most adorable way, but then the music began and Munthrope was forced to enter the circle with the other men, prancing and hopping like a dizzy court jester. If he must behave like a senseless goose, he might as well entertain his audience. He gave an exaggerated dip of his hand here, a kick of his toe there, and a lift of his arms in a swirling flourish.

Laughter ensued, followed by clapping as Munthrope skipped around a scowling Captain Nichols. When the men twirled back to the women, Munthrope purposely bumbled toward Miss Juliana instead of his own partner. He winked at her, injecting pink into her cheeks and flaming red into Captain Nichols's as the man shoved between them and took Miss Dutton's arm, all the while giving Munthrope a look of scorn.

Munthrope's innocent shrug, followed by a repeat of the same mistake in the next set, caused further jocularity amidst the watching crowd as well as further curses from the poor captain, who dragged Miss Dutton from the floor as soon as the dance ended. Handing Miss Wilson off to an interested gentleman, Munthrope followed the couple down the grand stairway onto the nearly vacant foyer below and finally out onto a private balcony overlooking the gardens.

He slid behind a large potted fern outside the doorway before they could glance his way.

"My dear lady, what an atrocious man. I do hope he didn't ruin your dance," Nichols said.

"Nay. I found him somewhat entertaining, albeit a bit ostentatious."

Munthrope smiled.

Miss Juliana drew a deep breath and gazed over the dark garden. "What are we doing here alone, Captain? 'Tis hardly proper."

She turned to leave, but Nichols grabbed her arm. "I bid you, grant me your ear for but a moment, Juliana."

"Miss Dutton to you, sir."

Nichols let out an exasperated sigh and moved to block the doorway.

Munthrope's fingers itched to teach the man a lesson in chivalry.

But the lady took charge and jerked from Nichols's grasp. "What could you possibly have need to speak to me about alone, Captain?" Her jittery voice betrayed her as her gaze took in the garden, no doubt seeking an escape.

"Miss Dutton." Nichols came to attention as stiff and purposeful as if he were standing before an admiral. Munthrope suppressed a smile at the poor man's nervousness. "I have concluded that you and I are well suited."

"Concluded?" She gave an uneasy laugh. "Have you been conducting some sort of experiment, Captain?"

"Nay, beshrew me!" He looked down. "But I—"

"If you mean we are suited as dance partners, I concur, sir." Juliana said rather hastily as she turned to make a quick escape. Nichols leapt in her path, a mere foot from where Munthrope hid.

He pressed against the wall. Was this the poor fellow's attempt at courting the lady? A dead fish could perform the task better.

"You mistake me, Miss Dutton. What I meant to say—"

"If this is about my venture down to the docks last night," Miss Dutton interrupted, eyes nervously glancing toward the now empty foyer. "I promise to be more careful in the future. Not that it is any of your affair."

"Why wouldn't it be my affair, dear lady?" Nichols took her hand. "Surely you know my feelings for you." The tune of a lively country dance trickled down from above.

"You have always been an agreeable friend." Miss Dutton tugged her hand away. "Now, if you don't mind." Once again she tried to leave.

Once again Nichols forbade her.

Munthrope could take no more. But how to relieve both him and Miss Juliana of the oaf's company? "The Pirate Earl! The Pirate Earl!" He charged onto the balcony, pointing his cane at the surrounding gardens.

Captain Nichols dashed toward the railing and peered into the darkness. "Where? Are you quite sure?"

"Indeed!" Munthrope exclaimed. "While your focus was on the lady, the ruffian appeared in the garden, cutlass drawn, staring at you both as if he would run you through where you stood. A horrifying sight, I tell you. Most horrifying." Munthrope threw a hand to his heart and winked at Juliana, who stared at him aghast.

"My dear." Nichols addressed Juliana, his voice charged with purpose. "He has no doubt come seeking you to finish the job from last night." Turning, he gripped the hilt of his service sword, eyes aflame. "That rogue! I'll not let him slip through my fingers again."

Nichols faced Munthrope. "Milord, will you help me dispatch this villain?"

Munthrope gave an incredulous chuckle and lifted a jeweled hand in the air. "I fear I have not wielded a sword in years, Captain. Hence, I leave the murdering to you."

With a grunt of disgust, Nichols sped away, shouting for assistance as he made his way to the front door.

Miss Juliana took a step back from Munthrope, the hint of a grin on her lips. "If I were to take a guess, milord, I'd wager the Pirate Earl is not here at all."

The sight of her showered in moonlight nearly stole his breath. He recovered with a smile. "Oh, I assure you, he *is* here."

She studied him, her eyes suspicious. And for a moment, Munthrope worried she saw through his disguise. But how could anyone see through the glittery garishness that transformed the Pirate Earl into Lord Munthrope?

"So what now, milord?" she asked. "You have chased away the wolf but have replaced him with a lion."

"A lion, you say?" He chortled. "You flatter me, milady. As you can see I am naught but a sheep. A sheep who is but your servant." With foot outstretched, he swept a bow before her.

"You wish to be my servant, is it? In all the festivities we've both attended, you have ne'er said a word to me."

"To my own sorrow, milady." And indeed, it was. He'd been enchanted with Miss Juliana Dutton since the first night he'd seen her more than two years ago. But the lady's obvious repugnance and repeated dismissals had prevented any conversation. A gentle breeze swirled about them, sending a wayward strand of gold dancing across her forehead.

She narrowed her eyes. "Why do you address me as titled?"

"I find it suits you." He feigned a look of nonchalance, though inside he chastised himself for the mistake.

"Hmm."

Captain Nichols's excited shouts drew her gaze to the garden, where he and several men spread out in search of the nefarious pirate.

"Regardless, I thank you for liberating me from the captain." She clutched her skirts and started to leave.

"I have a proposition for you, Miss Juliana."

She halted, her sharp eyes assessing him as disgust shadowed her delicate features.

"Begad!" He forced a look of shock. "Not that sort of proposition, I assure you. Oh, what you must think of me." Pressing a lace-covered hand to his chest, he leaned toward her and whispered. "I speak of a bargain that benefits us both."

"You have nothing that would benefit me, milord. Return to your fawning coterie." She forged past him in a whiff of vanilla and cherry that brought back pleasant memories of the night before.

"Ouch, miss. I am sorely wounded." He fell into step with her.

"You will no doubt recover in time," she quipped as she appeared to be searching for someone among the few people loitering in the foyer.

Ah, such wit! Munthrope stopped beside her. He must find a way to tame this wild cat. "I beg you—allow me to escort you home, Miss Juliana? I believe Captain Nichols will be otherwise engaged for quite some time."

"My brother is here somewhere."

"He left with Mrs. Blanesworth, I believe. Her husband is abroad, you know."

Her mouth twisted in a knot.

"My footman will join us," Munthrope urged. "It will be entirely proper, I assure you. Do hear me out, I beg?"

"Begging does not become you, milord." Finally the semblance of a smile curved her mouth.

"I cry pardon! The lady has discovered me." He laughed. "Upon my oath, there will be no more begging this night." He lifted one gloved hand toward her and raised his painted brows in a ridiculous attempt to appear harmless.

It elicited yet another smile from Miss Juliana. "Very well. But I assure you, milord, if you seek a tryst, you will be sorely disappointed."

Disappointed? Munthrope doubted it. Nothing about this woman disappointed him.

Not even when she refused to look at him in the carriage as it ambled toward her home. Though small in stature, this was no frail lady. Straight back, shoulders lifted, she sat with dignity as she gazed out the window at the passing scenery. A warm breeze danced among the soft waves of her coiffure and sent one golden strand dangling again across her forehead. How he longed to touch her porcelain skin, if only to see if it felt as soft as it looked. With a gloved hand, she brushed the lock away. Passing streetlamps sent wavelets of golden light over her, drawing his gaze to the healthy blush of her cheeks, and the silvery fringe of her neckline, rising and falling beneath each strong breath. He wondered if she was frightened of him, but thought better of it. She had not shown fear the night before when faced with the dreaded Pirate Earl, why should she be alarmed in the company of such a dainty nincompoop?

Yet despite the lady's strength, she seemed to bear the weight of the world upon her delicate shoulders. Finally she faced him, cynicism in her eyes.

"What is it you want, milord?"

"Want?" His voice came out too low. He coughed into his hand, forcing it higher. "Rather, Miss Juliana, you should be asking what I can give."

She merely stared at him.

"Can I be forthright?" He set his cane atop the seat while he rested a hand on his silk breeched knee.

"I do not know, can you?" she returned with a lifted brow.

Munthrope hid his smile. "I could not help but notice you were—how shall I say—not entirely receptive to Captain Nichols's advances."

Her lips tightened. "I don't see how—"

"I know the man." Munthrope withdrew a handkerchief and waved it in the air. "He will not give up. He will pursue you until you give in to him out of sheer exhaustion."

"You do me a discredit, milord, if you find me so weak."

"On the contrary, I hate to see such a strong woman abused."

The carriage pitched, and she gripped the seat. "I can handle the captain."

"But why endure the struggle?" He leaned forward, tossing the curls of his blasted periwig over his shoulder. "Why not put an end to this annoying insect?"

The carriage lurched to a stop before her house. She hesitated, staring out the window at her home. "What do you propose?"

His footman, leapt down to open the door, but Munthrope waved him off. "A betrothal to me, Miss Juliana."

Fie, she knew she shouldn't have allowed the fop to bring her home. Huffing at his impertinence, she reached for the door. "Good night, milord."

He touched her hand. "Not a real betrothal, of course. A charade. A pretense to keep Nichols at bay until he sets his sights on another lady."

She hesitated, studying him, but his eyes were lost to her in the shadows. A cloud of his perfume—a mixture of cinnamon and rose—enveloped her. Nearly gagging, she opened the door and attempted to step from the carriage, refused the footman's hand, and tripped on her voluminous skirts.

Munthrope grabbed her elbow and settled her. How had he leapt from the carriage so fast when he'd seemed unable to dance a minuet without bumbling?

He released her arm. She felt his eyes pierce her. He stood so close—much closer than at the party—and she hadn't realized how tall he was, how unsettled she felt in his presence. She took a step back. "And just what does this charade entail?" she said, mainly to fill the uncomfortable silence.

"Begad. Nothing untoward, I assure you." He raised a hand in the air, returning to his foppish stance, which did much to allay her fears. "I propose only that you allow me to escort you to society's functions, accept my protection once there, and join me in an occasional stroll through town as required to satisfy flapping tongues."

She watched him adjust the ribbons at his cuffs. Protection, indeed. Should they ever be accosted, no doubt he'd be the one screaming in the corner while she fought off the villains. How could she court, even in pretense, a man whom she found so fluff-headed and effeminate?

"I mean no disrespect, milord, but I am not"—she bit her lip and studied the way moonlight made the scarlet hibiscus lining her walkway look like blood—"I simply do not wish to …" Fie, how could she best put this?

"Engage yourself to me?" He chuckled. "'Twould that other ladies in town were of the same mind. I grow weary of their attentions." He gave a sigh.

His vanity annoyed her. "Oh you poor man." She turned to leave, but he caught her elbow.

"I chose you precisely because you've made your disinterest in me quite clear. Believe me, the last thing I desire is to marry. Nay, 'twould be like caging a wild falcon." He twirled a lock of his white periwig and gazed up at the night sky. "And this falcon is having far too much fun flying free."

"So the lion that turned into a sheep has now become a falcon. Soon we will have an entire jungle full of animals at our disposal."

She thought she saw one side of his mouth curve upward. Still, she didn't trust him. What possible benefit would this charade be to him? Moonlight shifted over his powdered face and landed on the small patch of a horse above his right eye. "If you wish to be free, be free, milord. Betrothing yourself to me would only hinder that." A breeze fluttered the filigree lace at his collar as a bell clanged in the distance.

His expression grew serious even as an intensity claimed his eyes. "In truth, I must satisfy my father, the Earl of Clarendon." He stomped his walking cane on the stone pathway. "He insists I choose a wife soon, or he threatens to bring me the first she-devil he finds in London."

Juliana nodded, still hesitant. "Word of our espousal would stay his hand."

"For the time being. So you see," He held her gaze, "my proposal 'twould benefit us both."

Her front door creaked open, sending a river of light onto the uneven stones. Mr. Abbot appeared, lantern in hand. "Miss Dutton, are you all right?"

"Yes, Abbot, thank you. A moment please." She returned her attention to Lord Munthrope as Abbot remained in the entryway. Though she was anxious to hear the butler's report of the day's business, Munthrope's proposal was not without appeal. How wonderful to be relieved of Nichols's persistence. She could far better keep her business a secret without his constant meddling— without *any* suitors coming around. In addition, a betrothal with Munthrope would surely satisfy her brother and keep his schemes to see her wed at bay. And if Munthrope was telling the truth, he would require nothing more than making appearances in society, which she was forced to do anyway. *If* he was telling the truth. But why would he lie? What purpose would it serve? He could have his pick of any lady on the island, yet he chose the one who wanted nothing to do with him.

An insect hovered near his face. Shrieking, he leapt back, withdrew a handkerchief, and swatted it away. "Dreadful beasts."

Juliana couldn't help but chuckle. If anything, the man's company would be entertaining.

He contained himself and handed the handkerchief to his footman. "If you would favor me with your answer, Miss Juliana?"

Chapter 6

MUNTHROPE AWAITED HER ANSWER WITH more anticipation than he cared to admit. Finally the lady raised her gaze to his, wiggled her pert little nose and said, "I agree, milord."

Before the lovely swan floated away, Munthrope raised her hand to his lips, wishing it was bare skin he touched rather than silk gloves.

She tugged it away. "I agree to a masquerade, milord— one in which you take no liberties."

"Ah, but the masquerade must be convincing, does it not? Pray, a simple kiss on the hand is to be expected." Though now, as a swath of light from her servant's lantern alighted upon her moist lips, Munthrope longed to do more.

"In public, only, milord. We've no need for pretense otherwise." She raised a brow before gathering her skirts and starting for the steps to her house.

"I do not gainsay it, Miss Juliana." He smiled. "However, surely I should speak with your father. To ask for your hand? Will he not suspect otherwise?"

Halting, she faced him. A nervous flicker appeared in her eyes. "What need of it when 'tis naught but a sham. I shall speak to him."

Munthrope dipped his head and started for his carriage, longing to extend the conversation with this enchanting woman. The footman opened the door. Munthrope spun back around, swinging his raised arms through the air. "Begad, we should announce our betrothal. Host a party. At my house, Saturday next. I'll send out the cards."

"Very well, milord." Her mumble was devoid of enthusiasm as she exchanged an anxious glance with her butler. "Good eve to you, milord."

"Good night, milady." He forgot himself momentarily and his voice deepened. Twirling around, he entered the carriage with as much aplomb as he could stomach to cover the mistake. After the footman hopped on, the driver snapped the reins and they started down the street. Only a few seconds passed when Munthrope thumped his cane against the roof to stop him. "Wait here a moment."

Munthrope didn't move. That "moment" turned into several minutes as nothing but the neigh of horses, distant lap of waves, and hoot of an owl drifted through the carriage. But then it came, floating on a salty breeze, the most delightful sound he'd ever heard. Like the sweet caress of a lover's touch, it swirled around him, easing his taut muscles, uncoiling his nerves, lifting unknown burdens from his heavy heart. The delicate siren of the violin. *Her* violin. The one she oft played before retiring. No doubt it helped her fall sleep as much as it soothed his soul.

Easing back on the leather seat, he closed his eyes and allowed the melody—a sad one tonight—to perform its magic on him. As it had so many nights before. But the pleasant notes ended abruptly, leaving him empty and forlorn.

Back at his home, he charged up the porch steps. The door opened as expected, and he marched inside, tossing his cane into the corner. He tore off his plumed tricorne and idiotic periwig and cast them over his shoulder to Mr. Whipple, who he knew would be behind him. The smug valet/butler followed Munthrope up the stairs into his bedchamber.

"Unpleasant evening, milord?" Whipple's tone mocked.

"Aren't they all, Whipple?" Munthrope snorted as he approached his wardrobe and began shedding his silly attire.

Whipple stood staunchly by. "If you would take a breath, milord, I could help you."

"I loathe being attired like a swaggering popinjay!" Munthrope ran a hand through his hair.

"'Tis the fashion, milord. Albeit, you do take it a bit too far."

"A fashion for fools."

Mr. Whipple, a superior look on his face, opened the wardrobe and pulled out a pair of leather breeches, jackboots, a white shirt, and leather jerkin, "And yet you prefer to dress like a reprobate."

Ignoring the man, Munthrope approached his chest of drawers and began scrubbing his face over a basin of water, ripping off patches and fake moles. "The itch and stink of this paste drives me mad."

"Then don't wear it. Most gentlemen do not."

"You know I must or I might be recognized." He grabbed a towel and dried his face, then stood staring at his image in the looking glass. No longer a dainty princock, Alexander Edward Hyde, Lord Munthrope, son of Edmond Merrick Hyde, the Earl of Clarendon reflected in the dim lantern light. He slicked back his moist black hair.

Also known as the Pirate Earl.

"Why you carry on with this pretense, I have no idea. Your father would be appalled."

"My father is not here." Alex spun and took the clothing from Whipple.

"A fact I regret every day." The valet stared at him with more boldness than a servant should.

But he wasn't truly a servant.

Indeed, Alex's father had sent him to Jamaica with the title of valet, but Mr. Whipple had been with their family for as long as Alex could remember. A trusted confidant of Alex's father, he'd been a valet, butler, protector, even school-master whenever Alex's father had been away. He'd also been a friend. Why, he'd even spent some time sailing on Alex's father's ship, *The Redemption,* years ago.

However, his present assignment was to help Alex do God's work in Port Royal. How long had it been since they'd arrived in the "wickedest city in the Caribbean" full of foolish hopes and unfounded zeal to save the lost? Five years? Alex could hardly remember those days, though Whipple reminded him of them often. Still, the valet was the only man Alex could count on, the only one besides Alex's quartermaster who knew of his dual identity. He took care of Alex and kept his secrets. No matter how far Alex descended into the pit of hell.

Shaking off the thought, Alex quickly donned his leather breeches, jerkin, and cotton shirt, then stretched his back, relishing in the familiar feel of comfortable clothes.

"Why bother with the charade? Why not just remain"— Whipple scrunched his nose in disdain—"*what* you have become."

"A pirate you mean?" Alex grinned, shoved his feet into his jackboots, then strode to a cupboard and flung open the doors. Inside, rows of cutlasses, short swords, pistols, and muskets stared back at him.

"Let us not mince words, Whipple." He selected a cutlass and shoved it into his scabbard then picked up two pistols and hooked them in his baldric. "Just because I am a pirate doesn't mean I wish to spend my idle time cavorting with ignorant curs. My intellect requires more stimulating conversation."

"And have you found it in society?" The chink of glass sounded.

Alex frowned. "Very little, I'm afraid." He closed the cupboard and faced Whipple with a grin. "I do, however, find myself entertained by the imbecilic performance most of them put on for one another. Besides there are only so many ships to plunder. What else am I to do when I'm in port?"

"Your brandy, milord."

He took the glass and sipped the amber liquid. Heat stroked his throat and radiated through his belly as he strode to the open window and gazed at the distant bay. Bare masts rose like candlesticks dripping with waxy moonlight—dozens and dozens of them. Merchant ships from England, the colonies, East Indiamen, fishermen, privateers, and *pirates*. He couldn't locate his ship among the others, but he knew she was out there. He could hear her call to him on the wind.

"I'll be taking the *Vanity* out tonight, Whipple."

"Very well, milord. No doubt there are ships desperate for your gentle hand at plundering. When shall I expect you back?"

"A few days." Alex longed to be at sea—where he could be himself, where life made sense, where he could taste danger and assuage the emptiness inside.

"Do you require my presence?"

"Nay. I need you here. We are hosting a ball next Saturday. Hire a bevy of servants if you must, but I want it to be a lavish affair."

"And what, pray tell, is the occasion?" Mr. Whipple began picking up Alex's discarded clothes.

Alex's gaze shifted south of High Street, where Miss Dutton lived, but nary a light lit the shadowy scene. "A betrothal! Mine, in fact, to a Miss Juliana Dutton."

Silence met his proclamation. The click of Mr. Whipple's shoes grated over Alex before the man appeared beside him.

"A wife?" Whipple's voice rose in shock. "Will you finally put an end to this roistering, milord, or do you dare drag a lady into your sordid existence?"

Sordid? Alex chuckled and stared at his valet. Barely a handful of dark hair remained atop a head whose expression beneath bore a nobility the man's status would forever forbid him. Thick shoulders spanned above a portly body that remained strong despite his eight-and-fifty years. "'Tis a favor I am doing her, Whipple."

One thick eyebrow rose before the man spun around. "Lavishing her with your charm, no doubt? Your astounding wit? Offering her the prestige of your association?"

Alex took another sip of brandy. "Though I hardly owe you an answer, I am protecting her."

"Pray, who will protect her from you?" The clack of the door sounded as Whipple closed it behind him.

Alex grinned. Indeed. He wondered that as well. Across the shadowy island, trees swayed in the trade winds, adding their soothing chorus to the distant swoosh of waves and rattle of a passing carriage. Down by the wharves—his territory—lights from hundreds of lanterns twinkled in an inverted dark heaven. Yet heaven had nothing to do with what went on there. A tune rode on the wind, along with the *pop pop* of pistols and a hollow scream.

He *was* protecting Miss Juliana. From that horrid man, Nichols. But in truth, he simply wanted to be near her. For two years, ever since she'd entered society, he'd been watching her, unavoidably drawn to her like a moth to a lantern. Even at eighteen she had stood out—a swan among so many swine. Refusing to dress and act like the rest of the bacon-witted minions, she almost seemed as bored as Alex was with the affairs of high society. Also unlike the wealthier of her class, she cared about those in need, spending hours at the Buchan orphanage wiping runny noses and ministering to castoffs that most of her friends wouldn't even notice should they pass them on the street.

Then, just last night, he realized her charity extended even to trollops. He could hardly believe his eyes when he'd seen her walk into The Cat and the Fiddle. If there was a God, Alex would thank him for putting him in that tavern at that precise time or the lady would have certainly forfeited her purity—or worse, her life. She was either very brave or very foolish. He imagined a bit of both. And such wit! He could spend a lifetime parrying her sarcastic quips.

For years, he'd wondered how to approach the swan without frightening her away. She had made it quite plain that a woman of her caliber and intelligence wanted naught to do with the pompous Lord Munthrope, nor would she associate with the scurrilous Pirate Earl. However, during the past few months, as he'd witnessed her disdain for Captain Nichols, an idea had formed in Alex's mind, a way to get close to the lady. And tonight he'd pulled it off—beautifully.

But why? Why go to such lengths to spend time with a woman he hardly knew?

Because Alex was so bored. So terribly bored. And she was the only spark left in the smoldering coals of his life.

Chapter 7

AN HOUR LATER, CAPTAIN ALEXANDER Hyde swung over the bulwarks of the *Vanity* and planted his boots on the sturdy oak deck. The night watch and those of his crew who were still awake scrambled to attention before their leader.

"Cap'n, we didn't expect ye tonight," one of the riggers said nervously as he shoved an open bottle of rum behind his back.

"I found myself with a sudden thirst for French treasure." Alex scanned his crew, naught but shifting shadows in the light of a single lantern hung from the main mast. "What say you?"

"Aye!" Shouts rang across the two-masted brig as sailors emerged from below, including Alex's master gunner, Bait, a massive one-armed Negro whom Alex had fished from the sea last year before the sharks could finish him off.

"Welcome aboard, Captain." Jonas, his quartermaster, smiled and fisted hands at his waist.

Alex nodded his greeting to his faithful friend—most likely his only friend in the world, besides Whipple. "Is Larkin aboard?"

"Aye, Cap'n," one of the crew replied. "He only jist arrived. A bit cupshotten, if ye ask me."

Larkin drunk? What else was new? Alex grumbled as he marched past the men. "Ready the ship. We'll hoist sail at first light." Which he reckoned to be in an hour by the looks of the gray lining the horizon.

"Spittal!" He swung to face the cook. "Brew coffee for Larkin. For all of us, in fact. And Riggs"—he turned to the bo'sun—"ensure Larkin is ready for duty."

"Aye, aye, Cap'n." The short, squat man dropped down a hatchway that barely fit his wide berth.

Leaping up the quarterdeck ladder, Alex descended the companionway and burst into his cabin, Jonas on his heels.

"Run out of doubloons already? We only arrived in port yesterday morn." Jonas shut the door.

Alex circled his oak desk, scanning its haphazard contents: open books, quill pens, parchments with odd diagrams of human innards. "What's all this?" His voice came out coarser than intended.

Jonas slid onto a chair before the desk, one hand fingering the thick brown whiskers angling down his jaw. "You told me I could attend my studies in your cabin, remember?"

Alex frowned, opened a drawer, pulled out a bottle of brandy, and poured two glasses full.

"I thought we were having coffee." Jonas raised a critical brow.

"Indeed. To counteract this." Alex smiled, then gestured with his cup to the volumes open on his desk. "It would behoove you to remove your physician manuals posthaste." He cringed as he looked at a drawing of what appeared to be intestines. "Else I cannot vouch they will remain unscathed should we encounter a prize."

"I will gladly do so, if you will tell me what has got you in such ill humor."

"You will gladly do so because I am your captain." Alex snapped back, taking another sip of brandy. He set down the glass and began sifting through the papers and books. "Ah, there." Finding a cord, he tied his hair behind him. "I fail to see why you study anatomy when you are the best quartermaster to ever sail the seas. You'll never suffer for lack of employment."

"Is that what you call this?" Jonas chucked and ran a hand through his thick blondish-red hair. "Odds fish, and here I assumed we were naught but thieves." Rising to his feet, he snatched a pair of spectacles from the desk and slipped them inside his vest pocket before he began gathering his books.

"I can hardly credit it!" Alex mocked. "We are the king's men at war with France." At least that's what Alex liked to tell himself. Though he supposed it didn't matter in the end.

"You have no letter of marque." Sharp green eyes assessed him from within the sarcastic yet kind expression of his friend—the man who had sailed with Alex these past four years.

"A trifle, dear Jonas. A trifle." Alex gulped the rest of his brandy and handed Jonas the other glass.

The quartermaster refused. "I prefer my wits about me when we go about murdering and pillaging. One of these days we may get caught and face the gibbet."

Alex tossed the man's brandy to the back of his throat and shrugged. "'Tis possible I suppose, though highly unlikely."

"I pray God revives your good sense before then."

"You may pray all you wish, my friend, but where I am concerned, heaven has always been silent."

Alex wished heaven was silent four hours later when the *Vanity* heaved through an agitated sea beneath skies bellowing with thunder. Still, the storm was just a minor squall from what he could tell, verified by Larkin, the ship's sailing master who'd been sailing these seas since before he was weaned.

No worries, then. Alex loved the spicy scent of rain in the air, the force of the wind flapping his shirt as he stood at the prow, arms folded over his chest, boots spread for balance over the heaving deck. What was it about the sea—the wild, adventurous sea—that stirred his soul and heated his blood? He supposed he'd inherited that love from his father, who'd once been the greatest pirate on the Caribbean some twenty-five years past. In fact, his father had rescued his mother off a deserted island not far from where Alex now sailed. Rescued her, and together they had become missionaries to the pirates. But that was a story for another time. For now, Alex liked to picture his father, Captain Merrick, standing in much the same position Alex now stood, commanding his ship of pirates as they scoured the sea for treasure. That was before his father had turned to God and given up the pirate's life for his namby-pamby religion.

The *Vanity* pitched over a roller, sending spray over the deck. Alex shook the water from his hair, wishing he could shake the memories of his childhood as well. It wasn't a bad upbringing. He and his two sisters had every need met, a good education, and the love of wonderful parents. When they'd been home. More often than not, his mother and father had been away on some godly mission, leaving Alex and his sisters in the care of wet-nurses and housekeepers. And of course, Mr. Whipple. Each charged on pain of death to keep the youngsters confined in a prison of religiosity and morality that had nearly strangled Alex. And though his parents espoused a loving God when they were around, Alex wondered if the Almighty was as absent from Alex's life as his parents had always been.

Lightning cracked the retreating dark clouds, followed by a low rumble of thunder minutes later. However, Alex had gained one valuable thing from his father—his ability to command a ship. When Captain Merrick had been home, he'd taken Alex out on *The Redemption*, taught him everything about a brig from keel to keelson: how to navigate, sail, determine weather, read the stars, smell danger in the wind. He'd even taught him how to load and fire a cannon, wield a cutlass, fire a flintlock, and make grenades.

And Alex had fallen in love with the sea. For it was upon her waters—and only there—that he'd had his father's full attention. During those countless hours together, Alex had come to know the honorable man who had sired him. Regardless of his father's belief in a nonexistent God and his life's useless devotion to the same, Captain Merrick was a brave warrior. A good man who cared for others.

Alex smiled. Such fond memories. Albeit short ones. For no sooner would they make port in Charleston than his father would leave again on some mission.

Movement broke his musings as Larkin appeared beside him.

"There's a ship off our starboard quarter, Captain."

Alex swung about, scanned the horizon, but saw nothing. Yet he trusted the sailing master, who seemed to have a talent for smelling a ship before it ever appeared. "I swear you're either part fish or part bird, Larkin." Alex plucked out his scope.

Larkin grinned and snapped dark hair from his face as the ship bucked over a swell and a blast of briny air struck them. Dressed in all black from his leather boots, breeches, and billowing shirt to his silver laced jerkin, the only thing of color on the sailing master was a red cravat and his stark gray eyes. Tall, muscled, and in possession of an inherent charm, 'twas no wonder the ladies flocked toward him like birds to their favored nest. The best sailing master on the seas, Larkin had sailed with Alex for two years, yet a slight hesitancy, an insincerity in his eyes, forbade Alex to completely trust him.

"A sail! A sail!" bellowed from the tops. Before the lookout announced the direction, Alex lifted his glass to the area Larkin had indicated. And there she stood, a three-masted, square-rigged Dutch Fluyt slipping through the turquoise water without a care in the world.

"Three points off the starboard quarter!" came the direction.

Alex shifted the scope to the ship's colors flapping from the mainhead. French. Good. A French merchantman. Snapping the glass shut, he shared a grin with Larkin. "I trust you've not partaken since last night. I need clear heads."

Larkin gave a shrug. "When have I let you down?"

Thus far, the man had not. Though a residual sting of alcohol still hovered around him.

Alex stormed to waist. "All hands on deck! Helm, hard aport! Up tops and gallants!"

Larkin nodded and turned, bellowing orders to the crew. Topmen leapt into the ratlines and raced up the shrouds.

"Stations for stays! Bring her about. Helms alee!" Larkin continued, sending more men scrambling over the deck. Within minutes, the ship tacked slowly about, cordage straining and blocks creaking, and the railing flirting dangerously with the rushing sea as the ship canted to starboard. Suddenly, nothing but the mad dash of water and groan of wood could be heard as sails drooped impotent, mourning their momentary loss of wind with angry flaps and flutters, only to glut themselves fully with a thunderous clap when the ship turned to catch the breeze.

"Brace up the weather yards! All canvas out!" Alex commanded. Then facing his sailing master, "Bring us to windward of them, if you please, Larkin."

Larkin examined the Fluyt before bellowing further orders to the excited crew. Jonas appeared from below. Strapping a belt and cutlass to his hip, he nodded to Alex. Though the quartermaster made no effort to hide his disapproval of pirating, he fulfilled his duties with more heart and skill than most of the crew, fighting alongside them during battle and stitching up the injured afterward.

Close-hauled to the eastern wind and listing to starboard under the force of it, the *Vanity* rose and plunged through the turquoise waters. Sunlight pierced the clouds overhead, stabbing the scene with shafts of light as the storm retreated on the horizon.

Grabbing the backstay, Alex leapt onto the bulwarks, allowing the wind to whip him as he gazed intently at their prey. The French merchants had spotted him, and with all sail crowded in a bloated mass of grey and white, they swung about, wagging their foamy stern in defiance. No doubt they had recognized the Pirate Earl's flag—a skull and a shield, both pierced by a sword—and were shivering in their froggish skins. Alex's reputation as a fierce and relentless pirate spanned the entire Spanish Main.

The *Vanity* dipped into the trough of a wave, and Alex tightened his grip on the stay, closing his eyes for a moment and relishing in the wind and salty spray and the smell of life and brine and the shouts of his men. Blood dashed through his veins, his senses heightened, his dormant heart sparked to life. Had his father felt this same thrill when he'd been king of the Caribbean? Would he be proud of his only son? Or would he feel naught but shame and disgust? Most likely the latter, which leeched some of his excitement. Would that his father had remained a pirate, and he and Alex could rule these seas together. But Merrick had taken another path, devotion to an invisible God. And though Alex had started down that path, it had ended in darkness and disappointment.

Nigh an hour later, as they fast approached the much slower ship, Alex gathered the men on deck and glared down at them from his position by the helm. They were a fierce crew, some barely wet behind the ears, some who'd lived on the sea more than on land—all with greed and malice dripping from their eyes. They were filthy, fetid, sporting mismatched articles of stolen attire, and adorned with every kind of weapon known to man, the metal of which now blinked in the sunlight. But they were *his* crew. Men he had made rich, and because of that, men who obeyed his every command. At first the power had intoxicated him. But after a while, even that had become commonplace. Nevertheless, he must use that power now to keep these miscreants under control.

"You well know the articles you put your mark to when you signed on with me," he shouted above the wind, scanning the mob and noting the faces of two men he'd recently recruited. "We are gentlemen of fortune, not savages. We are out for gold, not blood. Hence, you will avoid unnecessary violence to our dear frog friends." Bracing his boots on the heaving deck, Alex fisted hands at his waist. "We will take their gold and silver and pearls. And if necessary, we will take them prisoner. But there will be no slaughter. Or you'll answer to me!"

Jonas nodded his approval. Larkin crossed thick arms over his chest and scowled. And though groans of disappointment filtered through the crowd, all finally agreed.

Alex raised his cutlass in the air. "Let us be after our prey!"

"Aye! Aye!" Shouts followed as the men dispersed to their duties.

"Extinguish the galley fire. Sand the decks!" Larkin commanded.

Sails thundered in anticipation of battle. Wind whipped Alex's shirt as he made his way to the railing to glance at their fleeing prey. He grinned. Within seconds, they'd be well on her weather quarter. Scanning the deck, he found the master gunner. "Run out the guns, if you please, Bait!"

The one-armed Negro flashed two rows of blinding white teeth at Alex before issuing orders for the gun crew to ready the ten culverins housed at intervals along the bulwarks.

A flame shot from the hull of the Fluyt, followed seconds later by a shattering *boom*!

"To the deck!" Jonas shouted, and the men dropped to the planks. All except Alex, who stood firm upon the quarterdeck, glaring at his enemy. He cared not if the shot struck him. Many a day he had begged for a cannon ball to tear him asunder. He had no fear of death. Forsooth, he welcomed it. At least it would offer a change in his otherwise meaningless existence.

The shot splashed into the sea several yards from the ship, and soon the men were on their feet flinging curses at their enemy for daring to defend herself.

"Sweep across her bow to rake her!" Alex commanded, and Larkin marched over the deck issuing commands to the topmen.

With every stitch of canvas spread, the *Vanity* swung about, pitching over endless waves. The *pop pop pop* of musket fire showered them from the Frenchmen's tops, sending the pirates scrambling for cover. A scream drew Alex's gaze to one of his men holding his shoulder, blood spilling down his arm. Jonas sped toward him and gazed up at Alex, who nodded his consent for the would-be physician to take him below.

White foam exploding over her bow, the *Vanity* creaked and groaned and heaved as she sped across the Fluyt's stern.

"Fire!" Alex shouted.

The air ignited with ten blasts that shook the ship from truck to keelson. The culverins leapt back a good foot beneath the strain as smoke poured over the railing, dousing them in a stinging, blinding cloud.

Coughing and batting it aside, Alex peered toward their enemy. Shouts of anger and fright ricocheted across her decks as the Frenchmen rushed to and fro assisting their wounded. Above them, shredded canvas flapped, ropes parted, blocks hung, and jagged pieces of wood stuck out from a mizzen mast that wobbled beneath the weight. Within minutes a white flag inched its way up the main truck.

"They surrender, Captain!" Larkin shouted.

But another flag in the distance caught Alex's eye. The Union Jack blowing in the wind from the mainmast of a Royal Navy frigate. And they were heading straight his way.

Chapter 8

ALEX CURSED UNDER HIS BREATH. Where had the Navy frigate come from? 'Twas as if they'd followed him out of Port Royal. That's three times now that one of His Majesty's ships had come upon him while he was in the midst of capturing a prize. Such a thing happening in the vast Caribbean was unheard of. He narrowed his eyes upon the approaching enemy, gauging their speed and position. With the direction of the wind, it would take them at least an hour to tack their way to Alex's brig. He had time to plunder the French Fluyt. Not *much* time, but he knew his men could do it. Besides, the danger of it, the risk, ignited every nerve and fiber, bringing him back to life. Finally a challenge!

"Prepare to board!" he yelled as he leapt down to the waist of the ship. The crew stood still, shifting their wide gazes between the oncoming frigate and the French merchant ship.

"I said, prepare to board! And be quick about it!" Alex all but growled.

Grumbling, his crew obeyed. Sharpshooters sped to the tops while the rest further armed themselves and prepared the grapnels.

"Bait, reload the guns," Alex ordered the master gunner. They might need them against the frigate if time ran out.

Minutes later, the *Vanity* came alongside the Fluyt. Grappling hooks were thrown, the ships thudded together, and with cutlass drawn, Alex led his pack of pirates onto the deck of the merchant ship. He wished the French captain and his officers would have given some resistance—made things a bit more interesting—but even with the assurance of the British frigate approaching, they merely stood there, relinquishing their weapons and cowering like puppies. No doubt they believed the Royal Navy would capture the pirates and return their goods forthwith.

Obviously, they had not had the pleasure of an encounter with the Pirate Earl.

Alex grew bored. So terribly bored. He took up a position leaning against the rail while some of his crew guarded the French and the rest did what they did best—plundered the treasure below. Within a half hour, all the silver, jewels, valuable foodstuffs, spirits, and anything else they could sell for pieces of eight were hoisted above and carried to the *Vanity*. Thankfully there were no females on board, for Alex did not relish the thought of protecting them from his men. Though he did have to restrain a few pirates from harming a foolish French sailor who dared to spit at them as they passed.

Alex raised his scope to the oncoming enemy, when a gush of French stung his ears. "He will catch you and kill you, filthy pirate."

Lowering his glass, Alex eyed the captain of the French ship, a man too young to fully understand the threat he was facing. Slight of figure and sharp of chin, he raised a haughty nose toward Alex.

Alex responded in fluent French, "The Pirate Earl is never filthy, Monsieur, and neither will he *ever* be caught." Enjoying the surprise registering in the man's eyes at Alex's command of the language, Alex raised his scope again, focusing on the commander of the frigate. Lud, what devilment was this? He'd recognize that sturdy stance and grim face anywhere. 'Twas the idiot, Captain Nichols. Egad, the man was relentless! Would his grudge against Alex never cease? Cursing, he slammed his scope shut.

Larkin approached, the greed in his eyes of only moments ago transformed into fear. "Captain, we should leave."

Alex agreed. "Back to the ship, men!" he bellowed.

The crew happily complied, bidding adieu and tossing insults upon their victims as they hoisted armfuls of goods back to the *Vanity*. Alex leapt from the Fluyt to his own deck, regretting not having time to take the merchant ship as prize. Grapnel lashings were cut as the remaining pirates scrambled over the bulwarks.

"Lay aloft and loose main sail! Hoist away royals and jib!"

The crew scattered to do his bidding, and within minutes the *Vanity's* sails were raised, seeking the wind as the brig inched away from the Fluyt. With their guns flooded with water and their weapons confiscated, the defanged French could do naught but watch.

The Royal Navy was another story.

Bearing down on them at full speed, the frigate fired a shot from their bow swivels. It pounded the air and skipped across the sea just short of the *Vanity's* larboard quarter.

Finally the *Vanity's* sails caught the wind with a deafening crack as each canvas spread to the favoring breeze, full and taut. The brig tacked to larboard and shot a stream of seawater off her starboard quarter toward their enemy. Alex smiled. The fastest ship on the Caribbean!

Another boom labored from the frigate, but once again the shot slipped impotent into the sea. Bracing his boots on the canting deck, Alex turned a haughty eye toward his enemy. He needed no spyglass to see the fury twisting Nichols's face as he paced the quarterdeck spouting orders to his crew. Halting, he raised a scope toward Alex as another jet of flame and thunder of a shot cracked the air. This time, the splash lagged even farther off *Vanity's* stern.

Removing his plumed hat, Alex gave a leg and dipped a flourishing bow toward his archenemy. He could almost hear Nichols growl in fury—almost. When he righted himself, he gave a salute before turning and heading toward the main deck.

"Proud of yourself?" Jonas joined him, his shirt splattered with maroon stains.

"Yes," Alex returned, raising a brow at the blood. "How is Milford?"

"He will live. This time." Jonas drew Alex to the railing away from the pirates, some of whom were already passing around rum in celebration. "But how many more lives will be lost to satisfy your lust for adventure?"

"'Tis not my lust alone, but the way of pirates."

"But you don't even need the treasure, nor the—"

"I do it because I'm good at it," Alex interrupted, his anger simmering. "Because it is who my father was and who I am. I do it because I am free to do it should I choose. I need no other reason. If you detest it so, why sail with me?"

Jonas rubbed the back of his neck and gazed at his friend with amused irritation. "Call it fate, call it God, but I fear my destiny is to be by your side, Alex. Think of me as your conscience."

Alex snorted. "Faith now, my conscience, sir? I relieved myself of that damnable folly years ago." He laughed.

"Precisely my point."

Alex gripped the railing. "I fear you embark on an impossible mission, my good man. Mayhap you should choose another."

"I have not chosen it. It has chosen me." Jonas smiled with a shrug, then gazed across the blue expanse. "What now, my fearless pirate?"

Alex raised gleeful brows. "Back to Port Royal. I have a betrothal to announce."

Sweet innocence danced upon joyful laughter when Juliana opened the door to the Buchan orphanage. Once she slipped inside, the sounds and scents magnified and swirled about her like a cool mist on a hot day. Before she could utter a word of greeting, the pitter-patter of a dozen feet filled the room like raindrops on a tin roof, and a swarm of excited children of all ages swamped her, leaping for joy. "Miss Juliana! Miss Juliana!"

Dropping her pack, she lifted the tray she carried above the sea of reaching hands as she wove around books and toys and pails of water to a table in the corner, upon which she lowered the sweet cakes Cook had made for the children. Dozens of hands reached for the treats, but she carefully ushered them back, smiling while trying to be stern at the same time. "Now, now, children. We must take turns and share. There's one for everyone. Hello, Rose." Juliana leaned over to say hi to the shy little girl. "Hello, John." She tousled a young boy's hair. "'Tis good to see you all."

The sweet faces stared back at her as Eunice entered from a side room. "I knows it must be you, Miss Juliana, from all the hollarin' I was hearin'." The elderly lady smiled and eased a lock of gray hair into her bun. "Children, let Miss Juliana breathe, fer goodness sakes." Rubbing her hands on her apron, she approached the mob of expectant faces. "Seems Miss Juliana has brought some cakes fer us." Several children eyed the sweets and nodded. "A'right. One by one, you kin come take one cake, and then go into the garden and finds a place to sit an' eat."

As the children formed an orderly line and came forward, Juliana was impressed with their discipline. Aside from being thin and wearing shabby clothes, they all looked happy, clean, and healthy. Smiling, she greeted each by name. James, Elizabeth, Arabella, Jackson, Mitzy ... Oh, how she'd come to love these children. Fourteen in all, ages three through eight.

Nearly half of them had chosen their cake and darted outside when screeching raked over Juliana's ears and a flash of brown swooped down from above her. Startled, she had no time to react to the spider monkey before he grabbed a cake and leapt onto the rafters stretching across the ceiling. The remaining children broke into a fit of giggles, while Eunice grabbed a broom and began furiously swatting at the creature.

"You flea-infested varmint! I told you t' stay away!" Pieces of straw showered down on them from the broom as she continued chasing the tiny monkey back and forth across the rafters. Climbing higher where she couldn't reach, the mischievous critter settled down to eat his cake and grinned down upon them with aplomb.

Juliana stifled a giggle. "Where on earth did he come from?"

Eunice lowered her broom and shook her head. "I knows not. He seems to have adopted us. Or mayhap we adopted him. He showed up a week ago, an' Isaac keeps puttin' him out, but he keeps findin' his way back in." She shook her head. "The children find him entertainin'."

They did indeed, as still giggling, the rest grabbed their cakes and scrambled outside.

"He *is* adorable, in an impish sort of way." Juliana gazed up at the monkey, who gave her a wide, innocent grin framed in cake crumbs. "However, I am of the same mind, Eunice. This is no place for a wild beast. I can bring my groomsman next time. He's good at trapping animals." When he wasn't besotted, that was.

"That be a fine idea, Miss Juliana." She set down the broom and gazed out the open doors to where the children enjoyed their treats on benches placed across grass. Beyond them, bean stalks from a vegetable garden climbed a wall that made up one side of the old church Reverend Buchan used to run. The building was used for storage now until a new preacher could take over. The man who had been sent to replace Reverend Buchan had run off and abandoned, not only his post at the church, but the orphans as well. Juliana's face grew hot with anger at the thought.

A sigh brought her gaze back to Eunice Tucker and her anger fled. No one could be angry looking at the kindest woman Juliana had ever known. Half-Negro, half-white, she was as round as she was tall, but she packed more spirit, spunk, and love in her short frame than most people held in their earlobe.

"You *do* spoil 'em so," Eunice said.

"If I don't, who will?" Juliana smiled and grabbed her satchel. "I've also brought two blankets, old clothing, and some books."

"Ah, good. The children love their readin' lessons wit' you. I don't know what we'd do wit'out you, Miss Juliana. Thank you fer carryin' on wit' your mother's work."

"How could I not? She loved these children with all her heart."

"And you do too, I kin tell."

"Yes." Juliana nodded, her eyes misting. "I have come to." In good sooth, she cared for all of them so much, she could hardly choose a favorite, though little three-year-old Rose held a special place in Juliana's heart.

"Reverend Buchan was sich a good man." Eunice pressed a hand to her back and lowered into a chair. "God rest his soul. He'd a hated it if we'd closed the orphanage. An' what would have happened to the children?"

"If only that new preacher hadn't run off … abandoning them all to starvation." Juliana's jaw tensed. "If I ever meet him, I intend to …" She slammed her mouth shut to avoid using words no lady should.

Eunice waved a hand through the air. "He's long gone by now, miss. Back t' a more comfortable lifestyle across the pond, no doubt."

Juliana couldn't help but loathe the man, though she had repented of her hatred more than once. But how does one forgive a person who left innocent children to die? A man who left them without anyone to care for them, and thus drew Juliana's mother here to offer her services. Services that eventually led to her death. Yes, Juliana hated this preacher, whoever he was, and God forgive her, she would have no compunction to tell him just what she thought of him, should their paths ever meet.

Juliana knelt beside her friend and took her hand in hers. "You and your husband were so kind to take over after he left. I know neither of you were prepared for such a responsibility."

"Nay." Eunice chuckled. "We already helped out now an' then when Reverend Buchan was alive. So when word came the preacher left, well, it jist seemed the right thing t' do. We ain't got much, but God provides."

Did he? Juliana wondered. Her mother had taught her to believe that, but recently with her father's illness, Rowan's dissolute lifestyle, and the tenuous future of Dutton Shipping, she had begun to doubt.

Rising, she backed up a step and bumped into something. A pail of water. One to match the dozens framing the walls of the large room where the children played and ate and took their lessons. "What are these for?"

Eunice smiled with a sigh. "You remember Lucas?"

"The boy that sailor brought here two weeks ago? Has he said anything yet?"

"Nothin'. I fears he's a mute. The sailor said he found the lad in an abandoned shack on an island offa the coast o' Carolina, tied up, dyin' o' thirst, and near shiverin' to death. He tried t' give the boy work on his ship, but the boy don't seem able t' talk." She shook her head and sighed. "But he sures made it plain t' us, usin' frantic gestures an' sich, that he needs these buckets filled wit' water stashed all o'er the house. To make sure we ne'er run out, I 'xpects. Same wit' 'em blankets. He insists on havin' stacks o' 'em. In the main parlor here and in the sleepin' quarters, even tho' it be too hot t' use 'em. Every time I's try t' take 'em or the pails away, he throws sich a fit, I fears he'll make hisself ill or worse—fall over dead."

"Poor boy. I can't even imagine being abandoned to starve and die in the cold without even being able to call out for help. It must have been terrifying." Juliana glanced out the window for the seven-year-old and found him sitting by himself, head down, savoring every morsel of cake as if he'd never see another speck of food. She kicked the pail, jostling the water. "But surely they are in the way?"

"The children have gotten used t' 'em. Besides, we have ladles they kin use to get drinks from 'em. When the water gets low, I send Mr. Tucker t' the docks t' get more that's been rowed o'er from the mainland."

"And where *is* your husband?" Juliana glanced around for the tall, lanky man who had given up a lucrative inheritance to marry a servant in his father's household.

A few children shuffled inside and surrounded the two ladies.

One of them tugged on Juliana's skirts. "Are you gonna read to us, Miss Juliana?"

"O' course she is, Emma. Now, you git the rest and set down in the corner there." The children ran off and Eunice stood. "Mr. Tucker is buyin' food wit' the money our secret benefactor sent o'er yesterday."

Opening the satchel, Juliana withdrew two books. "And you still don't know who gives you such a large sum? Two pounds every month, is it?"

"Yes'm. It's such a huge help." Eunice shrugged. "But the note the servant leaves wit' the money is jist signed Mr. A."

"Well, praise be to God for this Mr. A, whoever he is!"

"Amen!" Eunice added.

Two hours later, after giving the children their reading and writing lessons, Juliana held young Rose in her arms, attempting to help the child fall asleep with a lullaby Juliana remembered her mother singing to her when she was young. After only a few choruses, the child snuggled against Juliana and drifted off, despite the noise of children playing in the room. Juliana smiled. According to Eunice, Rose rarely slept peacefully. Nightmares plagued the three-year-old, who had been discarded in a filthy alleyway six months ago with a note pinned to her chest saying, "Her mum is gone an' I can't care for her. God forgive me." Anger and a host of other emotions she couldn't name had riddled Juliana at the discovery. Mayhap 'twas because Juliana's own mother had died and her father wanted naught to do with her that she felt drawn to young Rose above the others. They had both been abandoned.

Still, as she embraced the thin child, she couldn't help but wonder what it would be like to hold and love a child of her own someday. Chastising herself, she quickly banished the thought. She had no time for marriage or children. She must devote herself entirely to her father's shipping business or she would not only never marry, she would be on the street. Just like her friend, Abilene.

Marriage brought thoughts of Lord Munthrope to mind and their recent bargain. She refused to call it an engagement. Not with that cheeky coxcomb. She'd not seen or heard from him in a week, and the thought had occurred to her that mayhap he had changed his mind. No matter. She wasn't altogether sure she'd made a wise choice.

A knock on the orphanage door startled her. Isaac, who had since returned, ambled to answer it. At five-and-sixty, his years of farming had taken a toll on his body in the form of callused hands; skin the sun had turned into parchment; and a slight limp. Even so, the man always met each hardship head-on. He opened the door.

Juliana's groomsman, Mr. Pell, dashed into the room. "Master Rowan is hurt, miss. Beat up pretty bad. You must come home quickly."

Chapter 9

ROWAN, DARLING." JULIANA KNELT BESIDE the settee where her brother lay bruised and bloodied from head to toe. He moaned and cracked one eye to look her way, wincing from even that small movement. His other eye remained swollen shut beneath a gash on his forehead that dripped blood into his hair. He attempted a smile, but cuts across his lips prevented it. Instead, he groaned and whispered. "I shall recover, dear sister, never fear." His voice was gravelly and thick with pain.

"Who did this to you, dear one?" Juliana's eyes burned with tears. She took his hand in hers, but he cried out, grabbed his arm, and removed it from her grip. "Please. I'm all right," he rasped. "I beg you, acquit me. I just need to rest."

"You need more than that, Brother." Juliana stood and glanced toward the door. "Wherever is the doctor?"

"He'll be here soon," Abbot said, gazing out the window.

Ellie entered with a bowl of water and a towel. "It will be all right, miss."

Grabbing the cloth, Juliana dipped it in the water and dropped beside her brother again, her skirts puffing around her. "Who would do such a thing? Rowan, what happened?" She couldn't imagine who would beat her brother so violently. He was such a jovial, lighthearted soul. Harmless, really. But wait. Mayhap Mr. Blanesworth had returned from overseas and found Rowan with his wife. She dabbed the cut on his forehead, remembering the time a few years past when Lord Rathsford had called Rowan to swords for a similar offense. She ground her teeth together. If only her foolish brother would stay away from other men's wives!

"Who did this to you?" she repeated.

Rowan shook his head. "'Twas nothing. I owed them money."

"Money, how much? Who? Honestly Rowan, if this is about gambling!" She pressed the cloth a bit too hard on his lips. He grimaced. Standing, she tossed the rag into the bowl, her ire rising enough to cast aside her concern and instead berate her brother for his shameless behavior. But a knock on the door stayed her tongue and sent Abbot to retrieve the doctor.

"Come, miss. Let 'em do 'is work." Miss Ellie dragged Juliana from the room as Dr. Verns passed her with a look of concern before he stooped to examine Rowan.

"Doctor, please come by my father's study when you are finished."

He nodded but said nothing, then lifted Rowan's eyelids to peer within.

Back in the study, with Ellie gone to fetch some tea, Juliana could not concentrate on the documents scattered across her father's desk. Numbers and letters blurred before her into an unknown language that made no more sense than her life. Why, oh why, wouldn't Rowan behave? Wasn't it bad enough he wouldn't help her run the business? Did he have to gamble away her profits too? And then get beaten to within an inch of his life?

Standing, she moved to the open French doors and gazed out upon her mother's garden. A red-and-green parakeet landed on the fence and cocked its head curiously at her before warbling a happy tune and flitting to the branch of a palmetto palm. The scene brought to mind something Jesus said in the Bible about not worrying about what you would eat or wear because the birds don't worry about such things since their Father in heaven takes care of them. Was that true? Or mayhap God had no problem caring for innocent birds, but considered sinful humanity beyond the limits of His grace.

A warm breeze fluttered the hair at her neck and brought the scents of heliotrope and the sea. Oh that she might sprout wings and fly away like that parakeet, never to worry again about money or sick fathers or wastrel brothers or trying to earn a living in a male-dominated world.

A voice cleared behind her. She turned to find Dr. Verns standing in the doorway, one hand carrying his medical satchel, the other laid across a prodigious paunch bedecked in a silver-trimmed doublet. The curls of his black periwig made his face all the more pale, though a flat, round nose and chin gave him a look of kindness.

"Come in, Doctor." She gestured toward a chair, but he merely approached the desk and stood, head bowed in thought. Mr. Abbot followed him in.

"Pray, tell me, shall my brother be all right?"

"He will, Miss Juliana, though he'll be in pain. He has a broken arm, cracked ribs, and several bruises and cuts."

Mr. Abbot addressed her. "We've moved him to his chamber where he's resting now."

"Thank you." Juliana moved back to the desk, fearing the answer to her next question. "Did you check on my father, Doctor?"

He nodded. Lifted his gaze to stare at the painting of a ship hanging behind the desk, then swallowed and glanced out the window.

"Am I to guess that he is worse?" she said, clutching the desk.

"I cannot deny it, miss. His fever has risen, his legs have swelled, and blood appears in his spit. In addition ..." He glanced up at her as if just remembering he was speaking to family, then changed his tone. "Not to fear, Miss Dutton. Indeed some patients often get worse before they recover. I will come by and purge him again in a few days." He moved forward and laid a hand on her arm, sympathy filling his eyes. Eyes that betrayed his words of hope.

She tried to smile. "Thank you for coming so quickly, Doctor Verns. Mr. Abbot will see you out."

Benumbed, Juliana propped herself against the desk and hadn't moved an inch by the time Abbot returned. Was the look of despair on his face due to Rowan's condition or had something else gone wrong? *Please, God, I cannot handle any more bad news.*

"Never fear, Abbot, we will discover to whom my brother owes money and pay off the debt lest the villains cripple him permanently next time. Or worse, leave him for dead."

Abbot merely nodded. "I will have Mr. Pell ask around." Yet the butler's thin gray brows continued to collide.

"Pray tell, Abbot, what is it?" Skirting the desk, she lowered into the chair and studied him, trying to guess the cause of his distress. "Your great success last week in dealing with the incoming shipment gave me hope we can continue our charade and make Dutton Shipping more lucrative than ever. But here you are looking as dour as a goose before the slaughter."

"Yes, good news, indeed, about the shipment. I astounded even myself. I grow more comfortable in my role and become more accepted down at the wharves."

"But …?" She examined him. She'd known him too long to not notice the hesitation hovering around his mouth, the distress in his eyes.

"It may be nothing. Perchance I can put him off."

Juliana groaned inwardly. She wasn't sure she wanted to know to whom he referred, yet she found herself asking the question anyway.

"Mr. Wilhelm Edwards."

"Mr. Edwards, yes. He's a friend of my father's. Runs a merchant fleet from Dover to Barbados."

"The same. He oft comes to town to see a mistress he keeps here. One time when he saw the *Esther's Dowry* at the dock, he asked the shipmaster where to find your father. The man directed him to me. He told me many times to say hello to your father and asked to see him. On one occasion, he insisted on traveling home with me. I've been able to put him off with various excuses, but I fear the next time he sails into Port Royal, I will be out of excuses."

Did a cloud absorb the sun, or did the room suddenly become gloomier? Juliana closed her eyes. She knew Mr. Edwards. He and her father had been childhood friends in Bristol. He would not relent until he saw his old friend. And once he did, he was not the type of man to keep a secret. Even worse, he would never approve of a woman running a business.

She rubbed her temples, where a headache began to form. "What else can go wrong, Abbot? I fear I cannot tolerate any more bad tidings."

Miss Ellie entered the study, carrying a tray of tea and cakes and set it on the desk. "Here you go, miss. Oh, you do look tired. Poor dear. Never you fear about Master Rowan. Weel get 'im well soon enough, you'll see. But 'tis you who must stay well." She stopped to take a breath and dab the moisture on her neck with a handkerchief. "I must check on your father and Master Rowan. Cook says she'll 'ave dinner ready soon."

Rising, Juliana approached the flustered maid. "Thank you, Ellie, for all that you do. Mayhap you should get some rest as well."

"Naw, miss." She waved her away. "If *you* aren't restin' then I'm not restin'." And with that pronouncement, she hurried from the room.

"An' I 'ave," Mr. Abbot began, "I mean to say, I have business down at the docks. I'll return before sundown."

Juliana smiled. "I'm so proud of you, Abbot."

He halted midstride to say, "It is you we are all proud of, miss," before he marched from the room.

Proud of *her*? She shook her head and poured herself some tea. Plunking broken bits of sugar into the steaming liquid, followed by a dollop of cream, she stirred and watched the steaming tea spin round and round. Like her life was doing. Like her head was doing at the moment. She raised a hand to steady it, when she saw a post on the tray with her name written in stylish letters. In all the mayhem, Ellie must have forgotten to mention it. On the back, a red seal bearing a single initial M stared back at her as she broke it and opened the missive.

My coach will arrive at eight p.m. this Saturday to escort you to our betrothal gala.

Forever yours, Munthrope

Fie! She'd nearly forgotten about the ball on the morrow. She tossed the note to the desk. With all that was going on, the last thing she needed were the attentions of some jingle-brained fop. Yet how could she bow out now with the invitations already sent and the celebration already planned? She simply must speak with Lord Munthrope before the announcement, give her regrets, but tell him she has changed her mind. Then he could announce whatever he wished. With his vivid imagination and flamboyancy, he would no doubt invent a grand tale with which to fascinate the crowd.

She sauntered to the French doors and leaned on the frame, drawing in a deep breath of moist, tropical air. Above her, puffy clouds strolled across a cerulean sky as if they knew exactly where they were heading and were in no hurry to get there. Ah, her fortune for such direction and peace in her own life. *God, where are You?* Juliana had done everything right. She prayed, she read her Bible, she gave to the poor, helped the orphans and widows—just like God commanded. Yet problems and trials continued to plague her.

What am I doing wrong? She stared heavenward, hoping for an answer, but only the croak of a frog and buzz of insects replied.

Mayhap she wasn't doing enough. She needed to work harder, give *more* to the poor, help the orphans *more*, be a good example for her wayward brother, be kinder to the servants. Mayhap she needed to spend more time reading her Bible and praying. Then—maybe then—God would be pleased with her. Then He would shine His favor on her and all these trials would cease.

Before he even laid eyes upon her, Alex knew Miss Juliana Dutton had stepped into his home. Like one coming out of a deep sleep or awaking from the darkest of nights to the breaking of dawn, the world around him came alive. The lanterns glowed brighter. The air was fresher, the scents sweeter. The mindless cackle of his guests drifted into the background. Even the orchestra began to harmonize. He stood on the landing above the massive foyer, peering down at her as she entered through the front doors, taking pause at the anger weaving through her features. She wore a lavender tabby gown fringed in black lace, a jeweled stomacher bedecked with pink ribbons, beruffled bell sleeves, and a low décolletage pressing against her creamy breasts. Golden hair spiraled in delicate layers atop her head, sparkling as much as the pearls woven betwixt the strands. She floated across the coral stone floor like a swan, ignoring calls of greeting thrown her way. She scanned the crowd, no doubt looking for her host, and from the looks of her tight mouth and sharp eyes, it wasn't to give him a kind greeting but to chastise him for sending his man to escort her instead of picking her up himself.

Alex adjusted the silly wig atop his head. He couldn't blame her. It was beyond incorrigible, but what else could he do? He mustn't give her any opportunity to call off their betrothal, as he suspected she may attempt to do. A week's time, no doubt, afforded her enough moments of lucidity in which to regain her senses. After the announcement, propriety would forbid her to reject his suit—at least until enough time had passed. And time was all he needed. Time with her. Toward what end, he had no idea, save to satisfy a yearning within him to know this fine lady. But now, how to avoid her for the next thirty minutes or until he could gather his guests for *le grande declaration.*

Chapter 10

WHEN JULIANA FOUND THAT VAINGLORIOUS cur, Munthrope, she would forget her manners *and* her station and tell him exactly what she thought of his lack of chivalry. Never in all her years had she been kept waiting for hours to be escorted to a ball—not by previous suitors, not even by her indifferent father. And then to find that the cretin wasn't even in the coach but had sent one of his lackeys to escort her. If this was any indication of his skills as a cavalier, she should break her bargain with the man here and now. Which was precisely what she intended to do.

As soon as she found him.

Halting at the edge of the ballroom, she strained to hear his effeminate lilt, his shrill laughter at one of his own jokes. But nothing but the giddy tittering of the crowd and the melody of the orchestra resounded in the glittering room. Quite a good orchestra, she had to admit. Difficult to find such skilled musicians on Jamaica. Why, there was even a violinist. The sweet dulcet notes of one of Peeter Cornet's courantes caressed her ears, making her long to play her own violin in the privacy of her home.

Apparently, Lord Munthrope spared no expense for the announcement of their betrothal. Neither in the orchestra nor in the lavish display of delicacies spread across the long banquet table she now passed: banana custard, broiled fish with lemons and capers, roasted wild boar, turtle puffs, lemon cake, and her favorite, *mousse au chocolat*. Sweet and spicy scents stirred her stomach to life and lured her to stop and sample a bit of the mousse. But she was on a mission. In the drawing room, two jugglers entertained the crowd, while in the garden a trained monkey danced and performed tricks for a cheering mob. No expense, indeed. Whom was Munthrope trying to impress?

The sound of trickling drew her to the middle of the garden's courtyard, where a knot of guests circled a bubbling fountain. Curious as to what drew their attention, Juliana soon discovered 'twas not water that spilled from the carved angels atop the ornate structure, but sweet Madeira, into which several people repeatedly dipped their cups. She had never seen the likes of it. What an unusual man this Munthrope was.

Back inside the house, barefooted mulattos wove expertly through a crowd that barely noticed their presence—until a tray of drinks or pastries was held before their noses.

"Have you seen Lord Munthrope?" She stopped Sir Branwell to ask.

"Nay, my dear. Not since I arrived. But if you are looking for a dance partner?" His bloodshot eyes sparkled with interest.

She declined and hurried along. Another lady had just seen him in the billiards room, but when Juliana arrived, he was gone. A gentleman told her he was upstairs in the library regaling a crowd with his tales at court as a young man. But he was not there.

"Oh, fie!" She huffed as she stood on the upstairs landing and gazed down into the parlor on one side and the ballroom on the other. Heat flooded her as her anger inflamed. How dare the man throw a betrothal celebration and then ignore the woman he planned to betroth!

A familiar face drew her gaze to Captain Nichols in the parlor below, drink in hand, conversing with one of his naval officers. Why in the blazes would Lord Munthrope invite him when the very purpose of their courtship was to keep him at bay? He lifted his eyes just then and saw her looking at him. She glanced away, seeking her friends.

She found them in the ballroom. Lady Anne, Miss Margaret, and Miss Ashton were flirting with a group of gentlemen, who seemed more than happy to indulge their whimsical silliness for a chance to dance—or mayhap *more* as the night progressed. She started down the grand staircase, intending to ask them whether they'd seen Munthrope, when the man himself paraded into the parlor, a horde of admirers fluttering about him like pesky summer gnats. Indeed, he captured everyone's attention with his cocky gait and beribboned arms waving through the air he lavished an exorbitant tale on all within earshot.

"Oh, Munny, you are too much, too much I say!" one man cackled, holding his corpulent belly as Juliana descended the rest of the steps then forced her way through the crowd to stand before the pompous oaf.

"Ah, Miss Juliana. You are the vision of Helen of Troy, bringing gentlemen everywhere such joy. Why then must you be so coy?" His impromptu ballad sent the crowd into fits of laughter as he urged on their praise with one hand pressed to his bosom and the other wiping a feigned tear from his eye. From the tips of his red-heeled shoes to the top of his curled and pearled periwig, he was all silk and lace and gold embroidery. Juliana found disgust joining the anger in her belly. She merely stared at him, her face a mask of controlled civility, until his eyes met hers once again. They were so blue, like the color of the deep sea, and for a moment a flicker of intensity spanned their depths. Then it was gone, replaced by a languid haze.

He pressed a finger to a fake mole glued onto the white paste covering his face. "I perceive Miss Juliana is not pleased with me. La, what to do?" The mob surrounding them laughed.

"Alack, can a woman ever be truly pleased?" one man said.

"Indeed, my friend. I believe ships have been sunk, mountains climbed, rivers forged, and wars fought and lost over that very question!" Munthrope announced with a flourish.

When the laughter faded, Juliana did her best to control the fury stiffening every muscle and nerve. "May I have a moment of your time, your lordship?" She gave a tight smile.

"Do not steal him from us, Miss Juliana," one elderly lady begged. "The festivities would be so tiresome without him."

"I only need a moment, madam, and he shall be yours for the rest of the night." The rest of eternity, if Juliana had her way.

The portly woman fluttered her fan about her pasty white face and grinned. "Oh dear, do not tease me so."

Munthrope opened his mouth to utter some witty response, when the ground trembled. At first a violent jolt struck, and then it seemed the very floor melted beneath Juliana's feet. The chandelier above them swayed, scattering light and dark over the room. Somewhere glass shattered.

Lord Munthrope clutched her arm. Not a fearful grip but one meant to calm and steady her. A strong grip with a look of concern to match in his eyes. The quaking stopped. The orchestra faded into a discordant tune.

The crowd silenced around them, save for gasps and murmurs.

"My word," a lady panted out. "'Twas an earthquake."

"A small one," Munthrope assured.

"We get them all the time," Lord Gilfoil addressed the entire room. "A little shaking here, a little there. 'Tis nothing to concern ourselves with."

"Concern? Bah! I arranged it for our entertainment," Munthrope added. "I spare no expense for my guests!" This brought smiles from the crowd as he gestured for the orchestra to begin again. Soon, the room filled with idle chatter and music once more.

Juliana dragged him from his sycophants. "I must speak to you, milord. 'Tis urgent."

Munthrope extended his arm and placed her hand upon it, all the while nodding and smiling at the guests vying for his attention. "Can it not wait, my sweet?" His smile was forced.

"I am not your sweet, and nay, it cannot." Juliana seethed as he led her beneath the stairs to a private space.

He turned to face her. His right brow rose, lifting the silly horse patch he always placed above it. "If 'tis regarding my tardiness, I am deeply ashamed and beg your forgiveness, but it couldn't be he—"

"Though I admit to being angry regarding your ill-manners," Julianna interrupted, waving a hand through the air, "I have not given it another thought, milord. I must speak to you about your upcoming announcement."

Two gentlemen approached, both well into their cups. One of them slapped Munthrope on the back. "Munny, there you are. Do regale my friend here with your tale of the Fishmongers Tavern," he slurred. "The one where the crab crawled off the dinner plate and down a lady's bodice!" This caused the two slosh-numbed men to bend over in laughter.

Juliana frowned and tugged on one of Munthrope's massive silk sleeves. "I beg you, milord?"

"La, if you insist." He fingered a lock of his periwig and bent to whisper in her ear. "Behind the gardenia bush, there is a bench. Meet me there in five minutes."

Juliana thought it an odd place to meet, but she didn't have time to agree before Munthrope began to entertain the two men with the ridiculous story.

Clutching her skirts, she made her way to the veranda, ignoring the calls from acquaintances to come join them, as well as the desiring glances of more than one gentleman. A blast of heat swamped her as she stepped outside to a cloudy sky that hid the moon and stars. Neither the sweltering temperature nor the humidity kept the partygoers from flitting through the courtyard, filling their cups in the fountain and squawking like a flock of ducks over a fresh pond. They rather resembled ducks now that she looked at them, waddling to and fro, flapping their mouths and wings in an effort to gain attention. Despite her anger toward Munthrope, she chuckled at the image as she searched for the gardenia bush. There it was. Turning sideways to squeeze her hooped skirts behind the shrubbery, she slid onto the stone bench and drew in the sweet smell of the creamy flowers.

A minute passed, then two, then what must surely be five. And more. Several couples, fairly drooling over each other, happened upon her secret spot seeking privacy. But then upon seeing her, dashed away. A horde of mosquitos nibbled on her neck no matter how many times she swatted at them. The ducks stopped quacking, and she peered through the leaves to see people abandoning the courtyard to enter the house again. Odd. Why would they all leave at once?

Then she heard his voice, that insufferable dandy, Munthrope, his tenor high, his tone emphatic, his lilt entertaining. Why was he relaying yet another ludicrous tale to his guests when he'd promised to meet her? Blood boiling, she eased from behind the bush and marched across the courtyard, when a few of his words pricked her ears to alert. Words such as "grand event" and "announcement". The buffoon was going ahead without her! Clutching her skirts, she plowed into the mob that filled the veranda, shoving people aside, ignoring their oaths and protests, and burst into the front parlor to find His Lordship standing atop the landing as if he were king looking down on his subjects.

"I am thrilled to announce that Miss Juliana Dutton has accepted my suit!" the man bellowed, causing a stir of whispers and shrill of excited voices.

No! Perspiration moistening her neck, Juliana forged through the swarm of people, who now willingly parted for her, and started up the grand stairs, feeling all eyes upon her.

"Ah, there my sweetness comes!" Lord Munthrope extended a lace-veiled hand and perfected a gallant bow. Then gazing over the crowd, he added. "I dare say, the woman will be late for her own wedding!"

Laugher bounced among the guests as Juliana's fists and teeth clenched harder with every stomp she made up the steps. She stopped before him, barely able to contain her fury.

"To Munny and Miss Juliana!" one man shouted with a lift of his drink.

"Here, here!"

"Huzzah! To Juliana and His Lordship!" another man proclaimed, and soon the entire room was aflame with shouts of congratulations. Only a few of the women remained sullen, obviously none too pleased at losing a chance to catch the wealthy son of an Earl.

Fie, they could have him, for all she cared! Their jealous eyes pierced her as she attempted to get Munthrope's attention. He smiled at her now, the gray flecks in his eyes twinkling in mischief. Had he purposed to announce their betrothal without her? Did he know she'd intended to cancel their bargain?

"Milord, a word please?" Without awaiting an answer, she took his arm and dragged him to the side while the crowd below them continued to buzz with the news.

"My intention was to call off your announcement," she whispered intently. "If you had given me but a moment of your time, we could have avoided this unpleasantness."

"Unpleasantness?" His painted brows rose, incredulous. "Cancel, you say?" Pain glazed his eyes, though she was surely mistaken. "Beshrew me, milady, you do not intend to shame me in front of my friends?" He glanced around at his fickle acquaintances, though she saw no fear in his eyes. "And make me a laughingstock?"

She wouldn't tell him that he'd already achieved that on his own.

"Begad, I did you a favor, milady. Did you see Captain Nichols's face when I proclaimed our courtship?"

"How could I? I was sitting behind a bush in the garden!"

One side of his lips quirked. "Ah yes, I cry pardon, my sweet. I intended to join you."

"After you declared our bargain to all, I wager?"

Lord Munthrope gave her a listless look. "Our bargain would be impotent without an audience."

Releasing a heavy sigh, she took in the crowd again, most of whom had already returned to their revelry, stealing glances at the stairs. From beneath his curled wig, Captain Nichols leveled a gaze at her akin to two cannons ready to fire. Indeed, the man seemed well out of sorts.

"Our plan was to keep the good captain at bay, was it not?" When she didn't answer, Munthrope continued, raising a gloved hand in the air and admiring the rubies inlaid in the silk. "How now? Have we not achieved our goal? Do say you won't destroy our plans by announcing me a fool to everyone here."

A wave of his rose-cinnamon cologne engulfed her and she turned to face him. For his ill-treatment of her that evening, he more than deserved to be made a fool, yet something in his eyes—a genuine yearning, a desperation—softened her anger. Though she didn't need further complication in her life, mayhap their bargain would work to her benefit. If Captain Nichols let her be, that was. Besides, 'twas possible God wanted her to help this overstuffed princock. He'd said their courtship would aid him with his overbearing father, did he not? Surely her sacrifice on his behalf would please God. And she needed God's favor now more than ever.

"You have my word, milady, I will intrude on neither your kindness nor your life. Then after time has passed and Captain Darling has moved on, I will allow you to bow out of any obligation to me, and hence reserve your dignity." He adjusted the emerald pin adorning his fleecy cravat.

Juliana could understand why people hung on this man's every word. Despite his extravagant attire, grandiose ways, and outrageous tales, there was an excitement that hovered about him, a charm that lured, and an authority that made you want to trust him. And for the moment, Juliana had no choice but to do just that.

"Very well, milord."

"I am your servant, milady." He winked and gave a flourishing bow.

Before Juliana could react, Munthrope threaded her hand through his billowing silk-laden arm and was triumphantly escorting her down the stairs. When they reached the bottom, the revelers swarmed them: men dragging Munthrope off for a drink and the ladies hovering around Juliana offering their approval of the courtship. She soon found herself in a circle dominated by Lady Ann, Miss Margaret, and Miss Ashton, who were all abuzz with excitement over the news.

"You scamp! Why didn't you tell us about Lord Munthrope?" Lady Anne chastised.

Margaret slapped her with her fan. "The last time we saw you, you behaved as if you couldn't stand the sight of him."

"And all this time, hiding it from your best friends." Miss Ashton sighed and glanced forlornly in the direction Munthrope had gone.

"I wasn't hiding anything. It came upon us rather suddenly." Juliana extricated herself from their frenzied clutches and stepped back.

"Came upon you? You make it sound like a disease." Lady Anne laughed. "You are a treat, Juliana."

A disease, indeed. And one that was making her feel rather ill at the moment. "If you'll excuse me, I fear all the excitement has taxed me greatly."

"Where is your father? Why is he not here to share the joyful news?"

"He is not feeling well. Good eve, ladies." She hurried through the crush of people.

"You will attend the tea at Lady Hanes's house this week?" Margaret called after her, but Juliana merely waved over her shoulder. She felt a headache coming on and wanted nothing more than to go home to her soft bed and her violin.

Not run into Captain Nichols.

He pulled her to the side, his eyes stormy. "I cannot express my disappointment in your choice of suitor, Juliana."

"My choice of suitor is none of your affair, sir." She attempted to leave, but he held her back, pulling her closer and nearly suffocating her with his alcohol-laden breath.

"I thought we had an understanding." He narrowed his eyes.

"My apologies if you misled yourself in that regard, Captain. Now, if you please." She tugged from his grip.

"I paid your brother's gambling debts." The sharp words stopped her cold.

"What did you say?"

"Rowan's recent debts." Victory beamed from his brown eyes. "Twenty pounds, if you must know, lost in a game of Faro to the basest of fellows. A man who gladly tosses his debtors into the bay rather than see them live and not pay him."

Alarm buzzed across her skin.

"But he is satisfied now, Juliana." He looked at her expectantly.

"*Miss Dutton* to you, sir," she snapped, "and I have no idea if what you say is true. Even if it is, why would you do such a thing?"

"It *is* true, I assure you." Releasing her arm, he took her hand in his and placed a kiss upon her glove. Cunning eyes tainted with desire met hers. "And surely, you know why."

She yanked her hand away. Anger at the man's manipulation inflamed her. "It is most inappropriate, Captain. Twenty pounds you say? I will pay you back. Every shilling." Though at the moment, she had no idea how.

"Faith now, why must you be so stubborn?!" He exploded, his shout drawing a few curious glances. "I do not lack for money, nor do I want yours, Juliana. Please know, I *will* and can take care of you far better than anyone, especially that pompous jackanapes, Lord Munthrope."

She stood her ground and glared his way. "I have no need of your care nor anyone else's." She was just about to demand that he never pay off any of her family's debts again, when one of Lord Munthrope's servants appeared before her.

"A man is at the door to see you, Miss Dutton."

A man? Without saying goodbye to Nichols, she followed the servant through the foyer to the massive mahogany doors. Just outside, Mr. Pell stood, fumbling with his hat in his hands.

"I came for you right away, miss."

Regardless of the sting of alcohol lingering about him, her heart seized. "My brother?"

"Nay, miss." He glanced at the servant still standing behind her.

"Then what? Mr. Pell?"

He led her to the side. "You said you wanted to know if ever Miss Abilene came callin', miss." He swayed and grabbed onto the porch post to steady himself.

Fear surged. "Miss Abilene? Is she there now?" Juliana started down the stairs to the street.

"Nay. Another woman came. Said Miss Abilene is hurt bad. She was upset when you weren't home. She said something about The Black Dogg, miss. It's a bawdy hou—"

"I know what it is, Mr. Pell. Take me there immediately."

"It's dangerous this time o' night, miss." Stumbling after her, Mr. Pell quickly assisted her into the carriage.

"I care not! My friend is in danger, Mr. Pell. We must make all haste."

Chapter 11

"**S**HE WENT WHERE?" ALEX STORMED into his bedchamber, yanked off his wig and tossed it to his bed.

Whipple followed him in and shut the door. "To The Black Dogg, I believe was the name, milord." The butler's calm demeanor grated Alex.

"By herself?!"

"Her footman, a Mr. Pell, was with her."

Lud! "Pell? He's nothing but a besotted dolt."

"Indeed, he did appear to be deep in his cups, milord."

"Bird-witted woman, she'll get herself killed!" Alex began tearing through the buttons of his doublet as he kicked off his buckled red shoes. "Earn your salary, man! Assist me. I must be after her." He held up his arms to allow the butler to unlace and untie the incessant ribbons and silk-netting that decorated his ridiculous attire. But the man was not working fast enough. Jerking back his hands, Alex tore through the fripperies and ripped off his doublet, then tossed his billowy shirt over his head.

"If the lady causes you so much angst, milord, mayhap 'twould be better to end this spurious troth."

Alex growled as he removed his sash and untied mounds of his cravat, then stepped out of his pantaloons. Dashing to the bowl of water on his dresser, he pried the patches off his face, popped off the mole, then scrubbed the paint from his skin and lips, and ran a hand through his black hair. When he turned, Whipple had a towel in one hand and Alex's buccaneer clothing in the other.

"She may cause me angst, Whipple, but she also causes me to feel many other things." Things he hadn't felt in years. He donned his breeches, shirt, and leather jerkin.

"Mayhap 'twould be best to restrain those *other* longings, milord, as is befitting civilized men." His butler's nose pinched.

Alex chuckled at the wave of maroon flooding Whipple's face. "Not *those* kind of longings, dear man. Curse me for a rogue if that's all I'm about." Though he'd not deny they were present—very present. He donned his boots, belts, and baldric, then grabbed his weapons and stepped out on the ledge. "I'm off."

"You have my full agreement on that point. What should I tell your guests, milord?" The butler's tone sounded as though he announced dinner.

"Tell them I succumbed to too much drink and retired early." Alex winked, dropped to the ground and darted into the bushes before anyone saw him.

It didn't take him long to find Juliana's carriage parked along the side of the road, Mr. Pell snoring on the driver's box and the lady absent. And with another four blocks to go before she reached The Black Dogg! If the vermin on the streets didn't get her, the vermin within the notorious bawdy house would.

Grabbing the hilt of his cutlass, he cursed under his breath and stormed down the street, keeping a weather eye out for a flash of lavender skirts. Already he could hear the shrill of debauchery emanating from the taverns and bawdy houses inhabiting the wharves: a discordant fiddle, maritime ballads butchered by drunken sailors, evil laughter, the eerie chime of a sword, curses followed by pistol shots. Mad infuriating woman! She might as well deck herself in gold doubloons and stroll down the streets shouting, *Free for the taking*!

He turned the corner. Another pistol shot cracked the muggy air. This one closer. A tiny shriek drew his gaze to the right where a wave of blond hair drifted in and out of the shadows. Darting ahead, he kept his approach as silent as possible and slowed when the lady came in sight. Relief melted the tension from his body. She appeared as yet unscathed.

In her right hand, she carried a satchel—which no doubt Mr. Pell had brought her—with her left hand, she clutched her throat as if trying to steady her racing heart. At least the lady was not completely ignorant of the danger surrounding her.

Danger as in the two men across the street. They honed in on her like wolves on an innocent rabbit and started in her direction. Juliana took no note of them as she hurried along beside dark warehouses and shops. Drawing his cutlass, Alex closed the distance between them. They were nearly upon her, slithering behind her like the snakes they were.

Juliana stepped off the wooden walkway between two warehouses. One of the men raised his hands to grab her. Alex clutched both men by their collars and dragged them into the alleyway. Before the drunken wretches could react, he slammed the hilt-end of his sword onto one of their heads then leveled his blade at the other's chest. The one man fell to the dirt in a heap, the other began to blubber like a baby before he turned and darted away.

Alex peered around the side of the building. Juliana had stopped and was staring behind her, intently searching the shadows. A nearby street lantern flooded her in a cone of light, and she stepped backward into the dark as if she could hide such beauty from peering eyes. Finally, she spun on her heels and proceeded, the clip-clop of her shoes echoing a heightened pace.

A blast of salty wind cooled the sweat from Alex's brow as he slipped onto the street after her. He supposed he should reveal his presence, but he preferred she remain frightened and mayhap learn her lesson not to wander the dark streets of a town that had been deemed "the wickedest city in the Caribbean".

When she turned down Thames Street by the wharves, Alex braced himself for the onslaught that was to come. Thus far, only a few people had been wandering about, but nighttime belonged to Thames Street—the haunt of every vile and perverse soul who loved the darkness more than the light. This was *his* street, *his* territory. Most of the ruffians who dwelt here knew and feared him, respected his wit, his success at piracy, but most of all his skill with pistol and cutlass. But that all may fall to the wind when they got a glimpse of the angel drifting in their midst.

Ahead, a band of such degenerates spilled out of a tavern onto the street, shoving each other and hurling insults at the sky. Alex recognized the leader, Drake, a bull of a man with the body of a mastiff and the brain of a mite. With his arm around a scantily clad trollop, he led his minions into the darkness, bellowing a sailor's ditty. The song halted on his lips when he spotted Miss Juliana, the resulting evil smirk cracking his bearded face.

"What 'ave we here?" He stumbled toward the lady.

She froze and glanced about for somewhere to hide. Naught but a brick warehouse was behind her, so she merely raised her chin and stood to meet her fate.

She was brave, Alex would give her that. Yet fear ignited his heart. At least he thought it was fear. It had been so long since he'd been afraid of anything, so long since he cared about anything—or anyone. But there were eight well-armed pirates and only one of him. He'd defeated such numbers single-handedly before, but had paid for the encounter with a sword wound to his gut. He would gladly suffer that again—for her—but didn't relish the idea. Instead, he hoped his presence alone would dissuade the men from their vile intentions. Hence, he took a stance behind the lady, arms crossed over his chest, and his eyes aflame with warning.

The men approached Juliana, leering like a pack of dogs. A breeze tossed the strands of hair dangling about her neck and brought the stench of unwashed men to Alex's nose.

"Greetings, young miss." Drake released the trollop and swept his plumed tricorne before him. "Are ye seekin' a bit o' pleasure this fine evenin'?" His men chuckled as he began fingering the lace on her sleeve. The bald one on the left with two gold rings in his ear took a swig from a jug.

Alex shifted his stance, hoping the men would see him through the shadows.

Batting the foul man away, Juliana took a step back. "I am not, sir. I am on a mission of mercy."

"Mercy you say?" Drake snorted. "I see eight fine gentlemen o' fortune in need o' some mercy t'night. What say you gentlemen?" He glanced over the band, his tone dripping with lust.

"Aye, Aye!" shouts rang in the air as one of the men grabbed the trollop and began kissing her neck. She pushed him off and sidled beside Drake. "Leave 'er be, Drake. A proper lady like 'er 'as no clue 'ow to treat a man like you."

Drake shoved the woman aside and approached Juliana, shifting sultry eyes to the crest of her bosom. He leaned toward her and inhaled. "Mayhap not, but she smells better than you!"

Laughter filled the air. Alex stepped forward, clenching and unclenching his fists, restraining himself from charging the band and putting an end to their crude insolence. If they did not see him soon, he'd do just that.

One of the pirates, a rawboned fellow with hair to his waist, reached for Juliana. She retreated, hugging the satchel to her chest. "I insist you give way, sir. I am on my way to help a woman in need. Without me she may die." Her voice quavered, but she kept her shoulders high.

"But without ye, we all may suffer a broken heart," one of the pirates plucked the bag from Juliana's grasp and held it out of her reach. While she attempted to regain it amidst the pirates' laughter, Alex drew his sword. Drake must have caught the glimmer of street light on steel for he glanced over Juliana's shoulder.

And instantly stiffened.

Alex shook his head in a gesture he hoped Drake would interpret as a warning. The bullish pirate hesitated a moment, wiping his mouth on his sleeve. He fingered the butt of a pistol protruding from his belt, eyes locked upon Alex. But finally, he huffed. "Return the lady's satchel, ye ill-mannered dawcock!" Scowling, the pirate did as he was told.

Juliana, her chest heaving, her eyes wide, embraced the bag and tried to lengthen her stance, but it only made more visible the tremble in her legs.

Drawing the trollop back into his arms, Drake offered another bow toward Juliana before plopping his hat atop his head. "Then be about your mission, miss. We wouldn't want t' cause a woman's early demise."

Grumbles of dissent racked the band, but Drake silenced them with a threatening curse. Turning, they staggered away, passing the jug of rum betwixt them.

Juliana fell back against the brick wall and threw a hand to her throat. Her breath came hard and fast. She closed her eyes and moved her lips as if speaking—or mayhap praying. Encased in shadows, she was not seen by the men now passing on the street. Nor by the crowd forming on the steps of The King's Arms tavern across the way. If only she would stay hidden where she was. Two more blocks stretched betwixt her and The Black Dogg, blocks filled with roving buccaneers, their bellies floating in rum and their hearts sinking in mire.

Alex took a step toward her, intending to make his presence known, but she pushed from the wall and hurried on her way.

Another block down the road, three men slipped into an alleyway ahead of her, no doubt waiting to pounce on her as she passed. Teeth grinding, Alex turned and sprinted around the back of Massey's Gunsmith then up the next street until he charged down the passage where the men waited. They heard him approach and swerved, blades in hand. Alex cursed as he drew his sword and took on the first man, quickly knocking the cutlass from his hand and plucking it from the dirt before he could reach it. Now with two swords, Alex parried the three men, diving, ducking, plunging, and thrusting this way and that. The ring of steel on steel could barely be heard amidst the sound of laughter and a nearby harpsichord. Young ruffians, these men were novices with the sword, and Alex almost pitied them as their swipes and thrusts met naught but air and their hard breathing and groans betrayed their fear. Finally, one man fell, clutching a bloody wound on his leg, another ran off, and the third winced beneath the tip of Alex's blade at his throat.

"Take your friend and leave. If you harm the woman, there'll be hell to pay."

The man nodded. A sliver of moonlight revealed the terror in his eyes. No sooner had the villain grabbed his friend and scurried off, then Miss Juliana Dutton walked past the alleyway, completely ignorant of the danger from which she'd just been rescued.

Alex ran a sleeve over his sweaty brow, sheathed his sword, and slipped onto the street behind her. At this rate, he'd be fighting off half the miscreants in town. Thankfully, The Black Dogg was fast approaching. Of course the bawdy house presented quite another problem altogether. One which the naïve Juliana could only imagine in her worst nightmare. Her slight hesitation at the bottom of the stairs offered Alex hope that she retained a whisper of wits. The salacious invitations tossed her way from the patrons lining the porch added to that hope. Surely she would turn and hasten back to the safety of her home.

Instead she jutted out her chin, mounted the stairs, and entered the den of debauchery.

Chapter 12

A FUMING CLOUD OF BODY ODOR, tallow, and stale spirits enveloped Juliana as she shoved her way through the door of The Black Dogg, past the piercing eyes, through the gauntlet of lewd comments, and straight into a vision of Dante's hell. Two men fought in the center. A punch was thrown. One of them stumbled backward straight for her. She leapt out of the way just in time, but ended up in the arms of the worst-smelling creature she'd ever encountered. His stink—spoilt eggs and dung—made her gasp for air while she did her best to shove away from the man who grinned at her with what appeared to be rotted wooden pikes instead of teeth.

Breaking away, she scanned the room. The two men who'd been fighting were now arm in arm sharing a mug of ale in laughter. The rest of the mob had returned to their drinking and whoring. Some hovered around tables strewn about the room; others stood in groups, sloshing their drinks and boasting of exploits on sea and land. Lanterns hanging from rafters and candles on tables were the only deterrents against the darkness filling the sordid place.

But the light's reach did not extend to the corners where Juliana caught glimpses of vile things no decent person should witness. Across the main room, trollops—baring too much skin—sashayed through the crowd or perched upon men's laps, urging them with coos and flattery to relinquish their coin. A sour taste filled Juliana's mouth. She begged God to make her invisible. Instead, one by one, dozens of eyes swept her way, gaping at her as if she were a heavenly being dropped down from above.

Speaking of heavenly beings—*God, where are you?* She knew coming here wouldn't be easy. She knew she'd be walking into danger. Which was why she'd stopped and prayed outside, just to make sure she was doing God's will. Hadn't he shown his favor, his approval, by protecting her on the way to this depraved place? Surely he would protect her once inside, especially since she was helping a friend in trouble. Yes, God would defend her! He would not abandon her like most of the other men in her life.

Forcing back her fear, she met the men's gazes with boldness.

"Well, curse me eyes if I ain't seein' a real genteel lady all decked in her fripperies and finery right 'ere in the middle o' The Black Dogg!" one particularly rotund man sporting a purple vest shouted, eliciting shouts and whistles from the throng. Another man fingered the ribbons bounding from her sleeve. Someone played with her hair from behind. A gaunt-looking fellow with two earrings in one ear and a nose the size of Jamaica ran a filthy finger over the embroidery of her stomacher.

Juliana's head grew light. Batting aside the vermin, she held a handkerchief to her nose and pressed through the crowd to stand in their midst. Surely once she explained her purpose, these men—no matter how vulgar and grotesque they appeared—would allow her to proceed upstairs unscathed. Hadn't the pirates she'd encountered in the streets done exactly that? After all, she was here to help one of *their* own. Though she wished that weren't the case with her dear friend Abilene.

"Gentlemen, grant me ear a moment. I come to help—"

"Us? Indeed ye are." A man approached and seemed to be winking at her from a gaping hole where his right eye had once been. "An' we'll be acceptin' yer help, says I!" He grabbed her arm just as the door flew open, and all gazes shot toward the newcomer. Not able to see who it was through the throng, Juliana closed her eyes and prayed for deliverance. Boot steps clipped over the wooden floor. Silence swallowed the revelry until all she heard were a few belches and the nervous scraping of chairs on wood. Pain burned her arm where the man tightened his grip.

"The lady's with me." That voice—that familiar voice, deep and commanding like rolling thunder—drew her eyes open to see the Pirate Earl. Against her better judgment, a tiny shred of relief spread through her.

Releasing her, the first pirate retreated a step. An odd mixture of fear and spite crossed his rum-glazed eye as he fingered the hilt of a dagger stuffed within his belt. Moans of disappointment rumbled through the mob.

"Damn me eyes!" one man growled.

"That's the way ye be, eh?" another said. "No sharin' from the earl t'night, gents!"

The one-eyed man glared at the Pirate Earl, his eye simmering, his mouth twitching. His fingers rubbed the hilt of his rapier as if he could summon a genie from it. The crowd backed away.

The Pirate Earl tugged Juliana behind him and remained an immovable fortress of confidence. "Are you in need of another lesson in swordplay, Will? Or mayhap you've not had your fill of my blade in your flesh?"

The man shifted his boots over the floor. A flicker of fear crossed his one eye as a parrot squawked from above them. "Slit his gullet, slit his gullet!"

The pirate snorted and relaxed his stance. "Stint this foolery." He gave a nervous chuckle. "Let's have no harsh words betwixt us, Earl. I 'ave a dozen other doxies awaitin' me pleasures." He dipped his greasy head toward Juliana. "No harm meant t' ye, miss." Then swerving, he marched off, the crowd parting as he went.

The Pirate Earl dragged her toward the front door.

"Nay! Unhand me. I must see Abilene." She pulled in the other direction, causing some of the pirates to laugh, but most went back to their business. Soon the place resounded with the slap of cards, slosh of spirits, flurry of curses, and the beginnings of a discordant ballad.

Halting, Mr. Pirate drew her to the side. "I suppose this Abilene is the trollop you went to visit last time you foolishly ventured down by the docks? Or do you intend on risking your life for every wench in the city?"

Fie, but the man was handsome. For a pirate, that is. Her eyes barely reached a chest that spread to a wide expanse of muscled shoulders. Full sleeves of his white cambric shirt emerged from within a leather jerkin over which a brace of pistols was strapped. Tight leather breeches disappeared into knee-high Cordovan boots. Doffing his plumed tricorne, he ran a hand through ink-black hair, sending a few strands drifting back over his jaw, and stared at her with those stark blue eyes flecked in irritated gray, as if she were the most exasperating woman in the world.

"You make too free with your opinions, Mr. Pirate. Abilene is my friend. She is hurt, and I'm not leaving until I see her," she said with as much fortitude as she could muster. "Besides, I did not bid you come to my aid. I have no fear I could have convinced these men of my good purpose in coming here."

At this he laughed. And the sound of it did odd things to her insides. Someone bumped him from behind, uttering a "pardon me, milord," and pushing him within inches of her. He grabbed her arms to steady her, and then with an intensity that sent her skin bristling, his gaze roved from a strand of her hair drifting across her forehead, to her eyes, her nose, cheeks, and finally her mouth, where it lingered for a moment too long. The scent of cinnamon wafted over her, oddly reminding her of Lord Munthrope. Yet this man before her was nothing like the foppish lord. Nay, this man possessed not an ounce of feminine airs. He was all roughness and strength, commanding and decisive. He invoked fear in the most fearsome, and respect from the defiant. And the danger that hovered around him made her heart skip a beat.

"Come." He ushered her through the mob to the back of the tavern, where a rickety staircase led upward. "We will see your friend," he said as he escorted her up the sticky treads, shoving aside besotted patrons, some who gave them curious looks; others grins that made Juliana's skin crawl. "Afterward, you will go home and never return to the wharves at night again."

He tightened his grip on her hand as his commanding tone pricked her indignation. Who was this pirate to order her about?

They reached the landing and started down a dingy hall. Lanterns hanging at intervals cast shifting light over closed doors from which blared laughter and grunts that made Juliana's ears burn. She tugged from his grip. "You do not own me, Mr. Pirate. Ergo, I will go where I please when I please."

She wished her tone had not been so insolent, for the pirate turned, pressed her against the wall, then looked down at her from his towering height. Her heart raced. She stared at the brass skeleton adorning the baldric that crisscrossed his chest. Warm spicy breath wafted on her forehead. "Do you wish to die, Miss Dutton? Not just any death but one which comes at the end of a long, torturous tenure as mistress to half a dozen lusty curs?"

Her breath scrambled to her throat. Her head began to spin. "God will take care of me," she whispered out in a tone that bore little faith in that fact.

"God?" He snorted. "A pretty desire, milady. But alas, do you see the Almighty here?"

As if on cue, one of the doors flew open and a man emerged, two women on his arms donned in nothing but thin chemises. The smell of brandy and something foul followed in their wake as they staggered past. One of the women winked at Mr. Pirate.

Ignoring her, he faced Juliana. She narrowed her gaze, trying to hide the repulsion—and fear—brewing within her.

"I make no doubt God is with me, Mr. Pirate. How do you suppose I came to this gruesome place unscathed? 'Twas the Almighty's doing."

For some reason, this made him laugh again. When he recovered, he shook his head. "Milady, your faith in the unseen astounds me."

"As your ignorance of it does me." She bit back further insults, not wanting to anger the only man who apparently had no interest in dragging her into one of the rooms lining the hall. A shrill tune blared from an organ below, accompanied by the clang of swords and vulgar shouts as no doubt another brawl ensued. "You would be best served to call upon God, Mr. Pirate, rather than waste your life in dissolute living. I fear you have lost your moral compass."

A scream resounded from one of the rooms. Mr. Pirate didn't flinch. Instead, one side of his lips quirked in a grin. "Milord Pirate, if you please. And I prefer my dissolute living to serving a capricious God."

She pursed her lips. "How sad."

The scream turned to laughter as other moans echoed from a room across the hall.

He huffed. "You would be the sad one, and far worse, if I hadn't walked into this bawdy house when I did. Are you aware, milady, of just who it was who had you in his grip when I arrived?" He leaned one hand on the wall beside her and gestured toward the room below, where the ruckus increased in sound and intensity. "That was William Delong. They call him Henry the Eighth. Can you entertain the reason?"

"Because he possesses an ego the size of England?" she returned with a smirk.

Mr. Pirate chuckled. "Forsooth, I believe you know the man." He pushed from the wall and crossed arms over his chest, suddenly sobering. "The blaggart harbors a penchant for light-haired women. Care to guess what he does with them after he has used all their wares?"

Juliana swallowed. *Actually no.*

"He passes them amongst his crew for months before he hooks them and drags them behind his ship as bait for sharks. Of late, a delicacy among pirates." His dark brows rose. "Sharks, that is. Women always have been."

A tremble coursed through her legs, making her glad she had the wall behind her for support.

"Another second and that would have been your fate." He leaned to peer in her eyes. "Still believe God is protecting you?"

In an attempt to calm herself, she drew a ragged breath. "I do," she said. "For as soon as I prayed for help. He sent you."

"Me?" He chuckled. "From God? Lud, milady, you disarm me with your wit."

"Mayhap you need to be disarmed, Mr. Pirate."

A mischievous grin twisted his lips. Planting his hands on the wall on either side of her, he barricaded her in and studied her intently. "Indeed, for who's to say I do not present as equal a danger to you as any man here?"

The heat from his body filled the air between them, his smell of leather and brine filled her nose, as his presence, so close to her, sent dizzying eddies through her head. Though he had done her no harm—yet—he could very well have some nefarious purpose in mind. Why else would he be protecting her from the others? He fingered a lock of her hair as he took in every feature of her face—a habit of his, it would seem. Her blood dashed madly through her veins. Not wanting him to notice the effect he had on her, she shoved one of his arms down and stepped to the side.

He raked a hand through his hair and gave her a cynical look. "If this God of yours is protecting you, then what need of me?" Turning, he started toward the stairs.

Her heart stopped. Her insides screamed, *Don't leave me*! Not in this hellish place where she had no idea where to look for her friend, where the sound of unspeakable acts leeched from behind closed doors, and where a pack of wolves prowled below awaiting their prey. *Oh, fie!* Where was her faith? Yet ... mayhap God had, indeed, sent this man to protect her. "You wouldn't leave a lady here alone," she shouted above the din as he reached the top of the stairs.

"I wouldn't?" Halting, he faced her. "I'm a *pirate*, remember?" He patted the pockets of his jerkin and breeches as if searching for something. "Lud, and I seem to have lost my moral compass."

She frowned at his impish grin. She would not give way to a *pirate*. She had announced her faith in God and would not besmirch his name by asking for this vermin's help. She was about to tell him that very thing, when a man draped in a doxy appeared at the top of the stairs. The woman, a russet-haired beauty who was all but bursting out of her tight bodice, veritably lit up upon seeing Mr. Pirate.

"Milord!" Extricating herself from her consort, she flew into Mr. Pirate's arms, squealing and flopping like a deranged pig. He shoved her back.

"Where 'ave you been, Your Lordship?" Not put off in the slightest by his brusque dismissal, she gave him a coy glance. "You told me you would come an' see me soon, but that was a fortnight ago."

"Forgive me. I fear I have been otherwise engaged." He nudged her back toward her patron.

She giggled. "Milord, my, but you 'ave such fine speech." Only then did the woman notice Juliana standing there. The glimmer left her eyes, replaced by cannon fire as she scanned Juliana from head to toe. "I see."

Her besotted customer, who'd been swaying in place and eyeing the scene with curiosity, came out of his daze, and with a disgruntled curse, dragged the woman into one of the rooms and slammed the door.

"Pray, do not allow me to keep you from your debauchery, *milord.*"

Frowning, he took her hand in his and led her down the hall. "The sick wenches are housed above."

She wanted to ask him how he knew that but thought better of it. She wanted to tug away from his grip, but the strength of his hand around hers brought her more comfort than she cared to admit. She wanted to run back to the safety of her home and forget the vile things she'd witnessed, but love for her friend drove her onward.

Thankfully, the third floor was devoid of bestial grunts and bawdy laughter, replaced by a single moan coming from the last room on the left.

"Abilene!" Juliana darted forward, but Mr. Pirate rushed ahead of her and knocked lightly, nudging her firmly behind him. The door cracked and a woman peeked out, her suspicious gaze taking in Mr. Pirate. But upon seeing Juliana, she swept it open, grabbed Juliana's arm, and dragged her inside. A wall of heated air tainted with a putrid odor blasted over Juliana as her eyes grew accustomed to the dim light of a single candle.

"Miss, ye came! God bless ye, miss. God bless ye." A bouquet of brown curls tumbled over the woman's threadbare gown and framed a face that would have been comely save for the bruise circling one swollen eye. But Juliana didn't have time to concern herself with the woman's condition as she rushed to the barely-recognizable form of her friend, Abilene—or at least she thought it was Abilene—lying on the cot.

Dropping to her knees beside the bed, Juliana coughed back the metallic odor of blood while she brushed strands of dirty hair from the woman's face. Yes, it was Abilene. She'd know those long lashes and full lips anywhere.

"Abilene, Abilene, oh dear, what happened to you?" A bloody gash tore across her forehead and another one sliced her arm. Bruises marred her swollen face and neck, and her gown was ripped down the front, revealing a stained petticoat. Worst of all, her wrists bore bloody grooves of harsh restraints.

"'Twas that beast Riley," the woman offered. "When she refused 'is money an' 'is insistence t' go upstairs, 'e dragged 'er out into the streets to God knows where." She began to sob. "I tried t' follow but couldn't find 'er anywhere. She showed up like this an hour ago … must 'ave dragged 'erself back somehow."

Mr. Pirate stepped in and closed the door, a scowl forming on his face.

Juliana squeezed her friend's limp hand and stood. "Why isn't she waking up?"

"He hit 'er on the head, miss. See?" The woman circled the bed, and grabbing the candle, pointed to where a pool of blood spread across the pillowcase.

Gasping, Juliana tossed a hand to her mouth. Mr. Pirate touched her elbow to steady her and tried leading her to a chair.

"Nay, I'm all right." She faced the woman who stood over her friend, wringing her hands in worry. "We need water and clean cloths, if you have them. And a doctor if you know of one who'll come at this time of night."

"Miss, I only knew t' get you. Abilene said if e'er she was in a bad way to get you, but no doctor will set foot in this place."

Alarm fired through Juliana. "None?"

Mr. Pirate shook his head. "The women have too many diseases. No respectable doctor will come here, especially not after dusk with the unruly throng below." He glanced out a glassless window so small, barely a breeze squeezed through. "But perchance, I can carry her to a doctor, if you know of one who'll attend her."

Juliana sighed. Would Doctor Verns be willing to help a trollop? Would he even be awake at this hour? "I dare not move her unless we are sure to find one who will agree to help. She could have broken bones, damaged organs. She may not survive the journey."

The woman gathered a bowl of water from the dilapidated chest of drawers along with several not-so-clean rags, and set them on the bed stand. "Please 'elp 'er, miss."

Rolling up the lacy sleeves of her gown, Juliana went to work cleaning the wounds as best she could, ensuring Abilene was breathing well, and checking her pulse. But it was weak, terribly weak. No doubt from the loss of blood still dripping onto her pillow, despite Juliana's attempt to stop it. The gouge in her head was deep and would need stitches at best. Another cut on her arm wouldn't stop bleeding either. And the poor lady was still unconscious.

"We need a doctor." Juliana tossed a bloody rag into the bowl and wiped her forehead with her sleeve.

The woman stared at Juliana, the tears in her eyes glittering in the light of the candle she clutched in her hands. "You 'ave to do something."

A noise drew Juliana's glance toward the door, where she was surprised to see the pirate had remained. With his brow furrowed and his jaw tight, it seemed he actually cared for the injured prostitute. But that couldn't be.

She faced Abilene's friend again. "I believe she has internal injuries. And I can't stop the bleeding." Juliana hesitated, her heart a heavy lump, but it was best to speak plainly. "If we don't get her to a doctor, she will die."

The woman broke into sobs, and Juliana went to comfort her, when the click of the door brought her gaze up to see Mr. Pirate leaving. Of course. Why wouldn't he abandon her? No doubt he had treasure to plunder, rum to drink, and other women to rescue. Who could trust a pirate, anyway?

Yet with his departure, all her remaining courage left as well. She was alone in a brothel atop a tavern filled with treacherous men. All alone with a dear friend who, before the night was spent, would most likely die in her arms.

Chapter 13

DESCENDING THE STAIRS TWO AT a time, Alex landed on the final tread and scanned the heads of the milling crowd, searching for one of his men. There, by the long oak bar talking to one of the serving wenches—Maine, his rigger from the *Vanity*. Sticking two fingers inside his mouth, Alex gave the whistle he oft blew aboard his ship—a loud shrill sound that rose over the clamorous din and even sent the parrot flying across the rafters. A few heads popped up and glanced his way, but it was Maine who stood at attention immediately, his eyes scouring the throng until he spotted Alex and headed his way.

He glanced up him. "Aye, Cap'n."

"Go fetch Jonas. Tell him be quick about it. And bring his medical supplies."

"Aye, aye, Cap'n." The young man nodded then scurried through the crowd and left. If he was disappointed about having his evening entertainment interrupted, he didn't reveal it. Alex demanded loyalty both on and off the ship. And in return he treated his men fairly and captured them many prizes. Prizes that also kept Lord Munthrope in his lavish lifestyle, among other things. Yet Alex found the fine clothes, culinary delicacies, beautiful home—all of it—trite and unfulfilling.

As he took in the riotous crowd, gulping down spirits, fondling strumpets, cheating at cards, bragging and shouting and strutting about in an exaggerated display of their egos, he wondered if they felt the same emptiness inside as he did. Were they simply putting on a show, feigning their enjoyment of life, fooling others and mayhap even themselves? Or did doubloons and immoral women and the freebooter's life truly satisfy their inward yearnings? If so, then 'twas not they who were the deviants of humanity, but Alex.

Turning, he started back upstairs, refusing one of the lady's offers to join her in a room. Even the occasional company of a female had lost its appeal. Had all the pleasures promised by life been naught but a lie?

He made his way down the hall and bounded up the second stairway. What wasn't a lie was Miss Juliana. No other lady would have been so brave in the middle of a bawdy house, hearing and seeing things no lady should. Then she'd faced the mutilation of her friend—all the blood and horror and pain—without swooning. Instead, she'd cleansed the wounds as if she attended such injuries every day. Half a smile lifted his lips. What a woman.

When he opened the door, she swerved about, the lace of her lavender skirts drifting over the stained floor like a swan over a cesspool. Shock flashed in her eyes. Had she really believed he would abandon her?

"I thought you'd left." She turned around and continued dabbing a cloth on Abilene's face.

"Gwen!" A male voice echoed from below, and the woman standing on the other side of Abilene jerked. "Gwen, get down 'ere, ye buxom wench!"

The poor woman instantly tightened. "I 'ave to go, but I'll be back."

"Thank you, Gwen." Juliana smiled and nodded. "We'll take good care of her."

"God bless ye, miss. An' ye too, milord," she said as she passed Alex and closed the door behind her.

"Why did you return?" Juliana knelt beside the bed, her tone both harsh and hopeful.

"I called for my surgeon."

She gazed up at him, her brows dipping. "*Your* surgeon? Oh, I see. Your *pirate* surgeon."

He crossed arms over his chest, amused by her disdain. "Shall I call him off?"

"Nay, forgive me. You are trying to help, and I'm being rude." She drew a deep breath. "I'm simply tired and worried, and I don't see how a pirate butcher can help, but—" She faced him again, a look of contrition on her face. "I'm sure this surgeon of yours is better than nothing." She sat on the side of the cot and stared at the bloody cloth in her hands. A breeze stirred golden wisps about her neck as candlelight caressed her cheek. Even with the blood splattered about her, she truly did look like an angel dropped into the midst of hell.

"You'll find him quite capable, milady. He has saved the lives of many of my crew."

"After your plundering and rapine brought them injury," she mumbled in disgust.

Lud, the vixen's tongue! Alex bristled, unaccustomed to being insulted. "Indeed. 'Tis part of the vocation."

"Pirating is no vocation, sir." Her eyes met his, and fear darted across them as if she just realized she was alone with a notorious pirate. She glanced at the closed door, beyond where a harpsichord and fiddle competed with the drunken shouts of men. "Why are you helping me? What is it you truly want, Mr. Pirate?" Rising, she circled the cot, placing it between them and lifted her chin in an attempt to appear unafraid, though her hands trembled as she dipped the cloth in the basin of bloody water.

He longed to tell her the truth, that he'd been watching her for years, that he found her a refreshing enigma among the frivolous women inhabiting the island, that she fascinated him, intrigued him, stirred his dead soul to life.

Instead, he merely gestured toward the injured woman and said, "I will gladly tell you, milady, if you will tell me who this trollop is and why you care so much about her."

Releasing a ragged sigh, Juliana wrung out the cloth and held it to the wound on her friend's head. "Her name is Abilene Hastings." Hesitating, she wiped moisture from her eye. "We met at a soiree at King's Hall. She and her parents had just arrived in Port Royal. Her father was sent by the king to ensure his interests were being looked after properly. Her mother was famed for her beauty and charity. Good people. Noble and honorable."

Alex nodded his agreement, then caught himself. The Pirate Earl would not have associated with such highborn people. However, he remembered the Hastings well, though they seemed to go out of their way to avoid Lord Munthrope. Which only reinforced Juliana's good opinion of them. However, if he remembered, the couple had succumbed to one of the many tropical diseases lurking about the island and died soon after they arrived.

"Abilene was not like the other ladies on the island," Juliana continued, easing onto the cot beside her friend. "She was humble and kind, not pretentious or shallow. She truly cared about others. We went everywhere together: strolls along Fisher's Row, horseback riding on the mainland, shopping at the Merchant's Exchange. She even made attending wearisome soirees tolerable. When my mother died, she was there to comfort me."

At this she stopped. Her lips tightened, and she seemed to be trying to control her emotions. Alex wished for nothing more than to take her in his arms.

But then she continued. "Her parents got sick—yellow fever, they said—and within a few months they were both gone." She withdrew the cloth. "Apparently, unbeknownst to Abilene, her father had amassed an enormous debt, and the creditors devoured what was left of the estate. With no family here or back home, Abilene had nowhere to go. I begged her to come stay with me, but her foolish pride refused any help."

Alex's stomach sank. He could guess the rest.

A pistol shot thundered from below. Juliana's shoulders jerked up as her eyes, brimming with tears, snapped to the door. Alex moved to stand before it in a gesture to reassure her of his protection.

She dropped the cloth in the basin. "She allied herself with a gentleman"—the features of her face grew tight—"or a scoundrel masquerading as a gentleman, who promised her employment as a house maid, when in reality he sold her as a prostitute to visiting emissaries in exchange for a better post in Barbados."

Alex clenched his fists. "Where is this *gentleman* now?"

She wiped a tear away. "He's long gone. Along with the emissaries." She caressed Abilene's hand. "Too ashamed to face anyone, she refused to come home with me. Said she was soiled, ruined, and that no decent home would hire her now. And without a skill, she had but one recourse."

Juliana glanced at him, her eyes glassy and sharp. "'Tis unfair for a woman, Mr. Pirate. We are completely at the mercy of the men who provide for us. Should that provision be taken away, or should they abuse us or deny us our living, what are we to do? What was Abilene to do?" She raised her friend's hand and placed a kiss upon it. And Alex wondered if she spoke from personal experience as well as for her friend.

His throat burned at the sight of her devotion to the lady, her willingness to risk her life to care for her.

"I would rather die than subject myself to the life of a trollop," she said.

Alex longed to approach her, to comfort her and tell her what a saint she was, but he dared not trust himself with this woman. Not alone. And not when she was so vulnerable. "She is fortunate to have you as friend."

"Is she? I fear there is not much I can do, save bring her trifles now and then and comfort her with empty platitudes."

"It is enough," he said. "It is more than most would do."

She barely nodded, then looked up and searched his eyes intently. "Now it is your turn, Mr. Pirate. Why are you helping me?"

"Milord Pirate, if you please." Alex rubbed the back of his neck, thinking of a clever response, when the door opened, pushing him aside, and in walked Jonas, medical satchel in hand.

The butcher surgeon actually appeared somewhat agreeable. And clean. No gaudy mismatched clothing, no rotted teeth, no glimmering baubles. No weapons, save for a cutlass at his side. In fact, his light hair was short cropped, the whiskers lining his jaw neatly trimmed, and an unsoiled white cravat bubbled over his stylish gray doublet. After a quick scan of the room, he nodded to Mr. Pirate, "Good evening, Captain," then brushed a glance over Juliana before centering on Abilene. Another pirate—one who looked the part—entered behind him and shut the door.

"What happened?" The surgeon knelt before the bed and laid a hand atop Abilene's forehead.

"She was beaten." Juliana rose to her feet.

"Jonas, this is Miss Juliana Dutton. Miss Juliana, Jonas Nash, my ship's surgeon."

Mr. Pirate's polite introductions reminded her to ask him how he came to speak so well. Her heart suddenly tightened. *And know her name!*

Shoving aside her alarm, Juliana focused back on Abilene and gestured toward the wound on her head. "I cannot stop the bleeding."

"Has she woken?" Prying her lids open, Mr. Nash examined her eyes.

"Nay, not since we've been here."

"Very well." He glanced at the bowl of bloody water. "I'll need your help removing her bodice and skirts." He swung to face Mr. Pirate. "Leave or turn your face, Captain, if you please. And you, Maine, go fetch some water and rags."

The surgeon's take-command attitude, and the fact that he seemed sober, did much to allay Juliana's fears.

Maine darted out while Mr. Pirate surprisingly obeyed and faced the wall.

An hour later, after the butcher surgeon poked, prodded, stitched, and mended, Juliana slouched on the bed beside her friend and took her limp hand in hers. Mr. Nash cleaned the blood from his hands as best he could in the dirty water, then stretched his back and moved to the window, no doubt to clear his nostrils of the same metallic stink that had also taken residence in Juliana's nose.

Mr. Pirate spoke up first from his seat by the door. "What say you, my friend? Will she live?"

The surgeon drew a deep breath and faced them. "Broken ribs, bruised liver from what I can tell, but no other internal injuries of note. I stitched up the gash on her head and the one on her arm, but what worries me is that she hasn't woken. A concussion, most likely. And she's lost a lot of blood. If she is allowed rest and receives good fare, she should recover in time."

"How is she to receive *either* in this place?" Juliana shook her head.

"She must." Mr. Nash tossed dirty tools into his satchel, then took one last swipe of a cloth on his forehead before facing his captain. "Corson is ill. If you'll permit me, I should return to him."

Mr. Pirate nodded. "Thank you, Jonas."

"Miss Dutton. A pleasure." He bowed toward her.

"I don't know how to thank you, Mr. Nash. You saved her life."

To that, he merely smiled, plopped his castor atop his head, and left, closing the door behind him. Leaving her alone again with the notorious Pirate Earl. Though the notoriety of his carnal exploits she could hardly imagine, his behavior toward her had been monkish thus far. Unless he was the type to lure a lady into his trap with kindness. If the raw masculinity of his presence and the intensity of those piercing eyes weren't enough to send a feminine heart aflutter, surely saving the life of a good friend would send a weaker woman swooning in his arms.

She was not a weaker woman.

He was a pirate—a thief and liar by nature. And she'd had her fill of untrustworthy men. Tearing her gaze from him, she studied Abilene, bruised and swollen but bandaged and sleeping peacefully now. "I cannot leave her here. Who will look out after her?"

"Do not fear, milady," He approached, each thump of his Cordovan boots increasing the beat of her heart. "I will arrange for her care. Several of the ladies here are in my debt."

"I can well imagine they are, milord." She spat out with disgust, glad for the reminder of his character.

He stopped within a foot of her, unruffled by her insinuation. Forsooth, did anything ruffle this man? The air heated between them. He lifted his hand. To do what, she did not stay in place to discover. Stepping aside, she busied herself with collecting bloody rags. "But surely the owner of this place will demand payment." A price she'd be willing to pay, of course—if she had any extra funds. Mayhap she should just bring Abilene home. The woman was in no condition to argue at the moment.

"Have no care, the room will be paid for, and I will send word to you of her progress." The depth of his voice rumbled through the chamber, a trumpet of assurance and comfort.

She gathered the rest of the rags, then dropped them in the basin, searching her mind for an explanation for his charity. He wanted something from her. But what? She had no wealth, no land, no real position. And if he'd wanted her purity, he'd have stolen it already. Hearing him approach once again, she spun to face him. "Why would you do this? What sort of pirate are you?"

"A successful one, it would seem." He gave a rakish grin.

"At thievery, I'll not gainsay it. But what of the raping and murdering your reputation expounds?" She slammed her mouth shut. *Fool!* Why remind the man?

"I have my moments." He closed the distance between them, running a forefinger and thumb down the sides of his mouth as his grin remained. A spark of familiarity shot an image of Munthrope into her mind, but she shook it off.

Heart thumping against her chest, she inched to the side, hoping to skirt around him. "Men fear you. Entire throngs of pirates obey you with one word. And yet you care for an unknown prostitute."

With one move, he blocked her path, trapping her against the dresser. "Nay, milady." Before she could stop him, he ran the back of his fingers over her cheek. They felt rough and strong and smelled of smoke and Madeira wine. "I care that *you* care for her," he whispered in her ear.

His gentle touch left her breathless, and she hated herself for it. Imprisoned by the sheer strength and size of him, she was at his mercy. He could do whatever he wished with her. In this place, no one would hear her scream or care if they did. She should be frightened. Why wasn't she? She closed her eyes.

The heat and strength of him enveloped her. Warm, spicy breath drifted over her cheek … onto her lips.

She snapped her eyes open. His mouth was but inches from hers. She jerked from him. The wooden knobs on the chest of drawers stabbed her back. "How dare you! I am betrothed." She attempted to get past him, but he took her by the wrist.

"Indeed?" His right brow rose, lifting a scar on his forehead. "Then why does your fiancé allow you to wander the streets at night?"

"He doesn't know where I am." She struggled against his grip.

"Hmm." He caressed her cheek once more. "'Twould seem a man who can't take care of such a precious treasure hardly deserves to keep it." He released her.

She found no mocking within his deep blue eyes—eyes that lured her into their depths with the promise of protection and comfort. Nay. She tore her gaze away. 'Twas the spell of a demon or warlock, that was all.

A swath of gray illuminated the window. Dawn's ribbon of light eased over the ledge and into the room before landing on the man. Taking a step back, she faced him, chin raised.

"I am no man's treasure, Mr. Pirate! Besides, what would you know about deserving—"

She gasped, staring at his face. "What, pray tell, is that white paste on your cheek?"

Chapter 14

ALEX CLUTCHED JULIANA'S HAND, HALTING her before she touched the white residue on his face and realized it was the paste Port Royal gentry used to make themselves appear pale and unblemished. Turning aside, he brushed it off. "'Tis only sand."

Lud, he'd have to be more careful.

Fortunately, Gwen returned at that precise moment, giving Alex an opportunity to slip downstairs and make arrangements with ol' Gengis, the tavern owner, for the room above, as well as procure some of the doxies' help in caring for Abilene. After ensuring no further paste remained on his face, he returned, and under much protest from Miss Juliana, dragged her away from her friend.

"'Tis nearly dawn, and your footman has no doubt woken from his stupor and will be worried about you," he announced as they descended the stairs.

She didn't reply, just trudged numbly beside him down into the main room. Though a few hardy souls still nursed mugs of rum and a man in the corner mumbled a dour tune, most of the patrons lay draped over chairs and tables, unconscious. Snores replaced the raucous din of the night, save for a few lewd comments some of the pirates tossed their way as they passed—comments about their supposed "activities" upstairs—comments Alex hoped Juliana was too tired to hear.

Unfortunately, the lady didn't miss much. Her tiny gasps and the red hue creeping up her face were evidence of that. The fresh morning air seemed to revive her as she halted on the porch and speared him with her gaze. "You should have corrected those men. They are now under the impression that we … that I …" She looked away, the red deepening on her face.

"That we know each other in the biblical sense?" He grinned.

"How dare you say such a thing?"

"We have spent the night together, milady. Why put on such airs?" The morning sun transformed her eyes into fiery turquoise.

Snorting, she proceeded down the steps and into the street. "I have a reputation to uphold, Mr. Pirate, even if you do not."

"Milord Pirate, if you please. And trust me, 'tis best they think you belong to me."

"I belong to no man."

"I suggest you inform your betrothed of that immediately."

Halting again, she tightened her lips in that frustrated, patronizing way of hers. "Mr. Pirate, you have been a great help to me this evening. A hero who came to the rescue of not only me but my dear friend Abilene. Though I fail to understand your reasons, I owe you my gratitude. But now, however, I fear we must part ways. You have your life here among the verminous hooligans, and I have my life"—she paused and stared into the distance—"somewhere else. Good day to you, sir. I shall find my way home." With that, she spun in a swish of skirts and flounced down the sandy road.

What an adorable, delightful woman! Alex fell in step beside her, taking liberties with his gaze as the first rays of the sun slipped over the horizon and showered glittering light upon this angel who dared stroll through the streets of hell. A pink glow hallowed the delicate layers of her hair, while the luster of pearls woven amidst the strands faded in comparison to her tresses of spun gold. Roses bloomed on a face tinged by the sun, her flawless complexion marred only by the shadows hovering beneath her eyes. And what eyes! Azure blue with streaks of green that matched the color of the water caressing Jamaica's shores. The blood splattered on her lavender gown only endeared her to him more. The woman was a saint. Alex felt like a filthy troll as he strolled beside her, a supplicant begging her favor.

And he'd never been good at begging.

Upon finding him beside her, she gave an exasperated sigh, but at least she made no further attempts to be rid of him.

They finally found Mr. Pell, who was, indeed, in a dither having woken to find Miss Dutton gone. The relief shouting from the footman's bloodshot eyes was nearly comical. After assisting her into the carriage, and receiving a rather snub look from Mr. Pell, Alex watched them drive away. The carriage wheels cranked and screeched down the sandy lane, and he found himself longing for one last glance from Miss Juliana. If she would but look his way, it would give him hope that mayhap she harbored a smidgen of affection for him. He'd happily settle for such a trifle. Which was why he stood staring after her like a fool. The carriage was nearly at the end of the street when the lady turned in her seat, shielded her eyes from the sun, and glanced his way. Alex couldn't help but smile. So, she *did* find him intriguing. It was a start. A start toward what, he had no idea, but just being with her made him feel like a better man. Mayhap it was possible, after all, that a lady like her could redeem a wicked pirate like him.

Two days later, as promised, Juliana opened the door of her home and received a missive from a rather slovenly-looking fellow, who tipped his hat above a leering grin before turning and stumbling back down the steps. It was from Abilene. She was recovering, well taken care of, extremely thankful for Juliana's help, but wanted her to promise she would never set foot down by the docks at night again. Not for her. Not for anyone. She signed it, *Affectionately your friend always, Abilene.*

Juliana wiped a tear away. 'Twould that the stubborn woman would accept more of her help, would come home with Juliana, allow her to care for her. Though how Juliana could feed another mouth, she had no idea. Business was down. A few of her father's long-standing customers had switched to Masters Shipping for the transport of their goods. Nervous, no doubt, in the absence of her father's presence in town. Dutton Shipping was but one summer squall or one pirate attack away from folding completely. How had Father stood the pressure?

Coughing spiked down the stairs from above. Not well, apparently. Was it the stress or his crotchety personality that had opened the door to such a gruesome illness? An illness that leeched away more of his life every day, according to Dr. Verns who had bled the man just that morning.

Folding the note, Juliana slipped it inside the pocket of her skirts and headed back toward her father's study, where a stack of documents awaited her. Up at dawn, she'd barely gone through a quarter of the writs of lading, and it was already noon. Her eyes hurt, her neck ached, and she longed for a nap. But at least not everything was bad news. Rowan had nearly recovered from his beating, and now Abilene was on the mend as well. She quietly thanked God for the small blessings. Mayhap caring for the orphans and risking her life for Abilene had won her a speck of favor with the Almighty.

Unbidden thoughts of the Pirate Earl barged into her mind. *Again.* Truth be told, she couldn't stop thinking of him.

The way he'd protected her, called his surgeon, paid for the room, and hired women to care for Abilene. The way he looked at Juliana with those penetrating eyes the color of the deep sea—as if she was more precious than all the doubloons he'd ever pilfered. The way her insides inflamed when he'd caressed her cheek. *Shameful!* Why did he affect her so? She moved to the French doors and hugged herself, staring out into her mother's garden.

Another knock on the front door spun her around. Restraining a growl at not having a butler—at least not when Abbot was down at the wharves—she headed back into the foyer. A few seconds later, she wished she hadn't opened the door. Captain Nichols, a silly grin on his lips, removed his cocked black hat and bowed to kiss her hand.

"Miss Juliana, you are a breath of fresh air."

She sighed. "I imagine you get more than enough fresh air on board your frigate, Captain."

He rubbed his smooth jaw, his brown eyes assessing her. "Tis not the same as the invigorating sensation of seeing you."

Nausea soured her stomach. "You flatter me overmuch, Captain. However, I fear I have no time for visitors today." Especially not visitors prone to snooping around asking too many questions.

"Miss Juliana." Nichols held the door firm against her attempt to shut it as his expression turned to one of pleading. "Pray, since you give me no choice, I must make bold. I insist you reconsider your engagement to that buffoon, Munthrope. I know you have no affection for him. Why, you never gave him a moment's notice, even shriveled in disdain whenever you saw him. Faith now, this effort to make me jealous has gone too far."

The flat line of his dark eyebrows indicated the man was serious. Juliana could not decide between feeling sorry for him or being angry at his overinflated ego. "You make too free with your opinions, sir. I cannot in good conscience allow you to continue under such a misguided perception. My engagement to Lord Munthrope is real, I assure you. And though I am sorry for your jealousy, in good sooth, I beg you to turn your affections elsewhere."

Spite appeared in his eyes. "As you already have, my dear?" He shifted his stance and raised a wooly eyebrow. "Word about town is you've been seen with the ignoble Pirate Earl. Late at night and even"—he curled his lip—"before dawn."

Blast that Mr. Pell! Juliana flattened her lips and made a note to chastise the footman for his loose tongue. "I never took you for a man who dabbles in gossip, Captain Nichols."

"Then, it is not true?"

"Do you take me for the type of woman who associates with pirates? Now, if you please." She started to close the door, when Rowan's voice boomed from behind her.

"He's not come to see you, dear sister."

Gripping the banister, her brother limped down the stairs, wincing with each step, and halted beside her, a playful grin on his bruised face. Despite his black eye and swollen nose, he was the epitome of fashion from the heels of his Turkish shoes to the gold-laced edges of his silk cravat. "The captain and I have business to discuss."

Alarm prickled her skin. "What business could you possibly—?"

Captain Nichols brushed past her and entered the foyer, greeting her brother with a dip of his head. "Mr. Dutton, thank you for seeing me." He glanced at the carved crown molding circling the room then up the mahogany staircase. "And how is your father these days? I heard he was ill."

"You heard incorrectly, sir. He is quite well, I assure you." Juliana shut the door, forcing a causal tone. "However he is overwhelmed with work at the moment. I'm sure you understand."

"Rowan, may I have a word?" She gave a tight smile toward her brother before facing the captain. "Captain

Nichols, would you care to wait in the sitting room?" She gestured toward the right, where two doors opened to a colorful, sunlit room.

The naval officer pursed his thin lips. "Wherever is your butler? 'Tis unseemly for you to be answering your own door."

"Surely as a Post-Captain in his Majesty's Navy, you can navigate to the sitting room without him?" She smiled sweetly.

"Of course." He gave a stiff bow and marched away as Juliana dragged her imbecilic brother aside, not caring when he winced in pain.

"Why did you agree to see that man in our home? Are you daft?"

Rowan swept aside strands of light hair from his face and smiled. "Daft? I believe we established that long ago." He kissed her cheek. "But 'tis you who will lose your youthful beauty with all this unnecessary fretting. Why, dear sister, you already have shadows beneath your eyes. We wouldn't want Lord Munthrope—excellent catch, by the way"—he winked—"to change his mind. "

"I care not what Lord Munthrope does, and I have shadows beneath my eyes because I forfeit my rest to keep this family afloat!"

"And you are doing an excellent job at it. Excellent, I say. Now, if you'll allow, whatever business Nichols has with me, I'm sure it has nothing to do with you."

"I doubt that. Do you realize—" Juliana slammed her mouth shut, forcing back her rising fury. "Do you realize that the captain has been most curious about our shipping business and our family as of late? Always asking questions, sticking that pointy nose of his where he has no right?"

Rowan shrugged and laid a gentle hand on her shoulder. "Don't vex yourself so, Sister. The man is harmless. His curiosity stems from his interest in you. Once he accepts your betrothal to Munthrope, he'll relent, to be sure."

"What if he sees me in father's study behind his desk doing his work? What if he notices our depleted staff? Hears father's sickly cough? He should not be here at all. If he continues to visit, he'll wonder why father never comes out to greet him."

"Becalm yourself, dear sister, I have the situation in hand."

"What you hope to have in hand is the dear captain's money. Of that I am sure," she spat, crossing her arms over her chest. "I don't like him paying off your gambling debts. I'll not allow it, do you take me?"

Rowan fingered the lace at his cuffs. "Would you prefer I be tossed into the bay?"

"I would prefer you not gamble away our fortune." She settled herself. "Can you not see I'm trying my best to provide for us? I could use your help, Rowan. At the very least, if you would not resist me." She sighed in weariness at the same look of remorse he always gave her. "We must pay Nichols back. I cannot be in his debt."

Rowan took her hand in his. "That is precisely why I received the good captain's request to meet. To repay him."

"With what?" Juliana huffed.

Before he could answer, Nichols stormed back into the foyer impatiently, pocket watch in hand.

Another knock on the door brought Juliana's frustration to a boil. How was she ever to get anything done today? "Faith now, who could that be?"

No sooner did Rowan fling open the door than Lord Munthrope swept into the hall in a tide of billowing silk and lace. Tight ringlets from a long periwig flounced over his shoulders. White paste coated his face, perfected by a well-placed mole above the right corner of his lips, a horse patch above his right eye, and circles of rouge on both cheeks. He extended a leg, both hands elevated, and bowed grandly before Juliana.

Oh, fie! His Lordship was the last person she wished to see. Or was he? Captain Nichols immediately lengthened his stance, grabbed the hilt of his service sword, and gave Munthrope a scorching look. Munthrope, however, barely acknowledged him before greeting Rowan and turning back to Juliana.

"Miss Dutton, Lady Milson has invited us to tea. 'Tis a breezy afternoon. I thought a ride about town and then some refreshment at the Milson's would be utterly delightful. Do say you'll join me, sweetums."

Sweetums? Juliana resisted the urge to roll her eyes. "Your Lordship is too kind. However"—she clamped her teeth together—"you have caught me at a disadvantage. For I was not expecting to go out today. Nor to entertain guests." She directed a glare at Captain Nichols, whose slight smile indicated he was quite pleased with her curt tone toward Munthrope.

Which reminded her that, business with Rowan aside, her best chances of getting rid of Nichols once and for all was to ensure him of her love for this annoying dandy. Releasing a heavy sigh, she stared at the three men. She truly *did* have work to complete today. And spending time with the cheeky princock held no appeal whatsoever.

"You could use an afternoon of play, dear sister." Rowan winked. "Besides, how can you deny your intended the pleasure of your company?"

"'Tis most uncouth to barge in on a lady unannounced," Nichols ground out, causing Munthrope to spin his way, the lace on his elevated hand fluttering.

"Especially so when that gentleman is not her betrothed. I am glad your humility admits it, Captain Darling." His chuckle filled the room.

"My business here is with Mr. Dutton," Nichols retorted, eyes lines of disdain.

Ignoring him, Lord Munthrope hooked his jeweled walking stick over one arm and took in the foyer. "Ah, your father, sweetums? I trust he is feeling better?"

"I knew it!" Nichols exclaimed.

Miss Ellie, cotton skirts in hand, hurried down the stairs. "Beggin' your pardon, miss." Her gaze took in the crowd. "I 'ad no idea you were 'xpecting company. I'll go 'ave cook put on some tea."

"There's no need, Ellie." Juliana said, hoping everyone would take the hint and leave.

"Of course there is," her brother interjected. "Captain Nichols and I will take our tea in the sitting room, Miss Ellie."

"Begad, so your business *is* with the younger Mr. Dutton," Munthrope said. "Very good. Very good." He tapped his tasseled blue shoes over the floor as he recited a quick rhyme:

'Tis the son not the father
Or the father's son
Whoever it be
There's business to be done!

"Oh, very good. Very good," he commended himself.

Rowan joined in His Lordship's laughter while Nichols snorted in disgust. "Your wit, milord. 'Tis outstanding."

Shaking her head, Ellie headed to the cook room out back. Juliana wished she could follow her and leave this flock of bird-witted men. But she couldn't. She must play the doting fiancée in order to get rid of Nichols once and for all. Yet perchance she could do so and still remain at home to do her work. She glanced down at her plain walking gown. "I'm hardly dressed for a party, your lordship. Mayhap another time."

"'Tis but an informal tea. And as usual, you will outshine every lady there, sweetums." A flicker of something in his eyes kept her riveted to his gaze. A flicker that bespoke of control, intelligence, and a seriousness that was so unlike the cavalier lord.

She could see no way out of this. "Then permit me to gather my reticule." A few minutes later, she descended the stairs to find all three men still staring at each other, two of them like wolves baring teeth in defense of their territory. The third, her brother, with the usual look of vapid delight on his face.

Fools, all! Yet the look on Nichols's steaming face as she waltzed out the door on Lord Munthrope's arm was surely worth it.

Chapter 15

NICHOLS TOOK A SEAT ON the velvet-lined settee and lifted his gaze to Juliana's dim-witted brother. As soon as he'd heard of Rowan's *accident*, a plan had sprouted in his mind, a plan that—after Lord Munthrope had announced his courtship with Miss Juliana—had blossomed and grown thorns. Even now, he bit back a burst of fury at the remembrance of that night. How dare she lead him to believe they had an understanding and then attach herself to another man—a bumbling fool at that! The insult was beyond the pale. He could make no sense of it. He'd been told his appearance was exceptional. He was wealthy, stood to inherit his father's estate in Hertfordshire, and he was a captain in His Majesty's Royal Navy. Not a bad *précis* of achievements.

Especially for someone whom both his father and brother thought would amount to nothing.

And especially not someone whose situation and assets should be shunned by a lady devoid of title or fortune. Dozens of women vied for his attentions. All except the one he wanted.

"Drink?" Rowan poured himself a glass of liquor from the sideboard and at Nichols "nay", took a seat across from him, crossing one booted leg over the other.

"I thought we were having tea," Nichols said, disgusted at the man's infatuation with spirits.

"We are, but I find my tea always in need of embellishment, do you not?"

The maid entered with a tray, spotted Rowan with a drink, frowned, then slammed it down on the table. After briskly pouring the steaming liquid into cups, she asked if Rowan wanted anything else and stomped from the room before he answered.

Nichols smiled. "Having trouble with your staff?"

"Miss Ellie? Nay, she's been with us for years. A bit capricious at times, but she means well."

"I would dismiss her at once." One thing Nichols never tolerated was disrespect from servants.

Rowan poured the brandy into his tea and leaned back, sipping the potion while eyeing Nichols curiously. "Pray tell, Captain, surely you didn't request an audience with me to discuss my staff." He cocked one of his fair eyebrows and continued before Nichols could respond. "No doubt you wish to demand a favor in return for your generosity in paying off my debt. An action I did not request, by the by."

Nichols watched the steam swirl from his teacup, wondering how best to handle this pompous fop who was so much like his own brother, it twisted his gut in knots. Arrogant, conceited, self-serving, with a rapier wit, the physique of a god, and a face that made women swoon. Even the fair hair and green mischievous eyes were the same. Men like him thought they could rule the world with only their looks and charm. Yes, this man was much like Richard. But where Richard had been wise and industrious, this dizzard was lazy and burdened with an exaggerated belief in an intelligence he would never possess.

"As I have informed you, it was but a gift of my charity, from one gentleman to another. We cannot have that swine Bilford tossing one of our own to the sharks, can we?"

Rowan tilted his head, examining him. "But the sum was atrocious, Captain. I insist on repaying you. In fact, I shall put my skills to use post haste in the gambling halls."

Idiot. Nichols stared aghast at the numskull. 'Twas what got him in the mess in the first place. "And yet"—Nichols sipped his tea, then set down the cup—"I would hate to find you in a similar situation all over again."

"Never fear, I've learned my lesson in that regard. Besides"—Rowan lifted up a palm when Nichols started to speak—"I will not suffer your charity, sir."

Nichols growled under his breath as a muculent cough filtered down from above. "Is someone ill?"

"Nay … I mean, yes, 'tis but a servant. No one of import." Rising, Rowan went to the sideboard and filled his glass again, but his flustered behavior fed Nichols's suspicions. Another bout of coughing, followed by the patter of someone running down the hall, confirmed them. "Your father has not been seen in town for months."

The chink of glass sounded. "He is a private man, Captain. Who prefers to spend his dotage in peace."

"He has never been so before, and he's hardly entered his dotage. Why, he can't be more than fifty."

Returning to his seat, Rowan forsook the tea and tossed the brandy to the back of his throat. "He has worked hard his entire life. What is it to you if he prefers to allow his manager to handle business down by the docks?"

"Business manager? I had no idea. Who is the man?"

Sunlight spearing in through the window striped the young buck's coat in gold and brown. He hesitated, his jaw working. "My, my, Captain, why the curiosity regarding my family business?"

"You must pardon me there, Mr. Dutton." Nichols was quick to allay the man's temper. "'Tis a curiosity born out of my interest in your sister. I was under the impression you were my ally in procuring her hand."

Rowan flattened his lips with a shrug. "In truth, her interest in Munthrope came as a complete surprise to me. I hadn't given her the credit for brains." He seemed relieved at the change in topic. "There is naught to be done about it now.

Besides, Munthrope is a wealthy man—wealthier than you, I'd say."

Nichols grew livid at the man's superior attitude, one his brother had constantly assailed upon him in their youth. Always thinking he was the better man, more handsome, smarter, more successful. And lording it over Nichols whenever he could. Making him feel inferior and worthless. But Nichols had more than proven himself. He had succeeded in every area his brother had deemed him incompetent. And he was not about to allow this goose-witted carp to make him feel like a failure again. He would win Juliana. He would not be defeated. "Munthrope is a fool, as you well know. He'll abandon your sister as soon as he tires of her."

Rowan shrugged. "Mayhap. But 'tis her concern, not mine."

"What's this? No care for your sister's future?"

"Who can count on a future, Captain?" Rowan stretched his arms across the back of the couch on either side of him. "We don't know what tomorrow will bring. Enjoy the moment, I say, and take no care for things that may never happen."

"Tush man, what nonsense is this?" Nichols barked, disgusted by the man's cavalier attitude. "We can very well alter our course in life. We can choose our own destiny."

"And what do you choose, Captain?" Rowan grinned. "What is your purpose on this earth? Or perchance should I rephrase: What is the price of your charity?"

The man was not as dumb as Nichols assumed. "I wish for your help is all."

Rowan gave a cynical snort. "I'd rather repay you with coin."

"But how can you hope to win at cards when you have no money with which to gamble?" Nichols picked up his tea but found it had grown cold. "My offer includes a handsome salary, one which should keep you long into Faro each night."

A glimmer of desire flashed across the young rogue's eyes before he masked it with disinterest. "You would pay me? When 'tis I who owe you?" He brushed dust from his coat.

"Think of it as an advance on the money you'll repay me when you win."

Nichols could almost see the greed waving at him from the man's eyes.

Rowan's jaw clenched, those greedy eyes narrowed. He was caught and he knew it. "What is it you want?" he said in surrender.

"Two simple tasks which should appeal to your adventurous spirit. One, to follow Lord Munthrope, watch him, find something malicious with which to discredit the fop, something that will cause Juliana to come to her senses and find me the better choice."

"And the other?"

"To use one of your father's ships as bait to trap the Pirate Earl."

Though Alex knew Juliana had only agreed to come with him in order to convince Captain Nichols of the sincerity of their betrothal, he couldn't be happier to be in her company again. Even in the form of the ostentatious Lord Munthrope, even though she looked at him with an odd mixture of amusement and aversion. And even though now, as they careened down the sunny street in his carriage, she stared at the passing homes with an abject look of boredom.

"In good sooth, sweetums, we certainly fooled the poor captain, did we not?" He chuckled. "Did you see his face? Begad, I thought it would erupt in a torrent of green."

She gave him a lifeless smile as the sea breeze doused him with her scent of vanilla and cherries. "Indeed. Your timing was impeccable, milord. I feared I would have to endure his company all afternoon."

The thought that she felt the same way about him cast a shadow on the sunny day. "Our plan is working then, milady."

"It would seem so, yes. Hence, now my task remains to stop my brother from inviting the odious man to our house." She gave an exhausted sigh, which pricked Alex's concern.

A breeze ruffled the white fichu tucked within the neck of her blue camlet gown. She gazed at him from beneath her straw hat as anxiety tainted with sorrow rolled across her expression. He resisted the urge to take her hand in his.

Outside the covered carriage, rows of tall brick homes that were lined up like soldiers soon gave way to cabinet makers, bakers, a mercantile, and other shops, which then opened to a wide market square. The smell of roasted boar and turtle stew wafted through the windows as vendors hawked their wares, "Fresh meat, fresh pork, duck an' turtle! Swordfish! Snappers! Mullet!" And the ever present rum punch or Kill-Devil rum.

"You appear tired. Are you getting your rest, milady? I heard something about your friend—Miss Abilene Hastings, was it?—that she'd suddenly been taken ill?"

Suspicion spiked her gaze. "How did you hear of her?"

"You left our engagement fete so suddenly, I asked where you had gone."

"Then, you discovered her"—Juliana bit her lip and looked away—"her predicament, milord."

"That she has fallen from grace, indeed. That you have the heart of a saint, I find I am quite pleased."

"She has not fallen from grace. Merely slipped," she shot back.

He could not help but smile at this.

"She is a dear friend, milord. I will never abandon her like others have abandoned me." Sorrow shadowed her eyes as the carriage careened around a corner and a salty breeze replaced the smells of the market. She glanced at the ribbons of glittering turquoise spreading across Kingston Bay. "Are you familiar with the Pirate Earl, milord?"

He masked his nervous surprise. "Indeed! Who isn't? The king of the pirates, a swarthy fellow I hear, a giant of a man in both brawn and brains." He flung his hand through the air. "The scourge of the seas, the pillar of plunderers." He leaned toward her and winked. "And quite fortuitous with the ladies, I hear."

She stared at him quizzically even as a blush tainted her neck. "I wouldn't know about such things. But to my point, milord, he calls me milady just like you do, though you both know I am not titled."

Alex cursed himself for the mistake, but effected a shocked expression. "Begad. You know him?" He stomped his cane on the floor. "A *pirate*?"

The carriage jostled over a bump, and she lowered her lashes. "I have had some encounters with him, milord. Nothing untoward, I assure you."

Heat swamped the carriage, and Alex drew a handkerchief to the back of his neck, doing his best to appear justly shocked. "And he did you no harm? This ravisher of young women, this rogue of the night?" This time he *did* take her hand in his. "You must be more careful, sweetums."

She tugged away. "I beg you, do not call me that when we are alone. And nay, he did not harm me. In fact he was quite the gentleman." She stared out over the glittering bay with its festoon of ships as if searching for one in particular. The Pirate Earl's ship, mayhap? If so, the longing in her eyes heated Alex far more than the sun streaming through the carriage windows.

"Was not your father a pirate, milord?" she hissed, then snapped her eyes his way.

Alex bristled. "*Was*, if you'll allow. He traded in the trade, so to speak, to become a missionary." Though he tried to hide the disdain in his voice, it seeped in anyway.

She narrowed her eyes. "Then why, pray, did he send his son to the most wicked outpost on the Main?"

Think fast, Alex. Think fast. Though many people knew of his father's past, no one had been bold enough to ask the question. "To protect me from a scandal, if you must, milady … I mean to say Miss Juliana." He smiled and adjusted the lace at his cuff, feigning boredom as he thought up a story. "If you must know I was called out by a jealous husband. Though I assure you I had not touched his wife." He gave an indignant huff for effect. "But my father, knowing I possessed little skill with the sword, whisked me away to hide until the man's temper abated. 'Tis quite the tale. I should tell you sometime."

"The man must have quite the temper, milord, for you have been in Port Royal for years, have you not?" Her tone was sarcastic.

"I find the climate to my liking." Even as he said the words, he felt a drop of sweat slide down his forehead, and he quickly dabbed it with his handkerchief before it washed away his powder.

Disbelief edged her eyes as she shook her head and glanced away.

"But for now," he added with excitement, "when we arrive at the Wilsons, I insist you regale us with your adventures with the Pirate Earl!"

The squeak and grind of carriage and wheels entered on a wave of humid air. Miss Juliana shifted in her seat. "I'd rather not. It will do no credit to my reputation. Nor yours, milord, since we are now courting."

Ah, Alex liked the sound of those words spilling from her luscious pink lips.

"Besides, I will never see him again."

He didn't like the sound of those words.

The carriage lurched over something in the road, lifting them from the seat and tossing Juliana toward the open door. Clutching her arm, Alex drew her close, then chastised his driver, "Watch where you're going, man!" He didn't realize he'd used his real voice until the words had left his mouth. Beside him, still in his grasp, Juliana's leg rubbed against his thigh. She caught her breath and stared at him as if he had turned into a horny toad.

"Your voice, milord. What happened to your voice?"

Chapter 16

JULIANA DIDN'T KNOW WHAT WAS more upsetting—the rock-hard feel of Munthrope's thigh against hers, or the deep, powerful sound of a voice that seemed foreign on the pimpish goose's lips, yet so familiar to her ears. Not only the sound of it, but the tone: the authority of one in command.

An unexpected swirl of excitement sped through her, and she yanked her arm from his grasp, wondering if the sun and fresh air had the opposite effect on her reason than it did on most.

"What voice, sweetums?" he said in his usual high-pitch. The momentary authority that had appeared on his face vanished beneath a façade of giddiness. "Shall I sing you a ditty?"

Before she could beg him not to, he began.
Pirates come and pirates go
Lost at sea, nowhere to row
Beware, the earl has come to port
Man the cannons at the fort
When he looks your way, don't be afraidy
For only Juliana is a milady

Despite the lunacy of the ballad, or mayhap because of it, Juliana shook away her foolish notions. Lord Munthrope was a swaggering nimbycock, nothing more. Proven by their arrival at the Milson home for tea moments later—an arrival met with the pomp and enthusiasm that accompanied Munny where'er he went. His admirers, most of them women, immediately flocked around him like seagulls around a tasty fish. A very large fish, with a rather muscular thigh, unless Juliana was imagining that as well. What did it matter? She was here only to reinforce their courtship for Captain Nichols's sake. How long she would have to suffer Munny's company before the captain finally gave up, she had no idea. As it was, she was now forced to engage in idle chatter while she should be home running Dutton Shipping. Another secret to be kept from this loose-tongued crowd. Not easy to do when several ladies intrusively inquired why she'd been absent at so many functions of late.

"Why, there was such a grand affair for the governor's birthday at the king's house last week. Not to be missed. Everyone was there," one elderly lady prattled on, describing what the attendees had worn, what was served, who danced with whom.

"And tea at Mr. Skagway's the next day," another lady chimed in.

"And cricket at the commons."

"And games of whist at the Bells."

While the women babbled on about the benefits of coconut milk over palm oil for one's complexion, Juliana slipped away. Moving to the table, she set down her tea and watched Lord Munthrope, who, with flamboyant gestures, relayed some humorous tale of a duke's son caught with his breeches down at a cockfight in Bath. Everyone was riveted, chuckling as he carried on.

At the end of the story, exclamations of praise and jocularity abounded while Mrs. Milson invited guests to sample pastries in the next room. As the small crowd made their way through the arched opening, Munthrope, with forefinger and thumb easing down the sides of his mouth, scanned the room, looking for something. His tea, mayhap?

A twinge of familiarity struck Juliana—similar to those singular moments when one senses a reoccurrence of past events. Odd. His eyes met hers. A glimmer of strength was soon clouded by his normal limpid gaze. "La, have you seen my tea, sweetums?"

A knock on the front door echoed from the foyer. A pleading female voice followed, joined by Mrs. Milson's butler's stern reply. More pleading brought a harsher tone that ended in a shout. Lord Munthrope sashayed toward the altercation and stopped before the short squab servant, who although dressed in the pristine livery of a butler reminded Juliana more of a portly penguin.

"Alack, what is the problem here, Jenson?"

Juliana approached as the butler, upon seeing who addressed him, deferred his eyes and bowed. "Milord, 'tis naught but a beggar and her daughter."

Sunlight tumbled over a woman, not much older than Juliana, dressed in clean but stained canvas skirts, her dirty hair pinned up in an attempt at fashion, her face unsoiled but haggard as if she'd aged before her time. A young girl, no more than four, stood beside her, clinging to her gown.

Juliana's heart pinched in sorrow.

"Why must you be so cruel, Jenson?" Lord Munthrope said, astonished.

The man's eyes lowered. "Mrs. Milson ordered me to send all beggars away, milord. They affect her nerves for the worse, I'm afraid."

"Indeed?" Munthrope swept the curls of his periwig over his shoulder and gazed at the pathetic woman.

Juliana started forward, willing to give the beggar her share of the pastry being served in the other room, when Lord Munthrope placed his jeweled hands about his waist.

"Mrs. Milson would defer to such an honored guest such as myself, would she not?" he asked the butler.

"Yes, milord." Jensen's bottom lip shook.

Reaching within his green metallic-braided coat, Munthrope withdrew a pouch, opened it, and held it toward the woman. Her face aglow, she spread her palms wide as he poured dozens of glittering coins into her hands. Juliana blinked, not trusting her eyes. The loot looked to be around twenty shillings or so, enough to provide a roof over the woman's head and some food for a month, mayhap two. Then leaning toward the butler, Munthrope said something Juliana couldn't hear, sending the servant scrambling off, only to return within seconds with a bowl of fruit and pastries, which, upon Munthrope's nod, he gave to the woman as well.

Still trying to find a place for the coins in the pockets of her skirts, she looked up at the food and then over to Munthrope as though she were seeing an angel.

"Thank you, Gov'nor, God bless you, Gov'nor. You're a kind man." Tears spilled down her cheeks. Then taking the bowl in one hand, she grabbed her daughter with the other and headed down the steps to the street below.

Two hours later, when Juliana finally managed to drag His Lordship from the party, she could not shake the vision from her thoughts. In all her years associating with genteel society, she had never seen one of them—save her own mother—lift a charitable finger to help anyone. In fact, faced with disgusted looks and quick changes of topic, Juliana had given up asking any of her friends for help for the orphans. It seemed as if those without money or position were not only beneath her friends' help, they were also beneath their very notice.

Yet Munthrope had not hesitated before lavishing the unknown woman and her child with more money than they'd no doubt seen in one place before. Now, as he sat beside her in the carriage, he seemed pensive as he stared out the window at passing shops and warehouses—almost drained from the theatrics of the day.

Juliana broached the subject, desperate to discover his motive. "I've never seen such generosity, milord. When you assisted that poor woman and her child."

He looked her way, and instantly the giddy fool returned. "Have you not? You must get out more often, sweet—" He stopped at her look of reprimand. "Miss Juliana."

"I've been *out* quite enough to know such charity is rare among Port Royal society."

He waved a hand through the air, lace fluttering. "'Tis nothing I pray thee. I have plenty." His eyes met hers, a dark indigo blue that startled her with their intensity. Flecks of light gray rolled across them like storm clouds. Why hadn't she noticed that before? Mayhap because she'd never truly looked at him. 'Twas hard to get past the white powder covering every inch of his face, the red staining his cheeks and lips, the moles, the horse patch over his right brow, and the star cornering his lips.

"Beware such modesty, milord. It would have you cast from those whom you so enjoy to entertain."

He laid a hand flounced in lace on his chest and gave her a look of feigned indignance. "Do you take me for a common troubadour? I can hardly credit it." But then he winked. "Though I do believe any eccentricity, even of modesty, would equally entertain this fluff-headed rabble."

Juliana flinched. 'Twas an odd thing for one of that fluff-headed rabble to say.

He moved his gaze back to the window, and she found herself suddenly curious as to what he looked like behind all the adornment. His features were handsome enough she supposed. Strong chin and jaw, regal nose.

"What color is your hair, milord?"

He coughed rather violently before apologizing and clearing his throat. "My hair? Why do you wish to know?"

"Just curious, if you'll allow a lady to be so."

"You flatter me, mil—Miss Juliana." He chuckled, lifted his hands in the air, and swept them over his elaborate attire.

"This is exactly what I look like. And my hair is light, like the sun, if it pleases you."

Light? Hmm. Not how she envisioned. But no matter. Their engagement was as much a show as this man's appearance.

The carriage turned a corner, and a breeze ripe with fish and salt whipped in through the window. "I deem the afternoon a success, Miss Juliana." He smiled, his eyes aglitter. "I believe there is no doubt among those attending the tea today that we are happily betrothed."

"Then I owe you my thanks, milord. I pray the news satisfies your father as well."

At the mention of his father, a frown nearly cracked the paste surrounding his mouth. "Indeed." He gazed out the window, idly twisting a ring on his finger. Moments later he faced her. "You must be tired, milady. We shall have you home in but a moment."

She *was* tired, and she had work to do, but this ostentatious man's sudden pensive mood coupled with his unseemly charity bade her remain in his company a while longer. Could there be more to him than ungainly poppycockery? An intellect, a depth she'd had but glimpses of during their time together? Either way, the discovery seemed far more interesting than the mound of writs awaiting her at home.

She glanced out the window. "Oh my." Her hand flew to her mouth at the sight of two bodies hanging at the point beyond Fort Charles, their arms chained to a scaffold, their eyes gouged out by birds, flesh shriveling from their bodies.

"Do not look, sweetums." Munthrope touched her chin and turned her gaze away, though his own remained on the poor sods. Pain etched his eyes as he studied them, but then a wave of airy indifference flooded his features. "Just pirates getting their due," he said, settling back onto the leather seat.

The smell of roasted turtle lured Juliana to dare another glance. This time they passed Chocolata Hole, where fisherman harvested the shelled beasties from the sea. "Milord, can we walk along the shore by Fort Charles? 'Twill be sunset soon, and I am so rarely out to enjoy it."

"For mila—you, Miss Juliana, anything." He surprised her with the sincerity of his tone. But before she could turn and see his expression, he faced forward and gave the order for his driver to stop up ahead. Soon, they were strolling along the shore, away from the fort and the pirates and the crowds in the middle of town. A stiff breeze from the open sea kneaded water into foamy mounds that crashed upon the glistening sand with a thunderous boom. Lord Munthrope's periwig flailed about his head like the arms of an angry octopus, and more than once, she thought it would take flight, giving her the answer to her earlier question. She had given up chasing her own hat and held it tightly in her hand, allowing the breeze to tear her wavy tresses from their pins.

Oddly, Munthrope was quiet as he walked along beside her, hands clasped behind his back, the ends of his green coat flapping over white beribboned breeches. Making her way down a short outcropping, she clutched her skirts and leapt onto a flat boulder for a better view of the horizon, where remnants of the sun left brilliant trails of crimson, orange, and yellow in its wake.

"Begad, Miss Juliana. A pretty ambition for a lady, leaping upon rocks like an overzealous frog. How refreshing!" Munthrope jumped up beside her.

She smiled and drew in a deep breath of briny, tropical air and allowed the wind to swirl over her, fluttering her skirts and dancing through her hair. For a brief moment—if only a moment—she dreamed she was still a little girl, her mother was alive, her brother adored her, and her father loved her so much that she hadn't a care in the world.

Until Munthrope opened his mouth. "This calls for a rhyme, I'd say." He raised his hand in the air. "There once was a lady who leapt like a frog, she dared to—"

Juliana touched his arm, stopping him. "Pray, I beg you. No more rhymes today, milord."

He pouted like a little boy, though a glimmer of mischief appeared in his eyes.

She faced the sky again, admiring how it changed with each passing second as if an artist with an invisible brush added a bit of color here, a swath there. "Thank you for indulging me, milord. This was not part of our bargain."

"On the contrary, it can only aid the impression we give should anyone happen by."

"'Tis beautiful, isn't it?"

"Stunning. Simply stunning." The seriousness of his tone brought her around to see he was staring at *her*. He coughed and quickly examined the sky, holding one hand in the air as if he were posing for the queen. "A glorious way to end the day."

"And usher in a new one," Juliana added, glancing back at the horizon. "A new beginning. Perchance a better one."

"Why would an accomplished lady such as yourself have need of a better beginning? Surely with your father's thriving business, all your needs are met, all your desires fulfilled."

"Do not presume to know me, milord," she ground out. "Or anything about my life."

A rare glimmer of contrition waved at her from his blue eyes. "My apologies, milady. I meant no offense. You merely concern me with your words. Is there something I can be of assistance with, some problem which I can help solve? I do hate to see you vexed."

She studied him. *Fie!* Surely the man bore no interest in her romantically? "I am not vexed. Nor do I need your help," she replied rather sternly. "I do not want your friendship either, milord. You'll do good to remember 'tis but a business arrangement we have. Your attempts to woo me are doomed to fail."

An impish grin appeared on his lips. "Woo you? Begad, sweetums, were I to purpose such a thing, I fear there would be no hope for your heart."

She smiled. "Alas, your confidence is exceeded only by your vanity, milord. But not to fear, there are many ladies quite taken with your wit and charm."

"But not you." He raised his brow, that ridiculous horse patch leaping with the movement.

She lifted her chin. "It would take more than wit, charm, title, or wealth, milord, to win my heart."

He gave a hearty laugh. "Alas, what is left?"

"Honor, honesty, goodness, kindness, and trustworthiness ... to name but a few."

His eyes locked upon hers, and an admiration she had not foreseen appeared within them. But then it was gone. Stolen by the shadows slinking out to claim the night. The last vestiges of sunlight drifted over his jaw, where evening stubble broke through like crops in a field of snow.

"It grows dark." He leapt from the boulder and helped her down, then proffered his elbow to escort her back to the carriage. A cannon thundered from Fort Charles.

Juliana's heart leapt as she tightened her grip on Munthrope's arm.

"No worries, Miss Juliana. They are but signaling an incoming ship."

She knew that, but for some reason her nerves were atwist. Shadows seemed to leap at them from all around. How quickly it grew dark here in the Caribbean. A carriage ambled by. A group of sailors rushed past, laughing and shoving each other playfully.

Juliana startled at a quick movement to her right. A man leapt out from behind a large fern, his body a dark outline against the sand. He thrust a knife—a rather large knife—toward Munthrope. "Your purse, milord."

Juliana's breath rasped in her throat. She squeezed Lord Munthrope's arm. Why, she couldn't say. The milksop could not protect her any more than one of her lady friends. In fact, he merely stood there, no doubt frozen in terror.

"Give it to him, milord." Juliana nudged him.

"I'd do wat yer lady says, milord, or I'll gut ye bof like a fish." At Munthrope's silence, the man stepped closer and waved his knife across their chests in a taunting display.

Juliana's heart nearly burst through her ribs. Was this to be her end? Gutted on the shores of Port Royal, left for the birds to eat, like those pirates hanging at the Point? What had she done to deserve this? *God, please help us. I promise I'll do better, but please save us.*

Munthrope remained silent beside her. He didn't twitch, didn't flinch, didn't cry out for help. Juliana shook his arm, trying to jar him from his terror-stricken stupor, when slowly and methodically, he nudged her behind him.

"Ah, 'ow chivalrous." The man spat to the side. "But I'll still be takin' that purse o' yers." He lunged for Munthrope. In a move too fast to see, the pompous lord gripped the villain's wrist, twisted him around, and shoved him to his knees. He then kicked him to the sand, while somehow ending up with the knife firm in his grip.

Then, with a shoe upon the man's neck, he made him eat sand, while he flung the blade into the now-dark sea.

Chapter 17

A S THE CARRIAGE HOBBLED THROUGH the streets on the way back to the Dutton home, Alex bit his lip, gazed out the window, and cursed himself for a fool. He had hoped to spend a pleasant afternoon becoming more acquainted with Miss Juliana. What he hadn't planned on were his many horrific blunders. He'd played the part of supercilious Munthrope among society without incident for years now. But in the past few days he'd made one mistake after another: leaving paste on his face, using his real voice earlier in the carriage, describing his supposed peers as fluff-heads. And now, the worst bungle of all, proving capable of defending himself and his lady against an armed assailant—something Lord Munthrope should not possess the skill or bravery to accomplish.

Of course afterward he'd made light of the incident, claimed his rage and stupidity had gotten the better of him. But now as the carriage jostled down the street, Miss Juliana studied him as a naturalist would a new species of insect. He even perfected a little whimper here, a shaking of the hands there, a sweating of the forehead and neck, all enacted amidst fearful groans and mutterings. But the lady was having none of it. She was no dim-brained female. Not a word spilled from her lips as she continued to watch him with narrowed gaze and suspicious looks.

"I daresay, have you ever seen such inane absurdity?"

He waved his arms about madly. "That poor villain was obviously new to his breeches, an amateur of the lowest ranks, no doubt sent out by Uncle Blackguard in an attempt to train the lad. Forsooth, I can hardly gainsay it! Either that or the man was cupshotten with the worst batch of Kill-Devil rum ever made on the island! His ineptitude made Your Lordship look like a hero, I make bold to say. I cannot wait to blazon the exciting tale among our friends!" He forced a loud chuckle.

Miss Juliana's delicate brows rose. "You are pleased to mock me, milord." Her voice was curt and strong as she sat straight in her seat.

"Mock you? Curse me for a rogue if I dare such a thing!"

She gaped at him as if he was, indeed, a rogue. But what else could he have done? If he had continued his namby-pamby performance, allowing the thief to easily acquire his money purse, the precocious scoundrel might have thought the lady would be easily acquired as well. And Alex could not have allowed that.

Now, he had one last card to play. And it was not an easy one. Squeezing his eyes shut, he thought of the singular moment in his childhood when he had cried. That single moment in which he had vowed never to do so again. His fourteenth birthday, when instead of seeing his father and mother strolling toward the house from their long trip abroad—as they had promised—he saw a messenger with a post that said they'd been delayed several months. Months that turned into a year. There. The tears came, filling his eyes with burning. Withdrawing a handkerchief from his pocket, he fluffed it out and drew it to his moist face.

It had the intended effect.

"There, there, milord." Juliana touched his arm. "No need for tears." Her voice had softened once again.

"My apologies, Miss Juliana." He sniffed, held the cloth to his nose, and looked away. "I suppose the terror of the event has just struck me. How very frightening to think we could have both died there on the beach."

"We are safe now, Your Lordship. God protected us."

God again! Could the lady not see 'twas he who constantly kept her safe?

When they reached her house, she thanked him for the interesting afternoon, denied his escort to the door, and quickly slipped inside as if he had the plague.

He ordered the carriage brought to a stop farther down the street. It had been weeks since he'd heard her play the violin, and he hoped it would sooth his agitated mind. But after an hour, only the distant crash of waves and screech of a night heron sounded, and he headed home.

He knew he was playing a dangerous game with this wise lady—a dangerous game indeed. Yet he could not bring himself to stop.

Rowan slid onto the bench in the back of The Three Crownes and nodded toward Captain Nichols sitting across from him. Why the man wanted to meet here, Rowan could only guess. 'Twas probably because card games continued unhindered from dusk to dawn and were now at full force around them, offering incentive for Rowan to continue his alliance with the Royal Navy officer. Not that he needed any. Rowan would do just about anything to continue gambling. Despite Juliana's opinion to the contrary, he found he possessed a skill at certain games that far exceeded that of most men. One day soon, luck would sail into port, and he'd make enough money to not only help run his father's business but keep the family in luxury.

Then he'd finally win the respect of his sister and all those who thought him nothing but a wastrel, a lazy drunk who was doomed to fail. Mayhap he didn't have the aptitude for numbers like Juliana, but God had given him another equally important skill. And with Nichols's allowance, Rowan would hone that skill until he could provide for his family and relieve Juliana of the pressures she placed upon herself. Then perchance the poor girl could relax and enjoy life. Faith, life was far too short to waste fretting over such inconsequential things. Both his parents had proven that. His mother, always in a fluster over the poor in the city, had caught one of their diseases and died. And now his father, who'd spent a lifetime building up his shipping business, lay dying before he could reap the benefits.

Rowan would not end up like that. He would help his sister, yes. But after that, he intended to spend what time he had on this earth pursuing the pleasures life offered. Then at least when he died, he'd have no regrets.

Nichols grinned, poured rum from a bottle into a cup, and slid it to Rowan.

"What is the meaning of life, Captain?" Rowan took a sip, curious as to the coxcomb's response.

Nichols snorted as if the question were ridiculous. "To win, of course."

Rowan nodded. "As you intend to do with my sister? And this Pirate Earl you seek?"

"Precisely."

A barmaid sashayed past the table, carrying two mugs of ale and eyeing Rowan with approval. He winked at her, eliciting a smile before she continued on her way. The snap of cards, whisper of bets, and feminine coos and giggles permeated the dimly-lit room in which velvet-upholstered chairs perched across a somewhat-clean wooden floor. Sea breezes whisked through open windows, stirring lanterns on tables and chandeliers hanging from rafters, creating waves of light and shadow over the scene. Just as the lantern on Rowan's table was doing to the captain—making him look sinister one minute and harmless the next.

But Rowan knew the man was anything but harmless.

"You know what to do?" Nichols asked, sipping his drink.

Rowan nodded. "The ship is due to sail into port on the morrow. I've already given the customs agent the money."

"And he won't allow it to be unloaded until the next day?"

"That's what he said." Rowan sat back, impatient.

Nichols gave a malicious grin. "Good. Then spread the word by the docks, and I'll do the same."

Rowan nodded. An easy enough task. Pirates loved hearing about free booty, especially a fortune in pearls. Unusual guilt caused him to shift in his seat. "I have your word the pearls will not be stolen."

At this Nichols laughed. "Stolen? Forsooth! I assure you, the only thing that will be stolen is the Pirate Earl's freedom."

Rowan hoped he was right. But what choice did he have? He extended his open palm to receive his due, longing for his conversation with the annoying Navy captain to be at an end.

Nichols eyed it with disdain. "What of the other matter?"

"Never fear. I'm questioning all of Lord Munthrope's friends." Rowan held up his same hand as Nichols began to protest. "I'm doing it discreetly. And I'm following him when I can. Nothing yet, but I'll inform you of my findings."

Card games called to him from all around like wanton lovers. "Now, if you please?" He held out his hand once again.

Scowling, Nichols pulled a leather pouch from inside his coat and tossed it onto the table. It landed with a heavy *chink*, the musical sound causing Rowan's heart to leap. Downing the remainder of his drink, he grabbed the money and stood. The sooner he found a game of cards, the sooner his luck would turn.

What did he care whether the Pirate Earl would be hanging from Execution Dock by the end of the week?

Juliana hadn't been able to sleep in a week. Not since she'd last seen Lord Munthrope. Visions of the dandified lord invaded her mind: images of his rapid reflexes, the way he grabbed the thief's wrist and flipped him around with minimal effort, then subdued him and took his knife within seconds. It had all happened so fast, Juliana could recall only flashes. Where would a man of his breeding and lavish, lethargic lifestyle acquire such reflexes, such courage, such ability? She could make no sense of it, and her mind refused to put it to rest.

Tossing aside her coverlet, she rose and stood by the window. A breeze burdened with humidity, barely fluttered the cotton curtains as she gazed out over the sleeping city. Mayhap there was more to Lord Munthrope than he presented. His father had once been a pirate, after all. A very feared and successful pirate until he met God one day in the crumbling church that sat behind the orphanage. Reverend Buchan, the man who ran the church at the time and who later started the orphanage, became good friends with the wayward pirate, teaching him the things of God until he gave up his vile ways and became a missionary. She had wanted to ask Lord Munthrope more about his father, but for once, the bold question had remained behind propriety's doors. Especially after the mention of him had caused Munthrope to frown so deeply. Though he seemed not to have acquired his father's religious fervor, could a bit of that tainted pirate blood be flowing through Munthrope's veins?

A vision of him gliding through the Milson home in a dainty whirl of lace and silk, his high-pitched laugh cackling over her ears, and then of him sobbing in the carriage on the way home, invaded her nonsensical thoughts. Nay. No pirate blood at all. She chuckled and shook her head. Seems the son was nothing like his father.

Gathering flint and steel, she lit a candle. The light flickered over the dark wood of her violin, causing her fingers to itch to pick it up and play a soothing tune. The sweet tones of Jean-Baptiste Lully or Heinrich Schütz would do much to calm her restless nerves, regardless of the fact that it was considered uncouth for a lady to play the instrument. But it was well past midnight, and she didn't wish to rob anyone of the sleep that seemed to evade her.

After donning her robe, she took the candle and slipped from her chamber. She'd not had time to see her father all day, having spent hours doing paperwork and going over the business with Mr. Abbot. They had another shipment due tomorrow, and in the meantime, they needed to fill up the *Esther's Dowry* with enough goods to make it worth the trip to the American colonies and then back across the pond. Since they had recently lost two customers, Mr. Abbot was having some difficulty signing on new merchants.

But Juliana didn't want to think of that now. Instead, as she made her way down the dark hall, she silently prayed she would find her father much improved.

Yet when she entered his chamber, her prayers fell like so much dust to the floor. Miss Ellie, ever vigilant, sat slumped in a chair by his bed, snoring lightly. Her father, sweat beading on his face, seemed to have sunk deeper into the mattress, as if he had a rent in his hold and was slowly sinking into the sea. His face was dull and listless, his arms naught but bones and withered skin. A drop of blood seeped from the corner of his mouth.

Stomach convulsing, Juliana sat on the bed beside him and slipped her hand into his limp, fevered one and bowed her head. *Please God. Heal him. Deliver him from this affliction.* As much as she enjoyed her independence and not being castigated by the man at every turn, she wanted no harm to come to him. He was her father, and she loved him. Besides, the sooner he took back control of the business, the better for them all. "Please Lord. I'll do anything you ask. I'll give more money to the poor, spend more time with the orphans, find a way to help Abilene. Just please heal my father."

In answer, the man coughed—a ragged sound that scraped across Juliana's heart. He opened one eye and peered at her with disinterest as if he were dreaming. Then fire stormed across his face. "Come to finish me off, Daughter?" he rasped out.

"Don't be silly, Father. I've come to check on you and to appeal to the Almighty for your health."

He jerked his hand from hers and coughed again. Blood spilled from his lips. Gathering a cloth, Juliana attempted to wipe it, but he pushed her away. "'Tis the Almighty who cursed me with a flighty wife, a wastrel son, and a greedy daughter. Now he's stealing my life from me." A coughing fit ensued as he appeared to struggle for each breath.

Miss Ellie jerked awake and darted to his side, her sleepy eyes meeting Juliana's.

"Don't be silly, Father. God doesn't make people sick. He makes people well. And you will get well, you'll see."

Ellie took the rag from Juliana and wiped his mouth. "There, there. Miss Juliana is right. You will be up on your feet in no time."

His listless eyes found the lady's maid and remained upon her as if she were a nest and he a bird returning from a long flight. A tiny smile peeked from the corner of his lips as Ellie proceeded to wash out the cloth and dab it over his forehead and cheeks.

"You're the only one who cares about me," he mumbled.

"Now, you know that's not true, Mr. Dutton. Juliana is 'ere to check on you. She loves you."

One glance toward Juliana and he started coughing again, this time violently, spewing phlegm and accusations that she was stealing his business and poisoning him.

Finally unable to bear the heartache, Juliana rose, deciding her presence did more harm than good.

"I'm sorry, miss. He's been delirious with fever all day. I don't know why 'e'd say sich things."

"It's all right, Ellie. He's never had a fondness for me. Please let me know if there is any change."

"Shall I come up for your morning toilet?"

"Nay, stay with him Ellie. I can manage for now."

Taking the candle, she made her way down the stairs to her father's study, where she hoped to get some work done before the sun rose. An unusual chill slithered around her. She glanced over the dark foyer as a strong sense of foreboding weighed the air.

The front door flew open and in walked Rowan, or rather, in stumbled Rowan in a brandy-drenched haze.

"Ah, sissssster dear." He held his arms wide for an embrace.

She stepped aside in disgust. His arms struck air, and he spun around. "I didn't 'xpect you to be up at … at …" He fumbled to draw a pocket watch from his coat.

"'Tis three in the morning, Rowan," Juliana huffed in frustration. "And I thought you'd learned your lesson about gambling."

"Gambling, pshaw!" Grabbing the lapels of his jerkin, he attempted to adjust them but nearly fell over. "'Tis invessssting, says I, do you take me?"

Juliana closed the door before the neighbors saw her brother's disgusting display.

"I was meeting a friend, if you please." He spoke into the darkness, then whirled to find her behind him. He winked. "A friend of yours, dear sister." Brandy fumes enveloped her, stinging her nose and eyes.

"We shall discuss this in the morning. Let's get you to bed." Easing her shoulder beneath his arm, she held his waist and dragged him toward the stairs.

He raised a finger in the air. "Captain William Nichols."

She knew she shouldn't speak to her brother in his condition, but that name ignited a fire of angst within her. She spun him around. "Rowan, you are not to associate with that man! He is *not* my friend. He is *not* your friend. And I do not want him in this house, do you understand?"

His glassy eyes flew over her face as if seeking a place to land. "Humph. He's my friend, and I'll see him when I want." He adjusted his skewed brown periwig, his eyes pointing upward as if searching for the hairpiece. "Infernal thing." He tore it from his head.

"Please, Rowan. I beg you. Keep your distance from Nichols. For me?"

"I cannot, sissster. We are in business together. A very lucrative business for me, I might add." He patted his pocket, where a jingling sound emerged.

Anger followed by fear stormed through her. "He's a Post-Captain in his Majesty's navy. What business could you possibly have with him?"

Grabbing the banister, Rowan sank to the bottom step. "Are we having another earthquake?"

Juliana ignored him and began tugging on his arm, but he was too heavy.

"He's paying me to gamble, so you no longer need give me an allowance." He leaned back, elbows splayed on the tread above him, and closed his eyes. "I will win enough to help our family. Soon, sissster, soon. You'll see."

"Paying you?" Juliana hoped she'd heard him wrong. "What does he get in return?"

"Nothing to concern yourself wi—"

Snoring replaced words, and Juliana slumped down to the stairs beside him as a feeling of dread sent a chill through every bone.

A sweet, melancholy sound lured Alex from his sleep. He jerked his head from the tree trunk and gazed up at the light trickling down from the second-story window he knew to be Juliana's. It had been a long week since he'd seen her. His many invitations for her to join him at various society functions had been met with excuses of illness or exhaustion or business she must attend. Posh! Excuses all!

After a miserable evening at Sir Cramwell's ball, Alex had dressed in his pirate garb and taken to the streets. But none of his favorite haunts enticed him, so he'd ended up in front of Juliana's house, as he so often had on his loneliest nights. Perched in the tree's shadow, he sat and watched, saw her besotted brother stumble home, then caught a glimpse of her through the front door, her long golden waves tumbling over her white robe like a sunlit waterfall on snowy cliffs. And his heart had leapt into his throat. But then she'd slammed the door on the angelic vision, and the house grew dark.

Still, he could not bring himself to leave. So he'd sat and watched, finally falling asleep. Now, the sound of her violin pierced the night. Such a mournful tune! As if she poured every fear, every unfulfilled hope, every misery into the strings of the instrument. What could make such a privileged lady so sad? She had a home, a family who loved her, friends, and every luxury one could desire. Surely it wasn't her concern for her friend, Abilene, or her sponging idler brother. Minor problems both.

Yet Alex could not forget the look of utter despair on her face as she'd watched the sun set, declaring her hope that tomorrow would bring a better day. Something troubled her. He must discover what it was and do all he could to ease her burden, to make all her problems go away.

Chapter 18

A TIDAL WAVE OF BOBBING heads crashed over Juliana the minute she entered the orphanage. Setting down her valise, she opened her arms and tried to absorb as many of the little urchins she could, savoring their sweet kisses.

"Now, children." Eunice's voice resounded over the excited clamor, "You be smotherin' poor Miss Juliana. Back away. Back away wit' you." Pushing through the mob, she nudged them away before turning to greet Juliana with a huge grin and a clasp of her hands.

"Did you bring us sweets?" one little boy asked.

"'Ow about some new clothes, miss?" Emilie smiled and tugged on Juliana's skirts. "My dress is stained, see?" She held out her blue skirts to reveal a smudge. Yet neither the stain nor her bedraggled garb detracted from the girl's angelic face. Dark lustrous skin and a bouquet of curly black hair adorned the young mulatto, who'd wandered into the church at age five looking more like a skeleton than a girl.

"Not this time, darling." Juliana suddenly wished she had brought new clothing, though the girl's smile didn't fade.

"Ain't it nice to jist have Miss Juliana's company?" Eunice planted fists on her rounded waist and scanned the children with her scolding gaze. "Does she always have to bring you's somethin'?"

A chorus of "nays" rang through the room.

"But I *did* bring something." Juliana glanced over the darling faces with a smile. "I brought new sheets for your cots"—she turned to Eunice—"and I brought Miss Eunice and Isaac some cooking pans."

"Why, thank you, Miss Juliana." Isaac entered, wiping his hands on a rag, his lanky frame reminding her of a weathered ship's mast.

"Has Eunice been withholding your meals, Isaac?" Juliana smiled. "You're naught but skin and bones."

"She feeds me plenty, Miss Juliana." He winked at his wife, then cast a stern look over the children. "'Tis these ravenous children who eat all the food."

Some of the little ones giggled.

"'Tis a good thing, then, that I brought some salt pork, flour, sugar, and"—cupping a hand beside her mouth, Juliana leaned toward Eunice and whispered loud enough for the children to hear—"ground cocoa beans."

A sea of cheers enveloped her. "Cocoa! Cocoa!"

"Will you make a chocolate cake, Mrs. Eunice?" One of the older girls laid her head on folded palms and gave the mistress a pleading look.

Eunice smiled. "O' course, child. Now, come on in, Miss Juliana." Taking her hand, Eunice led her forward while Isaac attempted to corral the children. Juliana's foot struck something, and she stumbled. Fearing she'd stepped on a child, she turned around to see a pail filled with sloshing water.

"Apologies, miss." Eunice gave a slanted smile.

Juliana chuckled. "I see your battle with Lucas is ongoing."

"An' he be winnin' it too." Eunice gestured toward the buckets framing the room and the blankets stacked upon shelves above them.

"Poor child has been through so much," Isaac added. "If this is what keeps him calm, so be it."

Nodding, Juliana opened her valise and unloaded the sheets, pans, and food onto a table.

Eunice wrapped an arm around her and drew her close. "Thank you, Miss Juliana. You are yer mother's spittin' image, both inside and out. The good Lord done blessed us doubly today! We jist got money from our secret benefactor, too."

"Mr. A was here?"

"Nay, jist a messenger is what he says. Quiet man. Drops off the pouch wit' the same note and then leaves with ne'er a word."

"And his appearance?" Even if the man was merely a servant, mayhap Juliana would recognize him from one of society's functions. If so, she could place his master and finally be able to thank this Mr. A for his generosity.

Eunice's lips drew into a line as she thought. "Tall, sturdy, light hair wit' a bit o' red. Oh, an' he had spectacles in his pocket. You don't see those much in Port Royal. I tell you. An' he smelled o' the sea, that one. Must work down by the docks."

Disappointment drew a sigh from Juliana's lips. She could recall no one by that description. "You don't think this Mr. A could be the preacher who left the orphans in the first place?" she asked, feeling her blood boil at the mere mention of the man.

"Dunno." Eunice shrugged. "That man called hisself Mr. Edward not Mr. A. 'Sides, don't make no sense to leave 'em an' then provide for 'em."

"Mayhap not. But he should be loath to ever cross paths with me. 'Tis a bullet in the gut he'll get! Or worse."

"Ouch, listen t' you now." Eunice chuckled. "You know the good Lord 'xpects us t' forgive."

Which is mayhap why God's favor shone not on Juliana. She didn't have time to ponder that revelation for something dropped onto her shoulder. Something smelly with sharp claws! A rat? Nay, that pesky monkey! Bending over, she screamed and tried to shove it off. An uproar of laughter filled the room as Eunice shouted for Isaac while she chased the hysterical Juliana around the room. "Juliana—stop, child so's I can get that little beastie offa you!"

The little beastie scrambled across Juliana's back and then it was gone. She shuddered, placed a hand on her heaving chest, and backed away. The impish monkey grinned at her from Eunice's arms.

Restraining a smile, Isaac relieved his wife of the beast. "Bad, bad monkey," he scolded as he left the room.

"I'm so sorry, miss." Eunice laid a hand on Juliana's arm.

A tiny giggle escaped Juliana's lips, followed by another and another, until everyone in the room barreled over in laughter. "I had forgotten all about the creature. And about getting Mr. Pell to capture him. Forgive me."

"Think nothin' o' it, miss. I do believe he likes you. He's ne'er jumped on anyone like that before."

Wonderful. She'd add that to her list of absurd admirers: an obsessed Navy captain, a pompous buffoon, a nefarious pirate—and now an impish monkey.

"Now, get on outside, children," Eunice ushered the crowd toward the back door leading onto the garden. "Miss Juliana will read you a story in a minute. I needs t' speak wit' her."

All of them moped away, except little Rose, who clutched Juliana's skirts as if they were a lifeline. Juliana swept her up in her arms, and the girl laid her head on Juliana's shoulders and stuck her thumb in her mouth.

Eunice hesitated at the sight, then uttered a sigh and led Juliana into the adjacent room. "It's Michael." She gestured toward the corner, where a young boy lay curled on a cot. Releasing Rose to Eunice's arms, Juliana sat on the stool beside the lad and wiped sweaty stands of hair from his face. Heated skin seared her fingertips. The seven-year-old didn't move. She remembered the day he'd come to the orphanage a year ago, a stowaway on a ship from Saint Dominique. What had happened to him on that island was anyone's guess. But Juliana knew one thing. It hadn't been good. The only English word he knew at the time was "die." At least he had added a few, more cheerful, terms to his vocabulary since then.

"What ails him?"

Eunice shook her head. "Bin like that fer two days. He can't keep nothin' in his stomach, neither. Called on Doc Blane, but he says it's naught but a seasonal ailment. Barely looked at him afore he scampered outta here."

"Michael is sick," Rose's tiny voice chimed in, drawing Juliana's gaze.

"Yes, he is, but he will get well again. You must allow him his rest and pray for him. Will you do that, Rose?"

Nodding, she stuck her thumb back in her mouth.

"I'll ask Dr. Verns to come." Juliana attempted to keep her tone light. Such a high fever rarely accompanied a minor illness. And the vomiting gave her pause. "In the meantime, you know what to do."

"Keep him cool, get water down him, an' make sure he gits his rest."

"Yes, and keep the other children away from him as much as you can." A chill wrapped around Juliana's heart. Her mother had caught a disease from children and died soon after. "I'll bring some Fever Grass root the next time I come. Doctor Verns has been using it on Father's fever."

"I didn't know your father be ill, miss. I'm sorry."

"He's not. He was … 'tis nothing, really." Juliana caught herself before she continued stuttering like a fool. Not that Eunice would say anything to anyone, but the fewer people who knew her father was sick, the better.

She rose, feeling the boy's illness add to the burden already pressing on her shoulders. Then, suddenly, the ground rolled like a wave at sea. She grabbed hold of Eunice and Rose as the three of them tumbled to the side. Dust showered over them from the rafters. One of the children in the other room started crying. Then all was still again.

Handing an unusually calm Rose to Juliana, Eunice dashed from the room, no doubt to check on the children, shouting, "Jist another tremor."

Juliana could handle a little ground shaking. What she couldn't handle was the upheaval of her life.

Two hours later, she had barely entered the door of her home when Mr. Abbot burst into the foyer with Mr. John Kinder in tow. Thankfully, Juliana had not yet gone to her father's study or she'd never be able to explain to one of the top merchants in Port Royal why she was tending the business in her father's stead.

She hurriedly put on her best smile while casting Abbot a look of dismay. "Welcome, Mr. Kinder. To what do we owe the pleasure of this unexpected visit?"

Behind Mr. Kinder, the butler shrugged and shook his head as if to say he had no choice in bringing the merchant home.

"Always a pleasure to see you, Miss Juliana." Doffing his castor, Mr. Kinder reached out and planted a kiss on her hand. "I've come to see your father on a business matter."

"You are far too kind, Mr. Kinder. However, I fear you have come here for naught. Father is not home presently."

"As I tried to inform him." Mr. Abbot took the man's hat.

"Most curious. Where else would he be? I never see him down at the docks. Indeed, I miss our chats at Bennets over coffee."

"As he misses yours, I am sure." Juliana smiled sweetly. "But as you can see, he has appointed Mr. Abbot his manager of affairs in order to allow himself more time at leisure."

"Leisure!" The man chortled. "Egad! Astounding. I never thought to see the day. Why, your father works harder than any man I've known."

A raspy hack bled down from above, drawing Mr. Kinder's gaze.

"If you inform me of your business concerns"—Juliana heightened her voice to cover up any further coughing—"I'll relay them to Father when he returns."

"Nothing to worry your pretty head about, my dear." He adjusted the velvet sash at his waist and swept a glance toward the sitting room. "I shall be happy to wait for your father here."

Juliana's nerves tightened. How to be rid of this man without causing him insult? He was one of their best customers, and she desperately needed his business.

"He refers to the *Midnight Fortune*," Mr. Abbot interjected, sensing her angst. "She sailed into port two hours ago."

"Ah, indeed, I ... Father has been expecting her arrival." Juliana made no move to show him to the sitting room. "What, pray thee, is the problem, sir?"

Mr. Kinder flattened his lips and studied her as if wondering whether her female brain could assimilate the information. "The customs agent refuses to unload her goods. Can you believe it? I've been waiting months for their arrival, and my customers will buy from someone else if they aren't soon satisfied. Tallow, tapestries, lacquer panels from the Orient, silks, ivory ... ah yes, and pearls for Lord and Lady Salem from Rio De La Hacha."

"I am aware of your shipment, sir." Juliana bit her lip. "I mean to say, Father has discussed it with me. And I assure you, 'tis quite safe here in port." Though she couldn't know that for sure. As soon as the man left, she would send Abbot to deal with the stubborn customs' agent and ensure the safety of the cargo. "I am convinced my father will straighten out this misunderstanding before the sun sets."

He narrowed his eyes with a snort. "I should hope so. Regardless, I should like to see him. I fear our friendship suffers from lack of attention. " He gave her a look that said their business would suffer the same fate if she couldn't produce her father forthwith.

Miss Ellie drifted down the stairs and stood before Juliana, hands clasped before her.

Thankful for the interruption but fearing bad news, she faced the maid. "Yes?"

"Beggin' your pardon, miss, but you must prepare for Lady Cransford's birthday celebration tonight."

Oh, fie! She'd forgotten all about it. And she couldn't get out of this one like the past two soirees she'd managed to evade. This affair was being held at Munthrope's house, so as his fiancée, she was obligated to be present. But she'd so wanted to head down to The Black Dogg to check on Abilene before it got dark.

Hiding her frustration, she faced the merchant. "As you can see, Mr. Kinder, I cannot entertain guests at the moment, so if you please." She gestured toward the door.

"Mayhap I can meet your father here later. If he won't be attending Lady Cransford's with you?" he asked.

"I'm afraid he will," she lied. "I'll tell him you came by." She moved toward the door.

"I've a better idea." He took his hat from Abbot. "Get me an invitation to this soiree, and I shall see him there!"

The audacity of the man! "I fear I cannot. 'Tis a private affair." She nodded to Mr. Abbot, who opened the door, letting in a swish of sea breeze, a burst of sunlight, and Rowan, who sauntered in and greeted Mr. Kinder with exuberance.

"What's this about a celebration?" Rowan said. "Ah yes, at Munthrope's. Mr. Kinder, you simply must come. I'm sure Juliana's beau would love to have you join us."

If Juliana were not a lady, she would have kicked her beef-witted brother in the shin. Now, how was she going to explain her father's absence at the soiree to Mr. Kinder? The successful merchant was no fool, as evidenced by the suspicion flitting across his eyes. If he discovered her ruse, all would be lost.

Sitting across the rum-syrupy table of The Sign of the Mermaid tavern, Alex studied his most trusted crew members: his quartermaster, Jonas Nash; his sailing master, Larkin Slayter; and his bosun, Jeremy Riggs. Trusted, yes, but also possessing more brains between them than the rest of his crew put together.

"Are you quite sure?" he asked, studying their expressions as a lantern centering the table sent oscillating threads of light over their faces.

"Aye, Cap'n." Riggs rubbed his bristly chin. "Pearls is what I heard. At least fifty o' 'em, they say."

The other men nodded. Larkin gestured toward a barmaid for another drink. "The news is trustworthy, Captain. It hails from a reliable source who is a friend of one of the crew."

"An' they be just sittin' there on the brig, aptly named the *Midnight Fortune*." Riggs adjusted his red neckerchief, which looked more brown than red. "Ready t' be plundered." A gold front tooth made up for two missing ones on the bottom as his grin turned greedy.

The wench returned and began pouring rum into their mugs. "Leave the bottle." Alex flipped her a doubloon, which she expertly caught before leaning over and giving the men a peek of her boundless figure. "Can I git ye gentlemen anythin' else?" Her sultry gaze drifted between Alex and Larkin.

"Later, love," Larkin replied, winking.

With a satisfied smirk, she sashayed away as Larkin took no time tossing his rum to the back of his throat.

"It will be well guarded," Jonas said, raking back his light hair and meeting Alex's gaze with one of reservation. Someone began playing an out-of-tune harpsichord in the corner as men gathered around to sing.

"I would expect nothing less." Alex sipped his rum. "And not only by the shipping company, but also by marines."

Jonas sat back with a huff. Riggs gulped his rum, eyes wide, and Larkin snapped hair from his face and grinned. "The marines? Not the night watch? Pray tell, Captain."

"Word is Captain Nichols is behind the rumors." Alex stretched out his legs.

Jonas snorted. "If you already knew, why ask us to keep our ears open?"

A quarrel rose at the table next to them as chairs scraped and two men stood to face each other in a challenge.

Alex gave them a cursory glance before continuing, "Because I wanted to know if you heard the same thing. Seems you did."

"But why would a Navy cap'n do such a thing?" Riggs asked. "Surely every pirate in town will be lickin' his chops to get the loot."

Jonas snapped accusing eyes toward Alex. "Because only a fool would attempt to board such a well-guarded ship."

"Yet fools are so underrated." Alex grinned.

Curses were spewed and punches thrown beside them. One of the pirates went flying across their table. Larkin picked up the bottle of rum just in time as the man sped across the stained wood, knocking over the lantern before thumping to the floor on the other side.

Upon seeing Alex, the man scrambled to rise and wiped the blood from his mouth. "Beggin' yer pardon, milord." He circled the table and charged his assailant once again. The mob broke into cheers.

Larkin replaced the bottle on the table as if they hadn't been disturbed. "If Nichols is behind this, then it's a trap."

Alex nodded. "So it would seem."

"An' there may be no pearls at all!" Riggs cursed.

"They'll be there," Alex said. "Of that you can be sure." Nichols's impudence would demand it.

Jonas snorted and gave him an incredulous look. "You aren't considering it?"

"Why wouldn't I?" Alex tossed rum into his mouth, then sighed as the spicy warmth sped down his throat. "We are pirates, after all."

"Indeed, we *are* pirates"—Jonas's jaw tightened—"but pirates with discretion, plundering French and Spanish goods, but never our own." He glared at Alex. "'Tis a British ship, is it not?"

"I have no idea whose ship it is," Alex shot back, irritation rising. "Nor do I care. Nichols has laid down the glove, and I intend to pick it up."

"To the Devil with your pride," Jonas spat. "I want no part of it."

"To the Devil with your impertinence. I am still your captain!" Alex poured himself more rum, if only to keep from pounding his fist on the table. A few men around them turned to stare. Riggs scratched his whiskers, while Larkin's gaze shifted betwixt Alex and Jonas, a smile on his lips.

Alex glared at him. "Then don't join us." Finishing off his rum, he turned to Larkin. "Gather twenty more of the crew and arm yourselves. We'll meet outside The Three Mariners."

Jonas sat back in his seat, a frown on his face.

Riggs rubbed his hands together. "When? At nightfall?"

"Nay. I have something I need to do." A soiree, in fact, at his house. Bad cess to the timing, but it couldn't be helped. The brig might very well be unloaded on the morrow. And he couldn't resist the temptation to outwit his dear nemesis.

"We'll meet at midnight. The guards should be lulled into complacency by then." And the celebration at Alex's house should be well over.

"Aye. Midnight then, Cap'n."

Larkin poured himself another drink and raised his glass to Alex. "Egad, sounds like a fun night."

"Let that be the last of the rum." Alex fingered the hilt of his cutlass. "I need you all sober."

Larkin huffed his displeasure and brazenly sipped the liquor, eyeing Alex over the rim of his glass. "Whatever you say, Captain."

Alex spun and marched from the tavern. Regardless of his sailing master's effrontery, tonight should not only offer a distraction from Alex's usual boredom but teach that clodpole Nichols that he was no match for the Pirate Earl.

Chapter 19

ALL LIARS GO TO HELL. Isn't that what the Good Book said? Hell was exactly the place Juliana felt she entered as she mounted the stairs to the Munthrope home, her goose-brained brother by her side. She'd long since berated him for his invitation to Mr. Kinder. He'd long since apologized. Yet now she must face the consequences of her lying heart.

As she greeted friends on either side of her, she breathed a silent prayer for a merciful punishment for her deceit, not one that revealed the true condition of her father and tossed all of them onto the streets.

But how was she to trick the pernicious Mr. Kinder into believing her father was an invisible guest at this soiree? How was she to detain him from storming back to their home to seek her father out for himself? All while she played the doting fiancée to a bloated fool. It was too much.

A headache formed between her eyes, and she squeezed the bridge of her nose. She had no time for pain or fear or exhaustion or despondency—all four of which battled for dominancy within her. She must be strong or all would be lost.

"Sister dear." Rowan, ever dashing in his black suit lined in crimson taffeta, escorted her through the crush of people at the front door. "No need to fret. I told you I would come to your aid. As soon as Mr. Kinder arrives"—a passing lady fluttered her lashes at him above a silk fan, distracting him for a moment—"I will entertain him, get him drunk, whatever it takes." He patted her hand. "All is well."

All might be well if she believed her whimsical brother. "Pray, Brother, for once I hope you mean to follow through. I truly need you tonight."

But her pleading tone seemed lost on the young man as a flock of befeathered young ladies flew by, giggling and casting him looks of interest.

He tugged from her, but she held him fast, giving him a stern look.

He offered with a wink. "Mr. Kinder has not yet arrived. Mayhap he won't even come."

"Oh, God, be merciful." She breathed out a prayer and gazed above.

"In the meantime"—Rowan flashed his brows at a passing coquette—"I intend to enjoy myself."

Whimsical laughter resounded from the top of the stairs, and all eyes lifted to see their host, Lord Munthrope, descend the grand staircase. With both hands raised to his sides, his bell sleeves hanging nearly to his embroidered shoes, he regally strutted down to the reception room in a dazzle of white satin and silver brocade. He scanned the crowd, his eyes alighting on Juliana.

"Ah, there you are, sweetums." He extended a leg, one hand on his heart, and bowed before her. But as he went down, his eyes held a glimmer of delight that could not be denied. Had he missed her the last seven days? Surely the man was not forming an attachment. She could not bear another complication in her already troubled life.

Taking her hand, he brought it to his lips. The surrounding ladies sighed at the exchange.

"You look ravishing."

Juliana gazed down at her clothing. She'd been so numb with worry while Miss Ellie assisted her in dressing, she barely noticed what she had put on. The bodice of her red velvet overgown sat low across her shoulders and extended down her arms to belled sleeves adorned with ribbons. A single pearl hung around her neck, matching her earrings. She supposed her attire was lavish enough to be His Lordship's fiancée. Even though, much to Miss Ellie's dismay, Juliana refused the itchy white paste on her face. Just a crescent moon patch on her chin, labeling her discreet.

For the next hour, she greeted guests alongside Munthrope, until her feet ached and her heart began to settle, for there was no sign of Mr. Kinder. She was about to thank God for the reprieve, when the wealthy merchant strolled through the front door. Heart in her throat, Juliana dragged Lord Munthrope back through the arched doorway into the ballroom, then through another side door to a large dining hall, where refreshments were being served. She must keep him out of sight of Mr. Kinder, who would no doubt wish to greet him, and therefore inquire after Juliana's father. A crowd of punch-laden guests immediately swamped him.

"Oh, Munny, there you are! Do tell Miss Halen the story of how you were attacked by smugglers off the Carolina coast."

Juliana took the opportunity to slip away and seek out Rowan. But he was nowhere to be found. Not near the table where they served unending spirits, and not in the ballroom, the portico, or the garden out back. Not even upstairs in the game room, billiard room, or various tea rooms. No doubt he'd taken off with some man's lonely wife.

Abandoned again in her hour of need.

She growled inwardly while ignoring calls here and there from friends begging her to join them. Forsaking the search for her brother, she spotted Mr. Kinder weaving through the crowd looking for someone—her father, no doubt, or mayhap Munthrope. The longer she delayed their encounter, the more of the night would be spent, and the less chance there was that he'd seek out her father at their home. Of course there was always tomorrow and the next day, but mayhap with Abbot's help, they could put Mr. Kinder off until her father regained his health and could sit and chat with him.

Oh, fie! Abbot! She'd forgotten to ask him to sort out the mess with the *Midnight Fortune* while he was down at the docks on another matter. She sighed, chastising herself. She would have to deal with it on the morrow. Now, she'd gone and lost sight of Mr. Kinder. Nay. There. She spotted a flash of his gray doublet. Following him, she slipped through the mob and turned a corner into the dining hall, when he suddenly appeared before her. She leapt back with a start.

"Miss Dutton. Why ever are you following me? And where, pray tell, is your father?"

Something had Miss Juliana all in a twitter tonight, and Alex intended to get to the bottom of it. Repeatedly he tried to extricate himself from clusters of admirers, demanding he entertain them with his embellished fables. Repeatedly he failed. Unfortunately as host—not to mention one of the most celebrated members of Port Royal society—it was not easy to slip away unnoticed, nor to deny his guests their due amusement. Fortunately, his height offered him the ability to watch Miss Juliana while he regaled and playacted and otherwise elicited belly-aching merriment from all within earshot. The poor lady flitted about like a goose chased by a jaguar, a look of angst marring her delicate features. One moment she was in the parlor, another in the foyer, then in the ballroom. Another time he saw her speaking with her friends Lady Anne and Miss Margaret—more like hiding behind their voluminous skirts until she dashed off again. She seemed to be looking for someone. Or perchance hiding from someone? Mayhap both. Fascinating woman! Did she never cease to intrigue him?

Finally, he begged leave of a group of elderly ladies— much to their effusive disappointment—with the excuse he must attend to Miss Dutton. He found the lady in question, her face pale, one side of her highly stacked coiffeur drooping, and her eyes glazed as she spoke to a gentleman Alex had never met.

Relief appeared on her face when she saw Alex before unease seized her features again.

"Lord Munthrope, may I present Mr. John Kinder," she said a bit breathless, "one of Port Royal's most prestigious merchants."

"Milord." Mr. Kinder bowed. "I thank you for the invitation to your home."

Alex raised his brows. He had never met the man and therefore could not have invited him, but Juliana's desperate look kept those thoughts unspoken. "'Twas my pleasure, Mr. Kinder." He nodded and flipped a curled strand of his periwig over his shoulder. "I do hope you enjoy yourself."

"I have every intention of doing so, milord." He turned to Juliana. "Now, if you would simply point me to your father, miss, I shall begin that enjoyment presently."

Her father? Here? Alex would be most pleased to meet the man. "I don't recall—" he began, but a sharp pain through his foot brought his glance down to Juliana's shoe slipping back beneath the fringe of her skirts.

"My father?" She addressed Mr. Kinder. "Yes. I believe I just saw him. But where?" She laid a finger on her adorable chin and sent a frenzied look toward Alex. Now he was beginning to see things clearly, though the why of the matter eluded him.

"Ah, Mr. Kinder." Putting one arm behind his back, Alex drew the man aside and gestured toward a linen-clad table lining one side of the room. "Allow me to show you the delicacies I had shipped in just for this occasion. No doubt we'll encounter Mr. Dutton along the way."

"We have *torta del Casar* from Spain, *canneles de bordeaux* from France ..." Munthrope's voice trailed off into the muttering crowd, and Juliana felt as though her legs would collapse beneath her.

She found a chair and slid into it, hoping no one wished to converse with her. Thankfully, most of the guests seemed otherwise engaged in dancing, conversation, or shameless flirtations. Munthrope's laughter echoed through the room. She shook her head. His Lordship surprised her. For such a ninny dunce, he'd picked up on her ruse immediately. Not only that, he'd played along and relieved her of Mr. Kinder's company for a time. A time of rest she very much needed.

But that rest didn't last long, as Munthrope soon returned.

"What have you done with him?" She grasped his outstretched hand and rose, wincing at the blister forming on her toe.

"Done? Begad, you make it sound so nefarious, sweetums." His mischievous grin shocked her. "I merely deposited your Mr. Kinder in the company of four elderly ladies who are enamored with his tales of merchant adventures." His blue eyes twinkled. "Or 'tis mayhap because they are all on their forth cup of rum punch."

Juliana gave him a coy look. "You are quite the scoundrel, milord."

"Alack, you have found me out!" He winked and adjusted the red silk bounding from his throat, then waved at a passing acquaintance.

For the next two hours, Juliana remained by Munthrope's side, all the while keeping an eye on Kinder, who seemed to flourish beneath what must surely be an unusual outpouring of female attention. More than once, Munthrope excused himself to offer the man and his companions another round of drinks, ensuring on her behalf that Mr. Kinder forgot all about her father. Why he was being so kind, she couldn't say. That it touched a tender spot in her heart, she dared not admit.

So they mingled among guests, nibbled on treats, and even took in a minuet in which Munthrope's usual entertaining style brought the crowd to laughter. Flamboyant in every move, with jeweled hands hefted in the air like a bird about to take flight, his white pasty face with that infernal horse patch over his right eye, and his cheeks and lips stained red, Juliana should have found his company irritating. Instead, she found it comforting. There was an authority, an assurance, behind the satin and lace she could not explain. Her nerves unwound, her breathing calmed, and thoughts of impending doom vanished when she looked in his eyes. Eyes of deep blue with specks of gray that reminded her of another man—a man opposite in every way from Lord Munthrope—the Pirate Earl. She'd been unable to shove the dangerous villain from her thoughts this past week, and had, much to her shame, secretly hoped to see him when she checked on Abilene. What a fool! How God must be frowning down upon her for such unscrupulous desires.

"So, sweetums, where is this mysterious father of yours?" Lord Munthrope handed her a glass of punch Madeira and drew her away from listening ears. "And why do you wish to keep Mr. Kinder from him?"

Delaying her answer, she sipped her wine, but her throat seemed to close, causing her to choke. "Father is home, if you must know," she managed to say. "He finds these affairs dreadful and didn't wish to see Mr. Kinder. In fact, he ordered me to keep him here." *Fie, another lie!* Now, she truly *was* going to hell. How many good deeds would she have to perform to cover up two lies in the same night?

"I fail to see why your butler cannot simply turn the man away."

Because her butler was on an errand, and the only other male servant who could stop Mr. Kinder from barging in was Mr. Pell, who was no doubt deep in his cups by now. "I fear Mr. Kinder can be quite persistent."

"Persistent, I'll not gainsay it, but still"—he cocked his head and fingered a curl of his periwig—"something else is amiss, I fear?"

Juliana gaped at him, taken aback by his discernment, and then by the look of concern in his eyes. Oh, how she wished for someone to confide in, someone to lend a caring ear. "If you must know, our family business has suffered a few setbacks of late," she blurted out, then bit her lip, suddenly regretting the disclosure. But the worry lining his face bade her continue. "Father has been taken ill with worry." Only a half-lie this time, but it provided an excuse for why the man never appeared in public.

Munthrope took her hand in his. "I am truly sorry to hear of it. Mayhap there is something I can do to help?"

"Nay." She pulled back her hand, flustered at the comfort of his touch. "I beg your pardon. I should not have mentioned it."

"I should hope at the very least we could be friends, milady." His voice lowered a bit, and there was a seriousness to his tone that sent confusion spinning through her.

She gave a little smile but said nothing.

He frowned and stared across the chattering mob for several seconds before pulling his watch from his pocket and glancing at it—for at least the tenth time in the past hour.

"Perchance, am I keeping you from some other engagement?" she asked, teasing.

He gave a nervous laugh. "Nay, just wondering where Lady Cransford is. 'Tis past eleven, and I've not seen glimpse nor glance of the birthday lady. And we must have the cake before everyone leaves." Munthrope drew his lips tight, stretching the mole at the corner of his mouth.

"Milord, 'tis so unlike you to fret so." Juliana studied the momentary flash of intensity that made him look almost authoritative as he stood there scanning the throng. "I imagine Her Ladyship wishes to make a grand entrance. You know how ostentatious she is."

He gazed at her curiously before a limpid gaiety overtook his features. "Oh, indeed! Indeed! I make no doubt!" He winked at her as he belted out a rhyme. "I simply do not wish people to pout and go out."

Juliana felt a twinge of disappointment at his silly behavior. "Go out? When have you known this crowd to abandon a lively affair such as this? Why, I doubt anyone will think of leaving for hours."

Chapter 20

"Y OU'RE LATE." LARKIN SNEERED AS Alex fell in step beside him, breathless from running across town.

"Couldn't be helped." Alex gripped the pommel of his sword and quickened his step. Street lanterns cast flickering skirts of gold onto the soggy ground, where an early mist formed.

"What is it you do, Captain, when you're not on board the ship?" Larkin cast him a sideways glance.

"Same as the rest of the crew: drinking, wenching, gambling. What else?" No one but Jonas knew of Alex's alternate identity, and he intended to keep it that way.

"Yet I rarely see you in any of the bawdy houses around town." Larkin's tone taunted.

Ahead, raucous music spilled from one of those bawdy houses, along with a throng of drunken men, doxies draped on their arms. Across the street, two men clashed blades in some mindless altercation. This was Alex's world. A world of darkness, violence, and debauchery. The world he'd plunged into after he'd realized God was but a myth. Yet it hadn't taken him long to realize that the happiness promised by wealth, women, and pleasure was also a fable.

Larkin chuckled. "Aha, I have it. 'Tis a lady. Aye, it must be a lady who occupies your time."

Alex snorted. If the man only knew.

"Some genteel beauty stashed away in a mysterious mansion."

"A mansion in Port Royal?" Alex snickered. "You dream too much, Larkin." Desperate to change the topic, he scanned the buildings that rose out of the darkness like tombstones in a misty graveyard. "Where are the others?"

"Waiting at The Three Mariners as you ordered." Larkin brushed dust from his black coat and dipped his plumed hat at a passing group of giggling strumpets. "I have no need of a genteel lady when I have my pick of any of these luscious fruits."

Indeed, the man spoke the truth. There wasn't a fallen woman in town whom the sailing master hadn't sampled. And continued to sample. Why, then, had Alex grown so bored with it all while Larkin seemed more invigorated with each passing month?

Thankfully, the conversation was cut short when they came upon his men—at least twenty of them—standing in the shadows beside the tavern, pistols and swords at the ready. The long sturdy plank Alex had told them to bring leaned against the brick wall beside them. Nodding his approval, he gave them final orders for their mission—a mission that, if he admitted it, stirred his blood to life. Finally something to break the tedium.

Though Juliana was doing a fair job at that. Unfortunately, he'd been forced to slip away from his own soirée with instructions for Whipple to keep the crowd occupied in his absence. Bad cess to it! Just when Juliana seemed willing to tolerate the doltish Lord Munthrope. He only hoped she would forgive him. But if all went well, he'd be back within the hour, and none would be the wiser.

Bare-masted and unsuspecting, the *Midnight Fortune* rocked idly at the end of King's Wharf. If not for Port Royal's deep harbor, the brig would be anchored at a distance in the bay, and they'd be forced to take a boat to board her. As it was, they needed to only leap onto her deck from the wharf.

"There are ten guards above deck," Larkin said. "All armed."

Alex nodded as he checked the pistols stuffed in his baldric.

"But we don't know how many is below," Riggs added.

Thunder growled in the distance. "There will be more," Alex said. Nichols would probably stuff the hold with Royal marines. "You all know what to do."

"Aye, Cap'ns" whispered through the midnight fog.

Riggs, knapsack over his shoulder and lit cigar betwixt his lips, hobbled down the long wharf, effecting a drunken stumble that would fool the most hardened souse. Keeping to the shadows, Alex and his men followed at a distance. A half-moon cast a milky glow over whiffs of fog icing the bay as a gust of chilled wind loosened hair from Alex's queue. He only hoped his father's tale of how his men had rescued him on the way to Execution Dock had been true. If not, the smoke grenades would possibly cost Alex and his crew their lives.

He knelt behind a stack of crates at the edge of the dock and gestured for his men to do the same. Silent as the grave, they waited, gripping swords and pistols, anticipation strung tight in the air between them. Lightning wove a silver thread across the dark sky.

"You there," a heavy voice shouted from down the wharf. "Aye, you. You aren't allowed on this dock. Begone with you, man!"

Riggs's slurred reply came fast, "What d'ye say thar, my friend?"

"I ain't your friend. I said begone with you, you drunken swine! Or I'll put a hole in your arse."

Laughter rang from the ship.

Riggs let out a loud belch. "Apologies, sir. I was lookin' fer me cat. Have ye seen me lost kitty, Puffins?"

A chorus of chuckles followed—along with the cock of pistols as the men pointed their weapons at Riggs. "Go on now. Yer cat ain't here."

Riggs waved a hand in their direction. "Very well, gents. Stay yer tempers, now. I'm leavin'. Can't a man look fer his cat wit'out bein' threatened fer life and limb?" He stumbled, tripped over his own feet, and plopped to the wharf with a thud, causing more laughter to fill the air.

Alex tensed. He glanced at his crew, their breaths heavy in the misty air. His best fighters, courageous all. He only wished Jonas were by his side. Though the man abhorred violence, for a sail-maker-turned-doctor-turned pirate, he possessed more skill with a sword than Alex had ever seen.

Muttering, Riggs twisted away from the ship in a feigned attempt to rise, reached into his knapsack, lit a grenade with his cigar and tossed it toward the *Midnight Fortune.* A good ten yards. But he made it. The hollowed-out two-pounder landed with a *thunk* on the wooden planks, sizzling like pig fat on a griddle. The stunned guards merely stared at it as the wick burned down, giving Riggs the chance to light and toss another one.

Alex gave the signal. He and his crew burst from behind the crates, carrying the plank between them as the first grenade exploded. Thick smoke enshrouded the guards. Yellow flashes peppered the air as shots cracked the night sky, directed toward Riggs. But he was no longer there.

Alex and his men slammed down the plank between the dock and bulwarks, then ducked as the second grenade exploded. *Boom!*

Curses and shouts shot from the gray cloud. Drawing his cutlass, Alex led his men over the plank into the waist of the brig. Riggs followed, lighting another grenade as he went. Smoke stung Alex's eyes. He blinked and coughed as his men let out a war cry that would frighten the bravest soldier. Riggs dropped the grenade down a hatch, then started to light another.

The disoriented guards were easy to find bumbling about the deck, rubbing their eyes and spewing curse after curse. Easy to find and easy to strike unconscious with the hilt of Alex's sword. Two more explosions rocked the brig. Smoke billowed from the hatches. A flurry of red coats buzzed on deck like angry bees from a hive. At least fifteen well-armed and well-trained Royal marines. Raising his blade, Alex took on the first man.

During the next few minutes, *clinks* and *clanks* rang through the darkness, joining grunts and screams and the occasional crack of a pistol. Sweat streamed down Alex's neck, dampening his shirt. He'd already taken care of three marines. A quick glance across the deck showed Spittal in a fierce battle with two men. Alex headed that way, when a tall major came at him, blade raised. Alex swung low at his opponent, who, though young, wielded his sword with a fair amount of skill. The boy blocked the strike and shoved Alex back. Their hilts locked in battle. Both grunted. Alex twisted his cutlass and drove the man to the side.

Swooping in from the left, the major intended to catch Alex off guard with his speed, but Alex leapt out of the way, swung about, and spanked the lad on the rump with the flat edge of his sword. His chuckle seemed to infuriate the boy further. He charged Alex like a bull, nostrils flaring. Alex met his parry with full force. The *chink* of their blades chimed into the night.

Sweat stung his eyes. Thunder bellowed in the distance. Alex shifted to the right and dipped his blade low. The major shrieked as a line of red appeared on his white breeches. He backed away, eyes seething. A breeze tossed the lapels of his red coat.

All around Alex, his men battled with swords and knives and some with fists. Grunts and groans bounced over the deck as their enemies dropped unconscious to the wooden planks. He'd instructed his men not to kill unless necessary. And he could see they were obeying. All but Larkin, who had declared that he "saw no need in saving men whom they may have to fight in the future."

A flash of light brought Alex's focus back to the fight at hand. He met the lad's slash and shoved aside his blade. Then, having his fill of this tomfoolery, Alex grabbed the backstay, swung onto the bulwarks, and leveled the tip of his cutlass at the boy's back. The young major dropped his sword and raised his hands as a barely noticeable tremble shimmied down his body. Leaping to the deck, Alex circled the man, pressed the tip of his sword to his chest, and pushed him toward the railing. "How about a little swim, Major?"

The man stared at him as if he were joking, but then quickly scrambled over the railing and dove into the bay.

Pain seared Alex's left arm. He swung about and met the point of a blade hovering over his heart.

"So this is the great Pirate Earl," the marine said between heaving breaths. Lightning flashed over his sweaty face. "Not so hard to catch, after all."

"At your service." Alex dipped his head even as he wondered whether the man realized his men were all but defeated and he was surrounded by pirates.

The marine ran a sleeve over his forehead. "I should run you through right here, but I'm under command to bring you in."

"I find your exemplary obedience to my liking, Lieutenant." Alex smiled.

Over the man's shoulder, he saw Bait creeping toward him.

A scream and a splash sounded as yet another man was tossed overboard.

Alex held out his hands. "I insist you clap me in irons at once."

The man's brow wrinkled. He pressed his sword deeper on Alex's chest. It pierced his leather jerkin, causing a prick of pain. "You are either a madman or a fool." The lieutenant snorted.

Alex cocked a brow. "Mayhap both."

Bait slammed the handle of his pistol on the man's head. With eyes rolling backward, the lieutenant crashed to the deck.

Thanking his friend with a slap on the back, Alex assisted his crew with the rest of the marines, and soon they had the men who were still conscious bound, gagged, and lined up against the bulwarks like a firing squad.

Ignoring the looks of hatred flung his way, Alex leapt down the companionway, which was still hazy with smoke, and made his way to the captain's quarters. Riggs and Larkin followed. There, they met one lone marine guarding the door, but at the sight of three armed pirates, he quickly surrendered and was escorted above.

"Yer wounded, Cap'n," Riggs said after he groped through the darkness, struck flint to steel, and lit a candle on the captain's desk. He held the light up to the bloody sleeve on Alex's arm. Caught up in the excitement, Alex had all but forgotten it, though now the pain begged his attention. "'Tis nothing." He tugged the cravat from his neck and tied it around the wound. Not deep, but he'd have Whipple dress it later. "Now let's find this treasure, shall we?"

He didn't have to issue the command twice before Riggs and Larkin began tearing the cabin apart from the deckhead above to the deck beneath their feet and everything in between. Once they found the pearls, Alex would let the rest of his crew loose in the hold to gather whatever else of value they could find. Either way, they would have to act fast before Nichols discovered his plan had been foiled.

A few minutes later, their search revealed the object of their quest—a lockbox stuffed behind a bottle of port in a drawer of the captain's oak desk. Plucking Riggs's boarding hatchet from his belt, Alex struck the lock and opened the box. Dozens of lustrous pearls stared up at them.

"You would think they'd have kept such a grand treasure better protected," Larkin said, rubbing his hands together. "Especially if they knew we were coming."

"'Tis precisely *because* Nichols knew we were coming that he believed the pearls secure." Alex picked up one of the gems. "The poor man has so little respect for pirates." He chuckled as he held a pearl to the light and saw his image reflected back at him from a creamy smooth surface that was perfectly round. Good quality.

"What would ye say they's worth, Cap'n?" Riggs was nearly salivating.

"A fortune, my good man," Larkin replied with a twinkle in his eyes. "A fortune." He reached to take the pearl from Alex, but it slipped from his fingers and fell onto the desk. When Alex went to retrieve it, two words shot like hell-fire at him from a piece of parchment. Two words that branded his mind like hot iron.

Dutton Shipping

He stared at the paper. There it was, plain as day: a writ of sale from Dutton Shipping. This was Juliana's father's brig! Of all the ships ... Alex sank into a chair.

Larkin plucked the pearl from the desk and held it to the candle. "Aye, these will bring a pretty price, I'd say."

Riggs's gold tooth twinkled in the light. "How much wou' ye say? Fer each of us?"

While Larkin guessed the pearls' value and spouted off several numbers that caused Riggs to squeal with glee, dread crept over Alex. If there was a God, there was no further doubt that He enjoyed toying with Alex to satisfy some sadistic pleasure.

Larkin scooped a handful of pearls and shifted them between his palms. "I'll wager these will bring some three hundred pounds, mayhap more."

Alarm pricked Alex. Why had Juliana's father allied himself with that braggart, Nichols? Why would he put such a fortune at risk? Especially when Juliana had just told Alex that Dutton Shipping was in trouble.

Riggs scratched his chin. "An' ow much will that put in me hands? Thirty pounds, wou' ye say?"

"Nay, you dull-witted fiend," Larkin snorted. "Divided amongst twenty-five men, and with the captain taking two shares"—he paused, thinking—"that should come to around eleven pounds each."

Alex couldn't steal from Juliana's family! A loss like this could put them in the poor house. And if Juliana ever discovered the Pirate Earl was behind it, she'd never speak to him again.

Riggs fingered the pearls still in Larkin's hand. "Eleven pounds. A fair wage fer a couple 'ours o' work, says I."

Alex ground his teeth together. 'Twas too late. If he denied the men their treasure, they'd mutiny and kill him—of that he had no doubt. However, he might be able to salvage the goods in the hold.

Nichols, the squirrely nodcock! This was all his fault! Alex slammed his fist on the desk, drawing the curious gaze of his men. Ignoring them, he found a quill pen and ink and scribbled a note on a scrap of foolscap, then glanced at the table clock. 1:15. *Lud!* "Put them back, Larkin," he ordered, slowly rising.

Larkin's scowl turned playful. "Don't trust me, Captain?"

Alex held up the open box. "I trust no one."

His sailing master eyed him for a moment as if actually considering whether to obey. Then he tilted his hand and allowed the pearls to slide into the box.

"Get the men back to the ship. I'll meet you there at first light."

"But what about the rest of the goods below?" Larkin asked.

Alex closed the box, tucked it under his arm, and circled the desk. "There's nothing else of value here."

"How d'ye know, Cap'n?" Riggs brow wrinkled.

"Because I do. Besides, the pearls are more than enough for tonight." He headed for the door.

"And yet, you seem to be running off with them." Larkin's boots thundered over the deck.

Alex spun on his heels and found the man standing behind him, fingering the hilt of his cutlass, a look of challenge on his face.

"What is this devilry?" Alex met his torrid gaze. "You will be paid your share, Larkin. As always." He gestured toward the man's blade. "If you intend to draw on me, you best do it now. Or back down before I teach you your place."

Anger flared in Larkin's eyes, anger that seemed to burn hotter with each passing second. Abruptly, he smiled and lifted his hands. "I wouldn't dream of it, Captain."

"Leave the ship at once. Nichols will be here any minute." Alex marched from the cabin, his mind a-spin with Larkin's defiance as he stomped down the companionway that belonged to Juliana's family. With a fortune in pearls that also belonged to them beneath his arm. How had such an adventurous evening turned so sour? He hoped his crew would leave the rest of the goods in the hold alone. He also hoped his guests would still be at his house and that Juliana had not discovered him missing and left. If so, she may never speak to him again.

If she discovered the Pirate Earl had plundered her father's ship, she may very well shoot him the next time she saw him.

Trouble was, he deserved it.

Chapter 21

"**W**HERE IS HE, MR. WHIPPLE?" Juliana glared at the pretentious butler. "I insist you tell me at once." She had searched the entire house for Lord Munthrope— except for his private chamber, of course—and not a speck of His Grace nor his lace could be found. How dare he abandon Juliana in the midst of his celebration of Lady Cransford's birthday? How dare he leave her to entertain his guests alone? In *his* home!

"I believe I just saw him discussing politics with some gentlemen in the garden." The butler looked bored.

"I was just *in* the garden, Mr. Whipple, and I assure you, your deviant master is not there." She glanced through the throng milling about the foyer toward the front door. She should leave. Courting the illusive coxcomb was turning out to be more trouble than it was worth. She faced the stodgy butler.

"It's nearly one-thirty in the morning. And Lady Cransford is asking about her cake. Where is His Lordship? With another woman?"

"I assure you, miss, you are the single object of his desire." He straightened his shoulders.

"Oh, fie, Whipple. We both know this betrothal is a farce."

One bushy brow rose.

"I'll have the cake brought out forthwith, miss. And I shall fetch milord. If he is tardy, please start the festivities without him."

The wooden butler was hiding something. She knew it. Behind that proper façade, he seemed worried. Or was it disgust? She couldn't figure out which.

Gathering her skirts, she flounced through the crush, pasting on a smile at those who greeted her as she passed. By the time she made it to the dining hall, after being waylaid by a few rather besotted guests, the cake was being wheeled in on a cart. A magnificent three-layered cake that looked as though it should be for King William instead of a mere baronet. But then, Munthrope always did everything to excess. Including his absences, it would seem. And, much to her delight, keeping Mr. Kinder occupied as well. She spotted the merchant deep into his cups, consorting with three doting dowagers across the room.

Forcing down her frustration, she headed toward the long table laden with now-empty silver trays glittering in the waning candlelight. Grabbing a glass and spoon, she thrummed them together, making quite a racket in order to get everyone's attention. The chattering slowed to a hum and people thronged into the room as all eyes sped to Juliana, including those of Lady Cransford, who clapped her hands in glee when she saw the cake.

Feeling conspicuous—not to mention nervous—in front of so many people, Juliana drew a deep breath, set down the cup and spoon, and clasped her hands before her. "It would seem I have misplaced Lord Munthrope," she began with a smile. Laughter bounded through the room, followed by whispered comments.

"Have you checked the mirror in the upstairs hallway? I daresay, he so enjoys preening himself," one man shouted, drawing more chuckles from the crowd.

"I did spot him with Miss Langston," one tipsy lady announced. "Mayhap you have some competition, Miss Dawson, eh?"

This elicited "ooohs" and "ahhhs" from the crowd.

Juliana frowned. "Nevertheless, we are here to celebrate the birthday of—"

"Lady Cransford." Munthrope's voice preceded his lavish entrance as the crowd parted to reveal the swaggering buffoon.

His eyes met hers. She scowled. He gave a little shrug and sauntered her way, then swung about and faced the crowd, bowing elegantly before the birthday lady. "Happy birthday, dear lady. We are honored you have allowed us to join in your celebration."

The lady in question returned his bow, her face pinking and giggles bouncing off her lips. "'Tis my honor, milord."

As Munthrope continued his speech, strutting before the mob like a popinjay, Juliana noticed something was different about him. Though he wore the same garish attire, his beribboned doublet sat on his shoulders slightly askew. His lace cravat appeared to be damp with sweat, his silk breeches wrinkled. Even the white paste on his face was blotchy and thin, revealing hints of sun-bronzed skin beneath. Sun bronzed? Couldn't be.

After he finished his whimsical soliloquy, he ordered the orchestra in the next room to play *Sweet Nightingale* in Lady Cransford's honor and then began to sing in his shrill voice. As the guests joined in, he conducted them with mighty sweeps of his arms.

This couple agreed;
To be married with speed,
And it's off to the church they did go.

He winked at Juliana over his shoulder, then swept Lady Cransford across the floor in a dance, delighting the crowd.

She's no longer afraid
For to walk in the shade,
For to lie in the valley below;

Finally, he halted, faced the mob, and with uplifted hands finished the last stanza with a flourish. Everyone clapped as the footmen cut the cake and the guests streamed forward to gather their piece. His Lordship slipped beside her.

"Where were you?" she demanded.

"Why, sweetums, whatever do you mean?"

She grimaced. "I told you not to call me that. And I haven't seen you for over two hours. That is what I mean." She smiled through gritted teeth at Mr. and Mrs. Ferrah passing by on their way for cake.

His grin lifted the mole atop his lips. Wasn't it on the other side earlier? "Dare I hope that milady missed my company?" He laid a bejeweled hand upon his chest. "My heart cannot take the thrill."

"I fear it will have to, milord." She seethed. "I care not whether you engage in trysts with every ample-bosomed sycophant who bats her eyelashes your way, but I would hope you would not do so when I am present, nor when I am required to entertain guests in your home."

"Trysts? Ample-bosoms! Oh my!" He laughed. "You use me monstrously, mil—Miss Juliana." His deep-blue eyes sparkled with mischief. "I may be many things, but I am loyal to a fault and would ne'er think to betray your confidence."

She was about to tell him that she had no confidence in him, simply an expectation not to be humiliated, when a red dot appeared on the sleeve of his otherwise pristine white shirt. A red dot that now expanded and streamed down the length of his arm.

"There can never be a tryst when Miss Juliana is in my midst." He began a ridiculous rhyme, then halted when he followed her gaze and saw the blood.

"You're injured, milord." Juliana gaped up at him.

"Nay. Just a scratch. 'Tis nothing."

But it didn't look like a scratch. In fact, from the amount of blood, it appeared to be a wound that ran deep across his bicep.

Excusing himself, Munthrope ploughed from the room, hand gripping his arm, his usual swagger replaced by a march of authority.

"What do you mean the pearls are gone?" Rowan stormed toward Captain Nichols, intent on shoving him against the wall of the punch house. But the man sidestepped him, snapped his fingers, and the two marines flanking him drew their service swords.

Growling, Rowan spun about, tore off his wig, and ran a hand through his damp hair. The other patrons who had glanced up, hoping for an altercation returned to their cups and cards as the normal clamor of strident voices and slosh of drink resumed.

Nichols stepped from between his lackeys, drew out a chair, and gestured for Rowan to do the same. "I suggest you keep your voice down, lest you want everyone in Port Royal to know of your loss. It certainly would not bode well for business."

"The news will spread soon enough," Rowan grumbled, trying to settle his breathing as a throbbing began in his head. He rubbed his temples. "You said the pearls were in no danger," he ground out in an angry whisper. "You said you posted enough marines on the ship to defeat a small army!"

Candlelight smeared blotches of gold and gray across Nichols's face, bringing to light the anger simmering just below the surface. "I did." His eyelid began to twitch. "'Twould have been impossible for anyone, even with fifty pirates, to overcome my marines." He pulled out a scrap of foolscap and perused it with a scowl. "To the Devil with the Pirate Earl!" He roared. "How did he accomplish it?"

Rowan snagged the paper from his hand.

Captain Darling, I could not accept such a gift without expressing my sincere gratitude.

Always your humble servant, PE

Rowan snorted. "So he knew about your trap."

"Apparently." Nichols dug his fingernails into the table, then grabbed the paper and held it over the candle. Within seconds, it burst into flames and disappeared.

"It would seem this Pirate Earl is not one to contend with." Rowan gave a bitter laugh. "He outwitted and outmatched you at your own game. And I played the fool for believing you the better man."

"I *am* the better man!" Nichols slammed his fist on the table, jarring the candle and nearly tipping over a pewter mug of half-finished ale. Gazes flung their way.

A sour taste coated Rowan's mouth. He cursed himself. Pearls worth more than three hundred pounds, and he'd trusted them to this fish-brained lout. How was he going to tell his sister? How would they be able to cover the loss of so great an amount when they were already struggling?

A tavern wench passed, and Rowan ordered a mug of Kill-Devil. The stuff could melt barnacles off a ship's hull, but he needed it tonight. "Now what am I to do?" he moaned.

But Nichols wasn't listening. He leapt to his feet and took up pace, a string of curses pouring from his mouth. "I'll catch him yet. He's not as smart as he thinks." He raised a finger in the air. "Pride goeth before destruction, and the Pirate Earl's destruction is fast approaching!"

"I said, what am *I* to do?" Rowan raised his voice over the din as the wench returned with his drink and slapped it on the table, holding out her palm. He slipped her a coin. "What am I to do to cover the loss of so great a fortune? You owe me, Nichols." He took a draught of the fiery liquor, choking it down.

"I owe you nothing!" Nichols halted, adjusted his periwig, and pierced Rowan with his snake-like eyes. "You knew the risks."

"Alack! You said there were none!"

"Any fool could see there was a chance this … this … base cullion would win." Nichols's face seemed to twist in the candlelight. "Nay, I must catch him in the act of piracy itself. Out at sea. Yes, that is it." He took up a pace again, the marines moving to allow him past. "One of your ships will do nicely."

Chuckling, Rowan leaned back in his chair. "Have you naught but seaweed for brains? I'll not risk any more of Dutton Shipping on your reckless schemes! I've already lost too much as it is."

Nichols snorted. "You mean to say you have gained too much, sir! Have you not been well paid for your endeavors?"

Rowan glowered into his drink. Indeed, the man had more than kept him in the many games about town.

Mocking laughter resounded through the room, followed by the chink of coin and chime of blade as some poor sod accused another of cheating. Shouts followed. Nichols ignored them. Taking a seat, he leaned over the table toward Rowan, a look of devious anticipation on his face. "Pray tell, what have you discovered of the priggish Lord Munthrope?"

"Nothing of interest." Rowan fingered his mug. "He's the son of an earl, an Edmund Merrick Hyde, Earl of Clarendon. An ex-pirate turned missionary, they say. He receives a stipend and post from the man every few months. He grew up in the Carolina colony with a mother, a Lady

Charlisse Bristol, and two sisters. I assure you, he is as unremarkable as he is ostentatious."

"Humph." Nichols's brow darkened. "Keep searching. There is something odd about the man. I know it." He leaned back in his chair and adjusted the cravat at his neck. "Now about that ship of yours."

"I cannot and *will* not risk my family's fortune again."

Fire simmered in the captain's eyes. "I underestimated this Pirate Earl, I'll not gainsay it. But he'll not beat me twice. A trap at sea using one of your ships and we'll have him, I know it!"

"Or he'll have my ship as prize." Rowan took another gulp of rum, finally feeling its soothing effects.

Reaching inside his jacket, Nichols pulled out a pouch and flung it onto the table. It landed with a mesmerizing *chink* that rang a sweet melody through Rowan's soul. He stared at it, knowing he should ignore it, knowing he should grab his rum and leave. One peek wouldn't hurt, would it? Loosening the ties, he peered inside at the doubloons winking at him in the candlelight. Enough money to mayhap make amends for the stolen pearls—*if* his luck at cards changed.

He shouldn't take it. He should have never allied himself with this man. Now, instead of helping Juliana, he'd lost a fortune. And their good reputation as well. What merchant would trust Dutton Shipping now with their precious commodities?

He glanced at the door, longing for the strength to resist, the honor he so desperately wished he had. But in truth, he possessed neither. He snagged the money from the cretin's hands before he changed his mind.

Nichols grinned. "I'll be in touch."

At well past three in the morning, with eyes as heavy as her legs, Juliana plodded up the steps to her home. She thought Munthrope's soiree would never end. Mr. Abbot opened the door, lantern in hand, and she held up a palm to stay his castigation. Her late revelry couldn't be helped—though she vowed never to host another celebration in her life.

Handing her hat and cloak to Abbot, she glanced up the dark stairway, hearing her bed calling to her. But she had a business to run, and it would be dawn in a few hours. She must rethink the benefits of this feigned betrothal with Munthrope. Surely, it wasn't worth sleepless nights. Even though—dare she hope—the pretense seemed to be working. Nichols had not made an appearance last night, nor had he sent his card requesting an audience with her in quite some time. Mayhap he'd finally given up his pursuit. *Oh, Lord, let it be so.*

She also hadn't seen Munthrope after he'd hurried from the dining hall holding his bloody arm. How could the man have injured himself so badly in his own home? He hardly seemed the type to invoke violence in others, nor was he clumsy. Oh, fie. What did it matter?

Before Abbot could shut the door, Mr. Kinder stormed into the foyer, his face flush with both alcohol and exertion. And with something else—

Rage.

"My pearls are gone!" he shouted. "Gone, I tell you!"

Realizing he was besotted from the long soiree, Juliana tried to placate him with a gentle smile. "If you please, Mr. Kinder, take a deep breath and calm yourself. What do you mean *gone*?"

"Stolen! Right off your ship!" He wagged a finger in her face. "Dutton Shipping guarantees the safety of their cargo at sea or at dock. And your father will pay, do you take me? He will pay!"

Dread soured in Juliana's throat as she tried to make sense of his words. Her father had always kept sentries aboard their ships in port. She had done the same. "There must be some mistake, Mr. Kinder. We keep our ships well-guarded." Why had she not taken care of the problem with the customs agent last night?

Mr. Abbot cleared his throat. "Yes, indeed, miss. There were several men stationed aboard."

Lantern light flickered over the veins bulging on Mr. Kinder's neck. "A hundred sentries would not have mattered. Not with pirates."

"Pirates?" The dread sank into Juliana's stomach.

"Aye, a nasty lot of them, word is."

"How did you hear of it?" *Oh, Lord, please let this be a mistake.*

"Hear of it?" Spit flew from his mouth. "Why, the news spread like the plague at Munthrope's! As soon as I was told, I left and verified it was true." He attempted to calm himself. "I have lost a valued customer. Lord and Lady Salem will never purchase from me again." He growled and shifted his searing gaze between her and Abbot. "Why am I even speaking to you?" He handed his hat to Abbot. "Where is your father, Miss Dutton?"

He started up the stairs, but the butler leapt in front of him. "I beg your pardon, sir, but Mr. Dutton has retired for the evening. If you would come back later ..."

"Nay! I will not come back later." He hesitated, glancing up the stairs one last time before stepping down in front of Juliana and thrusting a finger in her face. "Someone at Dutton Shipping disclosed the contents and value of my merchandise on board your ship."

Juliana swallowed, trying to accept that the pearls had been stolen, trying to accept that her business was most likely ruined. "Nay, sir. I resent the implication. I ... my father runs a reputable business."

"Then why did every sailor I spoke with tonight confirm rumors of a fortune in rare pearls hidden on your brig?"

Knees buckling, Juliana exchanged a glance with Abbot, who merely shrugged. She faced Mr. Kinder and forced a rigid tone. "We can hardly be held accountable for foolish rumors, sir."

"Yet, they were neither foolish nor rumors, now, were they?" Mr. Kinder's shoulders sagged. He searched the dark foyer as if expecting his pearls to materialize.

"Tell your father I will return later in the day." He grabbed his hat from Abbot and lifted a stiff chin toward Juliana. "At which time, I shall expect two things: one, to actually see the man in the flesh, and two, full reparations for my stolen pearls. If not—our friendship aside—I shall tell every merchant in town that Dutton Shipping is not to be trusted."

With that, he marched out the door into the darkness.

Chapter 22

THE FIGURES ON THE PAPER began to twist and curl and fade. Leaning back in her chair, Juliana rubbed her aching eyes and listened to the warble of afternoon birds in the garden. After sending Abbot to King's Wharf to ensure the safe unloading of the rest of the goods aboard the *Midnight Fortune*, she had barricaded herself in her father's office, searching through every line of his accounts to find a way to pay Mr. Kinder for his lost pearls, praying for God to insert a sum where she had overlooked it before, some overestimated expense, some underestimated credit. But after three hours, the only thing she discovered was a dwindling income that, if left unchecked, would sink the business to the bottom of the sea.

To make matters worse, from the sounds of the coarse hacking drifting down the stairs, her father's health worsened. When she'd visited him moments ago, he'd not even had the energy to insult her, only offering her a weak scowl. Which worried her all the more. So she'd sent Miss Ellie for Dr. Verns, though Juliana was beginning to doubt the man's curative abilities. However, she did wish to ask him if he'd paid a visit to young Michael at the orphanage as she'd requested.

More coughing echoed down the stairs, this time violent, sending a shudder through her and tears into her eyes. *God, please don't take my father.* She closed those eyes now, forcing back the fear. What would she do if her father abandoned her just like her mother had done? And like Rowan had done his whole life? Just like that preacher who had abandoned the children at the Buchan orphanage? Then she, too, would be an orphan, left to cope in this cruel world all by herself. How long could she run Dutton Shipping before people discovered her ruse? Not that she was doing that good a job of running things anyway.

Footsteps and the clank of glass opened her eyes to see Rowan gesturing to a cup of steaming tea he'd just set atop the desk, his normally cocky grin replaced by a slightly penitent frown.

A breeze quivered the calico curtains and teased the curled tips of his light hair, absent a wig at the moment. She much preferred his natural hair anyway. Dark stubble peppered his jaw, and though he wore the same lavish suit from last night and shadows hung beneath his eyes, he still presented a handsome figure.

"I brought you some tea, sister dear. I know how tired you must be."

She eyed him. "I've been tired on many an occasion and you've never brought me tea before."

"Have I not?" He shrugged. "Bad cess on me." Turning, he ran a finger over the bookshelves, pretending to peruse the titles, though Juliana had never seen him actually read a book before.

"What is it you want, Rowan? I have work to do."

He strolled to the open French doors and leaned on the frame, gazing out upon their mother's garden, where afternoon sunlight angled over colorful flowers. Bees buzzed, birds flitted. All happy and carefree—completely unaware of the disaster looming in the house beside them.

"Do you ever think of her?" he asked.

"All the time." Juliana brought the cup to her lips. Peppermint and lemon filled her mouth, reviving her senses.

"'Twould that she had not died." He gave a listless sigh.

Juliana's chest tightened. "She loved you very much."

He snorted. "She's the only one who did." He glanced at Juliana over his shoulder, his eyes misty. "Besides you."

Juliana set down her cup, remembering all the times their father had spoken cruelly to Rowan. "Father doesn't mean what he says to you. You know that."

"Yes he does."

Poor Rowan. While Juliana seemed able to shrug off *most* of her father's abuse, Rowan took it to heart, allowed the man to trample his confidence and stomp on his hopes. "He's just an ill-humored old man who wants everyone to be as miserable as he is."

Rowan continued to stare into the garden. "He was unfaithful to Mother, you know."

She *did* know. Though she hadn't realized Rowan was aware of it. The smell of heliotrope filled the room, caressing her heart with memories of the dear lady. "She forgave him. As we should." Though Juliana wasn't entirely sure she had succeeded in that regard. Another blemish on her sinful soul. 'Twas no wonder the Almighty withheld his blessing.

"Never! He's getting what he deserves." Rowan spun, his face tight with pain and anger.

Sorrow burned in her throat. "You mustn't say that, Rowan."

"Why? Because we need him to run the business? We're doing fine without him."

"We?"

His lips slanted. "You then. And I in my own way." Moving toward her, he leaned his palms on the edge of the desk, looking more serious than he had in a long while. "The Devil's own luck about Kinder's pearls." Remorse burned in his blood-shot eyes.

Lowering her gaze, she examined the papers strewn across the desk. "We cannot afford the loss. Or the scandal. I don't know what to do, Rowan." She raised pleading eyes to his, hoping beyond hope that he would step out of his childish cloak and put on a man's attire—become responsible, as she so desperately needed him to be.

Instead, he reached inside his coat pocket and tossed a pouch of coins onto the desk.

"What is this?"

"Thirty pounds. I won it last night in a game of Faro." He smiled with pride.

"And you're giving it to me?" She raised a brow. That was certainly a first.

"To help cover the cost of the stolen pearls." He opened his mouth to add something, but shut it. Was that a look of guilt on his face?

She wanted to ask him where he got the money to gamble with in the first place but knew it was some hellish agreement he had with Captain Nichols. In truth, she didn't want to know. Grabbing the pouch, she thanked him. It was a start. A small start. Though she knew it wouldn't be enough to satisfy Mr. Kinder when he arrived. Which was why she'd instructed the staff not to answer the door to anyone. She couldn't put the merchant off forever, but she needed time to figure out what to do, what to say, how to appease him before he destroyed her family business.

Covering another yawn, Rowan started for the door. "I simply cannot keep my eyes open another minute, sister dear. I'm abed." And off he went without a thought that she, too, had not slept all night.

A lightness in his step, despite his lack of sleep, Alex took the stairs up to the Dutton home two at a time. He knew Lord Munthrope was being rather presumptuous in calling on Juliana uninvited, especially when she was no doubt still asleep, but he couldn't help himself. Something in her eyes last night—a flicker of admiration, a hint of camaraderie in their banter—gave him hope that even dressed and behaving like a silly fop, Juliana might find him agreeable in some respects. Besides, he wanted to see how Dutton Shipping fared after the loss of the pearls. He hoped the business hadn't suffered overmuch. He hoped they could hold out another day or two until he could put his plan into place. Had Miss Juliana heard 'twas the Pirate Earl who'd become her enemy? That, too, disturbed Alex more than anything.

Yet no one answered the door. He knocked again, tapping the hilt of his cane on the wooden portal over and over until hurried steps sounded on the other side. The door flung open to reveal a plump woman, face flushed and red curls poking from beneath her mob cap like a sea urchin.

"Yes?"

"Lord Munthrope to see Miss Dutton." He flung his cane over his arm.

"Oh, forgive me, milord." She bobbed a curtsey and wiped her hands on her stained apron. "I believe she's in the master's study. Let me fetch 'er." She started toward a room on the left, when a woman's voice barreled down the hall from the back of the house. "Marcie!" The scent of something burning tickled Alex's nose. The woman flung her hands to either side of her head then darted away, exclaiming. "My bread! My bread!"

Alex stared after her. Why would the cook be acting as butler? No matter. In the study, eh? Mayhap he'd finally get to meet Juliana's father. Affecting a pompous walk in case anyone was looking, he crossed the foyer and stopped before the closed door. Snoring met his ears. Not loud obnoxious snoring like the men on his ship, but soft snoring that was more like a deep rumbling sigh.

Opening the door ever so slightly, he peered inside. Miss Juliana sat behind her father's desk, her head lying atop a pile of papers, her pink lips slightly open. Golden waves spilled from their pins over the desk like a waterfall of sunlight. A pen perched in one hand, while her other lay limp beside a cup of tea.

A dozen questions stormed through him, but none of them mattered at the moment as he stood mesmerized by the sight. The lady astounded him. She enchanted him. And he suddenly felt unworthy of her. He inched inside the room for a closer look, when the toe of his silly red shoe struck a chair.

Her head jerked up. Her eyes met his, dazed at first before a line formed between her brows and she shook her head. "Oh my. Lord Munthrope." She stood, wobbled, and gripped the edge of the desk. "How, why? I didn't hear you come in. Where's … ?" She glanced out the door as if looking for a servant. "Oh, fie! They weren't supposed to answer the … never mind."

Odd. She wore the same gown from last night. "Your cook let me in." He smiled, taking in the bookshelves lining the walls, the elaborately carved wainscoting, oil paintings of the English countryside. "Your father's study, I presume?"

Juliana brushed her skirts and attempted to stuff her wayward hair back into her coiffeur. "Yes … I … uh … he asked me to find … to bring a document to him. And well, I must have fallen asleep." She lifted up a few papers and released them, sending them fluttering back to the desk. "I can't tell one writ from another. They all look alike." Her giggle was forced. What was she hiding?

"Looking for a document with a pen in your hand?"

She stared at the quill, still gripped in her fingers, before tossing it to the desk with a nervous laugh.

Alex raised his brows. "I was hoping to meet your father, sweet—Miss Juliana."

"He's not home, I'm afraid." She wouldn't meet his gaze, but instead began shuffling books about the desk.

"Hmm." Alex scratched his chin, then remembered the blasted white powder covering it. "Did he request you send him the document by post?"

She lifted narrowed eyes and frowned.

He swung a long curl of his periwig over his shoulder. "However, it pleases me to know he has recovered from his illness." A humid breeze blew in through the open doors, showering him with the same scent of vanilla and cherries that so often lingered around Juliana.

Pasting on a smile, she skirted the desk, took his arm, and led him out of the room. "Forgive me, Your Lordship, but what exactly *are* you doing here?"

Rays of sunlight floating in through the front windows dappled her in gold. A few strands of her flaxen hair danced about her waist. Her cheek bore the imprint of the document she was lying on, and he reached up to smooth it out. If only to touch her skin.

Coughing sounded from upstairs. She jerked her gaze upward. So, her father was not well, after all. Mayhap news of the stolen pearls had sent him back to his bed. Guilt tightened across Alex's chest at the look of fear on her face. But how to inform her that he knew what he wasn't supposed to know and that all would be well?

She ushered him to the door as if she couldn't get rid of him fast enough. So much for their friendly banter last night.

He halted and faced her. "I came to beg your forgiveness, milady, for dashing out on you last night. It was beyond incorrigible, and I owe you an explanation."

"You owe me nothing, milord. I hope you have recovered from whatever wound your arm suffered." Yet she seemed as disinterested in his injury as she was in spending another moment in his company.

"I have, indeed, thank you. A sword wound, Miss Juliana. From a playful joust with a friend. You see, that is where I was during my absence. Another thing for which I must beg your forgiveness. I simply cannot turn down a challenge, once presented."

At this, she gaped at him and laughed. "You? A sword fight? With whom?"

He waved an arm through the air, avoiding her eyes. "An old friend. 'Tis sort of a tradition."

Her face twisted in unbelief, but she gestured once again toward the door. It flew open, admitting a middle-aged woman in a maid's uniform, who was followed by a tall, lithe man with graying temples, carrying a satchel.

"Dr. Verns," Juliana swept toward him. "Thank you for coming. Miss Ellie will show you up." She all but shoved the man toward the stairs.

"I saw your father yesterday, Miss Dutton," the man said as he mounted the steps. "I'm not sure I can do much more for him."

Juliana's shoulders slumped as the doctor turned and finally saw Alex standing behind the open door. He sent her a look of apology before continuing upward.

She approached the bottom of the stairs. "Dr. Verns, did you have a chance to see the young lad, Michael, at the orphanage?"

"Not yet, Miss Dutton. I intend to visit him later today."

The orphanage? Alex swallowed. Were the children struck with more disease?

The maid glanced at Alex before giving Miss Juliana a look of sympathy and continuing to lead Dr. Verns up the stairs.

Juliana stared after the doctor, wringing her hands until he was out of view. Then, turning, she gazed at Alex with contrition. "I beg your pardon for my untruth, milord. I simply do not wish it known that my father is ill. He is recovering and will be back to himself in a matter of days."

He studied her. The catch in her voice and shift of her eyes told him otherwise. Was this dear lady running Dutton Shipping on her own? It certainly wasn't being managed by her wastrel of a brother. Alex had seen him on multiple occasions deep into his cups—and his cards—down by the docks. If that was the case, the loss of the pearls would be her undoing.

Her gaze met his and a brief acknowledgment of the truth spanned between them. "Please tell no one, milord. I beg you."

"Of course." He sobered and took her hand in his. "Nary a word 'twill escape my lips."

She gave a sigh. "Now if you don't mind. I am quite busy."

Alex risked a serious tone. "Is there something I can do to help, sweetums? Is there some problem you need advice on?" He resisted the tug of her hand, desperate to hold it awhile longer.

She stared at him, searching his eyes, a longing in hers that nearly forced him to confess the truth of who he was and reassure her all would be well. But he feared her hatred more than anything. He feared it would be his undoing.

For a second, he thought she would unleash her burdens on him and receive his help, but then she shook her head as if remembering he was but a buffoon.

"It would help me if you would leave."

His heart collapsed. And for the first time, he truly loathed himself. "Mayhap later? A ride through town? Supper at my home?" Anything to see her again and offer his comfort.

"I'm afraid I cannot, milord. I promised to visit a sick friend." She ushered him out the door onto the stoop.

"Pray tell, who?" He twirled about, rubbing forefinger and thumb on the sides of his mouth. "Should I accompany you?"

"Nay, 'tis but an old friend, Miss Abilene."

He started to insist that he escort her, when she spit out a "Good day, milord" and closed the door with a clap.

Running a shipping business or not, there wasn't a saint's chance in hell he would allow her to venture to The Black Dogg alone.

Chapter 23

*O*H, *FIE,* HOW HAD THE day gotten away from her? Juliana had meant to set out much earlier in the afternoon for The Black Dogg, but Abbot had returned and she'd become entangled in keeping the accounts on Mr. Kinder's recent shipment. All was in order, save the missing pearls, of course. Mayhap Mr. Kinder would accept payments? Nay, he didn't seem the type to be that obliging. In fact, he had pounded on their front door late that afternoon for nigh twenty minutes before she heard him curse and march away. She hated being so rude, but what else could she do?

Clutching her satchel to her chest, she glanced at Mr. Pell bumbling along beside her. The useless footman had already been too fuddled with rum for her to trust him driving the carriage, so she'd asked him to accompany her on foot in a pretense of safety she didn't feel in the man's presence.

Yet it was only five o'clock. Though the sun hung low over the horizon, they still had a few hours before it dipped into the sea, luring out the vermin that occupied the port at night. They turned down Queen Street, and Mr. Pell released a putrid belch.

"Pardon me, miss." He slogged beside her.

"At least try to pretend you aren't inebriated, Mr. Pell. For both our sakes."

He grunted, attempted to obey by steadying his teetering, but only managed to trip over his own feet.

It may have been better if she hadn't brought him at all. Besides, God would protect her as he had done each time she'd visited the docks on a mission of mercy. Her thoughts snapped unbidden to the Pirate Earl. She hadn't seen him in more than a week. What an enigma the man was. She still couldn't sort out what he wanted from her, nor why her insides turned to mush in his presence. Did he think of her as much as she thought of him? Unlikely. No doubt he had many other women to occupy his time.

Two-story homes with white-gated yards gave way to warehouses and storefronts, the Merchant's Exchange, and then the customs house as the strong smell of fish and the sea swept over her in a welcoming breeze. Perspiration slid down the back of the modest muslin gown she'd donned so as not to draw unnecessary attention.

An impossible feat once they turned onto Thames Street from which wharf after wharf extended into the turquoise harbor like brown teeth in a gleaming mouth. Lined with taverns, punch houses, brothels, and shops, this was where every sailor and pirate squandered his pay and prizes on useless trinkets and dissipated living.

Dozens of eyes from those same men now latched upon her like grappling hooks, following her every move down the sandy street. Most of their comments were lost to the wind, thank God, but a few hit their mark, causing a flood of heat to rise up her neck.

Mr. Pell took no notice. Instead, he gazed longingly at a barrel of Kill-Devil rum that had been rolled into the street from a tavern and into which men dipped their mugs for a flip of a coin. Juliana should release the incompetent footman. But what would stop him then from telling everyone in town that she was managing Dutton Shipping on her own?

Adjusting her parasol to shield herself from prying eyes, she glanced over the glistening harbor, where ships of all sizes and shapes teetered in the choppy water, while others sat bare-masted, tied to the docks. Half-castes, their backs open to the sun, carried crates and barrels to and from the languid ships, while bare-footed mulattos scurried about selling fruit and rum to new arrivals. The crank of carriage wheels and stomp of horses' hooves joined the cacophony of shouts, curses, waves slapping against pilings, and the distant clank of a hammer on iron.

Stepping over a pile of horse droppings, Juliana stopped before The Black Dogg, not nearly as ominous-looking in the daylight as it appeared at night. She gripped Mr. Pell's arm as he led her inside—or rather wobbled her inside. Muddled sunlight sifted in through grimy windows, revealing the tavern for what it was. Not a dragon's lair filled with frightening specters but a dreary room filled with stained, chipped tables covered in melted wax and spilt liquor. Bugs joined rats nibbling on food droppings on a floor that stuck to one's shoes with each step, while a few patrons lay asleep in their own vomit. Behind the long counter, the proprietor stared at them dreary-eyed.

"We ain't open yet," he growled.

"I'm here to see Abilene." She deposited Mr. Pell in one of the chairs, praying this beast of a man would allow her upstairs.

But the scowl on his face suddenly lifted. "Yer the Pirate Earl's lady. Aye, aye, o' course." He poured rum into a glass, his demeanor instantly one of a servant. "Head on upstairs, miss. I'll tend to yer man." He scrambled around the bar, drink in hand, much to Mr. Pell's utter glee.

Wonderful. By the time she came back down, her footman would most likely be under the table. But she didn't wish to impugn the owner's attempt at hospitality, nor inform him she was not the blasted Pirate Earl's lady.

"I thank you, kind sir. I shall return anon." Thankfully all was quiet upstairs. No moans or groans penetrated the doors of the rooms she passed on her way to the third level. By the time she entered Abilene's room, her nerves had settled. Especially when she saw her friend sitting up in bed, the color returned to her cheeks. And a huge smile on her face when she saw Juliana. A bruise darkened one of her cheeks and one eye was still swollen, but otherwise, she looked well.

"Hello, Abilene." Setting down her satchel and parasol, Juliana scooted a chair close to her friend and sat, nodding at a red-haired woman who wrung out a cloth over a basin beside the bed.

"She gonna be all ri', miss. A tough one, she is," the woman said. "I 'xpect she'll be back to 'erself in jist a few more days." She hung the damp rag over the back of a chair and headed out the door, shouting to Abilene. "I'll check on ye later, dearie."

"Thank you." Juliana called after the woman before turning to her friend. "Seems you have been well taken care of."

Abilene took Juliana's hand in hers and smiled, though the effort seemed to cause her pain. "Because of you. You saved my life." Her brown eyes brimmed with gratitude.

Juliana shook her head. "Nay, 'twas … 'twas … a friend"—was the Pirate Earl a friend?—"and his doctor."

"Aye, so I heard." A twinkle now appeared in those eyes. "Is it true what they are saying, Juliana?"

She didn't know what they were saying. Didn't want to know. "No matter about that. How are you feeling?"

"Achy and sore, but stronger every day."

"Are you getting enough food?"

"More than enough. Why, I'll be as fat as a Christmas goose if don't get out of bed soon." She laid a hand on a belly that was still far too thin for Juliana's liking.

"Fat or not, you are staying right here until you are completely well."

Clanging bells and shouts rode in through the window on a gust of heated air, stirring up the stale smell of sickness.

Abilene stared down at her stained nightdress. "I don't want your charity, Juliana. Especially not since your father has taken ill."

Juliana squeezed her hand. She'd forgotten she had told her friend about her father. "'Tis not my charity." Which reminded her. She must find this Pirate Earl and pay him back. The last thing she needed was to be indebted to a thief and scoundrel. Mayhap that had been his plan all along. Then he could demand repayment in whatever form he chose. A shudder claimed her at the thought.

"So, 'tis true then," Abilene said, leaning back on the bed frame as if she suddenly grew tired. "My benefactor is the infamous Pirate Earl." Her brow crinkled in concern. "But what is he to you?"

"Truth be told, I have no idea. He seems to have formed some sort of attachment." Juliana adjusted the pillows behind her friend's head, trying to shove the vision of the handsome pirate from her mind. "Nothing to concern yourself with. We must get you well and ensure this never happens again."

"It won't. At least not from that fiend Riley."

"Why?" Juliana sat back. "What happened to him?"

"Beat to nary a spark of life left in him. Or so I heard."

"Indeed?"

Abilene nodded, studying her friend. "You must be careful of this Pirate Earl, Juliana. I know he appears charming and intelligent, even civilized, but he's not the sort of man you want to cross."

Charming, intelligent, civilized. Yes, he did appear to be all those things, along with protective and kind. Juliana swallowed. Yet she must not forget how he made his fortune: from murder, rapine, and thievery.

"In fact, you shouldn't have come here at all," Abilene continued, struggling to sit. "'Tis not safe."

Juliana forced her back down. "My footman is downstairs and 'tis not yet dark." Rays from the setting sun speared through the glassless window. She gripped both of Abilene's hands and leaned toward her. "I wish you would come home with me, Abilene. I've plenty of room."

Abilene lowered her chin. "It is too late for that. How can I face anyone after what I've … what I've become. Nay, I can never go back." She paused as if trying to force back tears. "But your friendship means the world to me, Juliana." She lifted glassy eyes. "You are the only one from my past who doesn't turn their nose away in disgust."

"How could I ever do that? You are my dear friend." Juliana lifted Abilene's hands to her lips as emotion burned in her throat. "I can't stand to see you live like this."

"'Tis my lot, I fear."

Juliana closed her eyes, wondering why God allowed such things to happen to his children. Was Abilene even his child anymore? Would the sinful life she'd been forced into forever keep her from heaven's gates? Juliana couldn't bear the thought.

Instead, she diverted the conversation to more cheerful topics, and they passed the next hour giggling at the silly antics of the city's elite—including Juliana's feigned betrothal with Lord Munthrope. However, the easy camaraderie that had always existed between them soon caused Juliana to spill all her current troubles to her friend, especially her father's worsening condition and the problems with Dutton Shipping. It felt good to confide in someone who cared, who understood, and whom she could trust.

"You were always so smart, Juliana. It surprises me not that you are able to stand in for your father and make a success of things."

"That's just it. Success seems rather elusive of late. And I don't know how much longer I can keep up the ruse."

Rising, she struck flint to steel and lit the lantern on the table to chase away the shadows. If only she could chase away her problems as easily. "Mayhap I shall be forced to join you here before too long." Juliana voiced her greatest fear. Abandoned by everyone. Left on the streets to rot.

"God forbid, my dear friend." Abilene's voice spiked with fear as she tried to rise, wincing in pain. "God forbid. Never! I won't allow it."

Juliana darted to her side, but the sound of boisterous laughter from below brought both their gazes to the door. "It darkens." Abilene gripped Juliana's hand. "You should get going."

Juliana nodded, saddened at the thought of leaving her friend in this place. "Oh, I nearly forgot." Opening her satchel, she pulled out a blanket, an old gown, some tallow candles, and a copy of *The Works of Sir John Suckling*.

Abilene received them with a smile, then shooed Juliana out before she could protest further.

With each tread of the stairs downward, her heart cinched tighter in her chest. The bawdy house was already brimming with patrons. An unkempt gentleman banged a tune on the harpsichord in the corner, while barmaids hoisted drinks on trays to thirsty customers. All eyes sped to her as she took the final step.

Mr. Pell was nowhere in sight.

Gulping down her fear, Juliana raised her chin and proceeded through the crowd as though she belonged there. Oddly, though the men gaped at her as if she were covered in gold, they made no move toward her nor uttered a single vulgar suggestion. Before she knew it, she stepped onto Thames Street and expelled a huge breath. The last remnants of the sun streaked saffron and magenta across the horizon, but soon the brilliant colors were swallowed up in gray as Juliana, heart still in her throat, gripped the high collar of her bodice and headed down the street.

Like cockroaches lured by the shadows, the port filled with an infestation of sailors, pirates, Navy men, and women of the night. A horse and rider clomped down the street, a carriage ambled by, bells tolled, hawkers shouted their wares, and off-pitch music blared from punch houses and taverns. The smell of manure and spirits assailed Juliana as she ducked beneath the covered porch of a butcher shop and prayed no one would pay her any mind.

No one did. They stared, some leered, but not a single man bothered her. She was about to turn the corner to make her way to Queen Street, when a man decked in tight leather breeches and jerkin, sporting a plumed castor, stepped into her path. Even in the shadows she could make out the mischievous grin of the Pirate Earl.

The jolt of her heart betrayed her. "Oh, 'tis only you." She kept the treasonous joy from her tone, while she cursed herself for her attraction to this ruffian.

"A pleasure to see you again as well, milady," he said in that unmistakable deep voice that never failed to melt her insides. He made a deep obeisance with a sweep of his feathered hat.

She brushed past him, knowing he'd follow as he always did. "I suppose I have you to thank for not being accosted."

"I accept your gratitude, paltry as it may be." He slipped beside her, the magnitude of his presence speeding up her heart.

"'Twould seem you have great power in Port Royal, Mr. Pirate. Perchance you could use it for less nefarious purposes."

"Milord Pirate, if you please, and alas, I believe I am. In protecting you."

She halted beneath a street lamp and studied him in its light. Coal-black hair stretched behind him in a tie, save one strand dangling over his forehead. Strong, shadowed jaw, aquiline nose, and lips that seemed stuck in a perpetual smirk. "I refer to halting your pillaging and plundering, sir."

His eyes twinkled. "One must start small on the road to redemption."

"And does bludgeoning a fellow pirate to near death suffice as a great start on this journey of light?" She tapped the tip of her parasol in the dirt.

For a moment he seemed perplexed. "Ah, you speak of Riley."

"Yes, Riley." She planted a hand at her waist. "You nearly killed him."

"*Nearly* being the operative word. And 'twas not me but my men who, dare I say, embellished a bit on my instructions." With finger and thumb he eased down the sides of his mouth, shooting a spark of familiarity through her.

And befuddling her mind. Still, hadn't Riley gotten what he deserved? She sighed. "It is unclear whether I should chastise you or thank you."

"Milord!" a man shouted from across the street.

Mr. Pirate nodded in return before he faced her again. "I much prefer your thanks."

His grin disarmed her. Clutching her skirts, she started walking again. Not because she wished to leave this man but because of the way he was looking at her.

As if she were a rare treasure he'd forfeit his life to protect.

"However, I do believe the weasel got the message," he said, keeping her pace. "I won't allow women to be thus treated in my town."

"Is it your town now?" She chuckled.

"Parts of it. The parts that you insist on visiting after dark." One brow lifted below a scarred divot in his forehead. Odd. 'Twas the same spot Munthrope always wore that silly horse patch. Why did she always think of that ninny when the Pirate Earl was near? Made no sense.

She frowned. "I was visiting Miss Abilene, if you must know. She looks well."

"I am pleased to hear it."

Stopping, she faced him. "'Tis due to your kindness, Mr. Pirate, though I have no idea why you would care for the wellbeing of a tavern wench."

"That kindness, milady, as foreign as it may seem for pirates, I owe to you." He rested his hand on the hilt of the cutlass hanging at his side. "I fear you bring out what little good remains in my dark soul." His tone lacked its usual taunt.

"Have a care, Mr. Pirate, I may reform you yet." She dared to smile.

"That is my undying hope."

His eyes pierced hers, the intensity within their blue depths sending her stomach awhirl.

What was she doing? She looked away. "Nevertheless, only God can cure a dark soul. I suggest you seek him out."

"I have, and alas, he is nowhere to be found."

"Then you have not looked hard enough." She hugged herself. "I intend to repay you for helping Abilene."

The touch of his finger on her cheek snapped her gaze to the mischievous glint in his eyes. "I can think of a number of ways." He smiled.

Jerking from his touch, she took a step back. "Money is all I have to offer." Though she had none at the moment. She started down the street again. A breeze stirred the hair hanging at her neck and brought an odd scent of cinnamon mixed with leather and gunpowder. It reminded her of something ... someone. But she didn't have time to ponder it before a band of colorfully-dressed men approached, spotted Mr. Pirate, and nodded toward him. Tipping their hats at her, they wove around them, one of them slapping Mr. Pirate on the arm. "Comely lass ye got there, milord."

Mr. Pirate winced and started to clutch his arm where the man had touched him, but then dropped his hand and acknowledged the men as they passed.

They walked on in silence. Light from street lamps gleamed off the brass-handled pistols stuffed in the baldric across his chest. His heavy boots crunched the sand. And Juliana desperately sought her mind for ways to be rid of him.

All the while desperately wanting him to stay.

"What is wrong with your arm?" she asked to break the silence.

"A bruise. 'Tis nothing."

"No doubt gained from murdering some poor Spanish sailor."

"I believe he was French, milady."

She knew he was teasing her. Or was he? No matter. It confirmed just how dangerous this man truly was. Something she must never forget.

She stopped in front of her house and faced him. "What is it you want from me, Mr. Pirate? And how do you know where I live?"

"I know everything about this town. And I merely seek your friendship."

"If you know everything, then you know that friendship is not within my power to give you."

He leaned toward her, his warm breath wafting over her cheek. "Oftimes friendship is not given but merely blossoms unannounced."

Stepping back from his nearness, she glanced at her home and released a heavy sigh. "I assure you nothing is blossoming in my life at the moment."

"Naught save the pink on your cheeks." He grinned.

"Merely from the walk, I assure you, Mr. Pirate." Though they both knew otherwise. The cocksure man could see how he affected her, just as he no doubt affected every woman in town. And she hated that. She would not be one the many ladies cooing and vying for a mere glance from the man. Then why was she standing here in front of her house like some lovesick minion unable to pull herself away?

"I have a gift for you." He reached within his jerkin.

She raised a palm to stop him. "Let me be unmistakably clear, Mr. Pirate. You are a thief and a murderer. I am a godly woman espoused to the son of an earl. I cannot—nor will I—accept any gifts from you. In good sooth, I must insist you leave me alone. In the future, should you happen upon me on the street, I beg, do not approach. You must never speak to me again. My reputation and my future insist upon it, sir."

Why was the infernal rogue still smiling? "I only wished to give you these." He pulled out a velvet pouch and handed it to her.

Setting down her satchel and parasol, she took it and loosened the string to peer inside.

Her heart stopped beating.

'Twas Mr. Kinder's missing pearls.

Chapter 24

THE SHOCK, DELIGHT, AND FINALLY appreciation beaming from Miss Juliana's face when she saw the pearls made Alex weak in the knees. And he was not a man given to being weak in the knees.

"Where did you get—" The delight vanished, replaced by reproach. "You!" Her eyes flashed fire. "You're the pirate who stole from my ship!" She punched him in the chest and then winced. It didn't stop her, however, from pounding him again and again, her frustration rising amidst groans and grunts and a few choice names such as "scamp!" and "vagabond!" and "miscreant!"

Alex heaved a sigh and stood his ground, allowing her temper to run its course, barely feeling her blows.

Which only seemed to infuriate her further.

"Ohhhhh!" She raised her fist for one more strike, when he caught it in midair.

"Milady, if you please. Hear me out."

"There is nothing to hear, *Pirate*!" She tore from his grip and grabbed her parasol, leveling it upon him like a sword.

Enchanting lady. Grinning, he ran a hand through his hair.

"You pretend to be my friend." She pressed the tip on his chest. "You pretend to protect and help me, while instead you seek information on the goods aboard my ships so you can pilfer them. Greedy, lowlife, son of a swine!" she seethed.

"Let's not bring my father into this, if you please," Alex remarked coolly. *Oh, but she was a wild cat, this one!*

She stabbed him with her parasol—hard—and he snagged it from her grasp. When she picked up her satchel and swung it at him, he ducked and took that from her too. Finally, she clutched the pearls to her chest, spearing him with a fiery gaze.

"I want nothing more to do with you." She turned to leave, but he snagged her wrist and held it fast. "Let me go, you beast. Mr. Abbot! Mr. Abbott!" But her home remained as quiet as a grave, the only sign of life a flickering light from an upstairs window.

"First of all"—Alex began above her protests—"you never told me of your shipment. I heard about it in town. All over town, in fact."

"What are you talking about?" She continued to struggle. "Who would know such a thing?"

"Your dear Captain Nichols, I'm afraid."

"Nichols?" She calmed and studied him. "Why would he …?"

Moonlight shimmered over her moist lips, and Alex licked his own, longing to kiss her. Instead, he released her hand and returned the parasol and satchel to her. She accepted them mutely, her eyes still interrogating him.

"As to how he obtained the information, I have no clue," Alex said. "As to the why he released it about town, 'twas to bait me, of course. He's been trying to catch me for years." He shrugged. "Some sort of personal vendetta, if you will."

"Then why were you the only pirate to attempt to steal the pearls? Surely every greedy thief in town would have converged on my ship that night."

"Because pirates may be many things, milady, but we are not bird-wits. Traps are something we can smell oceans away."

"Perchance there is something wrong with *your* nose then, Mr. Pirate?" She smirked.

"Nay"—he leaned toward her and drew in a breath—"your scent is quite lovely as usual."

She backed away while a divot appeared between her eyebrows. "Why take the risk of stealing the pearls only to return them to me?"

"For the fun, the challenge." He grinned. "The chance to infuriate that fluff-head Nichols."

Her jaw stiffened. "You play games with my family's future, sir."

"Lud, I knew not it was your father's brig, milady. Not until I had the pearls in hand."

A horse and rider trotted by as a burst of wind stirred the golden strands at her neck. She studied him. "What is it between you and Captain Nichols? Why do you hate each other so? It goes beyond his job as a naval officer to capture you."

Alex shifted his boots in the sand. "I have many enemies."

"Of that I have no doubt." She gave a ladylike snort, then clutched the pearls to her chest as if her life depended on them. Mayhap it did.

"Whether you believe me or not, I am glad to see the pearls back in your possession."

"What devilry are you about, Mr. Pirate? For I still cannot comprehend why you would return them. What kind of pirate are you?"

"A gentleman pirate, milady." He bowed. And one who now must pay his crew out of his own fortune—money he'd had to sell a few valuables to acquire since he rarely kept that large a sum in his house.

But it was worth the look on this lovely lady's face.

He no sooner rose from his bow when a roar much like thunder sounded, and the ground jolted beneath their feet. He clutched Juliana's arm. Sand rippled across the street like waves at sea. It lasted but a few seconds, then all was quiet.

She caught her breath, staring wildly about as if it would happen again. "We've been getting quakes a lot lately."

"Indeed, 'tis one of the exciting things about living in Port Royal."

Her chest rose and fell as she glanced at her house. "I perceive that your view of excitement and mine are quite the opposite, Mr. Pirate."

Reluctantly releasing her arm, Alex dared to raise his hand and run the back of his finger over her cheek.

She jerked back. "Do not presume, *Pirate*, that returning my pearls will grant you access to my bed."

Alex gave her an inviting grin. "Are you sure that is not what you want?"

"You brazen oaf! Of course not! How dare you!" She turned to leave.

He stopped her with a touch. A mere touch was all it took. Despite her bluster. And Alex longed to draw her close. To protect her. To comfort her. And to keep her with him forever. Instead, he backed away. "I will be away for a while. Weeks, mayhap a month."

"Pirating?" She raised one eyebrow.

"What else?" He grinned. "Never fear, I shall see you upon my return."

"Nay, you shall not, sir! I meant what I said earlier. You are not to speak to me ever again."

Yet she remained in place, staring at him as if she wished him to challenge such a ridiculous demand. Was it possible the lady felt something for him? He quickly prolonged the conversation. "Faith now, milady. How are you to reform my dark heart if we remain apart?"

"That is not my concern."

"Yet I thought 'twas a Christian's duty to save sinners from hell."

Her gaze skittered over the street. "For a heathen, you know much about Scripture."

Before she could stop him, he brushed fingers over her cheek yet again, murmuring, "I know that you are an angel sent from heaven."

To his surprise, she closed her eyes. Her lashes fluttered. He caressed her jaw. She trembled. He eased a lock of hair behind her ear. She gasped. He inched his hand behind her neck and drew her close. She did not resist. Then, leaning over, he gently brushed his lips over hers. Her breath caught. The pulse in her throat thumped madly beneath his hand.

Abruptly, she tore from him, raised a hand to her mouth, and dashed into her house.

Juliana burst into her bedchamber and closed the door quietly instead of slamming it like she desired. Leaning back against the sturdy wood, she flung both hands to her heaving chest as she gazed into the darkness. She'd allowed the Pirate Earl to kiss her. The horror! The shame!

The ecstasy ...

Yes, she'd enjoyed it. More than enjoyed it. Though it was but a whisper of a kiss, a bare touch of their lips, she'd felt like her spirit had left her body and soared through the heavens.

Falling on her knees beside her bed, she clasped her hands together and begged forgiveness for her wantonness with a heathen pirate while she was betrothed to another. Surely all her good deeds of late would make up for this one tiny mistake? Oh, she must try much harder to be good, to be chaste. How could she expect God to help her when she was so weak? *Thank you, Lord, for returning the pearls, but I beg you, please forgive me for my weakness.*

Even as she prayed, her traitorous body tingled in remembrance of the Pirate Earl's lips brushing against hers. Angry at herself, she rose, lit a candle, and took up a pace over her Turkish carpet, wringing her hands and biting her lip. Finally, she plucked her violin from its stand, grabbed a bow, and began to play—a lively tune she hoped would lift her spirits. But after a while, the melody turned melancholy until tears streamed down her face. She put her violin down and batted them away.

Sighing heavily, she strode to the window and pulled back the drapes. Clouds obscured the heavenly lights and oppressed the town with a darkness she could feel in her soul. How could she understand her attraction to him? A man whose vile deeds should send her running in the other direction. Not into his arms.

Thunder growled in the distance, and a burst of rain-spiced wind whipped around her, spinning loose strands of her hair into a frenzy. Street lanterns dotted the city like stars on a night sky. She hugged herself and leaned against the window frame. Confusion spun her thoughts into bedlam. Nothing in her life was going well. A strange ailment afflicted the poor orphans. Regardless of the return of the pearls, Dutton Shipping was failing. Rowan had some nefarious alliance with Captain Nichols that could only spell disaster—she would have to have a word with Nichols about using her ship as bait. And her father was not getting better.

Worse, Juliana had fallen for a pirate. Not just any pirate, but the most notorious pirate in Port Royal. No wonder God was displeased with her.

Nay! She stomped her foot. With the huge burden she bore daily, 'twas no wonder her emotions were riotous. Yes, surely that was the reason for her wayward desires. Besides, hadn't her heart recently softened toward Munthrope? He was a silly fop, to be sure, but nonetheless a gentleman with fortune and good breeding. Perchance her feminine compass was not totally askew.

Oh, fie, what was she thinking? She had no need of a man at all. Especially not one who would abandon her. And both Lord Munthrope and the Pirate Earl were temperamental enough to do just that. Nay, she could take care of herself. She would make Dutton Shipping successful if it was the last thing she did. Her father would recover soon. And then all would be well.

She gazed up at the dark, broiling clouds hanging so low she could almost touch them. "God Almighty, I promise to do better. I promise to care more for others, to be a better daughter and sister and friend and to help those in need. And I promise never again to … to speak to the Pirate Earl."

Movement below drew her gaze. A man dressed in leather stepped from beneath a tree into the light of a street lantern. Even from where she stood, she could feel his penetrating gaze upon her before he flipped his hat atop his head and strode away.

"Miss Juliana! Miss Juliana!" A voice, distant and hollow, pierced Juliana's blissful fog of sleep. She ignored it. She preferred the fog—the peace, the serenity of unconsciousness to whatever she would face when the day dawned.

Still the shouts persisted … desperate … tormented. Someone grabbed her shoulder and shook her, whisking the fog away and sparking her mind to life. What she wouldn't give for a few more moments, just a few precious seconds in which she didn't carry the weight of the world.

"Miss Juliana! He's dying. Get up. You must get up." Miss Ellie's frantic tone snapped Juliana's eyes open. The maid's face hovered over her—a round specter haloed by a candlelit mob cap. Shoving her quilt aside, Juliana flung on her robe and dashed to her father's room, Miss Ellie whimpering behind her.

The chamber smelled of death. Sour and rot and hopelessness. She knew the scent well. It had hovered over her mother for days before she passed. On one side of her father's bed stood Mr. Abbot, a mournful look on his face. On the other, stood Cook, wringing her hands. And in the middle, shriveled up like a used rag, lay her father, the slight rise and fall of his bony chest the only indication that he still hung onto life.

Miss Ellie ran to kneel beside him, gripping his hand and sobbing.

Horror numbed Juliana. All she could manage was, "Where's Rowan?"

"He's not come home yet, miss," Abbot said. "Shall I go look for him?"

"Nay." There was no point. Rowan would come home when Rowan was ready to come home.

Candlelight angled over Cook's face as she passed Juliana and murmured, "I'll brew some tea, miss." As if a cup of tea would make the world right again.

Juliana swallowed and approached her father, easing onto the bed beside him, expecting the usual castigation—and oddly feeling sad when it didn't come. Instead, he struggled to open his eyes and turned toward Ellie. "Ah, stop your crying, sweet Ellie. We knew a cantankerous old sod like me wouldn't live out his days." His voice sounded so very weak.

"Don't be sayin' sich things, sir."

"Henry. Please use my Christian name." He rasped out a cough that seemed to pain him. "Just once."

Juliana was stunned by the affection between the maid and her father.

"Henry." Ellie said the word with reverence, then took his hand and pressed her cheek against it, tears slipping from her eyes. "You cannot leave. I won't stand for it."

He squeezed her hand. "A man knows when he's done for." He coughed again, the effort exhausting him. He closed his eyes and his shallow breathing became hoarse and labored. Blood trickled from one side of his mouth, and Juliana dabbed it with a rag, forcing back her tears.

He slowly turned and faced her, surprise flickering across his expression as if he hadn't realized she was there. "Juliana."

"Yes, Papa. I'm here," she choked out as emotion seared her throat.

"'Twould seem you and Abbot got what you wanted." He snorted with his usual disdain.

"Papa, don't say such things. All we wanted was for you to get well."

He seemed ready to argue, but released a sigh instead as if he had no fight left in him. "I've not been a good father to you," he finally whispered and closed his eyes again.

Now the tears came, spilling down her cheeks and dripping from her jaw into her lap. All her life she'd waited to hear those words. All her life she'd desperately longed to hear his admission of guilt—that he'd treated her and Rowan terribly and was sorry for it, that mayhap somewhere deep inside, he loved them. But hearing the words now brought her no comfort.

"It doesn't matter, Papa. All that matters is that you ask forgiveness from God and go to him in peace."

He closed his eyes and frowned. "Never was much for religion."

"Papa, please." No matter how cruelly he had treated her mother and her and Rowan, she didn't wish him to suffer the fires of hell.

"Do as she says, sir—Henry. I want to see you agin." Miss Ellie drew his gaze, and there it remained, for only upon the sweet maid's face did a spark of joy touch his eyes. Never when he looked at Juliana. Had he ever loved her at all?

He drew a raspy breath. "I regret …" He halted and released a shuddering sigh. Then his eyes went hard and cold. A breeze fluttered the candle by his bed, flickering ribbons of light and dark over his still form.

"No!" Ellie lifted his hand to her lips. "No!"

Juliana bowed her head and sobbed. Now what would she do?

Chapter 25

A BLAST OF MUGGY AIR SWAMPED Juliana as she left her house and stepped onto the street. Mrs. Childers waved at her from across the way where she escorted her two children to their waiting carriage. Juliana waved back, forcing a difficult smile on her lips. She must keep up appearances. She must not let anyone suspect that her father had departed into eternity. For the past two weeks she had not put on her mourning gown, nor had she kept to the house, or called on friends for comfort.

Egad! She had not even put her father to rest.

Though she had wanted to do all of those things—wanted so desperately to allow herself to grieve. To grieve for the loss of her last parent, at being left all alone in the world, and for the responsibility that now weighed solely on her shoulders. But she hadn't. She had a business to run, mouths to feed, and appearances to make. How long she could do any of those things, she had no idea.

Especially not alone. Rowan had finally come home early the morning her father died, drunk as usual, though he appeared to sober up the instant he saw Father's body. Falling by his side, Rowan had wept far longer than Juliana would have expected for a boy who'd been nothing but belittled by the man. The sight had brought renewed tears to her eyes just when she'd thought she had no more to shed. Then, with more maturity than she believed he possessed,

Rowan assisted Mr. Abbot in washing Papa's body and dressing him in his best suit. Abbot quickly went to work building a simple wooden coffin and once finished, he coated the inside with the tar Dutton Shipping used on their brigs to preserve wood and rigging. Afterward, they wrapped her father in several clean quilts then carefully laid him inside and sealed the outside with the same tar. It was the best they could think to do in order to keep the odor down until they could bury him properly.

Hope waning, she turned onto High Street as a carriage clattered by. A bell tolled from the bay, while a flock of gulls soared overhead. Waves of heat rose from the ground and rippled through her as her guilt was doing. But what else could they do? Since there was only one cemetery in town, they could hardly place him there without the entire city knowing. Of course they could sneak him to the mainland at night and bury him in the jungle, but Juliana couldn't bring herself to force such an indignity upon her father.

Which is why she needed Lord Munthrope. He was the only one who had known about her father's condition, and his silence thus far on that matter engendered her to trust him once more. He had friends on the city council and surely could arrange a proper burial for an unnamed acquaintance. But after sending several posts to his home, begging to meet him, she'd not heard a word in return. Against all propriety, she'd even called upon him one day, only to be turned away by his impudent butler Mr. Whipple with the excuse that His Lordship wasn't home, and he had no idea when he would return.

Now, as she made her way to the orphanage, she wondered if she'd been wrong about Munthrope all along. Mayhap his kindness had just been part of their act to keep his father's interests in Munthrope's marriage status at bay. And when her company didn't aid that cause, he had no need of her.

The sweet smell of bananas, papayas, and breadfruit swept away her gloomy thoughts as she passed the market and waved at the plump mulatto woman standing behind her cart.

"Fresh mangos fer the young'nes, Miss Juliana," she shouted.

"Not today, Sally. Thank you," Juliana replied, wishing she *could* purchase some fruit. But she had only enough funds to pay her staff and provide food for the next few months. In a week, the *Esther's Dowry* would be loaded with sugar, coffee, yams, indigo, and logwood headed for the American colonies. The profit from their shipment should provide enough to live on for several months. Then, of course the *Ransom*, their third brig, was due to sail into port from Liverpool in thirteen days.

The *Ransom*. Just the thought of it sent warmth through her. Not the ship itself but the name her mother had given it. Her father had named their other two brigs, but had allowed his wife, after much pleading from her, this one privilege. When Juliana had inquired as to the meaning of the name, her mother had quoted from Hosea:

I will ransom them from the power of the grave; I will redeem them from death: O death, I will be thy plagues; O grave, I will be thy destruction.

A smile had graced her mother's delicate lips and a gleam sparkled in her eye as if she'd looked upon God himself as she spoke. Juliana had always been envious of her mother's relationship with the Almighty—one of love and companionship, not obedience and servitude.

Yet, as it turned out, God hadn't ransomed Juliana's mother from the grave at all.

Frowning, Juliana brought her thoughts back to Dutton Shipping. Everything was about perfect timing, good wind, and fair weather. And no pirates. Pirates like the Pirate Earl. Nay. In good sooth, he *had* returned her pearls. Or rather, Mr.

Kinder's pearls, who—praise be to God—had promptly forgiven all and went on his way.

Albeit with threats to return and visit her father.

Which now would never happen. She cringed once again at the thought of her father rotting away in a coffin in his bedchamber. Another blemish on her wayward soul. Along with the liberties she'd allowed the Pirate Earl. Not just allowed, but enjoyed! *The shame!* She made no doubt the rogue had all but forgotten the incident, so many were the kisses he likely received—or stole. 'Twas nothing to him. Just another lady overcome by his masculine charm.

She had begged God for forgiveness and for help to forget the scoundrel, and thus far, the Almighty had been silent. Just another sign she needed to try harder to behave.

Releasing a heavy sigh, she dabbed the perspiration on her neck.

Nevertheless, with the Pirate Earl out plundering, Munthrope ignoring her, and Rowan gone for days on end drinking and gambling, Juliana felt more alone than she ever had. Of course she had Abbot, who, though he was still learning how to manage the business, was an invaluable helper and friend. And also Miss Ellie, whom Juliana doubted would ever leave her side. Regardless, she could not stop the despondency that weighed on her as she passed Gallows Point on her left and Bridewell Prison on her right— a prison for lazy strumpets, or so they said. The orphanage certainly wasn't in the best part of town, but it was daylight, and Mr. Pell was nowhere to be found to drive her.

Hefting the sack filled with fabric, an assortment of bowls and spoons, and a few medical supplies, she made the final turn toward the orphanage. Crumbling stone walls enclosed a front yard filled with palms and a weed-infested vegetable garden. To her left stood the old church, used only for storage now, and toward the back was the brick building, where she could hear young ones playing. She opened the door to an explosion of happy greetings and smiling faces. It had been far too long since she'd visited, and the children's yelps of delight did much to soothe her agitated soul.

Kneeling, she dropped the sack and opened her arms to embrace as many of the sweet urchins as she could in one swoop. The scent of lye and sunshine and innocence filled her lungs and put a smile on her face. The first one since her father had died.

But Eunice's frown, when she entered from the side room, quickly dissipated Juliana's joy. The woman attempted a pleased expression, but Juliana had known her too long to be fooled.

"What is amiss?" She stood and hoisted little Rose into her arms.

Eunice wiped her hands on her stained apron as the monkey skittered across the rafters, chattering and eliciting giggles from some of the children.

"You haven't gotten rid of the beast yet?" Juliana asked as the creature jumped onto her shoulder and swung one hairy arm around her head and one around Rose's. The little girl laughed, and the monkey leaned against her cheek to cheek.

"You see why I hasn't, Miss Juliana. He's a smart one. He knows if he wins the children's hearts, he ain't goin' nowheres."

The monkey planted a kiss on Juliana's cheek, and then gave her a wide grin as if he understood everything Eunice had said.

"Now, children, go play fer a minute. I needs to talk wit' Miss Juliana." Eunice clapped her hands, and the children obligingly scattered. The monkey too. He leapt into the rafters as Juliana deposited Rose on the floor. Then, stepping over a bucket filled with water, she followed Eunice into the other room, where not only Michael lay on his pallet, but three other children as well.

"Oh no." Juliana dashed to the first one, Moses, a two-year-old Negro, and laid a hand on his head. Hot as a griddle.

And young Mable, too, on the pallet next to his. Along with Gordon, not yet six. Lastly, Michael, who had grown even more gaunt and listless since the last time she'd seen him.

"I kin hardly keep anythin' down him that he don't spit right back up," Eunice said, her face scrunched in worry.

Isaac entered. "We're keeping the other children away from them as much as we can. Do you think it's the pox?"

"What does Dr. Vern say?"

"He ain't been here."

"Not been here?" Juliana shook her head, disgusted. She knew some doctors refused to care for the indigent, but she had thought Dr. Verns a more charitable sort. Gazing over the sick children, her stomach sank like a rock. She would not lose these precious children. She could *not* lose them. She must find a way.

Alex stood at the bow of the *Vanity*, hand gripping the back stay as the ship rose and plunged through the agitated sea. Agitated like his heart, his spirit—if men actually possessed such things. Wind flapped his shirt and whipped strands of hair across his cheek. He drew in a deep breath of the briny sea and waited for the sense of satisfaction that normally filled him when he was on his ship.

It never came.

It should have come, for it had been a successful raid. Very successful, indeed. They'd captured a Spanish merchantman headed for Santo Domingo loaded with spices from the Orient, fine china, silk tapestries, silverware, and best of all, a chest of rare gems. All of which they had traded in Tortuga for pieces of eight, along with the ship itself. No sense in returning to Port Royal loaded with plunder that would give Nichols cause to search Alex's brig. He supposed, due to the hostilities with France, he should acquire a commission to privateer from the Jamaican Council and do away with his illegal trade. But where would the fun be in that?

The brig dove, sending water over the bow. Sea foam snaked about his boots. Alex snorted. Staying one step ahead of Captain Nincompoop offered no challenge at all. At the very least the man should try harder, seek advice from more intellectually-endowed men, in order to hatch a plan that would not bore Alex to his grave. Lud, was there no one who could surprise him?

Visions of Miss Juliana Dutton filled his mind. As they so often had these past three weeks. He missed her. Terribly. Which surprised him. But why should it? Everything about her surprised him. He hoped she fared well in his absence. He hoped she hadn't visited Miss Abilene alone. And with the pearls returned, he hoped her shipping business thrived.

All questions that had prompted him to tack the *Vanity* about and head home. Another question that had burned on his mind since they'd left Port Royal was why information about the shipping date and cargo of one of Miss Juliana's merchant brigs had been on the lips of every shop owner, tavern keeper, and hooligan in town. The *Esther's Dowry* should have set sail yesterday, in fact, from Port Royal to the American colonies. Local wealthy plantation owners, Mr. and Mrs. Gerald Hornspike were listed as passengers, bearing a chest full of coins meant as a dowry for their eldest daughter in Boston. Information neither a merchant nor a shipping company would want leaked to every greedy sot in town.

Alex guessed it to be the workings of Captain Nincompoop.

But what the scatter-wit didn't realize—or mayhap didn't care—was that in his paltry efforts to capture Alex, he'd alerted half the pirates in Port Royal, especially those clumsy sluggards who sought an easy prize. None of them would attempt to approach the *Esther's Dowry* until she was at least a day's journey from port. And by Alex's calculations, they should be upon her general position any time now.

Larkin appeared beside him. "We should arrive in Port Royal by tomorrow evening, Captain."

Alex nodded, staring out over the expanse of glittering turquoise, then up at the sun atop their heads. "Maintain course."

The sailing master hesitated, then crossed arms over his chest. "But why go back to Port Royal? We are well supplied from our stop in Tortuga. No one is injured, and the men are itching for another prize, Captain."

"They'll get another prize soon enough."

Sails thundered overhead. Larkin's jaw tightened. "The crew will not be pleased."

The brig pitched over a wave, and Alex braced his boots on the deck as seawater sprayed them. He was glad for the cooling effect on his rising temper. He turned to Larkin and eyed him curiously, wondering why his one-time friend seemed to defy him at every turn. "They know who brings them their prizes. As do *you*. If any are dissatisfied, they are free to join another captain."

Wind whipped Larkin's dark hair into his eyes. He snapped it away as a tight smile strung upon his lips. "Of course, Captain."

Something in the man's expression irked Alex, reminding him of a similar expression he'd born when Alex had demanded the man turn over a piece of treasure from the Spanish merchantman. "You didn't keep that silk tapestry from Madrid you were salivating over?"

Larkin kept his face to the wind, his jaw flexing. "Would I disobey my captain?"

Alex feared the answer to that was a definite yes. Especially when it came to something Larkin had taken a particular fancy to. The tapestry was small, old, and not extremely valuable, but Alex's crew was forbidden to keep any treasure not divided equally among them. Doing so was punishable by death. Not to mention, Alex must have nothing on board that would implicate them in piracy.

Larkin had not hidden his anger at Alex's command to sell it along with the other goods.

A call came down from the tops. "A sail. A sail!"

Plucking the scope from his belt, Alex leveled it on the horizon and was about to ask the direction, when another call came down. "Two sets of sails. Two sets!"

Which meant there was either a convoy or one ship pursued the other.

He shifted the glass until the tall masts and bloated sails of a ship came in sight. No, a brig, a merchant brig. And the other one a smaller ship, a sloop most likely. Turning, he marched across the foredeck and leapt into the waist, Larkin on his heels.

"Step lively, men! I want every stitch of canvas spread!" Alex turned to Larkin. "Bring us to windward of them, if you please."

"To windward, Captain." Larkin faced the crew. "Lay aloft, topmen! Man top halliards and sheets! Let fall main and fore-topsails!"

Pirates flung into the shrouds, scrambling aloft, and soon all sails caught the stiff breeze in a thunderous snap. Hauled to the wind, the *Vanity* tacked toward the ships. Blocks creaked and sails rattled as the brig rose and swooped through the foamy sea. Alex took his position on the quarterdeck by the helm, scope pressed to his eye to survey the oncoming ships.

An hour later, with all sails glutted and black squalls crashing over the bow, Alex could make out the Dutton Shipping ensign as well as the name *Esther's Dowry* painted in red on the hull of the first ship. The poor merchant captain marched across the deck in a frenzy, barking orders to a crew that darted about like ants whose hill had been stepped on.

Fast pursuing on his stern, *The Sea King* bore down upon her, captained by that heartless toad Snead, whose lack of intelligence was only exceeded by his girth.

Jonas appeared from below, where he'd been keeping accounts of the divided treasure from their last prize. He slipped beside Alex and gripped the railing, refusing to look his way. He didn't have to. Alex could feel his disapproval from where he stood. Sunlight glinted red streaks in Jonas's light hair as the wind tore strands from its tie.

Alex grew impatient. "Well?"

"Well what, Captain?"

"Surely you have some opinion you wish to lavish upon me."

The ship bucked, and Jonas gripped the railing tighter. "Only that you are, yet again, plundering your own countryman's goods, I see."

"Things are not always what they seem, my friend." Turning, Alex scanned the main deck for Bait, his master gunner. "Bait! Ready the gun crew! Clean the tackles and load and run out the guns!"

The large Negro saluted with his one remaining hand and lumbered off.

Larkin approached, greedily eyeing their prey. "Seems we aren't the only ones interested in capturing this rare prize. Swounds! The *Sea King* will get to her first!"

Indeed. Alex stared at the *Esther's Dowry,* who now lowered sails in a sign of surrender. With nary a shot fired! No doubt the poor captain assumed he faced two pirates instead of one. The *Sea King* also lowered sails and would be alongside the merchantman in minutes.

"Orders?" Larkin said, his tone both angry and excited.

Jonas shot Alex an incriminating glance. "Be done with this pirating and let's be away, Captain."

Ignoring him, Alex slapped the spyglass against his palm. "Let us inform our dear friend Captain Snead that he has trespassed onto our hunting grounds, shall we? Lower fore and main. Bring her in slow under tops," he ordered Larkin before moving to the quarterdeck railing and shouted down at his master gunner. "Bait, a warning shot over the pirate's bow when you have it."

"Aye, aye, Cap'n."

"I see, Captain! Get rid of the competition, and we shall take the spoil." Larkin flashed delighted brows at Alex before he began spouting orders to the crew.

Alex didn't inform him that they'd take no spoil today.

Within minutes a thunderous boom etched across the sky and quaked the ship from bow to stern. Gunpowder stung Alex's nose as he peered through the gray smoke. Would the inbred captain heed the warning? Surely he'd spotted the Pirate Earl's flag. Not many would dare cross a man whose reputation at sea battle was the talk of Port Royal. Besides, Alex wouldn't mind a joust with one of his own. He'd been battling merchants far too long and could use a challenge.

But true to form, Captain Snead withdrew like the coward he was. After staring at Alex through his glass for what seemed like an eternity, he turned and stomped across his deck like an obese duck, all the while barking orders to his crew that sent them flinging aloft. Soon, with all sails to the wind, he tacked aweather, flashing Alex his stern as he tucked tail and ran.

Alex was about to bellow orders to put the helm over and leave the *Esther's Dowry* behind, when another shout came from above. "A third sail!"

White canvas gleaming in the afternoon sun, a Royal Navy frigate, blue-and-white flag flapping from the masthead, dipped and plunged toward them, a mustache of foam spread across her bow.

Alex gripped the railing and shared a glance with Jonas.

"Nichols," they both said at once.

"We can take the merchant before he arrives," Larkin shouted up from the main deck.

Alex eyed the frigate. Aye, he agreed. They'd have to be quick about it, but they could do it. And if it were any other merchantman, he'd welcome the thrill of trying. But not Miss Juliana's brig. Before Alex could issue the command to turn to starboard, Larkin's voice thundered from below. "Arm yourselves, men. We've another prize to take!"

"Nay, belay that order!" Alex approached the railing, hands fisted on his hips, giving Larkin the full measure of an angry glare.

His crew, an assortment of slovenly, foul-mouthed men, stood on the main deck with greedy grins that soon turned to frowns as their gazes shifted between him and Larkin.

"We've enough spoils for now," Alex shouted above the wind. "What say you we go home and spend our wealth?"

This did not elicit the "ayes" and "huzzahs" he'd hoped for. Instead, a couple of the men spit on the deck. Others stared longingly at the merchant brig—which quickly raised sails in an effort to escape the remaining pirate—while a few glared at Alex as if they intended to hack him to pieces.

"I says we take 'er, Cap'n!" one man shouted.

"Aye! Aye! She's easy pickin's!"

"I say we put it to a vote." Larkin's eyes turned narrow and cold. "As is the crew's prerogative."

A grumbling of ascent waved through the crowd.

Larkin was right, blast him. It wasn't purely Alex's decision—not according to the articles they'd signed. As he saw it, he had two choices. Steal from the woman he loved and thereby aid in ruining her forever. Or risk a mutiny in which he'd most likely end up dead.

Chapter 26

IT'S A TRAP, YOU FLEA-INFESTED toads! Can't you see that?" Jonas stepped forward and gripped the quarterdeck railing, gazing down upon the crew. "That ship"—he pointed to the sails growing larger on the horizon—"is a Royal Navy frigate. And she's just waiting for us to capture the British merchantman so she can haul us in and string us up. Our captain here is attempting to save your worthless necks."

Some of the men rubbed their throats at the declaration while Alex gave Jonas a nod of thanks.

"But ye ain't never run from no Navy ship afore!"

"Aye, an' we's got time!"

"Are you as daft as you look?" Jonas bellowed. "The Navy will witness the crime and give chase. And when they catch us, you'll forfeit every last piece-of-eight you earned from our last prize."

This seemed to get some of their miniscule brains thinking.

"But ain't no Navy ship fast enough to catch the Pirate Earl!" Cheers and fists thrust into the air, making Alex proud of his crew's confidence in him. Though he wished they had less at the moment.

Larkin leapt onto the quarterdeck ladder and glanced over the men. "We chased off that toad, Snead, and I say we claim our prize!"

Roars of agreement followed.

"Unless you've gone yellow-bellied, Captain?" Larkin sneered at Alex.

And just like a fickle female, the crew spit and cursed their agreement.

Alex gave Larkin a smoldering look. How could his friend defy him so vehemently in front of the crew? And why was he gripping the hilt of his sword as if he would draw on Alex any moment?

Alex glanced down upon his men, most of whom were scowling his way. He roared above wind and wave, "This yellow-bellied captain has kept you all alive and swimming in gold. And you dare defy me now? I make no doubt Mr. Larkin is a great orator, but so is the Devil, and both will send you straight to hell."

The pirates' faces twisted as they pondered this new revelation.

Gaining Alex's attention, Jonas nodded toward the frigate—clearly Nichols's ship, HMS *Viper*—which was nigh upon the merchant brig.

And far too close to them now.

"Then let's have that vote, shall we?" Bracing his boots on the rocking deck, Alex fisted hands at his waist and waited for the pirates to realize they had lost their chance to take the merchantman and escape. One by one, their gazes drifted aloft and one by one their eyes widened until finally they sprang into the shrouds. Larkin—after casting a seething look toward Alex—began braying orders to hoist all sail.

Something sharp pounded through Rowan's head, like the galloping of a dozen horses. Horses with spikes on their shoes, apparently. He moaned and attempted to push himself up from the settee onto which he'd fallen late last night. Or had it been morning?

"I asked you a question, sir."

Rowan held up a hand at the hazy form of Captain Nichols, who had suddenly appeared before him—disturbing a rather pleasant dream of a tryst with two doxies. "Please lower your voice, Captain. No need to shout."

"I'm not shouting, you fool." The captain frowned. "You're drunk."

Nay, if Rowan was drunk, his head wouldn't be splitting and his stomach wouldn't feel like he'd consumed a keg of sour milk. He belched, the smell confirming his suspicion about his stomach. "To my utter dismay, I fear I am not drunk, Captain, but do give me a minute." Shoving to his feet, he ignored the spinning room and stumbled to the cupboard, where a decanter of rum sat sparkling in a ray of afternoon sun angling through the windows.

He tossed a glassful to the back of his mouth. "Ah …" The pungent liquid spiraled through him, untying knots where knots ought not be and numbing places that were too painful to consider. For the past two weeks—or had it been three?—Rowan had dwelt in a murky world of cards, rum, and women: the only alternative to facing the death of his father along with the mounting responsibilities left him for the welfare of his sister and Dutton Shipping.

"What has you in such a pother, Nichols?"

"What has me in a pother? I'll tell you. It's that infernal Pirate Earl. Do you recall the trap we set for him with one of your ships?"

Rowan searched his memory, dull as it was. "Ah yes. The rumors we spread about the dowry on board."

"Yes, that one. Does your curiosity not demand to know what happened?"

Rowan opened his mouth to inform the man that his curiosity had been sated with rum, but Nichols proceeded with his tirade as he took up a pace before the window. "He protected your ship."

Rowan poured another drink and lumbered back to his seat, unsure he heard the man correctly. "Protected?"

"Can you believe it? I certainly wouldn't have, unless I'd seen it with my own eyes." Sunlight gleamed off Nichols's white periwig as, with hands clenched behind his back, he made good work of the rug before the window. "He protected your brig from another pirate intent on taking her. And then proceeded to sail away, leaving her be."

"Astonishing." Rowan's chuckle faltered on his lips beneath Nichols's glare. He sipped his drink, relishing in the sudden apathy that swept through his brain, dulling his pain with it. "Seems your Pirate Earl has outwitted you once again."

"Don't be absurd. He has no more wits than morals." Nichols's face reddened. "Nay, there is something else afoot." Halting, he tapped his chin. "Why would a pirate not capture prey?"

"Mayhap he was tired."

Nichols's look of disgust could melt iron.

Rowan rubbed the bridge of his nose. "He must have spotted you."

"He had plenty of time, I tell you. Plenty of time! Nay, there is something going on here, and I intend to discover what it is." Nichols stormed toward Rowan and took a seat in a chair, leaning toward him. "In the meantime, what have you learned about Lord Munthrope? Or have you found time to pull away from your *affair d'coeur* with rum and gambling to earn your pay?"

Rowan frowned. He was going to need another drink if the man didn't leave soon. "I've done as you asked, but there's naught to learn. The man is simply who he appears to be: the wealthy son of an earl squandering his father's fortune on high living. Besides, he hasn't appeared in society for nigh three weeks. Every time I called upon him, he was not home. Nor has anyone in society seen him. He was neither at the Chilling's Tea nor the Bedford Soiree, nor the play at Chaucers. His butler merely says His Lordship is busy with business."

"Business? What business?"

"How should I know? Mayhap something of his father's."

"His father was a"—Nichols froze, a tiny smile forming on his impervious lips—"pirate." He grabbed his tricorne from the table and started for the foyer. Halting at the door, he glanced up the grand staircase. "I don't suppose your sister is home?"

"I have no idea."

"Your butler said she wasn't, but I haven't seen her in quite some time." Nichols gazed at him suspiciously. "Nor your father, for that matter. Odd."

His headache worsening, Rowan took another sip of rum and struggled to rise. "The whereabouts of my family is none of your business, Captain. And though I marvel at your concern, I assure you they are both well."

"Humph." Nichols assessed him for a moment, then slapped his hat atop his head. "Then I bid you good day."

"What of my pay?" Rowan held out a hand. "You promised me ten shillings a week."

Nichols snorted. "For what? You've produced nothing of value. We've not caught the Pirate Earl nor have you dug up any skullduggery on Lord Munthrope. Our deal is off, sir. And might I make a suggestion?"

Rowan would rather he not, especially after hearing he was completely and utterly destitute once again.

"Clean yourself up, man. Do away with this roistering and assist your father with the family business. Or better yet, join His Majesty's Navy. Make something of yourself. This idle dissipation is no way to live."

Rowan's glare followed Nichols out the door. His idle dissipation was a far better way to live than slaving one's life away at hard labor only to die young and leave it all behind. As both his parents had done.

Or perchance Rowan was simply what his father had always claimed—a useless sot.

Juliana gestured toward the stone bench in her mother's garden. "Won't you have a seat, Lord Munthrope?"

"I wish you'd call me Munny, sweetums, like all my friends." Sunlight dappled glitter over his beribboned sleeves as he twirled, arms lifted, and promptly took a seat.

"And I wish you'd call me Miss Juliana, as is proper."

He wrinkled his nose. "Not for my betrothed."

Turning her back to him, Juliana dipped her nose to her mother's heliotrope and breathed in the sweet vanilla scent. If only for the courage to ask what she must of this foppish man. "But ours is not a true engagement, milord, now, is it?" She spun to face him, her skirts brushing against a nearby shrub. "Otherwise you would have answered my many urgent requests to see you these past three weeks."

His dark brows rose, lifting the silly horse patch atop his right eye. "I came as soon as I could, mil—Miss Juliana." His frown held regret as he suddenly stood, flipped the long curls of his periwig over his shoulder, and took her hand in his. "I am here now." He leaned to gaze into her eyes, surprising her with how blue his were—deep blue like the sea, yet with specks of gray that glimmered with concern.

He pulled her down to the bench and sat beside her, still gripping her hand, running his thumb over the tops of her fingers. Odd, but his skin felt rough and scratchy. So unlike the hands of a man who lazed about town.

"Something has happened." He peered at her again. "Pray, what has you so vexed?"

Juliana swallowed, absorbing the strength of his touch—the strength that oddly surrounded the capricious man—and desperately longed for someone to lean on, someone to trust. But he hadn't been there when she'd needed him. Just like everyone else. "I had hoped to acquire your help, milord, with a personal matter." She looked down.

"Anything. I will do anything you ask of me." His voice caught, momentarily plunging into baritone. She raised her gaze to his, squinting at the sun reflected off the white paste on his face, off the glitter in his periwig and the satin cravat bounding beneath his chin.

But his eyes … his eyes held a strength, a conviction, an intensity he rarely revealed. They reminded her of someone … Nay. She nearly laughed. A foolish notion.

A bird landed on a branch above his head and began a cheerful tune, drawing both their gazes and a smile to his lips. "You see, sweetums, even the bird wishes to bring you good cheer." His voice raised an octave once again.

"I fear there's nothing to be done." Juliana drew back her hand, her eyes burning with unshed tears. She prided herself on being strong, being capable. In her world, there was no time for self-pity. Not when she had a business to run and a family to provide for. Regardless, sitting in the garden with her mother's love surrounding her and this man's genuine concern, a single rebellious tear slipped its lashy perch and slid down her cheek.

Raising his hand, Munthrope wiped it away with a calloused thumb as a rare seriousness came over him. She did not wish to be pitied. She rose and strolled to a gardenia bush, turning her back to him, collecting her wayward emotions.

"This was my mother's garden. She spent many hours here."

"La. I can see why. 'Tis lovely. And peaceful." She heard him move behind her. "You miss her."

Juliana fingered a leaf, still fighting back tears. "More than you know." The air felt as thick and heavy as her heart. Perspiration slid down her back. She had brought this man here to ask his help, but now she feared 'twas not wise. For all appearances he seemed capricious and whimsical, not someone worthy of her trust. Yet ... something in his eyes, in his presence, set her at ease. Oh, fie! What to do?

She spun on her heels. "Lord Munthrope. Do you have access to a grave?"

The man, who had inched behind her, leapt back in surprise. "A grave?" He gave a humorless laugh. "For whom, my pet?"

"Someone who has died, of course." She stared at him, hesitating. "Someone who needs to be laid to rest."

He ran a finger and thumb down the sides of his mouth and looked at her as if she'd gone mad. "A grave is no difficulty. The family has but to go to the city council and purchase a plot at the Palisadoes. Not someone close to you I hope?"

"I can't go to the council." She batted away a bug. "I must bury this person in secret."

"Indeed." One brow cocked. "Now you have me worried, sweetums. You didn't murder someone, did you?"

Juliana wove around him, in no mood for jokes. "Don't be absurd!"

"Then, who is it?"

"Milord, can I trust you?" She turned to face him, wringing her hands. "I mean, can I *truly* trust you?"

He studied her a moment, his brow darkening, his eyes searching hers. "If you would do me the honor of that trust, milady."

The sincerity in his tone sank her to the bench. "'Tis my father." Saying it out loud brought the tears back, this time shamelessly streaming down her face.

He moved toward her, and a handkerchief fluttered in her vision. Grabbing it, she wiped her cheeks.

"My utmost condolences, Miss Juliana. 'Tis a tragedy not to be borne alone."

"If word gets out ..." she sobbed. "I will lose everything and be tossed onto the streets."

"There, there, now." He sat beside her. "That will never happen." Circling an arm around her shoulder, he drew her close. She buried her nose in his silk doublet, drawing in the scent of rose and cinnamon that always accompanied him. Her tears flowed freely as he rubbed her back. Beneath the preened layers of fluff, his chest felt firm, not fleshy, his arm as thick and sturdy as a pole.

For the first time in a long time, she felt safe. And cared for.

"Where is your fa—where is he?" he finally said.

"In a sealed coffin in his bedchamber." She hiccupped.

"I'll make the arrangements this afternoon." He nudged her back, gripped her shoulders, and gave her a look of assurance. And, oddly, authority. "Be ready at midnight."

She sniffed and drew the handkerchief to her nose. "You won't tell anyone?"

"Lud, my pet. You do use me poorly." He tsked, then grew serious. "Nay, no one will ever know." He took her hand in his. "What about your father's shipping business?"

"It is well and not your concern." She didn't mean to sound curt, but the less the man knew, the better. Though, she could tell from the look in his eyes he understood the situation well enough. Thankfully, he intruded no further.

"You have naught to fear from me, Miss Juliana. Mum's the word."

"I don't know how to thank you, milord."

"Pshaw, 'tis nothing. I could use a little intrigue to spice up my life. Besides, we are friends, are we not?" He eased a finger down her jaw.

Were they? Where once Juliana thought him a selfish peacock, now she wondered at the lengths he went to please her. To help her. When it benefited him naught. She'd witnessed his charity as well. And despite his ridiculous attire and flamboyant gestures, she found herself drawn to him, even enjoying his company. "Yes, we are friends, Lord Munthrope."

"Then you must call me Munny." He smiled.

"Very well, Munny."

His gaze took her in as if she were a vision from heaven.

Warmth flooded her. Could she actually be falling for this ridiculous man? She felt herself drawn to him. Not physically of course, but to something deep within him… mayhap to the man himself. Nay. She shrugged it off. 'Twas merely gratitude for his help.

"Midnight, then, my pet?" He lifted her hand for a kiss and gave her a devious wink so contrary to the man's flippant attitude. Then swinging about, silk flapping in the breeze, he strode away, announcing he'd see his own way out.

Sliding back onto the stone bench, Juliana released a heavy sigh as a feeling of foreboding claimed her. Had she done the right thing in trusting Munthrope? Or would he abandon her like everyone else?

Chapter 27

A WISTFUL MOON CRIED MILKY tears over the fresh mound of dirt in the Palisadoes graveyard just outside Port Royal. Alex stood beside Juliana, unsure what to say. Two men from his crew—their identity unbeknownst to the lady—had just finished burying Mr. Dutton and were carrying their shovels back to the wagon. Waves crashed ashore in the distance, joining the serenade of crickets and frogs, a not-too-unpleasant funeral dirge for the man gone now nearly a month. Even tar-sealed in a coffin, the stench was insufferable. It had been difficult enough for Juliana to bear on the way there as the poor lady, sitting upon the driver's perch of the wagon, had oscillated between coughing, covering her nose, and sobbing uncontrollably.

But now that the man was settled four feet under, she had calmed considerably, merely staring at the mound as if expecting her father to break forth any moment. Alex had heard there'd been no love lost between the two, yet here she stood mourning him as if he'd been a doting father. Alex sighed. He'd had a different sort of father. A restrictive one—a man of many rules. One who had loved him when he'd been home, but who had rarely *been* home. On the other hand, Juliana's father had always been home, but uninvolved and unloving. Alex wondered which was worse.

Standing beside the wooden cross Alex's men had hammered into the soil, Juliana ran fingers over the name engraved upon it: Sam Mason. "I wish we could have buried him under his own name."

"Someday you will," Alex offered. "When all this is over."

She looked at him, her expression lost in the shadows. "Will it *ever* be over?"

The sorrow and desperation in her voice would be his undoing. How he longed to take her in his arms, to hold her while she spent her tears, to tell her that yes, life would get better. That if she allowed him, he'd care for her all her days.

But instead, he stood there affecting a nonchalant pose so as not to arouse her suspicions. Suspicions that he'd already witnessed on the expressions of her face, the flickers in her eyes. Suspicions that if confirmed would send her careening far, far away from him forever.

"At least he's at rest now," she said. "And buried as a loved one should be."

Which reminded Alex of Rowan. "Wherever is your brother? Did you not tell him of the burial?"

"Out filling his belly with rum, I imagine."

Alex shook his head. This poor lady. Not only bearing the responsibility of a shipping business but also the burden of a wastrel brother. If possible, his admiration rose even higher for her while his disdain grew for Rowan.

Mayhap Alex should simply disclose his true feelings—that he wished to make their betrothal real. Hadn't he seen sparks of regard—dare he say affection—in her eyes? Mayhap under the circumstances, she'd be amenable to becoming the wife of such a strutting fool. Alex would gladly give up being the Pirate Earl if he had a chance at gaining the love of such a woman.

The cards lying face up across the table rolled back and forth like a stormy sea in Rowan's vision. He blinked, trying to bring them into focus.

"Where are you placin' your coin, Dutton?" the man next to him drawled out. A gray periwig circled skin leathered by the sun and a brow that protruded like a monkey's. With the brains to match.

Rowan would have no trouble outwitting the baboon yet again. He'd already won more than twenty pounds with only two shillings to begin with. Grabbing his glass, he downed the rest of his rum and eyed the dealer—a rotund man across from him who ran the mercantile. Beside him sat Rowan's other competitor, a Mr. Camp, dressed in a Turkish garment of gold brocade, newly arrived from England with money to burn.

"Hurry it up, Dutton. I ain't got all night," Baboon man slurred.

A crowd formed around the table, all eyes locked on the high-stakes game. One doxy brought Rowan another glass of rum and sidled up beside him. A fiddle screeched in the background, joining the squawk of parrots that inhabited the rafters of the old tavern.

Rowan studied the cards again. The queen of spades focused in his blurry vision. Wait. Had she winked at him? He could have sworn she … He smiled. Of course. 'Twas the sign he'd been seeking. He shoved all his ivory chips—twenty pounds worth—to sit before her. He knew he would win. He felt it in his bones. Mr. Camp divided his chips betwixt the two and eight of spades, while Mr. Baboon laid all of his fifty pounds worth on the jack. Fools. Within seconds, all their money would be Rowan's—his and Juliana's, that was, for he fully intended to use his winnings to help support the family. Mayhap, finally, his dear sister would understand that his skills, though different from hers, were just as useful.

With a confident grin, he watched the dealer as he flipped over the first card. Whew. A two of hearts. Mr. Camp frowned at the loss. The second card would be a queen. It had to be. The doxy nibbled on Rowan's ear as he stretched out his arms to gather his winnings. He shifted his gaze between the men, waiting to see their looks of despondency and horror. The card snapped. Mr. Camp spewed a colorful curse. Waiting for Mr. Baboon to do the same, Rowan studied him with eager expectation.

But a grin slashed across the man's face.

What? Rowan stared at the jack of diamonds giving him a devilish wink from the top of the pile. The rum fired like hot lava through his mind. "Impossible!" he shouted.

"I assure you, sir, 'tis quite possible." Mr. Baboon gathered all of Rowan's and Mr. Camp's chips with an arrogant sneer as "ooohs" and "ahhhs" sounded from the crowd. The doxy shifted her attention from Rowan to the new winner, while Mr. Camp excused himself, scowling.

Desperation sent Rowan's heart racing. "One more game," he said. "Double the entire fortune."

"But you have nothing left to bet, my friend." The man's condescending tone scraped down Rowan's spine.

"Yes I do." Rowan attempted to sit up straight, though the room still wobbled. "I have a merchant brig. The *Midnight Fortune*. She's anchored in the bay as we speak."

Mr. Baboon chuckled. "Tush, man, you would wager your brig?"

"Is she even yours to offer?" The dealer cocked a brow.

"Aye. I'm the heir to Dutton Shipping and run much of the business now that my father … is … spends his dotage in relaxation. 'Tis mine to pledge, of that you can be sure."

"Very well, then." Greed took residence in the man's eyes. "One more hand. And the *Midnight Fortune* is on the table, gentlemen!"

It had been two nights since Juliana had buried her father, and the sting of its finality had not given her a moment's peace. In some twisted way, having him still in the house had made her feel as if she wasn't completely alone. Now that he was in the ground, the truth of her situation hit her like a blast of hot Caribbean wind. She had no idea how much longer she would be able to keep curious friends and insistent business acquaintances at bay. Sooner or later, someone would become suspicious and alert the authorities, thinking some foul deed afoot. Until that time, she resolved to make as much money as she could for her and Rowan's future. But with the business failing, she had about as much chance of that as she did of Rowan sobering up and coming to her aid.

In the meantime, she must keep up appearances, and part of that meant she must attend ridiculous parties on the arm of Lord Munthrope. As she was doing tonight. Only this night, due to the close proximity of Mr. and Mrs. Rosemere's home to Juliana's, Munthrope had sent his carriage ahead and insisted they walk. In truth, she was glad for it. 'Twas a pleasant evening with a cool breeze that swirled the scent of orange jasmine and hibiscus beneath her nose. The sky was ablaze with myriad stars while street lanterns lit their way like golden breadcrumbs on a dark path.

"How fair you, milady?" Munthrope asked after several minutes of silence. "How goes the business?"

Both the question and the concern in his tone caught her off guard, and she realized she oddly trusted this man to keep her secret. "It goes well enough, milord, though I fear my father was far more skilled at making a profit than I."

Light from a lamp shimmered over Munthrope's white periwig and pink satin doublet as they passed beneath. "Indeed. I heard he was a shrewd business man."

"And *I* am not?" She raised a brow, teasingly.

"You are not a man." He grinned. "Nor would I call you shrewd, sweetums. Though I have no doubt should you ever have the opportunity to deal with merchants face-to-face, they may find you so."

"Find me shrewd? I marvel you would say so." She laughed. "While most women would be insulted, I am flattered by the adjective, milord."

"Yet another reason I find you so enchanting, sweetums."

Heat blossomed up her neck. *Enchanting.* What a lovely compliment! She had no idea how to respond to such an endearing term. "Have a care, milord, or a lady might assume something beyond a feigned betrothal."

Though her tone was taunting, Munthrope didn't laugh. Instead he halted, hooked his cane over one arm, and took her hands in his. "The lady may assume as she wishes." There was no lift of his lips, no mockery in his voice—just an intensity in his deep-blue eyes that made her toes tingle. She tore her gaze from his, her heart a thrashing drum in her chest. What was the man suggesting? Did his interest go beyond their agreement? Yet even as the thought of possessing such security began to chip away at the uncertainty and fear that had hardened within her like a rock, she remembered how she'd sworn never to depend on anyone again—especially not a man. 'Twas a man, a cruel man, who had abandoned the children at the orphanage. And both the men in her life had left her, one initially in his heart followed by his body, and the other in heart and mind since they were both children.

Tugging from his grip, she gathered her velvet cape about her and continued forward, desperate to change the topic. "In truth, milord, I am still plagued with nightmares that one day I shall awake working in a brothel alongside Abilene."

He seemed about to say something but then flattened his lips. "Begad, milady! It pleases me that you mentioned your friend, for I believe I have a solution to her problem."

Juliana stared at the man aghast. Stunned he would even give a moment's thought to a strumpet he'd never met.

He halted once again, tapping his cane in the dirt. "I will hire her as my house maid." His red lips quirked, raising the mole he wore at the right corner.

"But milord, your reputation."

"Beshrew my reputation, sweetums!" He lifted a finger in the air as if making an announcement to the world. "The woman needs honest employment, and I can provide it. I care not what these society fiddleheads say, nor how many turn their backs on me because I hire a woman of ill repute. Besides"—his eyes twinkled in the lantern light—"the scandal may do well for my reputation."

She studied him curiously. The last thing the man needed was more tongues mocking him behind his back. "You are a most unusual man, milord."

"I am honored you find me so." He dipped his head. "I'll have my man Whipple attend to it first thing."

Excitement buzzed through her. She couldn't wait to see the look on Abilene's face. At last her friend would be in a decent home with good food and respectable employment. "I don't know how to thank you, milord."

"By calling me Munny, sweetums." He tucked her gloved hand within his elbow and gave her a grin that if it hadn't come from a man dressed like a trussed goose, would have stirred her body to distraction. It *did* stir something within her, something that went beyond thankfulness, beyond admiration.

He must have seen it in her eyes, for his smile widened and he placed a gentle kiss on her other hand.

"We'll take the lady from 'ere." A rough voice bellowed, jerking Juliana's gaze upward.

Three men emerged from the shadows dressed in the shabby attire of common sailors, two sporting blades that flashed in the lamp light and one pointing a flintlock at Munthrope.

Her heart took up a wild beat.

But no cry of alarm, no shriek burst from His Lordship's lips. Instead, with arms raised in his usual flourish, he moved to stand in front of her. "I cry pardon! What did you say, gentlemen? I fear I did not hear you correctly."

"Ye heard us, ye foppish nod." The man on the end spat into the sand. "We're takin' the lady an' ye have no say in it."

Cupping his ear, Munthrope took a step toward them. "Taking the baby, did you say?" He snorted. "There's no baby here, gentlemen. Begone with you." He flicked his jeweled hand at them. "Back to your cups, little pups."

The men stared at Munthrope, dumbfounded. One of them scratched his head. The other shared a glance with the third, and both started to laugh.

"Are ye daft, ye witless toad?" The leader lunged forward and pointed at Juliana with his sword. "The woman, the wench."

Her breath escaped her. Her mind raced. What did these men want with her?

"The French? Where?" Munthrope lifted his chin and spun on his purple-ribboned heels, searching the darkness and waving his cane, inadvertently knocking the man's blade aside. "Are they attacking?"

Gripping the hilt of his sword tighter, the leader let out a foul curse while chuckles bounced between his friends.

"Gentleman, if you'll allow—tsk, tsk. Such language in front of the lady."

Munthrope feigned indignance. Or was he serious? Juliana couldn't decide. Either way he was a fool! Did he think he could but put on a show as he did in society and beguile the crowd? For this crowd would take no thought to silence his buffoonery.

"Give us the lady!" They started forward, weapons drawn, but Munthrope stood his ground.

Juliana moved behind him. "Nay, milord." Her voice sounded as though it came through syrup. Her legs trembled. But she could not allow him to be hurt—or worse, killed—on her account. "I will go with them. If not, they will kill you." Yet memories of the way His Lordship had dispatched the thief on the beach resurged. Surely that had been pure luck, had it not? Even so, the pampered man was no match for *three* ruffians. Ruffians who, for all their demand to possess her, ironically seemed not the least bit interested in her at all.

Even so, the thought of going with them had her blood rushing so madly, she thought she might faint. She was about to touch Munthrope's arm to stay any further bravado, when he turned to face her. A calm assurance passed across his eyes. No fear or alarm. He nodded as if to say "obey me." Then he winked. *Winked!* As if this were but an act in a play. Gripping her shoulders, he nudged her back.

"I've 'ad enuf o' this," one of the men said as they swarmed toward Munthrope.

Juliana let out a shriek.

Munthrope twirled and flung his cane across the path. It struck the man's pistol, sending it into the air. Munthrope caught it. A shot exploded. Glass shattered and all went dark. Blood pounded through Juliana so fast, it buzzed in her ear. She stumbled, tripping over her voluminous mantua, and started forward with one thought in mind: help poor Munny before he gets himself killed! Shadows passed before her in a mad demonic dance.

A grunt, a groan, a shriek! Another pistol shot thundered the air. The ring of blades. The eerie squish of metal slicing flesh. A thud and moan. Curses. Footsteps skittering away. Then all went silent.

"Munthrope!" Juliana groped forward, her eyes still adjusting to the shadows. "Munthrope!" There. A pink lump on the ground. She dashed to his side and touched his arm. Moaning, he rose to sit while adjusting his periwig, his breath coming hard.

"Are you injured, milord?"

"Nay, nay, sweetums. Are the fiends gone? Oh, *do* say they are gone!" He allowed her to assist him up, then furiously brushed sand from his doublet and breeches.

"I believe so." She scanned the surrounding darkness. "But you … how did you?"

"Me?" He flung a hand to his ruffled cravat. "You think I … ?" He chuckled. "Nay, milady. In good sooth, I feared for my life. Those swag-bellied devils were nigh upon me when I dove to the ground in fear. If not for that other man …"

She felt a tremble wrack through him. "What other man?"

"A rescuer, milady. A champion," he breathed out. Plucking a handkerchief from within his doublet, he dabbed his forehead. "A man who appeared nigh as rough as the men who attacked us."

A champion. Juliana pursed her lips. She knew of only one man who would risk his life for her. "Did this rescuer have black hair and wear leather attire, milord?"

"How now? How did you know?"

"A guess," she mumbled. "And he said nothing?"

"Nary a word. Just dispatched the villains and left."

The Pirate Earl. It had to be. She'd not seen him in almost a month. Not since she'd told him to leave her be. And he'd done just that. Though not in her thoughts. Much to her shame, she'd been unable to banish him from those.

Munthrope began fluttering the handkerchief around his face. "A most frightening experience. I thought 'twas the end of ol' Munny."

"You were very brave, milord, to stand up for me." And she meant it. She'd not expected such courage from the man.

Leaves fluttered up ahead and more footsteps sounded.

"Let us be away." Juliana tensed. "I fear there are villains afoot this night."

"Indeed, I shall take you home." He bent to retrieve his cane, then placed her hand on his extended arm. "If I am so overcome, you must be all atwitter with nerves, sweetums."

"In truth, I *am* a bit shaken." And she would rather return home, but her absence from the ball would only cause curiosity among those with naught more to do than ponder the lives of others. "However, let us make an appearance, milord. Since we are almost there and our absence would be of note. If you are able?"

She sensed him smiling, but could not make out his face in the darkness. "Pray, milady, I am more than able."

After greeting the host and hostess, Lord Munthrope entertained several guests who begged for one of his humorous tales, looking and behaving no worse for his frightening ordeal. Juliana, on the other hand, had difficulty calming her heart, both from the fear at what the villains had wanted with her and from the gallant rescue by the Pirate Earl. She could make no sense of either, and instead, drifted listlessly through the crowd, sampling the treats, and avoiding her friends.

Now, as she watched His Lordship draw out the climax of a particularly fanciful story, his body a blur of flailing satin and gold trim, she wondered at her strange attraction to him. Perchance 'twas naught but the pressures of her life befuddling her heart and mind, for what woman in possession of all her wits would be drawn to such a silly man for anything save entertainment or—with the prospect of marriage—security.

Security. When was the last time Juliana had felt secure about anything? Especially her future? Save for that one moment in her mother's garden when Munthrope had held her.

He finished his tale, grabbed two drinks from a passing tray, and headed toward her, when two other ladies intercepted him and led him away. Shrugging, he cast a smile at Juliana over his shoulder.

Something in the way he glanced at her just then, a slight tilt to his lips, a mischievous authority in his eyes, reminded her of the Pirate Earl. Not that she needed reminding. Fie, did the rakish man follow her all about town? What kind of pirate was he? But the more disturbing question was why the idea thrilled her so.

Releasing a ragged sigh, she studied the life-size marble statue of an angel, complete with wings and peaceful smile, and realized she was probably doomed to hell for such wayward desires.

So absorbed in her thoughts, Juliana didn't see Captain Nichols until his shadow crossed her face and the scent of his bergamot cologne smothered her.

He smiled—that sickly sweet maniacal grin of his that always soured her stomach. He followed her gaze to Munthrope and gave an indignant huff. "You can't seriously be fond of that princock."

Juliana frowned and took another sip of her wine punch. "He is a kind man." *And twice the man you'll ever be,* she wanted to say, but that would be cruel.

"Kind, you say?" For some reason this sent the captain into a bout of laughter that took several moments to contain. She should have taken the opportunity to slip away, but curiosity at the man's hysterics kept her in place, waiting with a tap of her foot for him to finish.

Finally he drew a deep breath and begged her forgiveness, then leaned toward her and said something that froze every ounce of blood in her body.

"Lord Munthrope *is* the Pirate Earl."

Before the words had a chance to settle on her reason, she gave such a hearty laugh, several people turned to stare. "I had my suspicions as to the state of your mind, Captain. Thank you for confirming them."

His lips tightened. "The evidence is overwhelming."

"Pray, what evidence?" *You jealous whiffet.*

"Why, just tonight before you arrived, did he not overcome three armed men?"

Her heart canted in her chest. "How do you know that?"

"Because, my dear, I staged the altercation to prove to you who His *Lordship* truly is."

Raising a hand, she slapped him across the cheek. Her glove unfortunately softened the effect. "How dare you? You sent those bullies? Have you any idea how frightened I was?"

"My apologies, Miss Juliana, but it couldn't be helped." He rubbed his cheek. "I assure you, you were safe the entire time. Should my suspicions have been in error, my men would have brought you to me and done Munthrope no harm."

Juliana could hardly contain her anger. "You are quite wrong, sir. 'Twas not Munthrope who fought off your men, but the"—she gathered her breath—"another man who happened by."

He laughed. "Is that what he told you? I was hiding but a few yards from where he stood, and I can assure you 'twas Munthrope who overcame the men. And quite expertly, I might add. Much like a man experienced at fighting." He gave a grin of victory, then leaned toward her. "You do realize 'twas him who shot out the lamp so you couldn't see."

She backed away, her breath fleeing her once again. "You're mad! If I couldn't see, then how could you?"

"A different angle, my dear. One in which the lights from the house were behind him." He leaned back and puffed out his chest. "Oh, I assure you. There was no other man present."

His words stormed through her, stirring up her rage and refusing to attach to reason. She felt her face redden with heat at the man's audacity, cruelty, and lies. "Are there no lengths to which you will not go to make me yours, Captain?" She spun to leave.

He caught her arm, his eyes flashing. "Nay. There are not. I did this for you! To save you from the villain. Can you not see that?"

"They are nothing alike!" she spat. "Their appearance, their gait, their gestures couldn't be farther apart! Their voices are completely different. And besides, Munthrope is taller by at least a foot."

A satisfied smirk took residence on his thin lips. "Have you considered the man's heeled shoes and tall periwig?"

Nay, she hadn't. She jerked from his grasp. "Why would the Pirate Earl pretend to be Lord Munthrope? He would have no need for the charade. He has plenty of wealth and could have any woman he wants."

"Shall we test my theory, miss?"

"You may test whatever you wish. I want no part of it."

Ignoring her, he continued, "I intend to inform His Lordship that I issued orders for the Navy to search the Pirate Earl's ship within the hour. If he is not the notorious pirate, he won't give a care. If he is, I imagine he'll make some excuse to leave immediately. If I am wrong, we will know right away, and I will grovel for your forgiveness."

"And while you are groveling, you will promise to never speak to me again."

He winced at this but nodded his assent. "Observe, my dear." With chin high, Captain Nichols strolled to where Munthrope enthralled the elderly ladies with some lavish rendition of Shakespeare's *The Taming of the Shrew*.

Juliana sipped her drink. The punch soured in her stomach, and she set the glass aside. *Ridiculous, ludicrous notion!* Nichols's lust for revenge had turned his brains to mush. She stared at Munthrope, arms waving and gestures exaggerated as he acted out the play. The Pirate Earl, indeed.

Yet as she continued to stare, vague memories rose, dulling the chatter and music around her: the surprising feel of Munthrope's muscular legs and arms when she'd inadvertently touched him, the brief moments when his voice dipped in baritone, the way he fought off that thief on the beach, the horse patch he always wore in the exact same spot the Pirate Earl bore a scar. Visions flashed of both men rubbing the edges of their mouths with thumb and forefinger when deep in thought, both calling her milady, both smelling like rose and cinnamon. And the sword wounds! Fie, the sword wounds on Munthrope's right arm. The Pirate Earl also had a wound on that very same spot.

Nay, nay, nay!

She rubbed her temples. Just coincidences. Her breath heaved in her throat. She gripped her neck. She was being silly. She was not engaged to the Pirate Earl! Nor would kind, honorable Munthrope lie to her, deceive her in such a horrendous way.

Make a fool out of her.

She pressed down her satin mantua, drew a deep breath, and watched as Nichols leaned toward His Lordship, whispering in his ear. Ridiculous. Munthrope would brush the man away with an expression of bewilderment, and then she would be ashamed of even entertaining the preposterous notion.

A cloud of brandy enveloped her, and she knew before she turned that her brother had approached.

"Juliana, I need to speak with you."

When did her brother ever call her by her Christian name? "Not now, Rowan, I'm busy." She waved him off, keeping her eyes on Munthrope.

There it was. The look of confusion on Munthrope's pasty white face, followed by his exclamation, "Begad, man, what has that got to do with me?"

Then why did Nichols offer her a wink as he strode away, his eyes grazing over Rowan in contempt before he left the room.

"Juliana, I fear thisssss cannot wait." Rowan insisted, his words slurring.

"What is it Rowan? That you're going to spend the evening with Lady Crastmur because her husband is at court? When have you ever needed my permission for your sordid affairs?"

"'Tis not that." His words lacked the usual sarcasm.

She faced him, concerned.

He swayed and blinked at her as if trying to focus. "I lost the *Midnight Fortune*."

The words jumbled in her mind. "Lost? She's still anchored in Kingston Harbor. You mean at sea?" No doubt the alcohol had addled his reason.

"Not at sea." He stared at the ground. "In a game of Faro."

Juliana blinked, shock forbidding his words to enter her mind. Laughter drew her gaze back to Munthrope, who excused himself from the women and hurried toward her, waving and smiling at guests as he passed. He greeted Rowan then took her hand.

"Sweetums, I regret that I am called away on sudden business. I'll arrange for my footman to escort you home."

Chapter 28

ALEX HURRIED DOWN THE DARK street, wiping his face with a damp cloth as he went. There hadn't been time to change his attire, nor to wash the infernal white chalk from his skin. A pox on Captain Nichols! The man's suspicions would prove the end of the Pirate Earl. And Lord Munthrope with him. How a dimwit like Nichols could have put the pieces together of Alex's double life, he had no idea. Yet 'twas obvious the man wasn't fully convinced. Hence, this trap he laid.

Turning a corner, Alex stormed down Thames Street. Hopefully the servant he'd sent ahead had already reached Jonas, and his quartermaster was henceforth gathering Alex's crew from the various punch houses and brothels. Not that Alex planned to set sail, but just in case.

Another curse blasted from his lips. This time directed at Larkin. Had the sailing master done as Alex ordered and tossed the Spanish tapestry overboard? Alex had been so caught up in saving Juliana's ship and dealing with Nichols and a mutinous crew, he hadn't made sure. And he had no confidence that Larkin's greed had permitted him to obey. If Captain Nincompoop found the unique piece, he would have all the evidence he needed to drag Alex to the Jamaican council to be tried for piracy.

Ignoring the insults of "merry andrew" and "limp wrist" tossed his way, he charged onward, wishing he was still a praying man but knowing that if he was, it wouldn't be proper to plead with the Almighty that he not pay for his crimes. Yet, he could not deny that for the first time in four years, he wished he had committed no crimes at all. Wished he was an honorable man. For her. For the woman who stirred him in every way possible. If only he could be the man she needed him to be.

Two men leapt out at him from the shadows, one wielding a knife, the other a pistol, both reeking of rum and refuse.

"Look what we've got 'ere. A real gentleman, says I."

"Aye," the other man slurred, cocking his pistol. "Lost are ye, milord?" They both laughed.

"How's about ye 'and over yer money pouch."

Alex sighed and stood his ground. "And why would I do that?"

"Consider it yer payment fer encoachin' on our territory."

"Aye," the other added. "Consider us trolls guardin' the docks."The first man thrust the knife toward Alex and gestured for him to hand over his money.

Alex studied his assailants, their positions, their stances, the lack of intelligence in their limpid eyes. He had no time for this.

"I'll pay your toll, gentlemen," he said, and before they could blink, Alex caught the man's arm betwixt his forearms and twisted it until something cracked. The man yelled out in pain. As the knife clinked to the ground, Alex booted the other man in the groin and snagged the pistol from his grasp. Then turning, he rushed away, shouting, "Beware the price for encroaching on *my* territory."

Within minutes, he charged down the wharf and leapt aboard his ship, only to meet the barrels of at least a dozen pistols. "'Tis me, your captain," he announced, tearing off his periwig and tossing it to the deck. His crew stood frozen in place, eyeing him as if he were a ghost.

"Is Larkin aboard?"

One by one they lowered their weapons. "Nay, Captain." Riggs, the boson, approached. "I ain't seen 'im since last night. Why are ye dressed like a—"

"What of Jonas? Has he returned?"

"Nay. He gathered five men and took off like a nun in a brothel jist afore ye got here."

"Ready to set sail, Riggs." Alex faced one of his topmen. "Conlin, take a dozen men and search this brig from truck to keelson. Start with Larkin's quarters. I seek a rare Spanish tapestry. Bring it to me immediately."

"Aye, aye, Cap'n." Conlin seemed to be withholding a chuckle at Alex's attire but finally sped off.

Alex walked to the starboard bulwarks and gazed toward Thames Street, where lanterns winked at him maliciously and sordid laughter rode upon curses and ribald tunes. "Come on, Jonas." He squeezed the railing tight. Shorthanded or not, as soon as the brig was ready to sail, Alex would have to leave. Unless they found the tapestry first. Otherwise, he couldn't take the chance. Mayhap Nichols had discovered Alex's ruse as Lord Munthrope, but there was no crime in that. Though what the discovery would do to Juliana, he could not consider, so heavy did the loss of her weigh on his heart.

However, 'twas his throat and the throats of his crew that concerned him at the moment. Though Nichols had ordered spontaneous searches of suspected pirate ships before, he'd not done so in quite some time, and Alex had grown lax. His gaze sped to Execution Dock, where the gibbet swayed in the wind, some unlucky pirate's rotted flesh and bones hanging upon it. He'd not feared death before. Welcomed it, in fact, as an escape from the emptiness. But that was before Juliana Dutton.

Now, he'd give anything to live and prove himself a man worthy of her.

Drawing the hood of her cloak tightly about her head, Juliana tore down the street after Munthrope. Her heart crashed against her ribs as the moist night air saturated her face with a mist that chilled her to the bone. Or mayhap 'twas the way His Lordship now sped toward the docks, alone and without conveyance, that chilled her so. Why else would he do such a thing unless the words spoken by Nichols were true? *She could not believe it!* Even when her memories betrayed her unbelief. Even when everything within her shouted the truth of it. But she had to see for herself. Had to demand an explanation for why yet another man had betrayed her, played her for a fool, used her for some selfish purpose.

Just like Rowan. Had he truly lost the *Midnight Fortune* in a bet? Was he really that foolish and self-serving? She could hardly think of that now. Or the loss of revenue it would mean for the business. A third of the profits at least. *Lord, why are you allowing all these horrible things to happen to me? I've tried to be so good. What does it take to please you?*

Giving no thought to her safety, she sped onward, tripped over a loose brick, and nearly tumbled to the ground. She redeemed her dignity and caught a glimpse of Munthrope's white periwig up ahead as he rounded a corner. *Deceiving cullion!*

Darting forward, she turned the same corner to see him held at knife point by two ruffians. Nay, not held, it appeared—not by his cavalier, confident stance. More like annoyed, as one would be with two gnats. Halting, she slipped into the shadows beside a cooper's store. She couldn't hear the villain's words, but 'twas obvious their threat. And for a moment—a brief moment—she feared for Lord Munthrope's safety. But before that moment had even passed, the man who should be naught but flaccid and soft due to his pampered station in life, dispatched both thieves with more speed and skill than she thought possible.

With the speed and skill of a pirate.

Then, wiping his hands of them, he dashed off into the night.

Horrified, Juliana stumbled backward and fell against the store front, trying to catch her breath, trying to settle her heart and her mind. But instead, they only spun faster. She had no time for shock or even anger. She must finish this. She must confirm what her eyes had already told her was true.

Skirting the men still writhing in pain on the ground, she continued after Munthrope, keeping to the shadows. A band of knaves approached, drinks in hand, and a ribald tune on their lips, but as soon as the street-light crossed her face, they tipped their hats and went on their way. She was the Pirate Earl's lady and not to be touched. Why did that thought flood her with warmth when it should make her sick to her stomach? Mayhap that was the reason God was so displeased with her? For enjoying the attentions of such a sinful man.

The lap of waves and toll of bells grew louder, overtaking the merriment from town. Juliana halted and scanned the line of wharfs jetting out onto dark, misty waters. Where had he gone?

There. Moonlight flashed off his pink satin doublet as he stormed down one of the docks. Juliana clenched her jaw. What else would Lord Munthrope be doing down here unless he was indeed the Pirate Earl? Fury overtook her reason, and clutching her skirts she sprinted after him, not caring that she stormed toward a ship full of pirates.

Alex could hear the patter of feet behind him as his crew scampered across the deck and leapt into the shrouds to unfurl sails. He also heard cat-calls and whistles from the same men. Spinning around, he spotted a flash of burgundy satin and flaxen hair speeding down the wharf. The puff of silk and lace halted before his ship. His heart turned to stone.

He started for the lady, saw in a shaft of moonlight the fury pinching her lovely features, heard her call out, "Munthrope, you swine!" before she backed up, grabbed her skirts, and sped up the plank betwixt dock and bulwarks. Leaping over the railing, she tumbled onto the main deck with a thump and a groan that brought every man within distance to her side. Most of them not with the intent to help the lady but to stake their claim on the gift they no doubt assumed the good Lord had dropped in their laps.

"Back away!" Alex ordered, shoving them aside as he knelt beside her, his mind careening with thoughts and questions he hadn't time to entertain. "Milady." He extended his hand.

She slapped it away. Palms planted on the deck, she lifted her gaze to his. Eyes like icicles speared his soul, instantly freezing it.

"You!" She struggled to rise, refusing his help. "You!" She jabbed him in the chest with her finger.

Laughter bounded through his crew. "Get back to work!" Alex shouted, causing even Juliana to jump. As the men skittered away, another sharp finger stabbed his chest.

"You lied to me! You deceived me!" She picked up his periwig from the deck and thrust it in his face. "You're the Pirate Earl. All along, you've been one and the same!"

Fury melted her cold eyes into pools of pain and betrayal. A pain Alex felt deep within his soul. He grabbed her wrist to keep her from jabbing him again. "Aye, 'tis true. But not for the reasons you think."

"What other reasons could there be?" She struggled against his grip. "Let me go, *Pirate*!"

His crew continued to laugh.

Conlin popped up from below, a string of men on his tail. His eyes brushed over Juliana, first with delight and then with curiosity, before he faced Alex. "There's no sign of the"—he coughed—"item ye told us to search for, Cap'n, but we did find Larkin in his hammock. Out cold."

Alex glanced toward the city, where a group of men rushed toward them. From their erratic and somewhat besotted running, he guessed it must be Jonas and the rest of his crew. Juliana tugged on his arm, growling like a she-devil, then kicked him in the leg. Pain arched into his thigh, and he spun her around and shoved her against his chest, clamping an arm about her waist. She struggled, kicking and thrashing like a wild cat.

He faced Conlin. "Don't stand there like a washed-up carp! Wake him up, man, and ask him where it is!"

"We tried, Cap'n," another sailor offered, his eyes all over Juliana. "Threw cold water on 'im an' everything, but 'e's buried in 'is cups. Ye know 'ow 'e gets."

Yes, Alex did. He growled and ran his other hand through his hair. Now he had no choice but to set sail.

Chest heaving, Juliana continued to pitch and toss against him. In a rather pleasing way, he might add. Which, he was sure would only infuriate her further should she know.

"Let go of me, you fiend!" She lifted her leg to kick behind her, but Alex stepped out of the way.

"Very well, Conlin. Up to the tops with you, then."

"Aye, Cap'n."

Alex released Juliana. She spun to face him. Did the lady have any idea how beautiful she was when she was angry? How her delicate nostrils flared, her blue eyes flashed, and her hair sprang about her like a lion's silver mane in the moonlight?

"Now that I've seen for myself what a liar and cheat and deceiver and rogue and foul blackguard you are, I have nothing more to say to you. Nor your band of scurrilous fiends. In fact, I hope I never see you again." She started for the bulwark.

"Sorry to disappoint you, milady." He clutched her arm and drew her back. "But alas, I have plenty more to say to you."

She kicked him in the shin just as Jonas and the rest of his men leapt aboard. Alex moaned and held the wildcat at a distance.

"Captain." Jonas's gaze took in Juliana with a lift of his brow. "We haven't much time. Nichols and his men are on the way. Welcome aboard, Miss Dutton." He bowed.

"I shan't be staying long," Juliana hissed. "I merely wanted to see for myself what a lying cur your captain is."

Jonas laughed and glanced at Alex. "You had merely to ask me at our last meeting, and I would have gladly informed you of such."

The faint staccato of marching boots drew Alex's gaze to town, where a band of marines in formation emerged onto Thames Street. Above him, his crew stretched across the yards, unfurling main and fore sails. The canvas dropped, flapping in the faint breeze.

"Up tops and gallants, jib and staysail!" Alex bellowed. "I want all sails set to the wind! And loose the lines!"

"Set sail? What are you doing?" Juliana twisted in his grip.

"Jonas, take her to my cabin. And lock her within."

"You will do no such thing! I'm going ashore this instant." She started for the railing but Alex pulled her back, then bent over and hoisted her over his shoulder. "Never mind. I'll do it myself. Get the ship underway. And fast." He cast Jonas a serious look that he knew the quartermaster would heed.

Juliana flopped and flailed all the way down to the main cabin, calling him names he assumed no lady would know. He hated doing this to her, but there wasn't time to put her ashore. And he wouldn't leave her to the wolves of Port Royal—Nichols included.

He kicked open the door and set her down on the Oriental rug in the center of the room. Casting him a look of fury, she started for him, but he grabbed her by the waist.

The ship lurched. Musket fire peppered the air. He nudged her down in a chair. "Be good now, milady. I mean you no harm."

"Too late for that." She eyed him, her eyes swimming with pain.

Frowning, he backed out the door, then shut and bolted it, hating himself more than he ever had.

Chapter 29

JULIANA HELD THE PISTOL TIGHTLY to her chest and stared out the stern windows at the ebony sea rising and falling from view. A plethora of stars dusted the night sky, flinging snowy glitter onto crests of waves, creating a peaceful aura that betrayed the truth of her situation. For just when she thought things couldn't possibly get worse ...

She'd been kidnapped by pirates.

And not just any pirate, but the Pirate Earl, the ruler of all pirates. A man who had lied to her, betrayed her, mocked her, and used her. Though she'd seen it with her own eyes, she still could not believe the Pirate Earl was Lord Munthrope, or visa-versa. She rubbed her temples where a headache brewed. How cruel to foist such trickery upon her. And why?

She'd spent the first several minutes of her captivity oscillating between shouting and waving her arms at Captain Nichols and his marines lining the wharf, and ducking behind the large oak desk as shots from those same men tore over the ship. If only a few had pierced the windows, then she could have shouted out the holes. But they couldn't see her. Couldn't hear her through the panes so stiff with salt and sun that she hadn't the strength to open them. And though she'd searched the captain's quarters for flint and steel to light a lantern in order to draw their attention, she'd come up empty. Well, not entirely empty.

She ran fingers over the cold steel of the weapon she'd found in the Pirate Earl's desk. Thankfully, her brother had taught her how to load and prime a pistol last year. She'd also found a knife, which she'd stuffed in the sash around her waist, and a sword, which she could barely lift. What she intended to do with the weapons, she had no idea. They simply made her feel more in control and less like a frightened little ship's mouse with nowhere to hide.

The ship lurched, and she braced herself on the window seat, swallowing a burst of nausea. The last thing she needed was to become ill with *mal-de-mer*. Though tossing her accounts onto the Pirate Earl's desk was not without some appeal. It had been at least an hour since she'd seen the lights of Port Royal disappear on the horizon like so many candles snuffed out one by one. Leaving her alone in the darkness, sailing upon the vast sea to only God knew where.

A tear slid down her cheek. What had she done to deserve this? How was she to run Dutton Shipping? What would happen to Rowan, Abbot, Miss Ellie, Cook, and Mr. Pell? Not to mention that now that the Pirate Earl's ruse had been discovered, what would he do with her? *To* her? On many an occasion, she'd seen the longing, the desire in his eyes. Now that he had her at his mercy, what would stop him from doing to her what he'd no doubt intended all along? For she could think of no other reason the man had pursued her as both the Pirate Earl and Lord Munthrope.

And to think she'd found him kind and charming, even alluring. The horror!

Every time he'd protected her, every kindness he'd extended, every comfort he'd offered, had only been part of his nefarious plan to trap her. Now, as feet pounded on the deck above and the sails thundered in the mighty wind, she heard his rich, deep voice bellowing orders.

And her heart betrayed her with a tiny leap.

Within minutes, the door burst open, letting in a blast of salty wind, the glare of a bright lantern, and the immense form of the Pirate Earl. He no longer wore the ostentatious attire of Lord Munthrope. In its place were tight leather breeches stuffed within knee-high Hessian boots. A leather jerkin covered a white cambric shirt, over which crossed a baldric stuffed with pistols. His coal-black hair was tied behind him in a queue, and the cutlass at his side winked maliciously at her in the light.

He kicked the door closed, set the lantern atop his desk, and turned to her with smoldering eyes. He smelled of the wild sea and rugged man.

Juliana pointed her pistol at him. "Don't come any closer, *Pirate*, or I'll shoot you clean through!"

One side of his lips quirked in a grin as lantern light glinted amusement in his eyes. "You never cease to amaze me, milady."

"'Tis Miss Dutton to you, Mr. Pirate. Or should I say *Munny*?" The gun wavered in her hand.

He grimaced. "'Twas not my intention to deceive you."

"Nay? Was it your intention to kidnap me?"

"An unfortunate turn of events." Lifting his baldric, he drew it over his head.

She thrust her pistol forward.

He held up a hand. "Just disarming myself." He laid the pistols on his desk. "Shoot me if you will. I suppose I deserve it." Remorse stung his tone.

But she wouldn't be fooled again. "Suppose?" she snipped.

Grabbing a bottle from his desk, he poured the amber liquid into two glasses then handed her one.

She shook her head. "What do you want from me?"

He downed his drink, took hers, and plopped in a chair. Leaning back, he examined her with those eyes of his that never ceased to send her reason tumbling. The gun grew heavy in her hands. Not a trace of fear registered on his face.

Nor was there any of his usual pomposity. Instead, the longing appeared again, along with a hint of frustration and sorrow.

Water purled against the hull as the ship creaked and groaned on its course. Lowering the gun, she averted her eyes from his perusal.

"How did you find out?" he finally said.

"Nichols. He informed me of his plan to trap you."

"Ah. So when I left the party …"

"I followed you. You must think me naught but a silly woman for falling for your schemes."

"On the contrary." He slammed the drink to the back of his throat. "I find you more resourceful, perceptive, and astute than most men I know."

She snorted. "You can cease the idle flattery, milord. If you even *are* a lord. What have you done with the real Lord Munthrope? Tossed him in the bay, perchance?"

He set his drink on the desk and rose to his ominous height. "My flattery is never idle. Before you stands the one-and-only Alexander Edward Hyde, Lord Munthrope. Or Viscount Munthrope, if you prefer." He dipped his head.

She shook hers, unsure whether to scream or cry. How can a pirate be the son of an earl? The ship bucked over a wave, and Juliana braced on the window seat, noting Mr. Pirate had no trouble keeping his balance. She pressed a hand to her roiling stomach.

He moved toward her. She raised the pistol again.

"If your stomach bothers you, I can have our cook make some ginger tea." Why did his voice sound so caring? Fie, but the man was good at lying.

"I want nothing from you," she said, motioning with her pistol for him to back up. "So your father was indeed Edmund Merrick Hyde, the great pirate captain."

He leaned against his desk and nodded. "He is now the Earl of Clarendon."

"Hence piracy taints your blood, withal," she hissed. "How unfortunate you did not inherit his zeal for God and goodness as well."

"God and I had a falling out, I'm afraid." He crossed his arms over his chest and stared out the stern windows.

"Finally, a word of truth from your lips."

His eyes met hers. "I have told you many things that are true."

Lowering the gun to her lap, she glanced out the window, not wanting him to see the pain in her eyes. "'Tis what you did not tell me that hurts the most."

"That I've hurt you brings me great sorrow. But that you are no longer enraged gives me hope."

She snapped her gaze to him. The intensity in his eyes, the desperation, caused a flutter of sympathy to battle her anger. But she would not fall for his tricks again. "I would not underestimate my fury, *Pirate*! And whatever it is you hope for, prepare to be disappointed."

The deck canted. Creaks and groans joined the purl of water against the hull.

"I make no doubt I am a rogue, milady. But a rogue whose only desire was to be near you."

"Fie! By deceiving me?"

"By protecting you."

"By lying to me." She fumed.

He shook his head and took a step closer. "By arranging an engagement that would ease your burden."

"So you could play me for a fool."

"So I would have reason to be in your company. I knew you were too proper a lady to spend time with a pirate."

"That much is true. Yet dressing up like a primped dawcock and dancing around like a foppish jester was a better idea?"

He gave a little smile. "Nay, I had already created that role."

"To what purpose?" She held up a hand. "Never mind. I do not wish to know." She truly didn't. Besides, he would only lie to her again.

He took another step closer. Her nerves grew taut. She leveled the pistol at him again. "Stay back! I warn you." He had circled the desk and was within two yards of her now. Towering over her, all man and strength and confidence. She felt like naught but a scrawny bird in his presence. A rather foolish bird holding a pistol with a single shot she'd probably miss him with anyway.

"I see you aptly named your ship *Vanity* after your bloated opinion of yourself."

One dark brow raised. "'Twas in reference to the vanity of life, milady, the meaningless of it all, if you'll allow."

"Nay, I will not allow." The pistol wavered.

"Give me the gun before you hurt yourself." He held out his hand.

"If anyone's to be hurt, 'tis you, milord."

He raised his brows, humor appearing in his dark blue eyes. Raking a hand through his hair, he dislodged strands from his queue and frowned. "How can I make you understand that everything I did, I did for you?"

Thoughts filled her mind of how he'd helped Abilene, of all the times he protected her, of how he'd helped her bury her father, and kept her secrets. "Tricks to win my affection."

"Did I succeed?" He swallowed and raised a brow over which that silly horse patch still resided.

"How can you ask me such a thing when you have misused me so horridly?"

He took another step closer, his boots thumping on the deck.

Her hand ached from the weight of the pistol, but she held the gun up anyway, hating that her eyes moistened with tears, that he saw his effect on her. "Your intentions become clear to me, now, Pirate."

He folded his sinewy arms and stared at her, curiously. "And, pray tell, what are they?"

"You are a scoundrel of the worst kind. The type of man who takes advantage of a woman who has no father or brother to stand up for her, a woman who carries the burden of her family's support. Then you shower her with kindness, weaken her will." With each word, each revelation, fury inflamed every inch of her. "All so you can take her to your bed!"

His eyes latched upon her, gray raging across the blue like a thunderstorm. A muscle in his jaw ticked. "Do you find me so callow, so base?" Anger spiked his tone.

Ignoring the terror pinching her heart, Juliana thrust out her chin. She would not allow another man to abuse her—not with neglect and insults as her father had meted upon her, nor with fickle untrustworthiness as Rowan had done, and certainly not by ravishing her, as this pirate intended. Squeezing her eyes shut, she pulled the trigger. The weapon flew from her hand. A loud crack roared in her ears. Smoke bit her nose. Coughing, she pried her eyes open to see the Pirate Earl staring at her through the haze, the smoking weapon in his grip.

Fury tightened his lips and stormed across his eyes. Tossing the weapon down, he grabbed her shoulders, lifted her from the seat, and pressed her against the bulkhead, pinning her there with his body. His face was within inches of hers. His breath, hot and spicy, wafted over her cheek and down her neck.

Her breath came rapid. Her blood raced. What was he going to do? *Oh, God, have mercy!*

He plucked the knife from her sash and flung it over his shoulder. It stuck in the opposite wall with a thud, expertly placed. Why did she ever think she could out maneuver this man, this warrior?

Trying her best not to tremble, she raised her gaze to his, not wanting him to see her fear.

His eyes penetrated hers. "When are you going to understand how much I care for you?" His desperate whisper feathered over her cheek and sent a ripple down to her toes. Heat from his body infused her own. Strength from his arms kept her in place, but the look in his eyes stole her voice. A strand of black hair wavered over his jaw, where an evening shadow grew.

A patch of white clung to the area beneath the horse patch, inflaming her anger once again. Reaching up, she ripped it from his skin and threw it in his face. "Charlatan!"

He blinked as a slow grin lifted his lips.

The ship creaked over a wave as their breath huddled between them. He raised a hand and brushed the back of his fingers over her cheek.

Then lowered his mouth to hers.

Juliana lost all reason. Warmth and pleasure spiraled through her, coupled with a desperate need she'd never felt before, a need that if it was not met would surely cause her demise.

He opened her lips with his and deepened the kiss, gently loving her, each caress a promise of more—more intimacy, more joy, more love. More of him. He cupped her face in his rough hands as if she were a precious vase of gold and he a curator of fine art terrified to break her.

She groaned, searching through the pleasurable waters of her mind for a lifeline—anything to grab onto to pull herself from this sea of ecstasy before she was lost in its depths forever. There, a thread of anger appeared. She fed it with memories of betrayal and lies. It grew and she latched on. And shoved against him.

He withdrew and caught his breath, his eyes glazed with desire.

"How dare you take such liberties!" She raised her hand to slap him, but he caught it with a look of devilish delight. Moisture sat upon his lips, evidence of their kiss.

"I only took what was offered, milady."

"How could I offer anything when you have me imprisoned against the wall?"

"'Tis called a bulkhead, and your lips were not shackled. In fact, they moved quite freely." A grin peeked at her from the right side of his lips.

She gave a rather unladylike growl.

The door flung open and the doctor entered. "I heard a gunshot." His gaze scampered over the two of them and his brow raised.

Mr. Pirate glanced at him over his shoulder. "Quite all right, Jonas. The minx tried to kill me is all." He chuckled.

Juliana swept pleading eyes to the doctor. Surely this educated, somewhat-refined-for-a-pirate would come to her aid. "Doctor, if you possess an ounce of gallantry within you, you will rescue me from this man's vile intentions."

Instead of swooping in to save her, the doctor laughed. *Laughed!* Mr. Pirate joined him as Juliana's fury rose to near boiling.

When he finally ceased his laughter and faced her, she offered him a coy smile.

Before kneeing him in the groin.

Chapter 30

AN AGONIZING THROB SEARED DOWN Alex's legs and radiated into his belly. He bent over with a mighty groan and backed away from the vixen. A moment ago his body had been spinning in pleasurable ecstasy; now it pounded in fiery spasms. His vision blurred. The room tilted. He felt like a grenade had gone off in his groin. Drawing a deep breath, he struggled to rise, determined to regain his dignity and not allow the lady the satisfaction of seeing him suffer.

Too late. She crossed arms over her chest and gave him a victorious smirk.

Jonas scratched his whiskers. "Rescue you, miss? Of what need? You seem more than capable."

"Mayhap next time, Mr. Pirate," she snapped. "You shall consider the consequences before stealing a kiss from me."

"Milady." Alex attempted to contain the agony in his voice with a sly grin. "'Twas well worth it." Then storming toward Jonas, he dragged his friend into the hall and slammed the door behind him, instantly bending over with a groan.

Jonas clapped him on the back and chuckled. "She's a hellion, Captain, I'll give you that. I believe you've met your match at last."

Alex straightened and limped down the companionway, groaning with each step. "My match, Posh! The woman merely needs to learn her place."

Jonas was still laughing when they burst onto the quarterdeck to a blast of salty wind and a black sky sprinkled with stars. "If you're quite done ..." Alex glared at him as he took a quick account of the sails and the ship's position and made his way to the starboard railing.

"Apologies, Captain. 'Tis just that I've never seen anyone get the best of you. I'm finding I rather like it."

"Don't get used to it." Alex gripped the railing and allowed the cool evening breeze to tear over him. Blast the woman! How could his body throb both with pain and pleasure at the same time? Just as his heart was doing.

Jonas rubbed the whiskers lining his jaw. "Honestly, Captain, you can hardly blame her. You've put her in a rather precarious situation."

"What choice did I have? Leave her with that dog, Nichols?"

"I don't believe the man would have done her harm."

"Mayhap not, but I have no faith he would have protected her either."

"Hmm." Jonas braced his boots on the heaving deck as he stared out to sea.

His silence pricked at Alex's conscience. "I care for her. She's better off with me."

"On a pirate ship? Full of lusty miscreants?" Jonas nodded toward the crew, some of whom were even now casting furtive glances toward Alex's cabin. "Don't your own articles forbid bringing women on board?"

Alex clenched his jaw. "My men will not dare cross me. Not if they wish to live."

"'Tis true most of them fear you, but they are pirates, after all. And, pray tell, you've never brought such a worthy prize on board before."

Alex gripped the railing tighter. Jonas was right. His crew's loyalty went only as far as the treasure he gained them. If any of them thought they had a chance at more than that, at power or a comely woman, they wouldn't hesitate to band together and take it. Lowering his gaze to the agitated foam clawing the hull, he released a heavy sigh. What had he done?

"I intend to bring the lady back to Port Royal posthaste. Is Larkin awake?"

Jonas shook his head.

"As soon as he recovers himself, let me know. We can't return to Port Royal until I ensure the Spanish tapestry is not on board. Once I determine that, we'll turn about, and I'll deliver Miss Dutton safely to her home."

Moonlight broke through a rift in the clouds and shone on the disapproval lining Jonas's face. "I hope you're right, Captain. 'Tis a dangerous game you are playing. She's a proper lady who deserves better than this."

Alex growled, his anger rising. "I love her, Jonas."

"So, you deceive her? Pretend to be someone you're not? That's not love."

"And what do you know of love?"

"I know the Bible says love is kind, unselfish, and true."

Alex pushed from the railing and crossed arms over his chest. "Spare me your religious trifles, Jonas."

"Very well, but the truth remains."

The great Caribbean Sea spread before Alex, as thick and dark as ink, as thick and dark as his soul. Yet heavenly light dared to sprinkle silvery jewels atop the waves. Here and there. Not all, but only those swells that reached for the sky. Was that the truth Jonas spoke of? That one had to reach to receive the light? Nay, Alex had tried that. He had reached toward God and received only darkness. Regardless, his friend meant well.

"You're worse than a nagging wench, man."

"Alas, 'tis the task with which I am burdened." His tone was mockingly superior.

"And, pray, who burdens you with such a task? Certainly not me!"

"Nay." Jonas cast him a sideways glance. "I answer to a higher authority than the Pirate Earl. 'Tis the Almighty who has assigned me to steer you from this destructive course you've set upon and back onto the right way."

Alex chuckled. "Those hours poking your nose in medical journals have made you mad, Jonas. God, if he even exists, has naught to do with me. Nor would he assign anyone a task so doomed to failure."

"We shall see, my friend. We shall see." Jonas smiled as sails snapped and thundered above. The brig soared over a wave then plunged into its trough, showering them in salty spray.

"What will you do now that your ruse is up?" Jonas asked.

"That Lord Munthrope is the Pirate Earl?" Alex shrugged. "It will give society something to talk about for years to come, I'm sure."

"But you will be forced to choose an identity, will you not?"

"Munny was a mere entertainment. I am a pirate."

"But is that what you were meant to be?"

Alex glanced at his friend with a cynical snort. "There is no *meant* in life, my friend. Just a day-to-day existence."

"No rhyme nor reason, no purpose save one's pleasure? How sad." Jonas frowned, then bid Alex goodnight and walked away.

Infuriating man! Alex stared after him. Why he kept him on his crew, he had no idea. Nay, he did know. Jonas was a friend. Alex's only friend, it would seem. He gazed back upon the chaotic sea, feeling like his life mimicked the random waves tossed here and there by tides and wind. Nay! He pounded the railing. *He* was in control of his destiny. No

God would imprison Alex with his many restrictions. No God and no man. Alex was free.

After some time, the pain subsided in his body. But not in his heart. He supposed Juliana had a right to be angry at his deception, even though his intentions had been pure. Was he being selfish? Only thinking of his own needs and desires? But he'd helped her, protected her, hadn't he? Or had it been only to get close to her for his own enjoyment? And now, he'd put her in more danger then she ever had been in on the streets of Port Royal.

Sometime in the darkest hours of the night, the lock clicked on the cabin door and it creaked open. Juliana, lying upon the only bed in the room—a bed that smelled of salt and mold and the Pirate Earl—gripped the knife she'd pulled from the wall tightly to her chest. And waited. Boot steps thudded in hollow echoes toward her, then stopped. The mighty form of the Pirate Earl, silhouetted in moonlight streaming through the stern windows, stood just feet from the bed. Juliana's heart leapt to her throat and stayed there, choking her. The smell of rum, cinnamon, and the sea filled her nose. Then he retreated into the shadows. A groan, a creak of wood, and within minutes the sound of his deep breathing filled the cabin.

It took Juliana another hour before exhaustion finally tugged her into unconsciousness.

She dreamt of Lord Munthrope, a flurry of satin and glitter, dancing like a jester before a cheering crowd, his limp hands held high, his face a mask of absurdity. But then as he continued to leap and prance, the white paste on his face began to melt away, the satin and lace turned to leather, the white wig to coal-black hair, the ribbons on his chest to pistols, the fan in his hand to a cutlass. And the dance to the lithe movements of swordplay. Yet it wasn't play at all as he slashed and hacked through the crowd of Port Royal society, who continued to laugh and clap even as he drove his blade in for the kill.

She bolted from the bed, blood cycloning through her veins. Hazy morning sun peered in through the stern windows as she tried to focus her sleep-laden eyes on her surroundings: the large oak desk sprinkled with charts and instruments and trinkets from exotic ports; the mahogany sideboard against the far wall that held silver lidded flagons, a gold-plated tea urn, and several books; the carved wardrobe beside it; the leather-strapped chest with an iron lock; and the collection of fighting swords and paintings of ships mounted on the wall. At the foot of the bed sat a cannon, squatting like a bulldog, its barrel and breech gleaming black. No sign of Mr. Pirate. Mayhap she had just dreamed that he'd come in last night.

Mayhap she had dreamed the kiss they'd shared. *The utter shame!* What had come over her? Some wicked spell not of this world, to be sure, for she had no other explanation for her wanton behavior. Or the way his lips had made her feel.

The lock clanked and the oak door swung inward, admitting a squat black man wearing a red-checkered shirt, stained breeches, and a blue bandana wrapped around what she suspected was a bald head. His grin revealed brown wooden teeth as he set the tray he was carrying on the captain's desk. "Some tea an' biscuits fer ye, miss," he drawled out as he continued to peruse her, the whites of his eyes as wide as a full moon.

Unsure of what to say, or of the man's intentions, she remained silent, praying he would disappear. Thankfully, Jonas entered the room. "That will be all, Spittal."

The man growled, turned, and lumbered out the door.

"Spittal?" Juliana found her voice.

"Our ship's cook." Jonas smiled. "I had him make some ginger tea for you. The captain mentioned your stomach was giving you trouble."

Juliana stared at the tray filled with a cup of steaming tea and some crusty objects that looked more like rocks than biscuits. *Spittal?* She gulped down a burst of nausea and drew a deep breath of the fresh sea air gusting through the open door.

"Where is the captain?"

"On deck. He wishes me to ask you if you require anything, milady."

"Pray, do not start calling me that as well, Doctor. And all I require is to be set free. Can you not see he has kidnapped me? Locked me in his cabin for some obscene purpose?" She eyed him, expecting a response, but he merely stared at her in amusement. "And why does he have a lock on the outside of his door anyway? No doubt I'm not the first woman to be enslaved within his cabin."

She gave him her most pleading look, complete with tears pooling on her lashes. "You are an educated man, a doctor who has vowed to heal others, to do no harm. I beg you, please save me from this ruffian."

He seemed impervious to her feminine appeal. Stepping further inside the cabin, he glanced out the stern windows, where a ray of sunlight oscillated over him with each sway of the ship. Tall, built along solid lines, he wore not the garb of brigand but could pass for any gentleman on the streets of Port Royal. A pair of spectacles peeked at her from his coat pocket.

"Let me put your fears to rest, Miss Dutton," he said, facing her with eyes as green as sea moss. "Alex"—he hesitated, flattening his lips—"the captain means you no harm. In truth, quite the opposite."

Her skin tightened in anger. Her eyes dried. "I cannot believe a man of your distinction could be so fooled. But I suppose you are just a pirate like the rest of them."

At this he smiled. "You flatter me, Miss Dutton. I am a surgeon, indeed, but a *pirate* surgeon, as you have so aptly declared. My first loyalty is to God. My second to my captain."

"Ludicrous! They are on opposite sides!" This man was as mad as his captain. She stood, attempting to press down the wrinkles in her mantua. Was it only last night she wore this to the Rosemere's soiree? "Nevertheless, Mr. Nash, I insist on seeing your captain at once."

"Alas, he is busy at the moment and insists you stay below for your own safety."

We shall see about that! She squinted out the windows as if she spotted something on the horizon. As soon as his gaze followed hers, she made a dash for the open door, smiling to herself when she avoided the doctor's hurried reach.

A wall of wind knocked her backward as she emerged from the companionway to a jolt of the deck that nearly sent her careening overboard. Toppling to the side, arms flailing, she finally found a grip on a thick rope tied to a mast. She righted herself, held her heaving stomach, and squinted across the bright deck until she spotted the object of her fury—the Pirate Earl standing with his back to her at the head of the quarterdeck, boots spread apart, arms crossed over his chest, hair and white shirt flapping in the wind.

Jonas emerged from below and started toward her with a scowl. Cat calls and whistles shot her way like cannon fire as pirate after pirate halted in their tasks to gape at her. The Pirate Earl spun on his heels. His eyes narrowed. His mouth grew tight. Juliana ducked away from the leaping doctor and charged toward the nefarious pirate captain.

"You will return me at once to Port Royal, sir!" She halted before him, brushing hair from her face.

He grabbed her arm and drew her close. "You will return to my cabin, *sweetums*, or I fear neither of us may make it home alive."

She jerked from his grasp, causing a deluge of chuckles from the crew. "What are you talking about? You and you alone can order this ship to turn around."

"I'm sorry, Captain. She got away from me." Jonas appeared beside her.

"I can see that, Doctor. Now, if you will rectify your mistake."

Grabbing her skirts, she dodged the doctor's hand once again and circled the binnacle. "I will not be kept behind lock and key like some criminal!"

"Aye, I agree wit' the lady," the pirate manning the whipstaff announced as he cast her a look that chilled her to the bone. Shielding her eyes from the sun, she took in the ship and found that most of the crew's eyes roved up and down her as if sizing her up for some task. A task she dared not contemplate. Her pulse rose. Mayhap it hadn't been such a great idea to come on deck, after all.

"Yer articles state, Cap'n," one rather greasy-looking fellow shouted from the quarterdeck, where more of the crew congregated, "that yer t' share all the treasure wit' the crew!"

"Aye, aye," several pirates agreed.

Juliana gulped.

Alex faced the main deck, his jaw tight, his stance commanding. "She is not treasure, gentlemen. She is a lady. *My* lady. And her presence here is by accident. And by God she will be returned in the same condition in which she arrived." He gripped the hilt of his cutlass and scanned them all with biting eyes. "Or you'll answer to me. Do you take me, gentlemen?"

His voice boomed, and Juliana suddenly found herself glad he was in command.

"Now, back to work, or I'll leave you worthless maggots on the nearest empty speck of land!"

Though a few grumbled, and a few stared back at their captain in defiance, eventually all returned to their duties. All except one man who slowly emerged from below, shoulder-length dark hair tossed in the wind and a hand to his forehead as if his head pained him. When he finally halted middeck and glanced up, his pleasing looks did naught to suppress the chill that slithered down Juliana when his gaze met hers.

"Take her below," Alex ordered Jonas, then leapt down the quarterdeck ladder and approached Larkin. But the man's eyes were locked on Juliana like a bolt without a key.

"Scads! Do my eyes deceive me? Who is the beauty?" He snapped hair from his face and ran a hand over his mouth, swallowing as if he were dying of thirst.

"She's mine," Alex said, looking over his shoulder just in time to see Jonas and Miss Dutton slip below. "What did you do with the tapestry from Madrid?"

"Where did she come from?"

Alex jerked the man around to face him. "Never mind about her. What did you do with the tapestry?"

"No need to shout, Captain." Larkin scratched the stubble on his jaw and gaped at Alex with gray eyes streaked in red. "The what?"

"There is *every* need to shout!" Alex returned, his patience waning. "We were nearly boarded last night by the Navy. Confound it, man! If I could but trust you." Alex ran a hand through his hair and lowered his voice. "You put the entire crew at risk of the noose!"

Larkin closed his eyes and held up a hand. "You do me most unfairly, Captain. I have given you no cause for mistrust, have I?"

Lud, the man *had*. But only in Alex's gut. "A most damnable folly, Larkin. Where is that tapestry?"

"Tossed overboard, as you ordered." The creak of blocks and rattle of sails joined Larkin's painful groan as he rubbed his eyes and gave a snort of disdain. "I assume you executed a search? Wouldn't you have found it otherwise? Why such bad faith?"

Why, indeed. Yet the mistrust continued. Mayhap 'twas the malicious gleam in the man's eyes, or the defiance in his grin, but something had the hairs on Alex's neck standing on end.

"Very well. Set us on a course back to Port Royal." And, in the meantime, Alex would assign more men to search the ship.

"Aye, aye, Captain, Port Royal it is." As the man sauntered away, whistling a tune, several of the crewmen glanced up as he passed, a few with winks, some with knowing nods. All causing a knot to form in Alex's stomach. Was a mutiny brewing aboard his ship? Had Alex been so preoccupied with Juliana over the past month that he'd missed the telltale signs? The men had been disgruntled when he'd not attacked the Dutton merchant ship. And of course now having the lovely Juliana aboard didn't help. But surely those two things weren't enough to cause his crew to turn on him when he'd done naught but line their pockets with gold.

Yet pirates were a fickle lot. Fickle and greedy. Not just for gold and silver, but some for power as well. There could not be a mutiny now—not with Juliana on board. For he did not want to consider what the pirates would do to her once they got him out of the way.

Chapter 31

"**A**LEX IS NOT WHO YOU think he is," Jonas said as he escorted Juliana back into her prison.

"Yes, I believe I found that out recently," she quipped, running her hands over the oak desk, admiring the carvings of ships on either side.

"I do not refer to his role as Lord Munthrope. What I mean to say is that he's not barbaric or cruel. He doesn't murder his victims."

"After he robs them of all their goods, you mean? How comforting." She turned to face him. "A pirate is a pirate, Mr. Nash."

"We are not all alike."

This man who stood before her certainly wasn't a typical pirate. Intelligence and civility shone from eyes that were a pleasant mixture of green and gold. She could not fathom his purpose in aligning himself with such cutthroats and thieves.

Shouts filtered from above, sails roared, and the ship pitched to port with such violence that if Juliana hadn't been holding the edge of the desk, she would have tumbled across the deck. Mr. Nash merely braced his feet farther apart.

Her glance sped to the open door, and, no doubt surmising her zest for flight, he closed it and leaned back against the hard oak, arms over his chest.

Though they were alone and the doctor was no slight man, she bore no fear of him. There was something very calming and gentle about him. Even good. If a pirate could be called so.

"Alex is confused and a trifle lost, if you'll allow," he started, "but his heart is good. True, he steals, but never from his own countrymen. And it may surprise you to know he gives much of his plunder to those in need."

A vision of Lord Munthrope helping that poor widow and her child in town flashed through her cynical thoughts. "That the man is confused and lost, I will grant you, sir. For, to what purpose would a pirate risk his life for money he plans to give away?"

"As I said, he is not like other pirates." Mr. Nash glanced above, where Alex's voice could be heard bellowing orders. "I must attend my duties. Rest assured, Miss Dutton, Alex will do you no harm. He is no ravager of women." He winked playfully. "Especially those he's quite taken with."

"Taken? Fie! He cares only for himself and his own pleasure."

"If that were true, you would be a maiden no longer."

The declaration brought heat racing up her neck. She pressed a hand on her embroidered stomacher. "Then, pray, what does he want with me?"

"Why don't you ask him yourself?" And with that, he left and shut the door.

Against every impulse within him, Alex decided 'twas best to stay away from Juliana as much as possible. They'd be in Port Royal by early morn, at which time he'd escort her safely home. After that, she'd most likely never want to see him again. Though he hardly blamed her, the thought sliced through his heart nonetheless, and he wondered what purpose there would be to his life afterward. In the meantime, having her in his cabin was driving him to distraction. Especially after their kiss, the remembrance of which had finally overpowered the pain of her kick afterward.

The moon rose over a restless ebony sea, and Alex's longing to see Juliana rose with it. He wanted to explain, make her understand the reasons behind his duplicitous behavior. But he wasn't sure he could trust himself with her alone.

How could he blame his crew for ogling her when she'd come on deck? With her golden hair loose and flowing about her bosom like waves on a creamy beach, her sparkling gown flouncing over the deck like a ballet dancer with each move of the ship, turquoise eyes so full of spark and life, and those pink lips and flushed cheeks, she was more beautiful than any treasure they'd plundered.

Nay, 'twas best he stayed above at least until she fell asleep. Then he'd perch outside his cabin door alongside Bait, whom he'd already posted there to guard her. Together, they'd keep out all intruders. Even if that intruder was himself.

Sails snapped as the ship dove into a trough. Foam leapt up the hull, reaching for Alex, no doubt intent on dragging him to the depths for treating a lady thus. To his left, some of his crew huddled, passing a flagon of rum betwixt them. They nodded his way and offered him the bottle, but he declined with a heavy sigh. No doubt a drink would aid in loosening the knots that had formed in his gut, but it would also loosen the control that kept him away from the treasure below. Besides, he needed his wits about him. Not only because Juliana was on board but because there was something else afoot, some mischief he couldn't quite place. The sooner they reached Port Royal, the better.

A high-pitched squeal—or perchance a scream?—etched through the air. For just a second, and then it was gone. Probably the wind through the rigging. Alex glanced across the deck at his men drinking and playing cards, then above at those in the tops, then over to the pirate manning the whipstaff. No one else seemed to have heard. Jonas was no doubt below with his nose shoved in a medical journal.

Alex faced the sea again as an overpowering uneasiness coiled up his spine.

Go to her.

He rubbed his forehead. Now he was hearing things. Mayhap he *did* need a drink after all. Gripping the railing, he closed his eyes and allowed a blast of wind to rip over him, hoping it would steal away his agitation. But it only made it worse. Finally, shoving from the bulwarks, he stormed up the quarterdeck, leapt down the companionway, and headed for his cabin. Just to ensure Juliana was safe. And then he'd leave her be. God help him.

But the door was open, and Bait was lying on the deck, blood seeping from a knot on his head. Gripping the hilt of his sword, Alex rushed into the cabin. A barrage of lacy petticoats exploded from behind the form of a man shoving Juliana against the bulkhead.

Rage lashed through Alex. He grabbed the man by his jerkin and flung him across the cabin. Juliana screamed. Larkin crashed against the sideboard, jarring the tea urn and dislodging a few books from the shelves. One landed on his head.

Alex glanced at Juliana. Thank God her clothing was still in place. But her red-rimmed eyes stared at him in horror from a face as white as a virgin sail. Movement drew Alex's gaze back to Larkin, who rose, bearing an insolent smirk. He raked hair from his face, his gray eyes flashing. "A captain is supposed to share his treasure," he snarled.

Alex approached the man, cautious of his every move, every twitch of his hands, the hatred—and hint of fear—burning in his eyes. Then drawing back, Alex fisted him across the jaw. Larkin's head whipped around, spurting a stream of blood on the bulkhead before he crashed into Alex's desk and thudded to the deck.

"A captain's treasure is not to be touched!"

Jonas stormed in, Riggs on his heels, both men assessing the situation. "We heard a scream."

Alex shook his hand and gestured toward Larkin. "Take him below and lock him up. And see to Bait."

Riggs yanked Larkin up, while Jonas gave Alex a look of reprimand that only added to the guilt that was breaking through his rage.

Wiping blood from his mouth, Larkin shot Alex a look that would have killed him if it had been armed. Instead it only wounded his heart. He'd once considered the man a friend. Had even trusted him.

Jonas shut the door, leaving only the lap of waves and creak of wood filling the room. And the quiet sob of a lady. Not just any lady. His lady. His Juliana. If only it could be so.

Slowly, he went to her. She raised her gaze to his, her chest heaving, her eyes pools of terror, her lips swollen where Larkin's hand had held back her screams. Hesitant, cautiously, he reached for her hand. A tear slid down her cheek as she studied him, searching his eyes … for what? To see if she could trust him. How could he prove to her that he'd never hurt her?

Finally, with a ragged sigh, she fell against him. He enfolded her in his embrace, wishing he could barricade her from all danger, all calamity—forever. She wept bitterly, this woman who was all strength and confidence and bravery and goodness. She finally wept, releasing all the terror and pressures and misfortunes of life on his shoulder. And he allowed her, relishing that he was the one chosen to give her comfort, to protect her.

At least for this moment.

He rubbed her back and ran fingers through her hair, uttering comforting words, trying to squelch his guilt at having allowed this nightmare to happen. The ship swayed back and forth like a cradle, gently rocking them as lantern light from the deckhead washed them in waves of dark and light. She clung to him. Desperately, completely. Like he'd always longed for her to do. To rely on him, to trust him, to allow him to care for her.

Finally, her sobbing transformed to hiccups and then into deep sighs, and, much to his dismay, she shoved back from him. "Forgive me. I am not one normally prone to such bouts of sobbing." Lashes laden with teary diamonds fanned over her cheeks.

"Mayhap you should allow yourself the luxury more often." Placing a finger beneath her chin, he raised her gaze to his. "As you can see, I am in possession of a solid shoulder."

She gave a little smile, stepped back, and hugged herself. A tremble shook her. Taking her hand, he led her to a chair and knelt beside her. "Can I get you something to drink? Wine, mayhap? A sip of port for your nerves?"

She hesitated and glanced over the cabin.

"You won't go to hell, milady, for a sip of port."

She nodded her assent and he leapt up, poured her a glass, and returned.

"Can you ever forgive me, Juliana? I thought you were safe. I placed my master gunner at the door, and only Jonas and I have keys." He lowered his chin. "I shouldn't have brought you here." He rose, clenching his fists, longing to punch something, if only to spend his anger. Anger at himself.

She said nothing, only stared out the stern windows into the dark void of the sea.

"I am a fool," he fumed, silently cursing himself. "I put you in danger, when all I ever wanted was to protect you. Thank God you are unscathed."

Moments passed.

"I thought you didn't believe in God," she finally said, a hint of teasing in her voice.

Alex leaned back against his desk and rubbed the sides of his mouth. "I heard … up on the deck … I heard someone say 'go to her.'" He squeezed the bridge of his nose and sighed. "It sounds crazy."

Tears filled Juliana's eyes once again. "Nay. 'Twas God. Saving me from being ravished." Though her words were firm, doubt clouded her expression as another tear spilled down her cheek. Alex searched his desk for the cleanest neckerchief he could find and handed it to her.

"'Tis the first kind thing God has done for me in a long time." She dabbed her cheeks.

"Mayhap 'twas not God but merely my own intuition." It *had* to be. For surely God would not waste time speaking to him.

"Intuition doesn't speak," she countered, lifting the trembling glass of port to her lips. "Perchance I have finally done enough good to win His favor." The thought seemed to please her as her shoulders lowered and a sigh escaped her lips.

Alex snorted. "If someone as good and kind as *you* must work so hard for God's blessing, then I stand no chance with him." Yet even as he said the words, he knew how contrary they were to Scripture. He'd spent years studying the Bible before his father had sent him to this hellish British outpost. "To save lost souls," he had admonished Alex.

Instead Alex had joined them.

Juliana tightened her lips, a tinge of anger hardening her eyes. "You are correct. There is no chance with God for a thieving pirate, a liar, and a man who kidnaps women."

The cut sliced deep into Alex's soul. When she said it like that—with such disgust—it made him sound downright evil. "Alas, I am truly sorry for that last one." He poured himself a drink. With his rising guilt and all this God-talk, he was going to need it. She was wrong about the Almighty. And Alex couldn't stand the thought that her error would cause her to turn her back on God like he'd done. She was too pure, too innocent and good to end up like him—empty and lost.

So, he spoke the words of a holy book he no longer believed in. "You are mistaken about God, milady. You need not win his blessings. You *can't* win his blessings. You must simply believe in him and walk with him."

She stared at him quizzically. "Have a care, Mr. Pirate, you sound more like a preacher than a plunderer."

He wouldn't tell her he used to be just that. Before God showed him it did no good to serve him, to live imprisoned by his rules.

"You are an enigma, Mr. Pirate."

"Please call me Alex."

"Not Milord Pirate?" She teased him with her eyes before a frown formed. "You speak of a God's blessing whose existence you deny. And you hear a voice from the same God and immediately obey."

"If it *was* God I heard, He only spoke to me for your sake, milady."

"It would thrill me to believe that." She swallowed. "Yet with all the disasters that have stricken me and my family of late, I can only assume I have not pleased him. What could I be doing wrong?" She lifted questioning eyes to him as if he had the answer. Eyes swimming in tears and desperation, just like a similar pair of brown eyes from a young lad who had asked a similar question four years ago. Lud, did he have the word *preacher* emblazoned on his forehead? Who was he to explain the workings of a distant God?

He shrugged. He had given the expected platitude to the young orphan at the time, but it had turned out to be false. He had no answer now. Wanting to change the topic, he spotted the book that had struck Larkin now lying open on the deck. He knew the minute he picked it up what book it was—his father's Bible. He set it on the desk, not wanting to see the page it had opened to but unable to pull his eyes away. They landed on the last verse of Isaiah 48:

There is no peace, saith the LORD, unto the wicked.

He didn't know whether to laugh that such a prophetic verse had struck Larkin or weep at how much it reflected Alex's own life. For he'd had no peace since he'd forsaken God and plunged into a sea of debauchery and dissipation.

He faced Juliana again, trying to hide his discomfort.

She said nothing and took another sip of her wine. It caused a flush to blossom on her cheeks, making her all the more alluring, if that was possible. Even in her wrinkled gown and bedraggled stomacher. Even with a rent in one sleeve and the silk fringe circling her neckline frayed. Even with her lips swollen and her turquoise eyes swimming. Not to mention her golden hair tumbling over her shoulders. He remembered the feel of those silken threads in his hand only moments ago, and he swallowed his rising desire.

To think he'd almost allowed this precious creature to be violated. His eyes burned, and he turned away and began sorting through the papers on his desk.

Juliana stared at the pirate's back as he fumbled with something on his desk. She could have sworn she'd seen a mist cover his eyes before he'd spun around. Impossible. Pirates didn't cry. Certainly not the Pirate Earl who ruled an entire city full of pirates. Yet she could not deny the anguish that had come over him, tugging down features normally staunch with determination and pride. Nor could she deny the way he'd gazed upon her moments before, completely awestruck and adoring. Was it possible this man, this Pirate Earl, cared for her? That everything he'd done—the feigned courtship as Lord Munthrope, the protection down by the docks, burying her father, caring for Abilene—was all due to his affections? Not some prurient desire to lure her to his bed?

As he continued to sift through sheets of parchment, she—and mayhap the port—gave herself liberty to peruse the man intently. Thick muscled shoulders stretched wide beneath hair as black as ink. Dark stubble peppered a jaw that still twitched—from anger? Leather breeches gripped thick thighs as he shifted boots over the worn deck. A long knife clung to one hip while a cutlass hung at the other. There was an aura of power about him. Of control. Here was a man other men feared and obeyed. A man who could take whatever he wanted. She remembered his face, contorted in rage, as he'd lifted that horrid pirate from her and flung him across the room as though he were but a feather. Not the expression of a man protecting his concubine. But a man protecting his lady.

The words spilled from her lips. "Where were you tonight? Why hadn't you come below?"

He coughed, straightened his shoulders, and turned, leaning back on his desk. His eyes were clear once again. "I thought it best I keep my distance."

"I don't understand."

He hesitated, his gaze dropping to her lips. "I didn't wish to frighten you, Juliana. I didn't wish to 'take liberties' as you so frequently accused me of before." One side of his lips quirked.

Another flush of heat swamped her. Fie, she was not a woman prone to so many blushes. She stared down at the port swirling in her glass. "Would you have?"

"Not unwanted ones. Nay."

She swallowed, realizing he spoke of her shameless response to his kiss. "But I thought …"

"Don't be fooled by the pirate attire. Beneath it lurks a gentleman. Mayhap not the posh and polish of Lord Munthrope, but certainly a man who knows how to treat a lady."

She studied him, an odd sensation bursting in her heart. A sensation of trust and affection that surprised her. "So, if not to bed me, what was the purpose of your charade? Of being Lord Munthrope? Of protecting me at the docks?"

He searched her eyes, hesitating. "Have you not guessed it by now, sweetums?"

Juliana stood and set her empty glass on his desk. "That term sounds so odd in your natural voice." She approached him, desperate for a closer look in his eyes, to seek the sincerity she hoped to find there. She wobbled, unsure whether from the port or the teetering ship. Alex steadied her with one touch to her waist. Even leaning back against his desk, his chin was level with her forehead.

She studied the stubble sprouting on that chin and longed to run the tips of her fingers over it. "Please enlighten me," she whispered as she raised her gaze to his.

He cupped her face in his hands and drank her in with his eyes. That gaze dropped to her lips, and for a moment she thought he would kiss her again, but instead he kissed her forehead and then ran a thumb over her cheek. "I love you, Juliana. Ever since I first saw you two years ago at a soirée in town."

Love. She could hardly believe her ears. "I was but eighteen."

"Aye, and I was completely and utterly stricken."

"But you never approached me?"

"As that buffoon Munthrope?" He chuckled. "I knew you wouldn't give me a moment of your time."

"Indeed," she said. "I would not have."

"Nor as the Pirate Earl, I feared."

"Most definitely not." She smiled.

"So you see my dilemma." He eased a flaxen lock behind her ear. "I watched over you from afar. Then when I saw how Nichols pestered you, and how much you disdained him, I found my opportunity."

She could hardly believe it. Loved by this man for so long, watched over like a guardian angel. And she'd had no idea. A thrill spiraled through her, urging her heart to a faster beat. "Why, pray, lead the double life in the first place? What purpose was there to the flamboyant Lord Munthrope?"

He sighed. "I suppose at first 'twas simply for my own entertainment. I found I quite enjoyed making a mockery of society, at least some of its more pretentious members."

"You have an odd sense of sport, milord."

He grinned. "In truth, I was bored, and found ol' Munny an amusing diversion. Besides, no one would have ever suspected he was the Pirate Earl."

She laughed. "I still cannot believe it myself. Your movements, your voice, your foppish attire, and those ridiculous rhymes." She shook her head. "You have quite the talent for acting. You played us all for fools."

She'd not meant her words to sound so curt, but a sorrow and an emptiness she'd not noticed before shadowed his eyes. He took her hand in his. "Please say you will forgive my deception. It was not meant to hurt you."

She believed him. She could see the sincerity, the remorse, in his eyes. A pirate who didn't ravish women, a thief who gave to the poor, a rogue who cared for a battered trollop, and a man who went out of his way to protect a foolish woman who risked her life for a friend. There was goodness in him. Goodness and kindness and honor that defied both his reputation and occupation.

Before she'd discovered his ruse, hadn't she begun to care for Munthrope? And she'd even harbored feelings for the Pirate Earl, though she had been dreadfully ashamed to admit it. No wonder she'd been so confused. She'd been smitten with them both. For very different reasons. And could make no sense of it.

Now she was starting to.

This Lord Munthrope, this Alex, this Pirate Earl, had taken care of her, protected her, and loved her when everyone else had abandoned her. And he'd done it expecting nothing in return. Surely this was a man she could depend upon.

But could she love a pirate? *Should* she love a pirate? Oh, fie! Instead of giving him an answer, she did what every impulse within her longed to do: she placed her lips on his.

And the world spun out of control. Her mind, her thoughts, dreams, hopes, and desires all became one pleasurable eddy of warmth and delight filling every crevice of her being, lifting her from the confines of earth into another realm where there was only light and beauty and a love so intense, there was no cure but to become one with this man.

Alex's arms, like iron bands, wrapped around her and pressed her so close she could feel his rock-hard strength, the rock of safety that was the Pirate Earl, as he gently, passionately explored her mouth and fanned her cheek with whispered words of love. She had no idea one could feel this way from a simple kiss. As if her body would explode from within if she were denied his touch.

Gripping her arms, he nudged her back, his breath heavy, his eyes glossed with desire. He ran his thumbs over her moist lips and licked his own, then drew a sigh as if steeling himself against something. Releasing her, he stepped away.

"I should go." He started for the door as if he were escaping for his very life.

She spun to face him. "Please don't."

He halted. "Alack, my pet. You have no idea the effect you have on me." The ship bolted and she stumbled. He was by her side in seconds, clutching her arm.

Her skin buzzed beneath his touch. "I believe I might have a clue." She gave a tiny smile.

His eyes caressed her. "Then you know I cannot stay."

"I do not wish to be alone. Please. We won't kiss." Oh, fie, another blush! "Or touch." She pulled from his grip. "We'll sit apart. But please don't leave."

And so the evening went. Alex sprawled on the deck on one side of the cabin as Juliana sat atop the bed. With moonlight rippling in waves through the windows and the sway of the ship like a lovers' dance, they talked for hours. They shared their childhoods: his loving and good but often with absent parents; hers a mixed bundle of a stern, upbraiding father and adoring, charitable mother. They spoke of their love of music. Of William Young and John Milton, and how much Alex loved to hear Juliana play the violin—to which she was very much surprised and delighted. They shared their love of Shakespeare and Bunyan and the art of Rembrandt and Caravaggio and of the beauty and majesty of the sea. At one point Juliana leapt from her bed and gave a mock performance of Lord Munthrope relaying one of his embellished tales to his admirers, the act bringing them both to such laughter, they could hardly breathe.

Then as the first glow of dawn lifted the shield of night, they both drifted off to a deep, peaceful sleep.

Until the door crashed open, slammed into the wall and sent a tremble through the cabin. Juliana bolted from her bed, her heart racing like a rabbit's to find Larkin and several pirates marching into the room, fully loaded with scowls, fully loaded with hate, and fully armed with pistols. Their gazes brushed over her before landing on Alex, who was already on his feet.

Larkin grinned. "I believe we'll be taking over the ship, Captain."

Chapter 32

STRIPPED OF HIS WEAPONS, HIS dignity, and what remained of his trust in mankind, Alex braced his boots on the heaving deck of the *Vanity*. His brig. Not the brig belonging to the lowlife scum-sucking miscreant who now strutted before him like a peacock. Nor of the twenty or so crewmen who'd sided with Larkin in his mutinous scheme. That left fifteen men loyal to Alex. But all of them, including Jonas, now stood hands bound and weaponless beside Alex on the main deck. Why he'd been left free of binds, he couldn't imagine.

Regardless, 'twas Juliana's safety that ate away at his gut at the moment. She stood, her arms gripped by pirates on either side, looking like a ray of sunshine amidst two storm clouds. Her hair flailed about her in ribbons of gold. Sweat beaded her lovely brow as blue-green eyes screaming in terror met his. My, but she was being brave. Not a whimper, not a scream, had emerged from her lips when Larkin's men had ripped her from the bed and dragged her above. The only sign of her angst was a simple look she'd cast Alex—one of sorrow and deep loss as they both realized their one blissful night together would never happen again.

Yet now, in the blaring morning sun, Alex saw another look cross her face, one that he felt deep within his soul. These pirates would have their way with her at their first opportunity. And Alex could not let that happen. He didn't know how, but he'd die protecting her from that fate. Lud, but he was a dimwitted cur for bringing her on board. Lifting his gaze, he tried to give her a reassuring look, but the deck tilted, and she staggered. One of her captors jerked her arm so hard, she cried out. Alex started for her. Larkin blocked his path. Tall and sinewy, the man had a few years on Alex. But that was all he had on him.

"Uh, uh, uh, Captain. Or should I call you *Alex* now, since you no longer command this brig?" He gripped the pommel of his sword and blew a kiss toward Juliana, eliciting laughter from his men. "That particular treasure is mine."

The muscles bunching in Alex's jaw felt as though they would explode. But he would not allow Larkin the pleasure of seeing him squirm. "What do you want?"

"Why, isn't it obvious?" He fisted hands at his waist and glanced up at the furled sails and tall masts, then down over the deck. "Your brig. Or should I say, *my* brig now."

"Ye yellow-livered namby!" Riggs, the boson, shouted at Larkin. "Turning on the cap'n like this. Why, he's done good fer us!"

"Aye, aye," several of the bound men agreed, casting searing looks at the sailing master.

Spittal spat on the deck. "Slimy carp! An' ye, Henry, and ye, Miggs!"—he called to some of the mutineers—"shame be to ye!"

Larkin drew his pistol and oscillated it between Spittal and Riggs. "Which one of you wants to be shot first?"

Neither men responded, but neither did they remove their defiant gaze from the former sailing master.

Jonas groaned beside Alex, his eyes crazed with a fury Alex didn't know the man possessed.

The brig toppled over a frothy swell, creaking and moaning as if as unhappy with the change in management as Alex was. He stared at Larkin and remembered the many drinks they'd partaken of in his cabin, the battles they'd fought side by side, the confidences they'd shared, Alex once again cursed himself for a fool. "I trusted you."

"Aye." Larkin gave a lofty snort. "A mistake many men have made."

The sun, now a mast's length over the horizon, lashed them with cords of heat that even the steady breeze refused to cool. Yet Larkin had lowered sails. Why? Alex could think of only one reason. "Are you now to toss us to the sharks?"

The traitorous cad smiled and shared a glance with his men. "Nothing quite so dramatic, I assure you."

Then why hadn't he tied them all up below? Why had he stopped the brig and assembled them on deck? Alex could see no other reason than to make them walk the plank.

A call sounded from above. "A sail! A sail!"

Out of habit, Alex opened his mouth to ask where lies she, but Larkin beat him to it, and upon receiving the answer, he raised a scope to his eye and leveled it beyond the stern. Alex glanced over his shoulder but saw nothing. Whoever it was, the sight put a rather pleased smile on Larkin's face. Lowering the scope, he slammed it shut. Sunlight glinted off the hilt of the sword strapped to his side, and Alex stretched his fingers, longing to grab it and slit the vermin's neck.

But that would bring a dozen or so blades and pistols to bear on him. 'Twas a fool's action, and Larkin knew Alex was no fool.

"Right on time," Larkin said, his nod sending two of his men dropping down a hatch. "Never fear, *Alex,* your wait shan't be overlong. In fact, your fate will become all too clear in but moments. Along with the fate of your toadies. And of this sweet tart." He slid a finger down Juliana's jaw. The lady jerked away in disgust.

"And what fate is that?" Alex demanded, drawing the vermin's gaze from her.

"Why, the only one fitting a pirate of your caliber. The noose and gibbet." His grin was malicious.

Alex glanced at the horizon again, where he could now make out bloated sails and the faint red and blue of the Union Jack thrashing above the masthead. "A Navy frigate," he said to no one in particular.

"And you declared your captain naught but a feather-brain, Miggs," Larkin addressed one of his mutineers. Laughter ensued. "'Twould seem he begins to understand that he shall soon pay for his crimes."

Alex clenched his jaw. "There is no crime here save the doubt of your own omnipotence."

A chuckle erupted from one of Alex's men.

Snapping hair from his face, Larkin bared his teeth before a slow predatory grin formed on his lips. "Ah, but you forget the tapestry, my former captain. The one I swore I tossed overboard. The one that links you to the plundering of the *Aciano*, the Spanish merchantman from Cadiz—the country with whom we are not at war with at the moment."

Alex grimaced.

"My men are placing it in your cabin as we speak. Tsk, tsk, so careless of the great Pirate Earl to leave such an incriminating item in plain sight."

"If I am accused of piracy, then you will be as well, Larkin."

"Alas, I fear under normal circumstances, you would be correct." He glanced toward the oncoming frigate. "But there is nothing normal about my bargain with Captain Nichols."

Nichols! Bile rose in Alex's throat.

Juliana whimpered.

"Ah yes, I see you both know the man. Apparently he knows you as well. Informed me he'd do just about anything to see you hang. Something about a fiancée you stole from him. The man certainly holds a grudge, doesn't he?"

Alex's insides broiled.

"I hand you over to him"—Larkin gestured toward Alex—"and he hands your brig over to me." Fisting hands at his waist, he glanced over the ship with a satisfied sigh. "A fair exchange, I'd say. Finally I shall be the captain of my own ship. As I deserve."

"You deserve naught but Davie Jones's Locker, Larkin."

"That may be true." Sunlight glinted in his taunting eyes. "Someday. But not just yet. For the time being, I shall enjoy proving myself a far better captain than you ever were. To begin, I shall show the captain's woman how a real man feels in her bed." He turned toward Juliana, snagged a strand of her hair from the wind, and lifted it to his nose. "Ah, the sweet smell of a real lady."

Eyes blazing, she tried to kick him, but missed. More sinister chuckles abounded.

"If you do her any harm," Alex began, barely able to contain his rage. "If you so much as touch her, you're going to have to kill me, Larkin. Because I shall make it my life's goal to hunt you down and cut you to pieces, slice by slice."

A speck of fear crossed the man's gray eyes before his glint returned. "You mean like this?" He dove in to kiss her neck and Juliana shrieked and writhed in the pirate's grasp as the mutinous crew cheered him on.

Alex charged Larkin. Plucking his sword from his scabbard, he held the tip to the villain's back before any of his men could stop him.

Larkin froze. Within seconds, the laughter ceased, replaced by the cock of a dozen pistols and ring of a dozen blades. All pointed at Alex.

"I'll run him through before you fire a single shot." Alex pressed the point, piecing Larkin's jerkin.

The man slowly turned around, hands raised at his side. "Then we'll both be dead. And where does that put your lovely lady?"

Sweat dampened Alex's neck. The man had a point. "Then fight me. Man to man. For the brig *and* the lady. As it should be."

"But I already have both." Larkin gave an insolent shrug.

"I says he's right," one of Larkin's mutineers shouted. "It be the way of the code."

Larkin's face paled.

"Aye, a fight to the death, says I, to see who's fit to be captain!"

Further shouts of agreement filled the air, from both sides.

His lip curling, Larkin cast a quick glance over Alex's shoulder at the approaching ship, then narrowed his eyes. Fear thundered across his face. But then it was gone. "Very well." He shrugged out of his jerkin and shirt, and Alex did the same. One of Larkin's men handed him a sword, and he took a stance and leveled it toward Alex.

"To the death!"

Juliana was having a nightmare. A horrifying nightmare. No doubt she was still sound asleep in Alex's cabin, dreaming of pirates and mutinies and sword fights. What else would inhabit her dreams on board a pirate ship? But then, why was perspiration sliding down her back? Why did her heart feel as though it might break every one of her ribs? And why did pain scream up her arms beneath the men's tight grips? What a vivid dream!

Trying to settle the blood pounding in her head, she watched as both Larkin and Alex stripped down to naught but breeches and boots. Sunlight glinted off their raised swords as they sized each other up with glares as sharp as their blades. The pirates began cheering and cursing and placing bets, including the two who restrained her as they loosened their grips slightly.

Alex made the first move, thrusting his blade forward. Larkin stepped aside and gave a taunting chuckle as he swooped in on Alex's left. But the Pirate Earl was too quick. Leaping out of the way, he swung about and raised his sword high. Larkin met the attack, and their blades rang together in an eerie chime. Both men groaned. Both expressions grew tight.

The ship canted and the men parted. Larkin swept his cutlass through the air, slicing a line of red on Alex's chest. Juliana squelched her scream. She didn't wish to distract Alex as he slunk around Larkin like a panther on the prowl. Sunlight gleamed over his muscles surging from exertion, his biceps bulging, his stomach a rippling shield. Juliana had no idea the power this man had kept hidden beneath his clothing. Surely he could beat the thinner Larkin. Then why did Larkin already wear a confident grin of victory?

A blast of wind struck them as Alex dove toward Larkin's right. Larkin met his parry, and their swords clashed hilt to hilt. Jaws clenched, they both groaned, testing the other's strength before Alex freed his blade and snapped it down to strike Larkin's leg.

The man gaped in horror at the red stain blotching his ripped breeches before raising his blade and blindly rushing toward Alex. The Pirate Earl met his advance calmly and the two began to parry back and forth. The *chink* and *clank* of blade-on-blade filled the air, joining the pirate's cheers as they backed out of the way, giving the fighters room. Rays of burning sun reflected off the deck. Juliana squinted. Loose sails flapping above, the *Vanity* bobbed idly in the turquoise waters as if nothing of import was happening on deck.

The skill and speed with which both men fought astounded her. She'd never seen the likes of it, even amongst the young upstarts of the nobility. No wonder these pirates ruled the seas. She glanced at the oncoming ship, unsure whether she should pray for it to hurry on its course or not. Regardless of whether 'twas Nichols in command, if it *was* the Royal Navy, their arrival would mean Alex's certain death. But it would also mean she'd be spared from being ravished by these pirates. Instead, she breathed a prayer for God to intervene. To save Alex's life and her purity. Though she truly didn't expect him to do either. The Almighty had been so silent lately, it seemed he'd abandoned her like everyone else.

Dodging Larkin's strike, Alex dove and twisted around, swinging his cutlass down upon the unsuspecting man. Larkin met the blow with a shaky blade that Alex quickly shoved aside, sending Larkin scrambling backward. Catching his balance, he cursed and wiped sweat from his brow. "Death by my blade or by Captain Nichols's. 'Tis your choice, *Alex*." A slight ring of fear betrayed his otherwise pompous tone. "Either way, you are already defeated."

"I'll take neither," Alex returned, barely breathing hard. "But your end by my blade is certain." He swooped in and caught Larkin off guard, pricking his thigh. The sailing master groaned and batted Alex's blade away, springing back. Pain lanced his eyes as sweat streamed down his bare chest.

The pirates holding Juliana loosened their grip. She glanced at Jonas. He gestured toward something below her, and she followed his gaze to the hilt of a knife sticking out from one of the pirates's belts. Fie! Even if she was able to reach it, what did the doctor expect her to do with it, surrounded as she was by pirates?

The clang of blades continued. Alex leveled slash after slash upon Larkin, who met each parry with his own. Off the stern, the Royal Navy frigate loomed larger, along with a desperate choice within her: save her purity or try to save Alex's life? Her heart knew but one course of action. And the revelation astounded her.

She loved him. Alexander Hyde, Lord Munthrope, the Pirate Earl. All of him. And she would rather die attempting to save his life than try to save her own.

Larkin leapt onto the foredeck ladder and Alex chased him, dipping and striking as the hiss of steel filled the air.

The pirates cheered, releasing Juliana. Fear buzzed through every nerve. Her next move could quite possibly cause her death.

Drawing a deep breath, she lifted her leg and kneed the pirate beside her in the groin. He yelped and doubled over. She grabbed his knife and dashed toward Jonas, circling around him. Some of the pirates chased after her, but Alex's men clustered together in front of Jonas, shoving them back with their bodies. Her hands shook. A pistol fired. A man shouted. A thud sounded.

She sawed through the ropes binding Jonas's hands. He spun around, gave her a wink, and took the knife. "Stay out of the way." Then turning, he cut loose his friends.

The clash of swords, along with thunderous cheers, still rang through the air as Alex and Larkin continued their dance of death up on the foredeck. Blood pounded like a drum in Juliana's ears. On wobbly legs, she backed against the bulkhead and strained to peer through the mob.

Fortunately, only a few of the mutineers even noticed that Alex's men were being untied. Spinning about, they drew their weapons, their shouts for help lost in the tumult. Within seconds, Jonas had freed the crew, and they stormed the mutineers in a tidal wave of savagery, relieving some of their foe's weapons before they could react. One unfortunate soul cried out and dropped to the deck beneath a bloody sword. Juliana gasped.

Alex and Larkin parted for a moment, both eyeing the mayhem below—one with terror, the other with a mischievous grin Juliana knew too well. Oddly, it brought her comfort. Alex said something to Larkin. Whatever it was, it caused the man to dash blindly at Alex, curses firing from his lips. The Pirate Earl turned him aside with a quick shove.

A pirate flew toward Juliana. She leapt out of the way. He slammed against the bulkhead beside her and crumpled to the deck. Blood gurgled around the blade of a knife stuck in his throat. She screamed and inched away, only to be shoved aside by two battling men. The bitter stench of blood filled the air, joining the sweat of men and fear of death. Terror stole her breath and sent her heart into a panic. She should go below. But she'd have to run the gauntlet of twisting bodies, hefting swords and blades and pistols. Instead, she crept to the larboard railing, knelt and hugged the bulwarks, wanting so badly to close her eyes on the bloody scene but too afraid to do so.

The crack of a pistol echoed across the sky. Juliana jumped. A scream and a splash sounded. More men dropped to the deck, their bodies twitching in the throes of death. The brig tilted, and a stream of blood sped toward her. Nausea curdled her stomach. She scooted out of the way. More swords slashed, more knives hit their mark, and more men wrestled for victory. Juliana closed her eyes and prayed.

Alex's booming voice broke into her pleadings. The clamor of battle softened. She pried open her eyes to see him holding the tip of his cutlass to Larkin's throat. Blood spilled from a wound on the villain's shoulder as he tossed his blade to the deck and raised his hands.

"Drop your weapons, or I'll slice him through. And the rest of you with him!" Alex shouted, his chest pitching, his black hair dangling over his shoulders. The few remaining mutineers still fighting did as he ordered, and the air filled with the clanks and thuds of pistols and swords hitting the deck, and then with shouts of victory from Alex's loyal crew.

Juliana rose on trembling legs. Tension fled her body as her gaze sought Alex like a beacon on a dark night. His men made quick work of gathering the weapons and corralling the mutineers together on one side of the deck, while Alex shoved Larkin to join them. Then, wiping his bloody sword on his breeches, he turned to face her, such a look of love and relief on his face, it nearly made her topple to the deck again. He caught her before she did and swept her into his arms. Arms still rock hard and twitching from battle. She buried her face in his chest and drank in the smell of him, all blood and sweat and musk and man.

Taking a step back, he gripped her shoulders and scanned her from head to toe. "Are you hurt?"

She shook her head. "Just frightened."

"'Tis over now. You're safe." He drew her close again, barricading her with his arms, and for the first time in a long time, she truly believed that.

Until a thunderous *boom!* quaked the sky.

Chapter 33

RELEASING JULIANA, ALEX SPUN TO see Nichols's ship, HMS *Viper,* coming in under topsails just forty yards off their larboard quarter. A nearby splash revealed the shot's resting place. Gray smoke curled from one of the two swivels aimed at the *Vanity* from the warship's prow. A warning shot.

The next one would not be.

The mutineers cheered. Alex's men gaped at their most feared enemy, eyes wide and faces stark. Releasing Juliana, he brushed hair from her face. Terror streaked across her eyes as she gripped his hand. He gave hers a squeeze and forced himself away, shoving down the realization he'd most likely never hold her close again.

Jonas approached, his face streaked with blood and sweat. "Orders, Captain."

Before Alex could reply, a voice blared from the frigate. Nichols's voice, magnified and distorted by a speaking cone.

"This is the His Majesty's Ship, *Viper.* Surrender immediately and prepare to be boarded!"

Alex's men crowded around him, defiant and fury shoving away the fear on their faces.

"We can outrun 'em, Cap'n," Riggs said, scratching the hair springing from his bandana. "I can 'ave main and fore up in no time."

"An' I can load the stern chasers faster than Spittal here can spit," Bait declared, thumbing toward the cook.

"Do it!" Alex commanded, sending those men who weren't guarding the prisoners across the deck and into the shrouds. Yet even before he returned his glance to Nichols's ship, Alex knew he'd sent them on a futile mission. One more glance showed him the *Viper*'s bow tearing the sea into a wild foam and coming fast upon the *Vanity*'s stern.

"They'll get a broadside off before we can catch the wind," Jonas said, rubbing the back of his neck.

"And they're perfectly positioned to rake us," Alex added with a growl. Terror clamped every nerve—terror and anger. *Curse Larkin to his grave!*

"Seems your fate has found you, after all," the defeated mutineer boasted from where he stood pinioned by the barrels of several pistols.

Nichols's insidious voice echoed across the water. "You have three minutes to comply, Pirate!"

Hot wind lashed over Alex, doing naught to cool the sweat streaking his back. A thousand possibilities spun in his head, none of them ending well. Above him, his meager crew sped to raise sails, while at his stern, Bait and his gun crew loaded the chasers that would make but a dent in the warship's hull.

The ship creaked over a wave, and Alex raised his gaze to Larkin holding his bloody shoulder but grinning as if he'd just plundered a ship full of jewels.

"I'd wipe that smile off your face, Larkin, for if I decide to fight, you and your men will be blown to bits same as us."

The grin dropped from his face, followed by a bead of sweat as he glanced toward the warship, then over to where Juliana stood. "You wouldn't allow your lady to die, would you?" He cocked a brow.

Juliana. Brave, precious Juliana, standing where he'd left her, watching him with tremulous blue eyes and a lump in her throat. Surely Nichols had spotted her. Would he fire upon them and risk doing her harm?

Larkin, no doubt noting the direction of his gaze, answered him. "Aye, he'll risk the lady, Captain. He wants you *that* bad." He snorted a laugh, then winced at the pain it caused his shoulder.

"Two minutes!" the voice announced.

"They've run out their larboard guns, Cap'n," Bait shouted from the stern. "Permission t' fire?"

Alex grimaced. If they didn't stand down, Nichols would rake them with a broadside that would wound them severely and scatter the deck with their flesh. 'Twas a suicide mission.

Hot daggers of sunlight speared him. Topsails fluttered above, snapping in the wind. The ship lurched. But it wouldn't be enough.

"Orders, Cap'n?" one of the gun crew bellowed, desperation charging his tone.

"Better to fight than be captured!" one of his topmen shouted from above.

"I'd rather die like a pirate than dance the hempen jig!" another man announced.

Alex's sentiments exactly. He'd always known he'd die at sea, fighting, plundering, in command of his own destiny.

"One minute!" Nichols's voice thundered over the deck and clamped Alex's spine like a vise.

His gaze sped to Juliana, and his choice became clear. To die, and watch her die with him, or to be imprisoned and hanged? He'd always sworn he'd rather fall on his sword than be locked up like an animal, only to then be hanged in dishonor for all to see. But not if that meant the death of the woman he loved. She was an innocent in all this madness, caught in the web of betrayal and wickedness.

And all because of him.

He'd rather be hanged a thousand times then see one hair on her head singed.

"Cap'n?" Bait shouted, but when Alex didn't answer, he ordered his men to fire on the upsweep.

"Belay that!" Alex thundered across the deck. "Lower our ensign!"

Curses flew at him like grapeshot. Defiant scowls faced him. Men continued in their tasks.

"Do you wish to die?" Alex leapt up the quarterdeck ladder and clung to a line. Wind whipped around him as he shouted across the brig. "To fight when one has a chance, even slim, is bravery. To fight when death is assured is foolishness. Much can happen between now and the noose, gentlemen. Who knows? Perchance Lieutenant Governor Beeston will grant us pardon." Alex had heard he was soft on pirates.

"Or we kin escape," one of his men agreed, rubbing his neck.

As the men studied the oncoming frigate, more "ayes" tumbled over the deck.

Still a few of his men defied him. "I'm not fer havin' the crows peck me flesh!" one of them shouted, approaching Alex, hand on the pommel of his cutlass.

Alex leapt to the main deck and drew his sword. "Will you fight me now?" He swept the point toward their enemy. "While the frigate blows us to bits? Come now, use your head, if you've still brains within it." Alex stood his ground. "I said lower the ensign." He swept a hard glare toward Riggs. The man backed down, and Riggs finally complied.

Sheaving his cutlass, Alex's eyes sped to Juliana. Perspiration glistened on her forehead. Golden hair tumbled to her waist and danced in the wind. Admiration shone from her eyes—warming every inch of him—before worry darkened her brow. For him? He would have thought she'd have been relieved to be spared a battle at sea. Regardless, he drew a deep breath. Nichols would not allow Larkin and his men to touch her. She'd finally be safe.

Juliana paced the tiny cabin that was no bigger than a wardrobe. Two steps forward, two steps back. "Ouch!" Her toe throbbed, and she glanced down to see she'd bumped into the side of her bunk. Yet the pain was naught compared to the despair in her heart. No sooner had Nichols's ship come alongside the *Vanity*, than he'd ordered his men to bring her aboard. Her last glance at Alex had been of him being harshly clamped in irons by one of Nichols's marines. But his eyes had been on her. He'd smiled as if to reassure her all would be well.

But she knew better.

Since then, she'd heard the pounding of several boots and thudding of feet above, along with the shout of orders and the thunder of sails as they glutted with wind. The ship had lurched, and water purled against the hull. They were underway. To where, she had no idea.

One thought kept penetrating her fear. Alex had sacrificed himself for her. As his men argued to fight, she had seen the agony lining his face at the thought of surrender. He was not the type of man to submit to anyone. Not the type of man to quit, to give up, and hand himself over to be locked behind bars. Yet, he had done just that. For her. To save her from injury. To keep her safe. The thought caused tears to fill her eyes.

A knock rapped the door, followed by the clank of a lock, and a thin man in a crisp blue uniform poked his head inside.

"The captain requests your company for tea."

Wiping her face, Juliana pursed her lips. She'd like nothing more than to reply that he could drown himself in his tea for all she cared, but she was desperate for news of Alex, so she allowed the steward to lead her to the main cabin.

The room was clean, efficient, and as dull and uninteresting as its owner. The furniture was wooden, plain, and practical: a desk, three chairs, tidily-made bunk, and a cupboard filled with books and navigational instruments all in perfect order. No rug softened the hardwood floor, no paintings or tapestries hung on the wall, no exotic trinkets from foreign ports were on display.

A tea set, complete with cakes of some kind, two floral-painted china cups, and a silver-plated pot sat upon a mahogany desk, from behind which Nichols rose, straightened his blue service coat, and smiled. Afternoon sunlight filtering through stern windows behind him haloed his white periwig in gold. Circling the desk, he moved toward her, arms extended. "You poor dear. What a horrific ordeal. Kidnapped by pirates." He attempted to take her hands, but she stepped away from his advance.

"Yet it seems I am kidnapped once again," she retorted.

Halting, he studied her in confusion. "Hardly, Miss Dutton. I have saved you. Alas, I fear you must be suffering from shock."

"I assure you, I am quite well."

Sunlight glinted off the gold buttons lining his jacket as a frown weighed upon his lips. "You can't imagine how horrified I was when I saw you standing on that filthy pirate's ship."

"You threatened to blow me from the water, if I recall."

His thick eyebrows collided. "Blow that fiend, the so-called Pirate Earl, from the water, you mean. Alas, I had no choice. I'm under strict orders to capture all pirates upon these waters, and I could hardly allow the greatest pirate of all to slip through my hands." His expression softened. "I would have done everything in my power to avoid hurting you."

"I am sure." She kept her tone sharp.

He shifted his stance. "I hope you find your quarters comfortable?"

The ship canted, and he reached out for her, but she stepped back and caught her balance. "Quarters or prison? For I seem to be kept locked within."

"'Tis for your safety, Miss Dutton. Besides, you won't have to endure it much longer. We should be in Port Royal by dusk." He gestured toward the tea. "Won't you join me in a light repast? Surely you must be famished. My cook is quite good. I believe you'll find the mango cakes to your liking."

She remained in place. "Where is Alex?"

"To whom do you refer? The Pirate Earl or Lord Munthrope?" He snickered.

"Both."

"He and his vermin are in the hold with the rest of the rats." Turning his back, he marched to his desk.

"I wish to see him immediately."

He spun around. "Alack, the man who kidnapped you? And God knows did what else to you?" His lip curled in disgust as he perused her.

"He didn't touch me, Captain. He was a gentleman." She lifted her chin. "He always has been, both as a lord and a pirate."

"Hmm." His eyes narrowed. "As I said, you are no doubt suffering from shock, you poor dear. Please sit." He gestured toward a chair. She didn't move.

He leaned back against his desktop. "I had no idea you would follow the man to the trap I set for him. I do apologize for that."

The ship creaked and groaned over another wave, and she laid a hand on the back of the chair for support. "I had to see for myself. I must admit, I hardly believed you spoke the truth."

"He fooled us all, Miss Dutton." He gave her a look of understanding, even pleading.

"Nevertheless, I wish to speak to him."

"Not possible. I would never allow a lady to endure the company of such reproachful creatures, even for a moment."

"I have endured the company of such *reproachful creatures* for more than a day and have survived unscathed."

He studied her as a surgeon would someone with a contagious disease. "Survived, I'll allow. Though I fear you have not come away with your reason, Juliana. Your request to speak to that pirate is proof."

"Miss Dutton," she corrected him curtly, biting down her rising frustration. Captain Nichols meant well. True concern burned in his eyes, softened his voice. But when would the man accept she could never return his affections? Especially not when he had all but delivered Alex to the noose. *The noose!* She could hardly think of it without her head growing light.

"There, there, now, dear." Nichols rushed to her and took her hand before she had a chance to move away. "I see merely the mention of the vile man distresses you. You are safe now, Juliana. Don't give the rogue another thought. Anon, you shall be back in your own home, in your own bed, under the protection of your loving father." He caressed her fingers and shifted sincere eyes between hers. "A lady such as yourself has no need to concern herself with the affairs of men. Wars, pirates, business—these things are far too taxing for your delicate constitution. By tomorrow, you'll return to a life of leisure and free from worry, as a lady of your stature deserves."

Juliana yanked her hand away and retreated. Her Christian name on his lips only added to the nausea brewing in her belly. His insinuation that a woman was incapable of handling men's affairs pricked her ire. "You should know by now, Captain, that I'm not the sort of woman to fritter away my time on idle pursuits." She'd love to tell him that she'd been running her father's merchant business for the past three months, if only for the satisfaction of seeing his face crinkle in shock. But of course she couldn't. So she blurted out the only other thing she had to her credit. "In fact, I am most anxious to visit the Buchan orphanage upon my return where, as my mother did before me, I volunteer my time and energy to those in need."

His thick brows rose. "The Buchan orphanage, you say?"

"Do you know of it?" Though how this priggish man would be aware of such a place, she couldn't say.

"I do. In fact, I heard of it only recently." His expression lifted in utter glee as if he was about to disclose some divine secret. "A place your Pirate Earl is quite familiar with as well."

"Don't be ridiculous," she said. "What does a pirate have to do with an orphanage?"

"So, you don't know?" He shook his head and gave her a look of reproof. "I had thought you more wise, Juliana. How disappointing."

Juliana grew tired of this man's slanderous tactics to win her. "Say your piece, Captain, or I shall go."

"The Pirate Earl, also known as Alexander Edward Hyde, Lord Munthrope—"

"Of course I know who he is!" she snapped.

He grinned. "But did you know that he came to Port Royal five years past as a preacher? His father sent him to run Buchan orphanage and pastor the church by its side."

A preacher? Now, Juliana knew he was mad. She let out an unavoidable chuckle.

"I assure you, 'tis true, Miss Dutton. The selfish clod only lasted a year. He abandoned the church and all the children." He waved a hand through the air. "Just walked out on them one day and turned to piracy instead."

Juliana searched her mind for all the things Alex had told her about himself. "Nay, 'twas a Mr. Edward who ran the orphanage." Or so Eunice had told her.

Nichols snorted. "I suppose the pirate's son wished to keep his identity a secret. Quite a tale, wouldn't you say? What a—"

But she wasn't listening anymore. A memory pushed through the fog spinning in her head. Something her mother had told her. Something about the famous Captain Edmund Merrick and Reverend Buchan being good friends, closer than brothers. Horror ripped through her gut as she realized Nichols spoke the truth. Of course Merrick would send his son to take over the orphanage upon Reverend Buchan's death.

Alex was the man who'd abandoned the orphans.

Alex was the man who'd left them to starve. Alex was the man she'd hated from afar for longer than she could say. The man whose actions had caused her mother to sacrifice so many hours to the orphanage. Where she had caught the ague.

And died.

Her knees buckled, and she finally lowered herself to the chair.

How could she ever trust—how could she ever *love*—a man who would sacrifice children to starve on the streets while he turned to a life of debauchery?

Chapter 34

THANKING THE YOUNG MIDSHIPMAN FOR his escort, Juliana closed the door to her home and leaned her head back against the hard wood. She'd never been so tired in all her life. Her mind was numb. Her body ached from tip to toe from lack of sleep and trying to balance on a heaving ship for two days. And her soul was flooded with emotions in such a whirl, she couldn't settle them enough to make sense: confusion, fear, anger, frustration, sorrow. Yet one overwhelming feeling rose above the others. Abandoned.

Once again, she felt so desperately and utterly alone.

She hadn't realized until now how much she'd come to depend on Lord Munthrope. His influence, his power, his very presence—even dandified as it was—had brought her a measure of comfort, a feeling of having someone to call upon should disaster strike. Even as the Pirate Earl, he'd made her feel safe and protected. Deep down, she'd known that she had but to call on either man for help and they'd willingly and happily grant her whatever she needed. But now, in one fell swoop, they were both gone. Not only gone, but they—or rather he—had betrayed Juliana in the worst possible way.

Then, why did agony strike her heart at the thought of him hanging?

"Miss, miss, you are home!" Ellie, skirts in one hand and a bucket in the other, came rushing down the stairs, nearly tripping on the final tread. "We was so worried!" Setting down the pail, she swallowed Juliana in a comforting embrace that smelled of lye and papaya. "Where 'ave you been?" She nudged her back and examined her. "Your gown, 'tis ruined. Has some mischief befallen you? Oh my, your hair"—she fingered a strand—"crusty with salt. Poor, poor dear. The sun 'as burned your face an' you look 'ungry and tired."

"I'm quite all right, Ellie." Juliana sighed, then—against propriety—fell once again into the maid's embrace, this dear woman who'd been more like a mother to her since her own had died. It felt good to be held by someone she could trust.

"But where 'ave you been, miss? Mr. Pell's bin out searchin' for you since evening before last." She pushed back, her eyes brimming with tears.

"I'm so sorry to have worried you, Ellie." Juliana wouldn't dare tell the woman she'd been kidnapped by pirates. That would no doubt send her nerves into a spin. "'Twas unavoidable, but I'm home now."

"Unavoidable, eh?" She eyed her with suspicion and a bit of reprimand before she blew out a sigh. "Well, thank goodness, miss, because things 'aven't been so good around 'ere."

"What things?" Juliana rubbed her forehead. What could have possibly gone wrong in just two days?

"Miss Juliana." Abbot emerged from her father's study, his normally-pressed coat a wrinkled mass and his chin a field of stubble.

Releasing Ellie, Juliana approached him, noting the shadows hugging his eyes. "Abbott, whatever is wrong? Did the *Ransom* make port as expected? Did you handle the unloading and writs of sale?"

"I did, miss."

"Thank you for remembering, Abbot." Tension fled her shoulders as she attempted a smile. "We'll make a merchant out of you yet."

But he did not return her smile.

Neither did Miss Ellie, who had moved beside her, wringing her hands.

Juliana could take no more bad news. "Whatever it is, I don't want to hear it today. I simply wish to bathe and go to bed. Ellie, have Cook heat water for my bath." She started for the stairs.

Abbot cleared his throat. "Apologies, miss, but there's a post you must read."

"A post? From whom?"

"Ellie, would you bring us some tea?" Abbot directed the maid as he gestured toward the sitting room, where he quickly sped to light wall sconces and lamps, sending a flood of golden light spilling over the sofa and floor. Barely able to breathe, Juliana lowered herself onto the floral couch. A cloud of impending doom settled over her—a sort of numbness, a defensive stupor that deep down, she knew she was going to need.

Abbot withdrew a parchment from inside his coat and handed it to her. She opened the crinkled note and immediately recognized Rowan's flourished handwriting.

Dearest Sister,

'Tis with a very heavy heart and many tears that I write you this missive. I know I have been naught but a burden to you these past few years. Though I have tried to help in my own way, I have failed you more times than we both can count. I have no excuse for the last miscarriage of losing the Midnight Fortune. Forsooth, I was so overcome with shame and grief, that I spent the next week so inebriated I have no recollection of my doings. I'm sure this does not surprise you. What may surprise you, however, and what shocked and horrified me, is that during that time I must have disclosed to someone the facts of our father's death and your exemplary management of a shipping business on your own for several months.

Juliana's heart became a stone. Surely this was one of her brother's jokes. *Oh, God, let it merely be a prank.* Against her will, she continued to read.

To whom I disclosed such confidences, I have no idea, but soon the news spread like a cancer through town. And like a cancer, it deadened everything in its path.

Juliana's hands began to tremble. Miss Ellie entered, set the tray down on the table, and sat beside her, laying a gentle hand on her arm.

"So our ruse is up, Abbot?" Juliana gazed up at the stalwart man, a butler who had become a business manager; a business manager who had become her friend.

He gave a curt nod, his face engraved in misery. "Every merchant in town has sent posts expressing condolences over your father's death and regrets that they must take their business elsewhere."

"Every one?"

"I'm afraid so, miss."

Juliana sank back onto the seat and stared at the steam rising from the teapot, spiraling into the air and disappearing. Just like her future. "How much did we make on the *Ransom*'s cargo?" she said numbly.

"Thirty-seven pounds."

Barely enough to pay her business expenses, the staff, rent and food for another few months. But at least she still had two ships. If she couldn't use them as merchantmen, she could sell them and use the money to delay their poverty until she could come up with a plan. Though she hated to forfeit the *Ransom*, her mother's ship.

"There's more to the letter." Abbot sank into the chair across from her.

Yes, she'd seen that, but assumed it to be the usual nonsensical apologies and self-degradation that always accompanied her brother's indiscretions. She dropped her

head in her hands as her throat went dry with rage. "Where is
Rowan now?"

"Read," Abbot said.

Lifting her head, Juliana proceeded.

*I cannot express to you the depth of my sorrow and
shame. You may not believe it, but I truly wished to help you.
Instead I have ruined you. And myself in the process. If
Father were alive, he'd have much fodder for his ridicule of
me. Mayhap, he was right along. I am nothing but a
disappointment.*

Tears spilled down Juliana's face, blurring the rest of the
letter, and dousing the heat of her fury. Wiping her eyes, she
finished the letter, telling herself there could be no further
bad news.

She was wrong.

*I intend to make amends, dear Juliana, or die trying. I
have gathered a crew from among the most skilled seaman in
town and taken the Esther's Dowry. Piracy is my new game,
and a far more lucrative game than Faro it will be! I will be
successful at the trade, you have my word. And when I make
my fortune, I shall return and make all things right once
again.*

Forgive me,
Your adoring twin,
Rowan

Putting on a stiff expression, Juliana rose, handed the
letter back to Abbot, thanked Ellie for the tea, and excused
herself. No sense in alarming her staff any further with an
emotional outburst. They'd been through so much with this
family, and by all accounts should have abandoned Juliana
for more stable positions long ago. The least she could do
was maintain an attitude of confidence in front of them. Yet

no sooner had she closed her chamber door, than she fell to the floor in a puff of skirts and agony. Leaning her forehead against the rug, she sobbed uncontrollably.

"Oh Rowan, Rowan, you foolish, foolish boy! Piracy! Fie! How could you?" Anger battled with fear and sorrow until Juliana couldn't form a single coherent thought. How could this be happening? She was ruined. In a month's time she'd be on the street. Just like Abilene. And there was naught to be done about it. Her worst fears had come true, after all.

Pressing her hands against her tear-soaked rug, she pushed herself up and gazed out the window, where moonlight sent spears of silver into the room. They might as well be piercing her heart for all the pain she felt.

"Why, God, why? Why are you allowing tragedy after tragedy to strike me? Have I not given to the poor? Helped the orphans? Taken care of Abilene? Have I not done my best to be kind, charitable, to honor my father, to not covet what others have?" She searched her mind for anything she might have done to deserve such a punishment, but could find no deed so vile. Save her love for Alex. More tears streamed down her cheeks and dropped onto her bedraggled gown. "Are you not to be trusted as well? Have you abandoned me like everyone else?"

No answer came, save the call of a mockingbird and the distant clang of a bell. Struggling to rise, she made her way to the window and glanced at the street below, remembering Alex's story of how he'd spent many a night listening to her play the violin. She half-expected to see his shadow beneath the trees. But of course he wasn't there. He was locked up in Marshallsea Prison.

Where all pirates should be.

Especially ones who had broken her heart.

A month later . . .

Sunlight angled over Juliana, warming her skin, and bursting a collage of bright colors behind her closed eyelids. She drew a deep breath, inhaling the sweet vanilla fragrance of her mother's heliotrope. One final time. Tears burned behind her eyes, but she shoved them back. She'd spent enough time crying during the last month to fill Kingston Harbor. But no more. 'Twas time to stop pitying herself and move on. Alone. Not one of her friends had come to call. Not one had sent a post expressing sympathy for her situation. There'd been no invitations to teas or parties or games of ruff or cricket.

She was utterly and completely alone.

"Miss, Abbot and I are ready." Ellie's voice drew her gaze to the maid standing by the open French doors, a look of abject misery on her plump features.

Juliana stood, taking in the beauty of her mother's garden one last time, implanting it on her memory. How she hated to leave it in someone else's care. Would they tend to it well? Would they honor her mother's memory by keeping the plants she loved alive? Mayhap 'twas best not to think of such things. Juliana didn't need a garden to remember her mother. The wonderful lady would always occupy a huge part of her heart.

"Very well." She followed Ellie into the main parlor, now absent all its furniture save an old sideboard Juliana had been unable to sell. Their footsteps ran hollow across the tile of the empty room.

"I can't believe they won't allow you to keep the 'ouse, miss."

"'Tis the rules, foolish though they may be, Ellie." With the timing of her father's death making Rowan the legal heir, and then his pre-conviction of piracy on the evidence of two merchantmen whose ships he'd plundered, the Jamaican Council had ordered all of Rowan's property seized by the Crown.

"Pure thievery," Ellie grumbled.

"I quite agree." Abbot stood by the door, suitcases in hand.

"'Tis for the best," Juliana said. "How would I maintain the estate, pay a staff? Feed us? It would all eventually fall into disrepair, and I couldn't stand to watch that."

"But at least you would have a roof over your head, miss."

"I'll have a roof. Thanks be to Eunice and Isaac Tucker." Juliana opened the door, ushering in a stream of sunshine that defied her dark mood. "The orphanage is a fitting place for me—an orphan."

"Don't say sich things, miss." Ellie touched her arm, eyes glassy.

"'Tis true enough, Ellie." Though Juliana hated to burden Eunice with yet another mouth to feed. But the money from the sale of her furniture, cookware, and most of her clothing would help out with expenses for a while. Plus, not having found a willing buyer, she still had her ship, the *Ransom*. Perchance she wouldn't end up like Abilene.

At least not yet.

Ellie batted a tear away and tucked hair inside her mobcap. "We thank you jist the same, miss, for gettin' Mr. Abbot and me new positions. And ones for Cook and Mr. Pell."

"I pray you will be very happy at the Braidwin's home. They are good people." Juliana took one last glance around the stark foyer, sifting through memoires of happier times.

A roar thundered down the street. She hadn't time to consider it before the ground jolted as if a spring had released and everything shook. Then it was gone.

"Seems the island is as unhappy at your misfortune as we are." Abbot frowned.

"If so, I pray it would shower wealth upon me instead of dust." She quipped, brushing dirt from her bodice.

"Miss." Abbot's voice drew her gaze back to him. "I thought you should know that the word about town is that Lord Munthrope or the Pirate Earl, or whoever the man claims to be, is to be hanged on the morrow at Gallows Point."

Something sharp speared Juliana's heart. She had tried so hard not to think of Alex this past month. Though, in truth, her efforts had failed. Why did the man—the pirate, the rogue--the *liar*—still have such a hold on her heart?

"Thank you, Abbot."

Miss Ellie's eyes pooled, and she flew into Juliana's arms. "I will miss you so much, miss."

"And I, you." Juliana gripped her as tears slid down her cheeks. "But we shall see each other again."

"Indeed, we shall." Abbot bent to pick up Juliana's valise, but she stayed his hand, wiping her moist cheeks. "No need, Abbot. You are no longer my servant. I must grow accustomed to carrying my own things."

He nodded, and the three of them left the home they'd lived in for more than four years.

After a tearful goodbye, Juliana started down the street toward the Buchan orphanage. In one hand she carried her valise, which held everything she had left in the world: two gowns, underthings, her hairbrush, pins, mirror, and her Bible. And in her other hand, she held her violin case. She could have easily sold the instrument, but found she couldn't part with the only thing left that soothed her soul. Afternoon sun torched the air, heating the ground in waves of humidity until perspiration slid down her back and her rapid pace slowed to a slog.

And still, she thought of Alex.

She'd not seen him since Nichols had stolen her from the *Vanity*. Too angry with him and too preoccupied with her own survival, she'd avoided facing the man. The last look he'd given her—of assurance and love—was forever imprinted on her mind like engraving on stone. It tortured her during the day and woke her in sweaty dreams at night. Tomorrow, he would die. Mayhap then the memories would cease.

Mayhap then she would be rid of the Pirate Earl forever.

Somehow, she doubted it. Somehow, her feet passed the avenue on which the orphanage was located and kept going down High Street toward Marshallsea Prison.

Mayhap if she spoke to him—asked him about the orphanage—his admission of guilt would seal the tomb on her traitorous passions. Then she would see him for the scoundrel he was.

And she could get on with what was left of her miserable life.

Chapter 35

A DARKNESS JULIANA COULD FEEL invaded her soul. With each step she took into the confines of Marshallsea Prison, the sweet scent of goodness, mercy, and light was shoved away by the fetid odor of hopelessness, death, and excrement. Men materialized from shadows into dim lantern light and gripped iron bars, some gaping at her in misery, others possessing enough life in them to whistle and beg her to come hence and give them a kiss.

Among other things.

Nausea gurgled in her stomach, threatening to dislodge the dry toast and jam she'd consumed at her noonday meal.

The guard who escorted her shrugged. "Don't say I didn't warn ye, miss."

She nodded. She could handle it. As long as the bars kept the villains from following through with their promises. Ignoring the lewd taunts, she proceeded down the narrow hallway, bordered on her left by cells the size of wardrobes, and on her right by a stone barricade. High above the cells, tiny barred windows let in a modicum of light that was lost in the shadows below.

As the guard's lantern advanced over the wall to her right, the stone seemed to move like waves upon the sea. Juliana slowed, staring at the odd sight, thinking she'd gone mad, when another shift of light revealed the wall wasn't moving at all. Instead, waves of cockroaches fled like hell's minions before the light. She shrieked.

Laughter raked over her as the prisoners continued their vulgarities.

"They won't harm ye, lady. Good fer eating, says I," one of them said.

Her stomach lurched into her throat, and she halted, drawing a breath to still her nerves. Bad idea. The stench overwhelmed her, and she began to cough. If only she had a hand free to cover her nose with her handkerchief, but she'd been unwilling to leave her valise and violin in the guard house.

"You all ri', miss?" the guard said. "We kin go back."

"Nay. Thank you."

A rat scampered across her path. Suppressing a scream, she continued.

How could they keep human beings in such a place? No matter what these men had done, nothing deserved such barbarity.

They turned a corner and then another and finally halted before one of the cells.

"Pirate! Ye got a visitor." The guard hooked the lantern on a ceiling beam and then retreated to sit on a crate a few yards away.

Juliana set down her valise and case and took a tentative step forward, peering into the shadows of the cell. The rapid beat of her heart betrayed her with a desperate yearning she could not explain. A yearning that turned into terror when he did not appear. Had he died in this filth and squalor? Had he already been taken to the gallows?

"Alex," she breathed out, frantically searching for any sign of movement in the murky black.

He emerged from the darkness like a ship from a storm—a sturdy ship not easily sunk. All man and strength and courage. The whiskers lining his jaw and slight paleness to his skin were the only indication he'd been locked up for a month. Though he'd donned a shirt, it hung loosely about his hips, open at the neck where no cravat hid the crest of muscles beneath. His boots crunched over sand as he approached.

A flush of traitorous heat warmed her body.

"Came to say goodbye?" His lips quirked, but bitterness poisoned his tone.

"Nay." She steeled her resolve. "I came to ask you something."

"Ye kin ask *me* anythin' ye want, lovely," a man covered in grime shouted from a few cells down.

Ignoring him, Alex's glance took in her valise and case. "If 'tis to carry milady's suitcase, I fear I am otherwise engaged."

His curt tone did much to squelch her sympathy for the man. "Don't be a fool, Milord *Pirate*."

"Milord? At last." He snorted, studying her with those deep-blue eyes of his, the mockery within them transforming into an intensity that made her swallow. "You shouldn't have come. 'Tis no place for a lady."

"Tell me about the orphanage."

Something flashed across his expression. Guilt? Sorrow? He shoved a hand through his hair and looked away. "So, that is the reason you haven't come to see me. I assumed my sacrifice on your behalf would have warranted at least one visit before my neck is squeezed."

Juliana lowered her gaze. She had not forgotten what he had given up to save her. Could not reconcile it with a man who would discard children like so much refuse. "I realize you chose not to fight on my account." She swallowed and lifted her eyes to his. "And for that I am grateful. But one selfless deed does not cover a lifetime of wickedness."

"'Tis a start." He approached the bars, searching her eyes.

"Ah, give the man a chance, sweetheart!" a man shouted from down the hall.

Juliana drew a little closer and lowered her voice. "The type of man who would leave orphans to fend for themselves is not the type of man to trust with one's heart."

He frowned, shook the bars, then released them with a shove. "Who told you?"

"Captain Nichols."

Alex's eyes flashed fire.

"*You* should have been the one to tell me." Juliana took another step forward. "Since you followed me around town, surely you knew how much I cared for the orphans. How much my mother had."

Clenching and unclenching his hands, Alex stared at the dirt.

"How could you have done such a thing?" she demanded.

He lifted his eyes to hers, light from the lantern reflecting the angst within. "Reverend Buchan was a good friend of my father's. When he died, I was sent to take his place. But—"

"You got bored," she interrupted, her ire rising, "as you are so apt to do, is that it? Nothing to pillage or plunder, no women to ravish at the orphanage?"

A voice bellowed from another cell. "Aha, gents, 'tis the great Pirate Earl bein' chastised by a proper lady!" Laughter ensued.

A look of contrition softened Alex's features, and he grabbed the bars again. "It wasn't like that."

She should leave. She should grab her things and go. She had the answer she came for. This man was not to be trusted. He used people for his own needs and tossed them aside when they no longer suited his purpose. He was a pirate, after all, and deserved to die for his crimes.

But she couldn't force her feet to move, couldn't turn her gaze from his. Because she knew when she left, she'd never see him again. She lowered her voice. "Pray tell, what *was* it like then?"

"I wasn't good for the children. I was a horrible preacher and a worse caregiver. The children got sick. One of them, a young lad of only seven named Peter ..." His knuckles whitened around the bars. "I prayed and prayed. I did everything the Bible said to do. I beseeched God. I fasted. I used the name of Jesus. But still he died." He hung his head. Strands of black hair shifted over his stubbled jaw.

"There was no reason for God to take him. No reason at all. He was just a boy. An innocent child. And I had failed him. *God*"—he spat the word—"had failed him."

"So you abandoned them both," she hissed.

"I made sure the children were looked after," he said. "Who do you think sent word to Eunice and Isaac that I had left?"

"How honorable." She huffed, though part of her softened at the revelation.

There was that look again, the one beaming from his eyes, the one that made her feel as if she was a thing of great value. "You cared for them," he said. "Just as your mother did before you. I loved you for it."

"And I hated you for leaving them."

He nodded.

Was the remorse shadowing his face real, or was it just another one of his deceptions? "You kept this from me like everything else. When you knew the one thing I wanted, the one thing I desperately needed, was to be able to trust you— to be able to trust anyone." Juliana hugged herself and took a step back, battling the burning behind her eyes. Silence, save for the pitter-patter of rats and drip-drop of water, invaded the prison.

"What are those for?" he asked.

She followed his gaze to her valise. "I lost my home. Rowan told everyone about Papa's death and me running the business."

He shook the bars and let out a growl that startled her. Iron flakes sifted down to the muddy ground. The guard rose to his feet. Juliana waved him back down.

"Where will you go?" Alex finally asked.

"I'm staying at the orphanage for now. Some of the children are sick. A few of them very sick. And Eunice and Isaac need my help."

Alex's brow darkened. "Has a doctor seen them?"

"None will come. I don't know what we're going to do. Little Michael has been ill for nearly two months."

"Blast those pretentious doctors!" Alex shook his head and stared at the dirt. "I wouldn't bother asking God for help."

Much to her shame, Juliana hadn't even thought of it.

"Juliana." The tender way he said her Christian name drew her gaze up to his. Yearning and guilt and sorrow battled on his features. "I wish things had been different. I wish I weren't locked up and I could help you … take care of you." He reached his hand through the bars.

"I can take care of myself." Yet the defiance she forced into her tone faded into a quaver. "Trusting others has only done me harm."

He stretched his hand toward her. "I am to die tomorrow. Please let me touch you one more time."

Everything within Juliana longed to go to him, to feel the roughness and strength of him, his warm breath on her face. Just once more. What harm could it do to honor this pirate's last request? She stepped forward.

The strength of his hand enveloped hers, heating her senses and thrilling her heart. She came alive, as if she were the tinder and he the spark. His unique scent of cinnamon and musk broke through the odor of sweat and filth and filled her nose with promise—with dreams of a different ending to their story.

He rubbed a callused finger over her palm. "I am so sorry, Juliana. I hope you can forgive me one day."

She swallowed, her anger dissipating at the thought that this man before her, so vibrant and strong, would soon be no more—that the intensity in his eyes would grow cold and fade. She could not bear it. A strand of hair shifted over his cheek, and she longed to brush it aside. "I do forgive you, Alex. But I could never trust you again."

Reaching up, he wiped a tear from her cheek. "Then, mayhap, 'tis better I die."

She broke from him. She had to leave now or she never would. "Go with God, Alex." Then turning, she grabbed her things and hurried away.

Pressing his face against the cold, hard bars, Alex watched Juliana leave—an angelic swan floating on a sea of sludge—until a corner stole her from view, leaving him in the darkness once again. Alone with the rats and cockroaches and the moans of men who had long forgotten what the sun felt like on their faces. A chorus of whistles and scurrilous invitations followed her through the prison until all grew silent.

When she'd first appeared, he thought surely he must be dead, but then he quickly realized where he was going there'd be nothing as beautiful as Juliana. A vision, perchance, a dream? But then she'd whispered his name, and the dream became reality, sparking his heart back to life.

He could think of only two reasons she hadn't come to see him the past month: some tragedy had befallen her—the thought of which had cost him many a night's sleep—or because he could no longer help her, she had no need of him. Day after day, he'd oscillated betwixt fear and anger. Both emotions so overpowering, they finally twisted into one huge knot of frustration.

In the end, 'twas his association with the orphanage that had destroyed any regard she harbored toward him. Not the pirating, not Munthrope's silly antics, nor even his deception. Just the one thing for which he still felt deep shame. He deserved her scorn. He deserved hell for what he'd done. Which was precisely where he was heading on the morrow.

Regardless, *if* there was a God, Alex should thank him for allowing him to see Juliana one last time. For allowing him to feel her satiny skin, breathe a whiff of her sweet scent, drink his fill from those sea-blue eyes. Though he'd never really have his fill—not even with a lifetime of gazing at her.

Curse her wastrel brother. Alex took up a pace. If Rowan had been an honorable, hard-working man, he could have taken over the business, and Juliana's future would not be at stake. Curse Nichols for locking Alex in this infernal prison! Curse Larkin for his betrayal! Halting, Alex shook the bars until the iron cut into his skin and blood dripped down the spokes. Juliana needed him now more than ever, and he was as helpless as one of the cockroaches skittering across the wall. Even worse. For he was locked behind an iron gate. The loss of his freedom, a fate worse than death.

At least tomorrow, he would be free.

Sinking to the damp floor, he leaned against the wall and drew up his knees. Cold stone seeped into his skin, sending a shiver through him. How had he ended up in this horrid place? The great Pirate Earl. The invincible master of the seas. He snorted. Not so invincible after all. He wondered where his father and mother were at this moment. Still in England dealing with family business? He wished he could see them one last time, to say goodbye and tell them how sorry he was that he couldn't be the preacher they'd hoped he would be. More than anything, he regretted the depth of their suffering when they would discover he'd been hanged for piracy. They would wonder where they'd gone wrong. How a child raised in such a godly, loving home could have strayed so far from the faith.

They would not find the answer, for Alex had none himself. No excuse. His parents had loved him. They'd instructed him, guided him, cared for him. He had fond memories of sailing with his father and sword-fighting with his mother. Aye, he chuckled. Odd as it sounded, Lady Charlisse was quite good with the blade. Problem was, those memories were few. Most of the time, his parents had been gone. "Saving the pirates," they had said. "For God."

If Alex were honest—and a man about to die always was—he supposed he'd grown up not liking this God who'd stolen so much of his parents' time. Even so, when his father had sent him to Port Royal to preach and care for the orphans, Alex had truly wanted to succeed. He'd wanted to make his father proud. Mayhap then they could all sail the Caribbean and preach to the pirates together—as a family.

But God had not been with Alex as he'd always been with his father. The Almighty had not answered Alex's petitions. He had not done what the Bible said he would: heal, deliver, save. Mayhap like Alex's parents, God was off doing more important work. More important than helping him. Either that, or he did not exist at all. Which meant Alex's parents had risked their lives, wasted decades of their time, and abandoned Alex and his sisters—all for naught.

Vanity of vanities, saith the Preacher, vanity of vanities; all is vanity.

What profit hath a man of all his labour which he taketh under the sun?

Alex was surprised he remembered these verses from Ecclesiastes.

For what hath man of all his labour, and of the vexation of his heart, wherein he hath laboured under the sun? For all his days are sorrows, and his travail grief; yea, his heart taketh not rest in the night. This is also vanity. There is nothing better for a man, than that he should eat and drink, and that he should make his soul enjoy good in his labour.

Which was precisely what Alex had done. He'd forsaken this invisible God and plunged into a life of eating, drinking, and sensual pleasures. For if God was dead, what else was there? What other purpose was there in the short days of life than to seek to please oneself? If there was no judge, no afterlife, what difference did it make if Alex robbed and murdered and drank himself into oblivion?

A bug scrambled across the sticky floor. He squashed it with his boot. "I did you a favor, mate." For Alex had discovered, much like King Solomon in Ecclesiastes, that no matter how much wealth one had, no matter how many possessions, or power, or women, there was naught but emptiness. All was vanity.

Until Juliana.

Now, he'd give anything to live and spend his days protecting and loving her.

He rubbed his forehead and squeezed his eyes shut. "Oh, God, what have I done? If you're there, if you care, please help me."

It was the first prayer he'd uttered in four years.

And just like with all the others, God was silent.

The eerie drip of water continued, the flutter of cockroaches. The man two cells down belched loudly, and cursing echoed from somewhere deep in the prison. A rat approached Alex's cell, stood at the bars on hind legs and sniffed, then dropped to all fours and went on his way. Even the rats couldn't stand the sight of him. How could he expect God to pay him any mind?

Footsteps sounded. Not the heavy boot of the guards but a soft pad that gave him hope Juliana had returned. But instead of her lovely face, a man approached. A simple man wearing a homespun shirt, faded breeches, and buckled shoes. Despite his common attire, he moved with the grace of royalty. Though he was short and spare, authority seemed to emanate from him as he stopped in front of Alex's cell. A magistrate? A member of the Jamaican Council? 'Twould explain why nary an insult or jeer had been tossed his way as he'd passed the gauntlet of prison cells.

Lantern light revealed an expression of kindness on his face, so foreign in this pit of misery and despair.

Alex grew uncomfortable at the man's perusal. "What do you want?"

"I have a message for you, Alex." The man's voice bore the peace of his countenance.

Alex leapt to his feet and approached. "From Miss Dutton?"

The man merely stared at him, an odd approval, an odd welcoming, beaming from eyes that seemed brighter than most.

"Well, spit it out, man. As you can see, I'm quite busy at the moment drowning in self-pity."

"He has never left you."

Alex eyed him. "Who?"

"The One who knows all."

Alex blinked as his spirit leapt within him. But then releasing a heavy sigh, he turned away. Of all the prisoners to taunt, this muddle-brain had chosen him. He faced the man again, intending to tell him to go bother someone else with his lunacy … but the man was gone. Vanished. No doubt he'd slunk off as quietly as he had come.

Alex shook his head. Just some guard heavy into his cups, 'twas all. But the man hadn't dressed like a guard, hadn't walked like a guard. His eyes had not borne the haziness of spirits, nor his words their slur. Alex rubbed his eyes. A foolish vision. Then why did his heart stir? Why did hope flicker within? Returning to the shadows, he sat back down, his thoughts awhirl with possibilities.

"God?"

Warmth flooded his chest and sent ripples down his spine. Warmth like he'd never experienced. Not a physical warmth but a sensation that went much deeper and woke up something inside him long since dormant.

His breath crashed against his chest, his blood raced through his veins. "God?" Yet only darkness and shadows surrounded him. Still the warmth continued as if someone were embracing him. Tightly. Lovingly. Overcome with the sensation, he hung his head, closed his eyes, and began to pray.

Chapter 36

JULIANA LAID THE COOL CLOTH on Michael's forehead, but it seemed to bear no effect on the heat radiating from his skin. Long past midnight, the light from a single lantern enhanced the lad's sunken cheeks and pale face. His breathing was labored, he oft broke into convulsions, and Eunice said he hadn't eaten anything but broth for days.

"Oh, God." Juliana dropped her head in her hands and allowed her tears to flow. "Please. If you answer any of my prayers, I beg you to answer this one. Please save this child. He has done nothing wrong. Please heal him and Mable and Gordon and Moses and Arabella." Arabella being the last child inflicted by the strange disease. They'd placed these four in a smaller room, separate from the rest of the children, desperate to contain whatever ailed them.

She thought of the story Alex had told her. How he'd fasted and prayed and begged God to heal one of the orphans, but the child had died anyway. Would God allow the same thing to happen now? "Where are you, Lord? Where were you then?" If God had answered Alex's prayer back then, mayhap Alex wouldn't have turned to piracy. And then he wouldn't be facing a brutal death on the morrow.

Her mother wouldn't have died.

And Juliana may still be living in the comfort of her home.

So many possibilities, so many outcomes ... if only heaven had not been silent.

Footsteps jarred her from her prayer, and she quickly wiped her eyes, not wanting the children to see her weeping. But it was only Eunice, a tight robe wrapped about her plump frame and a look of exhaustion on her face.

"I thought you were asleep." Juliana took her hand as the woman lowered to a chair beside her.

"Haven't slept much since the children got sick."

Juliana stared at the ragged rise and fall of Michael's chest. "I was praying."

"Always a good thing t' do."

"I'm so sorry to burden you with my presence here."

"Burden?" The woman gave an incredulous snort. "We love havin' you. The good Lord will provide somehow. He always does."

For the first time in her life, Juliana doubted that was true.

"I still can't believe that preacher, Mr. Edward, turned t' piracy," Eunice whispered, shaking her head. "Or that he is the son of an earl ... or the son of Cap'n Merrick!"

"You knew of Captain Merrick, his father?"

"Knew o' him? I met him once. He vis'ted Reverend Buchan as oft as he could. 'Sides, everyone on the island knew 'bout Cap'n Merrick."

"I wonder why Alex ... Lord Munthrope ..." Juliana groaned, "whoever he is, didn't mention who his parents were when he took over the orphanage."

Eunice shook her head. "Beats the tar outta me. Ne'er told a soul who he really was. Jist plain Mr. Edward, a preacher from Carolina, was all we knowed."

"I suppose he had his reasons for not wanting people to know." Juliana dipped the cloth into a bowl of water and wrung it out. "Mayhap he didn't wish to be judged by his father's reputation. Merrick left deep footsteps in which to follow, 'twould seem."

"Regardless," Eunice sighed, gazing at Michael with worry, "it be a shame he be hanged tomorrow. Though I admit t' bein' right angry wit' him, I don't wish him harm."

Juliana's throat tightened. Neither did she. In fact, she'd been trying her best not to think about it. Every time she did, her stomach vaulted, tears flooded her eyes, and her heart shriveled in such agony, she feared she'd be of no help to Eunice at all. She must remain strong. For the children. Besides, there was naught she could do. Save pray. And lately, her prayers seemed to fall like so much dust to the ground.

A loud rumbling sounded, like an out-of -control carriage pulled by horses gone wild. The thunderous rattling grew louder. And louder still. The entire room quaked as if some mad giant shook the earth in a fit of rage. Pictures fell from walls. Books thudded to the floor from shelves. The chair Juliana sat on skipped over floorboards like a playful child. Glass shattered as the lantern slipped from the table and its flame sputtered out. Then all went dark. And silent.

With each word Alex spoke to the Almighty, with each whispered plea, each shameful regret, a sensation of hope and purpose burgeoned within him. Like a light chasing away the shadows, it advanced over his soul, filling him with a life he hadn't felt in a long time. Words washed over him from the Scripture his mother had made him memorize as a child. Words from the lips of a God who loved His children enough to die for them. Words of promise: abundant life, protection, help during times of trouble, comfort, strength, and a Presence that would never leave. A love that would never abandon.

The more Alex opened his heart to hear, the more the possibility rose that he had been wrong about this God his father worshiped. This God who was also a father. A perfect father.

Boom!

What sounded like cannon fire shook the prison. Bars rattled. Dust and rocks rained on Alex. The sandy ground shifted back and forth like dirt in a sieve. Alex was tossed on his side. Leaping to his feet, he teetered to the center of the cell just in case the walls caved in. A mighty roar stormed through the narrow hallways like a monster on the prowl. The stone walls groaned beneath the strain.

Then all was silent.

Coughing, Alex brushed dirt from his sleeves and batted the dusty air around him. He'd felt many tremors during his years in Port Royal, but none quite so violent. His thoughts sped to Juliana. Fear for her safety sent him dashing to the iron gate. To shake it loose, if only he could. To run to her and ensure her safety.

He clutched the cold metal and pressed his forehead against the unforgiving spokes.

To his surprise, the bars gave way and the door screeched open.

The padlock fell to the dirt, steel split as though someone had taken an ax to it. He stared at it, benumbed. He must have fallen asleep while praying and was dreaming. But other doors squealed open. Laughter and shouts gorged the dank air as prisoners fled their cells and dashed for freedom.

And Alex knew somehow, some way, God had freed him.

"What do you mean the Pirate Earl has escaped?" Juliana's heart leapt at the possibility, even as her mind rejected the news. No one ever escaped from Marshallsea.

"Don't pretend you don't know, Misssss Dutton." Captain Nichols shoved past her and staggered into the main room of the orphanage where Eunice and Juliana were having tea. After the quake, it had taken nearly an hour to settle the children back to sleep, but finally they all had drifted off, along with Isaac, leaving Juliana and Eunice too jittery to join them. When a knock had sounded on the door, Juliana supposed it was someone in need of help. Unfortunately, she'd been right. Just not the kind of help she could give him.

Closing the door, she spun on her heels. A stain marred the naval officer's normally white breeches, a gold button swung on a thread from his blue coat, and his cravat was untied and hanging to his waist. "You're drunk, Captain."

"Indeed." He dipped his head but nearly lost his balance.

"I insist you leave at once, sir, and return when you are in better form."

At this, he let out a hearty snort. "Not until I find that scoundrel, the Pirate Earl!" Grabbing the only lit lantern from a table, he tottered through the room as if the ground were still shaking, peering into corners, beneath tables, and behind chairs. More than once, he tripped over one of the water pails lining the wall. More than once, he let loose strings of curses so foul, Juliana's ears ached.

Even so, his search fed a hope within her that he spoke the truth. Could Alex truly be free?

The monkey scolded Nichols from the beams overhead, drawing the man's gaze. Picking up one of their tea cups, he tossed it at the animal, muttering something about a filthy, uncivilized orphanage.

As the cup shattered on the floor, Eunice slowly rose and exchanged a worried look with Juliana. Stepping toward the inebriated man, Juliana forced her sternest tone. "Captain,

Alex is not here, I assure you. He is locked up at Marshallsea. I saw him there earlier today."

"Vistiting a pirate? Tsk, tsk, tsk, my dear." He waved a hand through the air. "But what did I expect from a woman who has a vile insatuation with the fiend." He belched. "Which is precessly why I'm here."

"I fear you are making no sense, Captain."

He peered into her face as if searching for her eyes. "The tremor opened the cell doors. Every lock broken." He blinked, then staggered backward. "Unfathsomable."

Juliana bit her lip. Could it be? How could an earthquake cut through a lock?

"Faith now, don't prestend you haven't heard." He twirled around. "He's here. And I will find him!"

"I insist you leave at once, Captain. You're going to wake the children." She tugged on his arm, but he shoved her aside. Stumbling over a chair, she struck the far wall. Pain throbbed across her shoulders. Eunice scurried from the room.

"Hiding a pirate! I'll have you sanged alongside him!" Nichols continued his tirade, starting for the serving room to the left. Juliana shook the dizziness from her head, thankful he went the other direction from where the children slept.

Eunice returned with a sleepy Isaac, who immediately bellowed at Nichols. "Hold up there, sir. This is an orphanage, not a tavern. You are to leave at once!"

Nichols faced him, his eyes swimming over him as if looking for anchorage. "I'm not leaving until you hand him over."

"Whoever you seek, sir, he's not here." Clutching Nichols's arm, Isaac started for the door.

But the naval captain was having none of it. He grabbed an iron skillet from a passing table and struck Isaac over the head. Screaming, Eunice dropped to the ground beside her husband. Juliana's heart raced, her mind spun. She had to get rid of this man before he hurt the children.

"Go get help, Eunice," she whispered, pressing fingers atop a lump forming on the back of Isaac's head. "I'll distract him." 'Twas the only way. Rising, Juliana stormed toward Nichols, who had opened the pantry and was tossing sacks of food to the floor. She shoved him in the back, sending him crashing into shelves, just as she heard the front door close. Thank goodness at least Eunice was safe.

He swung about, teeth bared, and held the lantern to her face. "Pirate whore! And to think I wanted you for myself. I'll not let that lecherous madcap slip srough my fingers again. Where isss he?" Pushing her out of the way, he stormed back into the main room, heading for the children's sleeping quarters.

But she couldn't allow that to happen.

Grabbing one of the knives from the table, she rushed after him. "Stop right there!" She pressed the tip to his back, all the while wondering whether she could actually stab a man. But it didn't matter. The skilled naval officer twisted around and knocked the blade from her hand before she could find out. He gave a maniacal laugh, spewing rum-drenched breath over her face, murder in his eyes.

Juliana backed away, but he caught her by the throat. Tossing the lantern through the air, his thick fingers tightened. The glass shattered. She clawed at his hands, desperate for air. Flames shot up from the corner of the room reaching for the rafters. The monkey squealed.

Nichols gritted his teeth and clamped both hands on her neck. Her lungs screamed. Her mind grew numb. The room began to spin.

Then all went black.

Cloaked in the shadows of a warehouse, Alex gazed over the inky waters of Kingston Harbor, Jonas by his side. The *Vanity* was not among the ships idly rocking in the bay, nor among those docked at the many wharves. Not that he expected it to be. That pigeon-livered dog, Larkin, didn't have the spine to sail into port so soon after he'd betrayed Alex. He would wait until word reached him that Alex had been hanged. And even then, he might never return for fear of revenge by those loyal to the Pirate Earl. Of those there were many. The Brethren of the Coast scowled upon such treachery against one of their own.

A troop of red-coated marines marched down the sandy street. Alex slipped further into the shadows. They'd be searching for the escaped prisoners, no doubt, though most would be able to blend in with the usual riff-raff that gorged—even at two in the morning—the many punch houses lining Thames Street. A drunken ballad, laughter, shouts, and the sound of a fiddle accompanied the clip of the soldiers' boots as they passed.

Jonas folded arms across his chest. "What now?"

Alex drew a deep breath and ran a hand through his hair. Several of his crew had found him after they'd escaped the prison, but without a ship, Alex had nothing to offer them. Hence, he'd released them to the ravages of the city with a warning to stay out of sight for a few days and then find another ship to join. All of them left. Except Jonas, of course. Not that Alex intended to pirate any more. He could not deny that something had happened to him in that dark prison cell. Something not of this world, something deep and meaningful. Something that could quite possibly change his life.

If he allowed it.

But his brig had been his only means to gain wealth. And wealth is what he needed at the moment to help Juliana.

If she would even be willing to see him. Or speak to him again.

"I have no idea," Alex replied with a chuckle. "For the first time in my life, I have no idea what to do. Along with no ship and no money."

"Doesn't Lord Munthrope have a fortune stored somewhere?"

A heavy breeze smelling of salt and rum swept over them. "His home, *my* home, will be the first place Captain Nichols will look."

"Of course. So the great Pirate Earl suddenly finds himself stripped of title, power, ship, and wealth. Makes one wonder what God is up to?" Jonas grinned.

A week ago—lud, a day ago—Alex would have replied in sarcasm that God neither caused nor cared about Alex's situation, but things had changed. God had freed him from prison. And Alex didn't believe he had done so just to bring him to ruin.

"Indeed, my friend." He clapped Jonas on the back. "I can't wait to find out."

Jonas's brows shot up, and a gasp escaped his lips. "Pray tell, is this the Pirate Earl who speaks, or did some preacher crawl into his skin while in prison?"

Preacher. It seemed like an eternity ago when Alex had arrived at the orphanage to care for the children and save the lost. Wait. Juliana had said some of the orphans were ill.

"Come, Jonas." He started down the street. "We're off to the Buchan orphanage. There are sick children afoot."

"But isn't Miss Juliana staying there?" Jonas fell in step beside him. "Surely 'tis one of the places Nichols will search?"

Alex halted. The man was right, of course.

"He'll clap us in irons and toss us back in prison." Jonas rubbed his neck, absent its normal cravat. "I, for one, am glad to have escaped the noose."

A hot wind tumbled down the dark street, fluttering the streetlamp above them. "The children are ill. You're the only doctor who will offer them care. We must go."

Even so, the thought of being locked up again in Marshallsea kept Alex's feet nailed to the ground. But the children ... he'd already abandoned them once. Had run away like a faithless coward at the first tragedy. Come what may, he wasn't going to do that again.

"Alas, I cannot force you to come, Jonas, but I'm going to do what I can and leave my fate in God's hands."

Chapter 37

JULIANA STOOD AT THE BOW of the *Vanity* as the ship hefted and rolled over foam-crested swells. Sea spray misted her. Yet it did naught to cool her heated skin. *Hot!* She was so hot, so very hot. Shielding her eyes, she squinted at the sun high in the sky. Waves of heat rippled from the giant fire ball that grew larger and larger with each passing second as if it were descending upon the very earth itself! Perspiration gleamed over her arms and neck. Her gown pasted to her body. Smoke bit her nose. She lowered her gaze to see flames licking and leaping and devouring the deck all around her.

Coughing, she tried to stamp out the fire, terror numbing her mind. Was she going to burn alive on this dreadful pirate ship? Where was Alex? His crew? One glance told her the entire brig was ablaze.

And no one else was in sight.

Irritating chatter scraped her ears. Something pushed her head. Tiny fingers poked her eyes. Batting the menace away, she gasped for air, her gaze landing on a wall of fire not two feet from where she lay. The monkey jumped on her chest and grinned. Clutching him, she struggled to rise against her voluminous skirts. Heat broiled her skin. Her head plunged into thick smoke. Hacking, she ducked back down. Hungry flames surrounded her, dancing, crackling, burning everything in their path.

The orphanage was on fire! Terror strangled what was left of her breath.

A child screamed. She glanced toward the children's sleeping quarters. Flames glowed from within. A burst of heat enveloped her. She leapt out the way as the fire consumed the spot where she'd lain just moments before.

"Thank you, little one." She pressed the monkey to her chest then dashed down the hallway, dodging pockets of fire, dread nearly blinding her as she shot prayers to God that the children were unharmed.

They *were* unharmed. Frightened, sobbing, calling for help, yet untouched by the flames that circled the room. Shouting words of comfort, Juliana knelt to gather them in her arms. They clung to her like snails on a leaf, whimpering and crying and shoving each other aside to be included in her embrace.

"Shhh, now. Shhh. 'Twill be all right. No need for alarm."

But there was *every* need for alarm. How was she going to get all these children out of the house to safety? And—her heart collapsed when the realization struck her—the sick ones in the next room. No time for a plan. Hoisting two of the smaller children in her arms, she instructed the others to stay and made for the door.

A roar thundered through the room. Rafters crashed down in a blazing heap of flames—landing right before the door, their only exit.

Juliana sank to the ground and gathered the sobbing children close. So, this was to be her end. Burned alive along with all the little ones she loved. *God, where is your mercy?* Only the mocking cackle of flames replied. She closed her eyes and prayed for a swift, painless death for them all.

When the Almighty spoke her name.

The faint echo resounded from within the roar of the fire. She looked up. There it came again. "Juliana!" Louder this time. Not God's voice, but one she recognized. One that caused her to stare with hope toward the burning door, to watch as a man burst into the room, cloaked in a wet blanket.

He darted toward them, flung off the cover, and laid it atop her head. Cool moisture gave her a moment's reprieve from the heat. "Are you all right?" He knelt and shouted. Blue eyes found hers. It was Alex, the Pirate Earl, Lord Munthrope—all wrapped up in one glorious rescuer.

"The children!" she shouted. "Save them!"

Reclaiming the blanket, he wrapped it around little Rose sitting in Juliana's lap, hoisted her in his arms, and dashed back out the door. Moments later, he returned, Jonas with him, both carrying buckets of water and blankets. After wetting the covers, they slapped some on the blazing wood blocking the door, while they flung others around children. Juliana grabbed a blanket, drenched it in a pail, then covered James and lifted him in her arms. Dashing for the door, she attempted to duck beneath the billowing smoke. Fiery needles pricked her skin. Her lungs screamed for air.

"The sick children!" she shouted at Alex as he grabbed another child. "In the next room!"

Alex nodded. "Get outside and stay there!" Then handing his child to Jonas, he started down the hall and disappeared into the black haze.

The next few minutes sped past in a blur of searing heat, ravaging flames, billowing smoke. And mind-numbing fear. Unable to stand outside and do nothing, Juliana dove back into the fiery building and assisted the men, until one by one, they carried all the children to safety, including the sick. The last person to exit the orphanage was Isaac, his arms hoisted over Alex's and Jonas's shoulders.

"Thank God," Juliana breathed as she watched the flames spit and claw at the sky. By all accounts a fire that hot should have consumed the building within minutes.

Yet something or *Someone* had held it at bay.

No sooner had the men cleared the front door, than the entire structure collapsed in a thunderous crash, shooting sparks in all directions. Some landed on the nearby church, but stone walls forbade them to ignite.

Gathering the whimpering children close, Juliana glanced at Alex. Soot as dark as his hair lined his face, perspiration streamed down his neck, and his chest billowed like a storm as sea. But at that moment, she thought him the most handsome man in the world. She longed to run into his arms, to thank him for saving her and the children, but doubts kept her at bay. Why had he come? Would he leave her? Would he abandon the children again?

Jonas, equally covered in soot, slapped his friend on the back. "Praise be to God!" He swiped a singed sleeve over his face and coughed smoke from his lungs.

"Thank you, *both* of you, for saving us." Juliana's voice came out hoarse. Her gaze drifted to Isaac, who wobbled on his feet and then sank to the dirt, rubbing his head. Thank God Nichols's blow had done no permanent damage to the man. Beyond him, the sick children lay on the grass. She whispered a thank you to God for His mercy, even as she realized that now these precious orphans had no place to live.

A shriek, followed by footsteps, drew Juliana's gaze down the dark street to see Eunice, skirts in hand, rushing toward them, two men on her heels.

"Isaac!" she shouted, casting a horrified look at the burning orphanage before she dropped to her knees and swallowed her husband in her embrace.

"I'm all right, woman. I'm all right," he said. "Thanks be to these men."

"I went t' get help, but all's I found was these two neighbors." She gestured toward the men, who stood staring at the burning building before they shrugged and turned to leave.

Hefting young Rose in her arms, Juliana stood. "This is the infamous Pirate Earl, Eunice."

The woman froze, then slowly turned to face the men while struggling to rise. Alex held out a hand. She took it. "Well, if it ain't Mr. Edward. Come back t' save us after all."

Alex cleared his throat. "I have much to apologize for, Mrs. Tucker."

"Humph. I says you do. But you have bigger troubles ri' now. That horrible man, Nichols be lookin' fer you."

"Captain Nichols?" Alex jerked his gaze to Juliana, his stance immediately stiffening. "Was he here? Did *he* do this?"

"'Tis a long story." She shook her head, gazing at the flames, still unable to grasp that the orphanage was gone. "It doesn't matter now."

Eunice stared curiously at Jonas. "Since you both be escaped pirates, I seen soldiers headed this way."

Jonas cast a nervous glance down the street.

"You must leave," Juliana said, her fear rising. "Now."

Alex hesitated. "But where will *you* go? With all these children?"

She wanted to ask why he suddenly cared about the children's welfare. "We'll think of something. Please. I can't bear the thought of you in that prison again."

Alex stared at her, firelight reflecting determination in his eyes. "I won't leave you. And I won't leave these children again."

Something hard inside Juliana's heart softened.

"Mr. Edward?" Jackson, the eldest of the children, separated from the others and crept toward Alex, hesitant at first. "Mr. Edward!" Recognition lit his face, and he ran into Alex's arms.

The pirate stood stunned for a moment before he embraced the lad. "Yes, 'tis me, Jack." He tussled the boy's hair. Three more children darted for Alex, hugging him and asking where he'd been. The scene should have infuriated Juliana, but the affection the children bore for

Alex and his welcoming response, along with the contrition in his eyes, had quite the opposite effect.

The monkey emerged from the shadows and leapt onto Jonas's shoulder. He jerked with a start, then scratched the creature beneath the chin. "Where did you come from, little beastie?"

"This little beastie saved my life," Juliana said, shifting Rose to her other hip. "Woke me up just before I was burned alive." And to think she'd been trying to get rid of him for months.

Rose leaned her head on Juliana's chest and thrust her thumb in her mouth.

"We must find a place to hide," Jonas said. "Now," he added with urgency.

"Wit' all these children?" Eunice's tone was skeptical as she helped her husband to his feet.

Alex glanced about anxiously. "None of us have homes anymore. Or friends to take us in. I don't even have a ship ..."

"Wait!" Juliana said, excitedly. "*I* have a ship."

Alex leaned on the starboard railing of the *Ransom*, warm cup of coffee in his hands, and gazed at the city of Port Royal, forty yards off the bow of the brig. At nearly eleven in the morning—while pirates and other sordid creatures slept off their nightly roistering—the wharves were already abuzz with activity. In the past hour, one East Indiamen had hoisted sail and cast off into the glimmering Caribbean, while two ships—one a fishing sloop and another a merchant barque—had scudded into the harbor and docked. Crates and barrels and livestock were now being raised from the hold of the merchantman by a pulley flung over a yard, while Negros and half-castes unloaded smaller cargo. Bells rang and seagulls swept the open sky. In the distance, Alex could make out carriages rattling down the sandy streets as women and men dressed in sparkling bright colors mingled with those in plain homespun. He'd come to this town a preacher, but instead had become a pirate.

And a dandified buffoon.

He loved Port Royal. Even amidst all the greed and evil, there was something compelling about it, something wild and adventurous. He could see why his father had loved it here. And why he'd sent Alex to help those who lived in darkness find the light.

The *Ransom* rose over an incoming wavelet, boards creaking and loose sails flapping. 'Twas good to be on a ship again, with the familiar sounds raking his ears and the roll of the sea beneath his boots. It had only taken an hour and two trips under the dark blanket of night to row all fourteen children and five adults to the brig. Thankfully the ship was anchored far enough from shore to hide the faces of those aboard, but close enough to spot any marines heading their way. There'd been none at four in the morning.

It had taken another hour to settle the children in bunks and hammocks below deck and offer comforting words until they drifted to sleep. Juliana had been best at that. Her calm voice, her gentle touches and kisses, had instantly put the little ones at ease, causing Alex's affections to grow even more for the lady. If that were possible.

No words could describe the horror that had consumed him when he'd found the orphanage ablaze and heard the screams of the children. He knew she would not leave them. He knew she must have still been inside. He knew that if he didn't act quickly, he'd lose her and the children forever. So, it had been without an ounce of hesitation that he'd dashed inside that fiery furnace. That made twice Alex had sacrificed himself for Miss Juliana Dutton. Unfathomable for a pirate who'd spent the last four years only pleasing himself.

After the children had fallen asleep, and much to Alex's surprise, Juliana had lowered to sit beside him as he leaned against the bulkhead on the main deck. She'd laid her head on his shoulder, both of them too exhausted to speak. Wrapping an arm around her, he drew her close, and within minutes, heard her breathing deepen. Her actions sparked hope within him that she would allow him back into her life, back into her affections. Not that he deserved a second chance.

"Oh, my, wherever did you get that coffee?"

The object of his thoughts appeared next to him at the railing. Bright sunlight revealed the ravages of fire that had been hidden in the darkness of night. Black splotches covered her gown that was singed around the hem and cuffs and burned clear through in other spots, revealing petticoats beneath. The smell of smoke lingered around her, and a small patch of soot blackened her cheek where she'd missed in her cleaning. Golden locks of hair tumbled over her shoulders and down her back as her sea-blue eyes found his.

He swallowed his longing, and thanked God for allowing him to save such a precious creature.

He handed her the cup. "I stoked the galley's coals and managed to heat some water."

She took a sip and stared over the bay, rippling in ribbons of silver. "When did you carry me to the captain's bed? I don't remember a thing."

"Shortly after you fell asleep. I don't believe a cannon blast would have woken you."

Pink tinged her cheeks as she took another sip of coffee.

"Are the children still asleep?" he asked.

"Yes. And Jonas, Eunice, and Isaac too. 'Twas quite a harrowing night." She set the cup down on the bulwarks. "This is the worst coffee I've ever had." She smiled.

Alex laughed. "Cooking was never one of my skills."

A blast of hot wind swirled over them, dancing through her hair. "Your doctor gave the children some rice-bitters tea last night. Told me it might be cholera and that he'd heard about this local cure."

Leaning one elbow on the railing, Alex turned to face her. "Jonas has studied medicine for years. Never fear, he will take good care of them."

"I can't thank you enough for bringing him. I'm not sure what—"

She was still talking when, unable to stop himself, he reached up and wiped the soot from her cheek.

Much to his delight, she allowed his touch. Her voice trailed off, and she raised her gaze to his, eyes moist. "Thank you for saving us. For risking your life."

"How could I do anything else?"

"Jonas told me you suspected Nichols might search for you at the orphanage. Yet you came, regardless."

Alex lowered his hand. "The children were sick, and Jonas is a good doctor."

"You could have been captured and tossed back in Marshallsea."

He merely smiled, thrilled at the concern in her eyes.

"You could have burned alive rescuing us." A tear spilled over the edge of her lashes. She wiped it away with the back of her hand and studied him, sunlight bringing out the flecks of green in her eyes. "I don't understand."

Alex shrugged. "I risked my life, aye. But God helped. Without those pails of water and extra blankets scattered about, I would never have gotten the children out unscathed."

She nodded, and a tiny smile lifted her lips. "That was Lucas's doing. I insisted we get rid of them, but Eunice allowed them to remain—to comfort the lad. Now it seems 'twas God's doing all along." She gave a sigh of unbelief as she gazed over the bay. "And that silly monkey! We'd been trying to capture him for months. Yet, without him I would be naught but a crispy corpse."

Alex ran thumb and forefinger down the sides of his mouth and gave her a teasing look. "So, 'twould seem your God has not abandoned you after all?"

She leaned on the railing and gazed over the harbor, where several small fishing boats bounced among the waves. "We are all alive, thank God. But I still don't understand why so many tragedies have come my way." She bit her lip. "I tried to follow all the rules, do everything right, but hence, I have lost everything."

Alex could make no sense of it either. He was the one who deserved to lose everything. Not this angel beside him. He gripped the railing and followed her gaze to the city. "Mayhap 'tis not about what we can do for God, after all. As I said on board the *Vanity*, we cannot earn his favor."

Frowning, she snapped cynical eyes his way. "Then that would mean life is naught but random events which God neither causes nor forbids."

"Nay. After yesterday, I believe he is very much involved."

She flinched. "I am surprised to hear you say such a thing, milord."

Alex drew a deep breath, turned, and took her hand in his. "Juliana, I know I lied to you. I know I deceived you. I know I've been the worst sort of scoundrel. But something happened to me in that prison cell after you left. I don't know. God opened my eyes to many things."

Her brow wrinkled. "God?"

He smiled and caressed her fingers. "He exists. I know that now. I was a fool for turning away from him. And from the children." Shame made him release her hand. He leaned over the railing and stared at the murky water slapping the hull.

"I am happy to hear it." Though her tone was skeptical. He didn't blame her. Yesterday, he'd denied the very existence of God, and today, he was spouting his virtues.

The brig creaked over an incoming wavelet. With a sigh, she directed her gaze toward Fort Charles. "Regardless. We should set sail immediately. 'Tis only a matter of time before Nichols realizes I still have a brig and seeks you here."

"How now, milady?" Alex shot back in surprise, snapping hair from his face. "Nay, I shan't put you in further danger. Jonas and I will leave. This is your brig, and it will provide a roof over your head and the children's."

Sorrow claimed her features. "In truth, there is nothing left for me in Port Royal. And, clearly, you can't remain here with Nichols fast on your heels."

"I can take care of myself."

"Back to pirating?" she asked, her tone cutting, yet tinged with hope.

He gripped the railing. "Nay, I find I have no further ambition for thievery."

"But you were so good at it."

Her taunting gave him hope to turn and face her, taking her hands in his. "I can be good at something else."

"Like preaching?" She gazed up at him, her eyes shifting between his.

"Like loving you. If you'll allow me the privilege."

Chapter 38

JULIANA CLOSED HER EYES AS Alex eased a lock of her hair behind her ear. His touch never failed to send blissful warmth through her. She could get used to a lifetime of such bliss. When she opened her eyes, it was to a look of complete adoration. She could get used to that as well— along with the way the wind played among the strands of his black hair, the sheer breadth of his shoulders, the strength of his presence.

But could she trust him?

Had he really changed, or would he leave her and the children again when God let him down or he grew bored with life? He'd said he'd had an encounter with the Almighty yesterday, but had he? Was it enough to change his wandering ways? So many who started out with great zeal for God allowed it to fade over the years.

Yet …

"Something odd happened last night while you were on deck securing the ship," she began. "Once Jonas washed the soot from his face, Eunice recognized him as the man who brought her money every month. From the elusive Mr. A." At first Juliana could hardly believe that Mr. A was Alex, but then it slowly began to make sense: his charity toward the young widow in town, his kindness to Abilene, Jonas's admiration of him, and the way the children who remembered him had responded. Could goodness still exist beneath the crusty exterior of the most fierce pirate in Port Royal? Surely, his behavior hadn't all been a ruse to win her affections? Nay. For most of his good deeds had been done in secret. Upon that realization, the anger and mistrust in her heart had begun to melt.

Releasing her hands, Alex glanced over the harbor as if ashamed of the topic.

She laid a hand on his arm. "Why?"

His jaw bunched. "'Twas the least I could do after I abandoned them."

"The great Pirate Earl giving his money to a group of lowly orphans?" She grinned. "Why, if word ever got out, milord? Your reputation as a rogue would be in danger."

"Methinks that's one reputation I can afford to lose." He smiled wryly, then grew serious. "Giving to those children was the only decent thing left of me. That, and you." A cloud moved aside, allowing the full force of the sun to beat on him as he stared at the city, lost in thought.

Slowly, he turned to face her, a storm brewing in his eyes. "I know you have no reason to believe me, Juliana, but I will never leave you. I couldn't. It would be like ripping the heart out of my own chest."

Against propriety, she ran fingers over the stubble on his jaw, relishing in the scratchy feel. Even in the face of being captured again, even in the face of death, he had come for her. And even after the fire, when he could have run away, he'd stayed, made sure they got to safety. Emotion burned in her throat. "I want to believe you, Alex, I truly do."

He raised her hand to his lips for a kiss. "I vow to prove it to you the rest of my life. If you'll allow me."

Hope and sincerity burned in his eyes. Wind fluttered the hem of her dress as the brig rolled over a swell. He steadied her with a touch to her elbow just as he'd been steadying her since the night they'd met. Mayhap he'd disappoint her. Mayhap he wouldn't. Either way, Juliana could not fathom a life without him. "Yes."

"Yes?" Moisture gleamed in his eyes.

She nodded, smiling.

Cupping her face gently in his hands, he lowered his lips to hers. The world around her dissolved and swirled and spun in pleasurable eddies, transporting her to another place and time where pirates became gentlemen and abandoned ladies were cherished. Drawing an arm around her back, he pressed her close, drinking her in ... desperately ... lovingly ... as their hearts seemed to meld together as one.

Thunder rumbled. Nay, not thunder. A roar exploded as if a leviathan were about to surface in the harbor. Keeping an arm around her, Alex withdrew from their kiss and glanced over the water. Still. Calm like turquoise glass. Odd. Something was wrong. It was too quiet. Where were the sea gulls and pelicans that normally crowded the skies and fished among the quays?

Alarm prickled Juliana's skin.

Another roar sounded. The water in the bay leapt in the air as if some giant had dropped a boulder in the center. Grabbing the railing with one hand, Alex forced Juliana to her knees beside him just as a wave struck the brig. It canted to port, sending them tumbling across the hard wood. Alex tightened his grip on her. "Hang on!"

The ship rolled to starboard. The anchor held, and soon they settled into a rocking motion. Distant screams and shouts peppered the air. The sound of rushing water boomed, like a massive waterfall tumbling over a cliff. Alex helped Juliana stand and held her tight as he inched against the foredeck ladder for support.

Both their gazes locked on Port Royal.

All the wharves along Thames Street fell into the sea. Nay, not fell. They sank. Followed by the street itself, and then the two rows of homes and warehouses behind it. Plunk! Like blocks shoved over by an angry child. The sea rushed in to cover them, bubbling and churning and reaching for the roofs of those buildings that were sinking fast.

Juliana gasped, not believing her eyes. Shrieking, she broke from Alex and made her way to the railing. Horror numbed her mind, her thoughts. Alex followed and drew her close as another wave struck the brig, almost sending them tumbling backward.

Screams and howls of agony blared from the city, some instantly muffled by the crash of waves and gurgle of sinking sand. The ground shook again, shifting in Juliana's vision as if she peered through an unsteady spyglass. Sand rippled in waves on the remaining land, flinging people in the air, then dropping them into pits that instantly flooded with water. Survivors darted here and there as more of the city plunged into the sea—sucked below by the god of the underworld.

Women waved arms from windows, screaming. Mobs clambered for higher ground as the furious sea seemed all too happy to reclaim its territory. Juliana spotted one poor woman running for her life when the ground opened up before her and swallowed her whole.

"No!" Juliana screamed. "No!" Bodies floated to the surface, tossed about by incoming waves.

Alex drew her face to his chest. "Don't look." She felt the wild thump of his heart through his jerkin, his harried breath upon her forehead. "There's nothing we can do."

But she *did* look. She couldn't help it. More land sank. More holes opened, then squeezed, shooting saltwater high into the air. The impenetrable stone walls of Fort James, Fort Carlisle, and Fort Rupert dropped from sight, as if they'd never existed. The steeple of Christ's Church, barely a nob above ground now, reeled and pitched like a buoy at sea.

A thunderous crunch drew Juliana's terrified gaze to HMS *Swan*. The mighty ship broke its moorings and plowed inland atop sinking homes, crushing one of them completely before coming to rest atop another.

She couldn't move.

More screams. More howls. More shaking. Then it all stopped.

Alex held her tight. Their breath coming in gasps. Their chests pounding together. "The children!" Juliana started for the hatch when something caught her eye—a wall of water rising from the south.

"They're in hammocks. They'll be fine. Hold on!" Alex grabbed the backstay and tightened his grip on Juliana.

She wanted to close her eyes but couldn't. The wave swept over what was left of Port Royal, reaching for its center like beastly claws making one last attempt to annihilate its victim.

Then it struck the ship, shoving Alex and Juliana to the deck. They remained there in each other's arms, Juliana trembling, Alex breathing hard—both too afraid to move. The ship rocked violently, and Alex grabbed a hatch grating for support. Not until the brig settled and the squawk of a gull sounded did they dare to rise and creep to the railing.

It was over.

Too stunned to speak, they merely stared at the destruction.

Two-thirds of Port Royal was no more. A new shore had formed where the roofs of houses entangled with the masts of sunken ships. Only a few buildings remained on a small spit of land that had instantly become an island, separated from the mainland by the sea that now covered where Fort Rupert had stood.

"My home!" Juliana pointed to the place where her house had stood, just off High Street. Both street and home now covered by turbulent water.

"Was anyone there?" Alex asked, fear in his voice.

"Nay." She swallowed. "Abbot, Cook, Mr. Pell , and Miss Ellie went to the Braidwin's ..." Her gaze sped to the location of the Braidwin estate. Still there. She breathed a sigh. "Thank God."

Alex took her hand in his, his eyes burning with concern. "What of your brother?"

"Gone." Juliana tossed a hand to her throat where her pulse raged out of control. "Sailed away on the *Esther's Dowry* a month ago. To become a pirate."

Alex stared at her in shock, then ran a hand through his hair. "For once his foolishness saved his life."

"Abilene!" Juliana tugged from Alex's grip, her gaze running up and down the foamy water where the wharfs had once stood. "She was down by the docks."

"Nay." Alex drew her close. "She was at my home. Or Lord Munthrope's." He pointed to where his house still stood just past the Merchant's Exchange. "I had Whipple bring her there last week."

She eyed him, tears spilling down her face. "Just as you said you would. Even imprisoned, you kept your word."

He gave a sad smile. "You thought me such a monster."

"Nay. Not you. I didn't trust anyone." She scanned the city once again, still unable to believe what her eyes told her. The sea gurgled and sloshed over the spot where the orphanage had stood, along with Reverend Buchan's church.

As if it had never existed.

A realization slammed over her. "We would have all been killed. If I had been home or at the orphanage, then I and all the children would have been killed."

"As would I if I was still locked up in Marshallsea." Alex's stubbled jaw tightened as he glanced to where the prison had been.

Juliana broke away from him, her breath coming hard and fast as the truth stormed through her. "All the tragedies that came upon me the past three months." Her voice raised higher and higher with the revelation. "My father's illness, me trying to run the shipping business, Rowan's inability to help—all brought *you* into my life to keep Nichols at bay." Alex started to say something, but she silenced him with a raised hand. "Then Abilene's beating introduced you to her, so you could save her. Dutton Shipping failed, my father died, the orphans became ill—all of which caused me to leave my home. Even your capture and Lucas's silly pails of water and blankets were all part of the plan to save me and the children from the fire. Don't you see?"

Her legs wobbled, and she gripped the railing. Alex held her elbow. "If you hadn't met me," Juliana continued, breathless, "you wouldn't have been captured. And if you hadn't been captured, you might have been down by the docks, sunk into the sea with the rest of the pirates."

Alex stared at her aghast. Shock, confusion, and finally acceptance—sad, humbling acceptance—filled his eyes before he shifted them back to Port Royal.

"Everything that happened," Juliana added, "every struggle and problem happened for a reason. Even Rowan losing the *Midnight Fortune* in a bet. Otherwise he would have been in town, down at the docks, gambling. Everything was perfectly orchestrated to bring us—you and me and the children and Jonas and Eunice and Isaac—to this brig. On this precise day at this precise time. To save our lives!"

Alex shook his head, swallowing hard. "I can't believe God would go to such trouble for me. For you, mayhap. But for me?" His brow twisted.

"He loves you, Alex. And he loves me. All this time I thought he had abandoned me." Emotion burned in Juliana's throat, making it difficult to speak. "I thought he was unhappy with me, that I wasn't doing enough for him. When all along, he was saving me." Tears spilled down her cheeks and dripped from her jaw.

Alex caught them in his hand, then drew her close, wrapping his arms around her. "We can't do anything to win God's love. He just loves because … that's the way he is. He can't help it."

She nestled against him, feeling loved, truly loved, for the first time in her life. Not just by Alex but by God Almighty, her Father in heaven. Who promised to never abandon her. Somewhere along the way, she had forgotten that. She had forgotten that no matter what happened, God was with her and had a plan, and that all things would work out for good in the end.

"But what about all those who died?" She pushed from Alex and stared at what was left of Port Royal. "Didn't God love them?"

"Of course," Alex said, his voice tightening in pain. "He may have tried to get them to safety. Mayhap they didn't listen. Mayhap, it was their time. I don't know."

A morbid scream echoed across the bay. Juliana made out the figure of a woman and child climbing onto the roof of a home. "We must go to the survivors, help those we can."

Alex nodded. "Aye, I'm of the same mind."

Footsteps and a horrified gasp brought both their gazes to Jonas, bursting up the hatch and rushing toward them. "What's happening?" His eyes shot to the coast and his mouth went slack. He started to stumble.

"Earthquake," Alex replied, leaving Juliana's side to grab his friend's arm.

"Are the children all right?" Juliana asked.

"Everyone is still asleep," Jonas stuttered as he stared at Port Royal. "Nothing would wake them after last night."

"Go get Isaac," Alex said. "We'll take the boat into town and search for survivors. Bring your medical supplies."

Jonas nodded but remained in place. "God in heaven help us," he mumbled as he approached the railing. "God have mercy. Sweet Jesus."

"I'm coming with you." Juliana clutched her skirts and started across the deck.

"Nay." Alex stayed her. "Remain with the children. They will need you."

She frowned, and he brushed a thumb over her cheek and kissed her, disarming her protest instantly. "We'll bring back those in need."

"A brig," Jonas announced. "Coming around the point. Lowering sails."

Alex squinted into the sun. A flicker of excitement—or was it joy—crossed his eyes.

"You know the ship?" Juliana asked.

Alex grinned. "'Tis my father's brig, the *Redemption*."

Author's Historical Note

O N JUNE 7TH, 1692, AT AROUND 11:40 a.m., a jolt
struck the town that one preacher had deemed the
wickedest city in the world, Port Royal, Jamaica. Anglican
rector, Dr. Emmanuel Heath was having a glass of
wormwood wine at a local tavern with his friend John White
when the ground began to shake. White assured Dr. Heath
that it was only another earthquake and there was nothing to
fear, but then another shock struck and then another, until
entire buildings began to crash down around them. The
wharves and rows of homes behind them slid into the deep
water of the harbor as Dr. Heath fled for his life. An
eyewitness describes the scene:

*The sand in the street rose like the waves of the sea,
lifting up all persons that stood upon it, and immediately
dropping down into pits; and at the same instant a flood of
water rushed in, throwing down all who were in its way;
some were seen catching hold of beams and rafters of
houses, others were found in the sand that appeared when
the water was drained away, with their legs and arms out.*

More quakes struck as Dr. Heath made his way toward
Morgan's Fort, but the building crumbled before his eyes,
along with his church, the tower of which toppled to the
ground. In a panic, he made his way toward his home as a
wall of seawater came crashing in from the south, flooding
the fort and the houses in its path and drowning those trapped

in the falling debris. Finding his home still standing, he knelt on the street and, along with many neighbors, began to pray.

The earthquake lasted two minutes and during that time two-thirds of the town sank into the sea. Ships docked at the wharves capsized. HMS *Swan* broke its moorings and plowed through the city. The ground opened up and swallowed people and houses whole. A young Mrs. Akers was swallowed up in a gap on land and then was somehow ejected into the harbor where she was later rescued. A French Huguenot named Lewis Galdy was sucked out to sea by the first seismic wave and then miraculously returned to land by the second. In an instant, the peninsula on which Port Royal stood became an island.

Over 2,000 of the 6,500 inhabitants died in the earthquake itself and another 2,000 in the looting, violence, disease, and starvation that followed. Though many tried to rebuild Port Royal, it never returned to its former glory, and most of the merchant business that had made it great transferred to Kingston. History lovers and treasure hunters diving at Port Royal for years have found many fascinating artifacts. One item of particular interest was a watch that had stopped at seventeen minutes before twelve: the time of the third and greatest shock.

Natural calamity or act of God? Only the Almighty knows.

If you enjoyed this book, please check out *The Reckoning*, Book 5 in my Legacy of the King's Pirates series!

About the Author

A CCLAIMED AUTHOR, MARYLU TYNDALL dreamt of pirates and sea-faring adventures during her childhood days on Florida's Coast. With more than fourteen books published, she makes no excuses for the deep spiritual themes embedded within her romantic adventures. Her hope is that readers will not only be entertained but will be brought closer to the Creator who loves them beyond measure. In a culture that accepts the occult, wizards, zombies, and vampires without batting an eye, MaryLu hopes to show the awesome present and powerful acts of God in a dying world.

A Christy award nominee, MaryLu makes her home with her husband, six children, and several stray cats on the California coast.

If you enjoyed this book, one of the nicest ways to say "thank you" to an author and help them be able to continue writing is to leave a favorable review on Amazon! (And elsewhere, too!) I would appreciate it if you would take a moment to do so. Thanks so much!

Comments? Questions? I love hearing from my readers, so feel free to contact me via my website:

http://www.marylutyndall.com

Or email me at:

marylu_tyndall@yahoo.com

Follow me on:

FACEBOOK:
https://www.facebook.com/marylu.tyndall.author

TWITTER:
https://twitter.com/MaryLuTyndall

BLOG:
http://crossandcutlass.blogspot.com/

PINTEREST:
http://www.pinterest.com/mltyndall/

To hear news about special prices and new releases that only my subscribers receive, sign up for my newsletter on my website or blog! http://www.marylutyndall.com

21753039R00233

Made in the USA
Middletown, DE
09 July 2015